FERAL COURIER

CALM ACT FERAL AMERICA BOOK 3

GINGER BOOTH

ISBN-13: 978-0960068579

Maps by Ginger Booth
Cover design by www.rafidodigitalart.com

Model image © Vladimirfloyd (modified) | Dreamstime.com
Train image © Savannah Grandfather (modified) | Creative Commons
commons.wikimedia.org/wiki/File:VIA_Passenger_Train.jpg

ISBN: 1987764439
ISBN-13: 978-1987764437

Created with Vellum

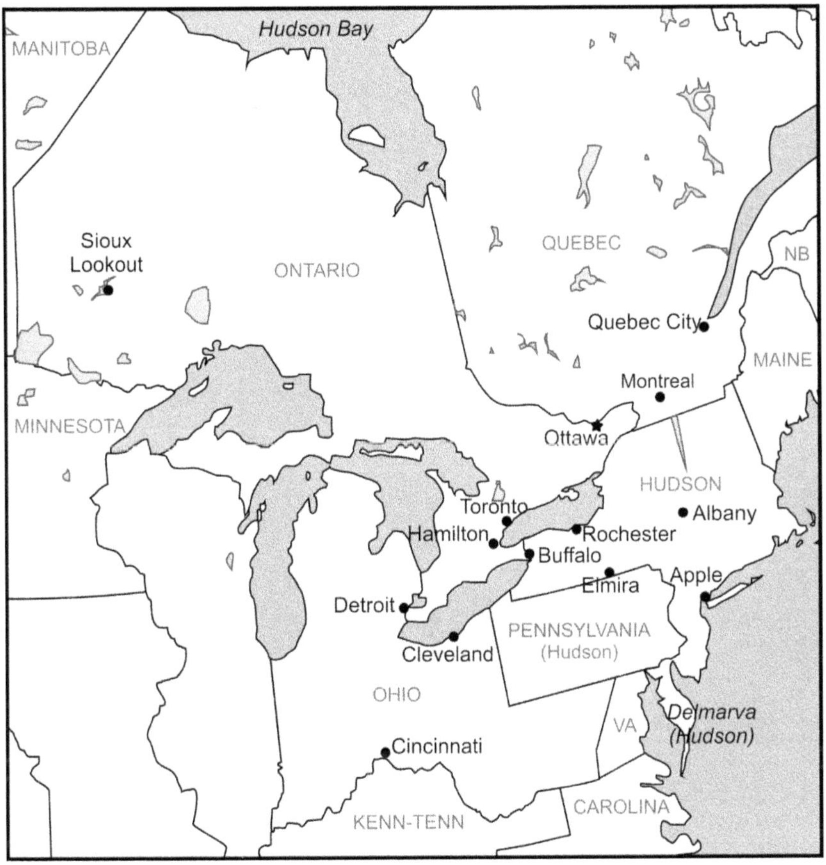

Additional maps are on pp. 173, 202, and 329.

PROLOGUE

THE CALM ACT

Climate change accelerated.
The tipping point came too hard, too fast.
Earth could no longer feed its billions.
America fared better than most.
Under a secret plan — the Calm Act.
Only half its citizens needed to die.

Young death angel Ava Panic is riding high.
Her first missions were a triumph.
But her partner, love of her life,
is seriously messed up.
Time to solo.

1

Interesting fact: At this time, the nation of Ohio covered the prior states of Ohio, West Virginia, Indiana, the lower half of Michigan, plus northwest Maryland and Virginia.

Ava Panic – currently using the name Bella – studied clear bottles of injectable livestock antibiotic.

Or rather, the bottle on the left was legitimate Nuvira. Ava-Bella considered this an awfully misleading name for an anti-bacterial drug that did nothing against viruses. The counterfeit bottle on her right contained the same inert base liquid, plain old propylene glycol, minus the antibiotic ingredients.

The printing job and packaging looked convincing on the fake product.

She paused in her study of the detailed warning label to glance around the Ohio barn the contractor used for their fake pharmaceutical bottling operation. In the event of accidental contact, this stuff advised immediate washing, removal of contaminated clothes, or a full 15 minutes of flushing for eye contact.

The fake antibiotic was perfectly harmless. She intended to open the real stuff.

"I need latex gloves and soap and water," Ava-Bella demanded imperiously of their host.

Williams was the local contractor's business manager. This particular fruitcake religious branch was called Four Horsemen. By whatever name, they were the same Sixers group she was familiar with from Pennsylvania – a sect that sought to hasten the End of Days. They were happy to doctor drugs for the company for pay. Mostly they produced poisoned opiates. But in this case they were un-medicating cattle.

The company didn't judge these requests from the martial authorities. They simply delivered.

Williams stonily ignored Bella's request and existence. As a rule, Sixers despised women. The feeling was mutual.

"Bella requires lab gloves and soap and water," KT repeated pleasantly. The ex-SEAL went by Cody in this part of Ohio. "Can you provide them? I think she wants to open the real sample for comparison."

Williams, a greying man in undertaker attire, rolled his eyes in impatience. "Antibiotics will do thy whore no harm."

"Debbie, Ed," Bella addressed the trainees. "Fetch me some sterile gloves from the car. Dish tub, soap and water. We'll wait." That last dig was for Williams. The car was parked on the far side of the farmhouse. They'd be standing here twiddling thumbs until the trainees returned.

Apparently Williams saw no need to hurry. He pressed his lips into a straight line and glowered into the distance.

That was fine. Between a career in the Navy SEALs for Cody, and Army Basic for Bella and the trainees, they were no strangers to 'hurry up and wait' while swapping gear.

Bella checked out the indoor distance as well. The barn air was replete with dust motes, she noted sadly. She ought to check the counterfeit bottles for visible inclusions. What she was trying to do here was quality control inspection.

Cody tossed the key fob to Debbie.

"How do you keep the dust out of the bottles?" Ava-Bella asked Williams.

After a suitable pause, KT-Cody parroted her question. Williams was willing to answer him.

The trio wandered over to observe one of the bottling machines in action, manned by a drugged slave. Bella peered into the device's plumbing. She checked the seal from the source propylene glycol barrel. KT-Cody had the mechanical and scientific aptitude of a guppy. But he forwarded Bella's questions affably enough.

The system looked reasonable to her. A few dust motes could float into the clean bottles. But they were only uncovered for a minute or two during the process.

"Do you wash the bottles as well?" Ava tried asking the slave this time.

Williams hand shot out to cuff the side of her head.

Caught by surprise, Bella failed to block the blow, which pissed her off immeasurably. *You nut case son of a –!*

She wheeled with a backhand to his gut, then a cross-punch to the sternum before KT-Cody could insert himself bodily between them.

"Don't touch my people again," Cody advised Williams. "If you don't want us talking to your slaves, just say so."

"Thou shalt not speak to the slaves!" Williams confirmed. "Thy whore should speak to no one! This is intolerable!"

Cody smiled lazily. "You want this shipment approved? You want payment? You'll just have to tolerate it." Cody didn't need to draw a gun. His physique spoke volumes. One blow from him could lay the old man out flat. "Bella is inspecting the shipment. You treat her with respect. Touch my people again and I will hurt you."

Williams and Bella glared at him equally. Bella would have preferred Cody deck the bastard.

It was a long morning. Bella finally approved the shipment and payment, and 30% bonus money. Every contractor got the same inflated payment these days. Now late May, the growing season continued to look dicey, agricultural forecasts grim, inflation mounting. But Cody managed to make Williams think he'd bargained for a major concession.

"How much of that is necessary?" Cody asked, as they drove away in his roomy Chevy Suburban, their ride in Ohio. He named the SUV

Rosa. "All that science-y stuff. I have no idea what you were doing there."

"Good question," Bella-Ava allowed sadly. "Did you hear Cody's question back there?" She craned her neck between the front seats to study her trainees. A month ago, Bella was meeting Sixers for the first time. She tried to get into the trainee's heads, but the occasions weren't very similar. This visit was routine and went according to plan. Her introduction to the Sixers was anything but.

As usual, trainee Debbie nodded, acting eager to please whether she heard Cody's question or not.

Ed was more honest. "Huh?"

"Cody asked what I was doing in the barn with the 'science-y stuff.' What you need to do. As an agent."

"OK."

"There's a contract," Bella attempted. "Those Sixers–"

"Four Horsemen?" Cody clarified.

"Right. Sorry. They have different names– Never mind. The religious fruitcakes prepare drugs for the company. We drop by and inspect their work. Can the buyers tell it from the real thing? Are the bottles marked so we can tell which is which? Stuff like that."

Ed asked, "What does a gang rat know about cow drugs?"

Like Bella, 'Ed' hailed from the tattered remains of New York City, the Apple. His Hispanic gang duked out their survival in Brooklyn, while Bella's corner of hell was in Manhattan's Chelsea neighborhood. Ed may never have met a cow personally.

"Not much," Bella allowed. "But you can't let that stop you. If you don't know much, study up before you go there. Read the contract. Ask questions. Look around, think it through. How could this go wrong? If I were a farmer, how would I know these were fake antibiotics? Count the bottles and the boxes. Match the manifest to the shipment."

"Manifest?" Cody asked.

"Remember the pages you plowed through with Williams?"

"I just parroted what you said."

"Any time there's a shipment, there's paperwork. What, how much, where, when. The carrier for distribution. Shipping addresses."

"Red tape," Cody said, nodding.

"Doing business takes a paper trail. Or email. Even when it's criminal business. I know. Surprised me, too."

"So how'd you know what's in the bottles?" Ed asked from the back seat.

"The barrels were propylene glycol," Bella said. "That's the same solvent real antibiotics would use. What Williams did was filling the bottles accurately, the labeling, and sealing. So it all looks legit."

"Prope-a-what?"

"The clear goopy stuff in the bottles."

"You knew that?" Cody asked.

"My parents were nurses," Bella explained. No, it wasn't her imagination. She'd lost control of this training session. Again. "They use the same stuff for e-liquid, too. For e-cigs."

"So why'd you open it?" Ed demanded.

"To make sure the real stuff didn't smell different," Bella said. "And see whether it had another seal under the cap." She rubbed her face with her hands. "Look, you'll do it your way. But that's what you need to accomplish. Otherwise the contractor won't respect you."

"Bella?" Ed said. "Newsflash. Williams did not respect you."

Cody chuckled. Debbie stared out her window in discomfort.

Bella felt her cheeks warm. Her hands itched to hit him. She was supposed to be training them. But her trainees didn't respect her any more than Williams did.

That had to change. But she couldn't figure out how. The car belonged to Cody, KT. She was 18. Cody was around 30. He was an ex-Navy SEAL, which impressed everyone, herself included. She was a vicious fighter for a hundred pounds and 5'1". But the runtiest guy alive had the reach on her. She was experienced at leading frightened kids, with her boyfriend backing her up. Cody had a sunny, laid-back personality. He was the kind of guy people simply enjoyed being around.

Cody-KT led this team. Not Bella-Ava. And there wasn't a damned thing she could do about it. She felt like she was letting Debbie down, too.

"Debbie, did that make sense?" Bella asked quietly.

Debbie kept her blank gaze out the window, and nodded. There was nothing out there to see except more young cornfields. Half an hour in Ohio, let alone a week, was enough to catch the gist of baby corn. Watching the geometric rows flash by the side of the highway was hypnotic.

Cody kept his eyes on the road, since he was driving. "It made sense, Bella. I just don't know that I could do it, if you weren't feeding me lines." He smiled disarmingly. "Girl, you make me feel dumb as a brick. What are we doing next?"

"Inspect the distributor," Bella said. "You want to ask the questions this time, Cody?"

"I have no idea what to ask a distributor," Cody said. "That's why you're here."

"Yup," Bella agreed. "Let's brainstorm it, gang. The distributor's job is to pick up the fake antibiotics, and get them to retail outlets. Veterinarians and feed stores, maybe? So there's a question I can ask. How do the drugs get to the farmers? The contract specifies, um, six counties. Ideas? Debbie, you first."

Bella felt like she was torturing them. But she managed to pry at least one question concept apiece from them for the vet supply distributor. Once they got there, she did the talking to the stolid ex-farmer. But the trainees were primed to listen and understand. The businessman automatically looked to Cody like everyone else. But he wasn't a lunatic like Williams. He readily switched his attention to the girl who acted like she knew what she was talking about.

The payment discussion was complicated by the fact that the task hadn't been performed yet. The distributor also raised a red flag in Bella's mind when he requested only 10% more money, where everyone else usually started at 50%. So Bella handled that negotiation, too.

As they rode off to seek the night's campground, Bella felt on the whole she'd done a pretty good job today. The company contracts for this job to un-drug the cows ought to proceed in good order.

"God that was boring," was Ed's verdict.

Cody smiled into the rear-view mirror. "Sometimes work feels like work, Ed. Rather go back to moldy salvage in Brooklyn?"

"Nope. Love my job," Ed agreed.

Bella said, "Guys? This was your first contractor visit. It was supposed to be easy. So you could learn what's supposed to happen. But think about how it could go wrong. Let me tell you about my first time –"

About to launch into her juicy tale, she stopped herself. A month ago, when she was the green trainee, her boyfriend Cade never did that. He didn't tell her stories of past jobs gone wrong. He let her experience the here and now, then made her ask the questions. Cade was a great teacher that way. He forced her to be the learner.

"Never mind," she said. "If you have questions about today, ask." When no one piped up, Bella consoled herself that she'd done her job.

BELLA CURLED IN ROSA'S PASSENGER SEAT FOR HER FAVORITE TIME OF DAY – talking to her boyfriend. The others huddled around a campground grill a stone's throw from the SUV, enjoying a before-supper beer to unwind. So far the only aroma of supper was the charcoal.

"You're upset," Cade noted. "What's up?"

Bella nursed her lite beer and shared her doubts about herself as trainer, and the leadership of the team. Cade made interrogative noises now and then. She could hear him chopping and sizzling his own supper at the company HQ resort camp in Finger Lakes, what was once western New York state. Home, for him at least. She hadn't spent much time there yet herself. But if Cade was there, it was home enough.

Weirdly, he could watch her via the dashcam, but she couldn't see him. She guessed he wasn't watching her anyway while he cooked.

When she wound down, Cade asked, "You want advice? Or just listening?"

"Do I need advice?" Bella asked defensively. He didn't reply, which made her answer her own question. "Yeah, I'd like advice."

"OK. First, baby, chuck your ego. This isn't about you. You're training them. Their training up to now wasn't like yours."

"Ed and Debbie won't tell me what they did last month." That was when Cade trained Bella-Ava in Pennsylvania, and then they swung through Virginia on a hair-raising prison break mission.

"They're not supposed to talk about it," Cade said. "But they were handlers. They monitored dashcams. Probably worked their way up to watching four at a time. The minute one got interesting, they had to hand it off to someone like me. God knows how many hours they watched you doze off, or stare out a window, or argue with me. They probably have to bite their tongues."

Bella wriggled to sit upright in discomfort. She hated the fact they were always spied on in their company car. She tried to forget the existence of the ever-silent watching handlers. The only one who ever spoke to Cade was Skull, Major Sullivan, their boss. For the Ohio trip, it was usually Cade who talked to them. He was Skull's assistant this month.

They were grooming KT-Cody to share that job. But he needed more field experience first. Hence this little jaunt in Ohio.

"Then there's Cody," Cade said, seeming to echo her thoughts. "So he's team leader. Why would you expect anything less? Baby, he joined the Navy before you started first grade. And he's a *Navy SEAL.* Best of the best. He's a nice guy. He'll humor you. But if you're smart?" He paused.

Bella scowled at the camera. "OK, I'll bite."

"Learn what you can from them. Especially Cody. It's the leadership move. Be the engaged student you wish they were. And enjoy them. Make friends. Be yourself. When you need to lay down the law, you will. You couldn't stop yourself if you tried. In the meantime, these people have your back. Are you willing to die for them? Would they risk their lives for you? That's what counts."

"I'm trying to be like you were."

"I was just being myself," said Cade.

"Oh."

"Baby, especially when it comes to bossing people around? I learned that back in the gang. It's impossible to be more strict, or less strict, than you really are. I'd try to be liked, be nicer than I felt. People didn't respect me for it. Did you have teachers like that in school? Sucked up to the kids?"

"Not at Brooklyn Tech. Earlier, though, yeah. A couple sergeants were too chummy at West Point, too. Not in my platoon, but others."

"We had one at St. Ignatius. Guys liked him, but took advantage. But when students came back to visit, when they were in college? The teacher they wanted to see again was Father Tanis. Religious studies. Toughest teacher in the school. We'd kill for his approval."

Bella frowned. "You took religious studies?" Cade wasn't Catholic. His high school was, and his best friends were. He went to Mass with them. But he claimed he wasn't qualified to take communion. She figured he'd signed a waiver to escape morning prayers or whatever at their top-notch prep school.

"Yeah. Really pissed off my parents at first. But the guidance counselor told me to try it for a semester and see. He was right. It wasn't catechism. Catholics made confirmation back in middle school. It was about ethics, leadership, understanding people, character building. Building a spiritual foundation for your life. Seriously, since Ebola broke out? Everything else I studied in high school? Useless. But we remembered Father Tanis every day."

"We," Bella echoed. *That's right.* The five guys who founded the gang were classmates at St. Ignatius. The two girls weren't. St. Ignatius was an all-boy school. "No wonder the religious crap in Western Civ class makes sense to you."

"Yeah, major advantage. But what I was saying. We didn't admire Father Tanis because he was easy, or nice. Or because he was hard. He was just himself. That's integrity. Back in the gang, sometimes I went the other way, tried to be more hard-ass than I really was."

Bella pursed her lips at the camera. As their gang leader Frosty the Snowman, Cade was tough as nails.

"Don't look at me like that." He was monitoring the dashcam after all. "Remember that guy who raped a ten-year-old? You wanted me to execute him. So I almost did, and then backed out of it. Remember how furious you were at me?"

"We gelded him," Bella pointed out. The furious girls, her in the lead, had taken matters into their own hands. Even now the old anger rose again.

"And I accepted that. I didn't agree. So I lost face. Not because I didn't agree, but because I flip-flopped."

"Oh. Yeah, I get it."

"So stop trying to be boss. Just be yourself. When you're the best leader, you'll be leader. When someone else has the hot potato, enjoy the fact it's burning his fingers instead of yours. Have I mentioned how I love having Skull as my boss?"

Bella grinned. "Once or twice. 'Orgasmic.'" She hadn't believed Cade at first on that score. She was starting to.

"Cody will make a good boss, too. That's why we picked him up."

"Yeah." Bella studied the affable man by the grill, with jaw-length light brown curls and great build, currently laughing with the others. If Cody was faking camaraderie with his young companions, she couldn't see it. "Miss you."

"Miss you, too. Not sure talking to me is good for you, though. They're not allowed to."

"Maybe it's OK to be an eighteen year old girl sometimes," Bella growled.

"Maybe it's awesome. Love you. Bye."

She took Cade's point. She waded back into the group by the grill. *Workout pointers,* she decided. If anyone could advance her physical training from where she left off in Basic, surely it was a Navy SEAL.

2

Interesting fact: Hudson was formed from the old states of New York, New Jersey, five of the six New England states, the Delmarva Peninsula, and soon to add Pennsylvania. Hudson had about the same population as Ohio. The two allied nations were the largest successors of the ex-United States.

Bella-Ava considered shooting at Debbie.

Yet again, the girl from mid-Jersey left her sidearm behind to visit the latrine. When Cade shot at Ava last month, he'd certainly made a lasting impression. She never made the mistake again. And while hiding from him, she took the opportunity to think through how she'd make it home to Hudson solo.

But Cade seemed to say that Cody was team leader by acclaim.

"Hey, Cody, could I talk to you?" She gestured away from the grill they ringed.

"Sure." He followed her lead twenty feet into the dark parking lot.

This was a low-end campground once. An empty in-ground swimming pool and large gravel parking lot were edged with some trees to keep the baby corn at bay. Assorted protuberances once provided power and plumbing hookups to RV's. Now they were just navigational hazards. Ed used a couple of them for awning tie-downs.

Between the warmer weather, claustrophobia, and a smaller vehicle interior, KT-Cody elected not to sleep inside Rosa-the-SUV the way Cade housed the team inside Darcy. Cody allocated more cargo space to creature comforts, and attached tents to either side of Rosa for sleeping. They each had a narrow air mattress to themselves, boys and girls on opposite sides of the car. Without the SUV itself providing protection, only three could sleep at a time while one stood watch. They split the night into three shifts, so that every fourth night they'd get uninterrupted sleep.

"What's up?" Cody asked genially.

"I was thinking about shooting at Debbie, and decided to run it by you –"

"Wait, what?"

"Whenever we're outside the SUV, we should go armed. She keeps forgetting her gun to go to the latrine."

Mouth slightly open, Cody pointed at the latrine. "Bella, I can see her. She didn't leave camp. Why would you shoot at her?"

"It makes a lasting impression?"

Cody continued to stare at her.

Bella sighed. "OK, no shooting at Debbie and Ed."

"No shooting at your own team. Ever. No. Bad idea."

"Cade– Never mind."

"Cade shot at you?"

"Yeah. I learned a lot that night."

"OK, Ava – Bella, sorry. Cade has some stability issues. Don't get me wrong, he's a great guy. And you, um, understand him. So maybe you could learn from that. Anybody else? No. Just, no."

"You're soft," Bella said. "Debbie could use some toughening up."

"Maybe. Not the way to do that. And Ed would never trust you again. Not sure I would either." Cody maintained his genial body posture. But his eyes were starting to acquire that glittery dangerous edge Cade's so often wore.

"OK. Another thing," Bella pressed on. "We've been camping like this, tents out. Cool. But I think we should hold a scram drill. You know, how fast we can go from asleep to buttoned up and out of here."

"You're just full of Miss Popularity suggestions tonight. Is Ed getting on your nerves again?"

"I'm supposed to be here to train you guys," Bella said mulishly. "Those were two ideas I had. Training that could happen tonight."

"OK. The tent scram isn't a bad idea. You shoot at anyone on the team and I take your guns away."

Bella glowered at him.

Cody sighed. "Bella, learning has active and passive phases. We had a big lesson today with the contractors. Tonight, everyone absorbs the lesson. Contemplate their moral reaction to withholding medicine from sick cattle. Or sleep and let the subconscious process the experience. Whatever. OK?"

Bella boggled. "You can only digest one lesson per day?"

"One big lesson, lots of little ones, kiddo." Cody's temper peeked out on that reply. He visibly tamped it down. "Tomorrow morning, when we break down the tents. You talk about how we'd do it in an emergency. We each pipe up. What we'd be in charge of. Where we need two people working together. Who's shooting, who's packing. What can be left behind. Stuff like that. Talk it through. It's a complicated evolution, Bella. We talk about it more than once. We practice it in the daytime. Next week, maybe we run a scram drill. It's a good idea."

"Maybe everyone should try doing it single-handedly."

Cody shook his head with a sad smile. "Miss Popularity, for sure. Let's talk about that after we've done it with four people. That all?"

"Yeah."

"Bella, you're doing fine," Cody said. "But not everything is an emergency, you know? Some people learn better in a crisis. Some don't. You were trained in the Army. Practice, practice, practice. So when it hits the fan, your reflexes do the right thing. That's the smart way to train."

Cody sounded so reasonable. Bella felt like an idiot. But at least she tried to work through him as the de facto leader.

THE NEXT NIGHT, A FEW CORN-FULL COUNTIES CLOSER TO TOLEDO, BELLA woke and stretched on her air mattress beside Debbie. The dew lay cool and clammy around her, beading on the tent fabric. Her phone thrummed on her hip again. Her mind finally focused on why she was awake.

She had the mid-watch.

Yawning, she pulled on a jacket against the night chill. She grabbed her Glock pistol and M4 carbine and some ammo, laid ready at the head of her bed. The dull khaki tent offered two exits – directly out, or into the car. They avoided opening and closing the car doors at night. In the pitch-dark silence, they sounded loud as gunshot and woke everyone.

Bella silently slipped out into the gravel parking lot. She lay the carbine down temporarily for some stretches and jumping jacks to wake up and get alert. A high haze dimmed the stars and thin moon above. Only then did she start to wonder.

Where's Ed?

He had first watch. By now he should be prodding her along so he could get to bed.

Thoughtfully, Bella slung her carbine and slipped silent and low around Rosa, crouching to keep her silhouette below the SUV hood and window level. No Ed to the front. She skirted the guys' tent on the left side and peered in through the window netting. Cody's side was full, as expected.

She slipped around the back. There, by the campsite's built-in steel-legged grill. Cody didn't bother to stow his beach chairs before bed. She snuck up to them.

Yup, Ed was sound asleep on the lounger. His hand dripped down toward an empty beer bottle on the ground.

Bella pulled out her Glock and shot the beer bottle.

Ed exploded from the chair, shaking glass shards off his hand. "You bitch from hell!"

Bella thwacked his head with a light backhand punch. "Asleep on guard duty. You pick up that rifle, idiot. Two hands, over your head. Pump that rifle! Up, down! Jog around the grill!"

Ed naturally felt more inclined to take a swing back at her. But Bella was in fighting form. Ed was rattled and reactive. She got in two kicks and connected with a nasty hook to his eye before Cody waded in and shoved them apart.

"What the fuck?" he inquired.

"The dumb-ass was asleep on watch," Bella accused.

Simultaneously Ed screamed, "The bitch shot a beer bottle out of my hand!"

"OK." Cody raised hands in the dark to halt the flow. "Ed. Sleeping and beer on watch? Really? Bella. We discussed shooting at the trainees. We said, *don't.* Drop your guns. Both of them."

"Like hell I will! Cody, *back down!* I've got this. And you know what? You can stow your god-damned lawn chairs right now! This isn't a picnic! Ed, I told you to pump your rifle over your head and *jog,* dammit. You jog til dawn! You take a swing at me again, you jog til sunset! And Debbie – thank God *someone* is thinking! Way to go, girl!"

Debbie was up and out. She had her M4 at the ready, and prowled around keeping watch while the other three were distracted. She wore her West Point standard sleep uniform – a T-shirt over stretchy workout shorts. Her bare feet were thrust into untied combat boots. Bella trusted she'd attend to her clothing along the way. Debbie was a thinker.

Unlike the two lugs before her.

Ed wasn't moving to comply. Bella darted around Cody and thwacked Ed's rump with her rifle, then scampered backward and aimed the gun at Cody.

"I told you to stow your damned chairs, Cody. Police the camp before bed. And neither of you needs your tent again tonight. Stow that, too. Do it now!"

"You're giving me orders now?" Cody demanded in disbelief. "And pointing a gun at me? *Me?!*"

"Yes I am. Move it!"

Ed tried to rush her. She shot the steel grill with impressively loud report. The ricochet grazed Cody's bare leg.

"Stop!" Cody yelled. The trio froze for a moment, breathing hard. Bella's frozen stance included an M4 pointed directly at Cody.

The SEAL raised his hands in surrender. In slow motion, he

grabbed the two chairs and collapsed them. He picked them up and popped Rosa's back hatch.

"Get that rifle above your head and start pumping," he advised Ed.

"Don't forget to jog," Bella added. "Around the grill. And oh yeah, you idiots forgot to apologize to Debbie and me."

"You're pushing it," Cody growled.

"Your goal is to stow that tent in under three minutes," Bella returned. "Keep practicing."

"I will discuss this with Skull in the morning," Cody vowed. "Ed, pump that rifle before I deck you."

Ed finally complied, swearing a blue streak.

"Why wait, Cody?" Bella demanded. "We can call Cade right now. Wake him up. Want to guess what he'll say? Because I'm trying to train you idiots. To keep you alive. It's *dangerous* out here! But you know better than me about everything. So you won't listen. And you prevent these other two from learning, too."

"I'll stow the effing tent," Cody agreed.

"Three minutes! That's your goal time. Ed, pump that rifle! *Up. Down. Up.* You've got *hours* to go!"

Debbie kneeled to tie her boot, yawning. "Are we all staying up?"

"Yup," Bella said. "I need to watch them. You watch the world."

"Then Cody can stow our tent, too," Debbie quipped, loud enough for Cody to hear.

Bella grinned at her. "Good idea. Hey, those shots might attract attention."

"That was my thought," Debbie concurred sourly.

Bella drifted over to watch Cody figure out that there was no way for one man to deflate two air mattresses and pack the tent in under three minutes. Under fire the best he could do would be to transfer the more critical gear into the SUV, detach the tent, and kick it away. His nice rainbow-striped fabric beach chairs, cook pots left on the grill for morning, and the beer cooler, would simply be left behind. Their combat boots and weapons were a priority.

She didn't let the SEAL off the hook that easy. He timed exactly how long it took to deflate the air mattresses, inflate them again, and deflate them faster.

A militia car did swing by after a half hour. Bella did the talking. Someone snuck up on their camp. A couple shots scared them away. Nope, sorry officer, didn't get a good look at them.

Us? The last cover story she worked up in Virginia dripped out of Bella's mouth on automatic. We were down in western Virginia trying to retrieve deadbeat relatives. Found them, but an indigent labor camp got them first. Couldn't get them released. Headed home to Cleveland now.

Ed? He fell asleep on watch. He's doing penance. "Up! Down! Pump that rifle! You're fresh from your nap, Ed! Too soon to slack off now!"

The sheriff's deputy laughed and drove away.

"You have a patch kit, Cody?" Bella inquired.

"Yeah. In the back."

She stabbed the air mattress he was deflating with her utility knife. "Quicker that way."

Cody shook his head in disgust. "Miss Congeniality. Not a team-building move, Ava. Sorry. Bel-la." He trilled the L's.

She squatted down beside him to speak quietly. "And you're not taking this seriously, Cody. How much money did we flash around today?" They'd dropped by a county farm market. Bella found a couple high-end leather briefcases to accessorize for their upcoming business meetings near Detroit. They all picked out business casual attire. Food? A week of eating high on the hog for four athletes. Toys? Beer? Whatever they felt like. None of the locals could afford to waste money the way they did.

"Yesterday?" she pressed her point. They'd paid off the Four Horsemen for three months of illegal manufacturing and supplies and subcontractors, plus a hefty down payment to the distributor. At current labor rates, they disbursed a generous annual income for over a hundred people.

"Cody, our *allies* are in organized crime. Our enemies include anyone who wants a free ride. The local cops. And oh, the Ohio Army if we piss them off. We carry enough money to *buy* one of these tiny towns. You keep thinking we're on friendly turf. But we're not. Because you're one of the bad guys now. You need to get your head in the game. I have so much to learn from you. But dammit, you need to learn from me, too. Capiche?"

"What's that? 'Capiche.'"

"It's New Yorker for 'do you understand?'"

"That Spanish or something?"

"I just said. It's New Yorker." Bella stood and sighed. "You know what your problem is, Cody? You're too damned likable."

"Not a fault you plan to emulate. Clearly."

"You got that right."

"Take a knee again, Bella. If you really believe you've got a thing or two to learn from me."

Bella scowled, but complied.

Cody punched the half-full air mattress into a folded wad and sat on it to hurry it along its way to flat. "Bella, here's the part you don't get. You cross the line, and your team starts to think how much better life would be if they just slit your throat in your sleep."

"Point. But none of us are that way."

"How do you know that? After tonight, Ed will hate you."

"No. Because Ed was a gang rat. Ed trained with us at West Point. Ed knows he screwed up. He doesn't like me. But he knows I'm right. We'll be OK in the morning. You, I'm not so sure about. We might need Skull or Cade to referee. Because some idiot down the line taught you that your feelings mattered. But you wouldn't slit my throat. Ever. Would you. You'd have my back. Because you know I'd have yours."

Grudgingly, the grown man nodded. "OK. And Bella? For the record. A guy who passed SEAL selection? We know better than you ever will, how to choose our own feelings."

Bella nodded, blowing out in satisfaction. Finally they'd turned the corner in this confrontation. "Cody, every bit of that you can teach me? I want to learn."

"Yeah, be careful what you ask for, little one. You learn that by enduring the suck."

"That's how Skull chose us," Bella said. "We endured the suck." She offered her fist for a bump. He punched it in accord.

They wouldn't need a referee.

"Are we really the bad guys, Bella?" Cody asked uneasily. "If the good guys hire us to handle their black ops?"

Bella studied him as best she could in the darkness. She couldn't tell whether his conscience was bothering him or not. She said gently, "I don't know, Cody. Could be that's backward. Maybe our team hires the good guys to manage the law-abiding for us. Way above our pay grade."

She left him with that beguiling thought. She wanted to keep Debbie company for a bit. The quiet girl deserved more recognition for doing the right thing. Mercifully, the Princeton New Jersey native had no midnight qualms of conscience, nor pangs of ego. She was just tired.

Around 0330 hours, there came a point when all gear was neatly stowed in Rosa. Ed was stumbling along exhausted. The raucous chorus of pre-dawn birds was starting to build.

Daylight savings time was history. Shopkeepers used to love it, to keep consumers out late spending while enjoying the summer evening sun. These days the martial Rescos preferred curfew and sending people to bed. Bella hated the birds waking her up so early.

She suggested they climb in, set the car alarm, and sleep the rest of the night inside. With so much stuff in the cargo hold, the seats couldn't recline.

Approval was unanimous.

At 0800, Skull woke them with new instructions.

3

Interesting fact: Canada picked up Alaska, Minnesota, Maine, and the Upper Peninsula (UP) of Michigan. The ex-states were still transitioning to provinces.

"Boss," Cody began, once they were presentable. "Before we get started, I think we need to talk about the command structure here."

On the road, they addressed Skull as 'boss,' not Skull or Major Sullivan. He used their current aliases.

"Why?" Skull inquired.

"We had an issue last night. The question is whether Bella or I have the lead."

"And the answer?" Skull asked.

Cody stared at the dashcam, mouth slightly ajar.

Bella offered, "I think it depends."

"On?" Skull prompted.

"We each have a role," Bella said. "I teach them the company ropes. Cody has more combat experience. Debbie was on watch last night. If she sees something while we're asleep, we have to follow her call. Same for Ed."

"OK," Skull agreed neutrally.

Cody said, "I told Bella a couple days ago that if she ever shot at Ed or Debbie, I'd take her guns away. That transpired last night."

"Transpired," Skull echoed.

Bella feared from Skull's tone of voice that Cody was rousing the boss's sense of humor. Bella found Skull hard to read through the Army officer facade. But she divined much from the way the man honestly enjoyed her boyfriend Cade's company and friendship.

"Ed made a mistake," Bella volunteered. "We corrected the mistake. I think Cody made a mistake, too. We hashed that out."

"Hashed," Skull repeated. "Ed?"

"We're good," Ed reported hastily. True testament to his inexperience, he failed to shut up at that point. "Bella didn't shoot at me, exactly. I mean, she shot a beer bottle out from under my hand. Then she shot the grill. I think the ricochet grazed Cody's leg. So there was some blood there, too. But by that point, she was pissed at Cody, not me. Um, sir."

"Debbie?"

"Ed fell asleep on watch, drinking beer. After Bella shot the beer, Cody stopped a fight between her and Ed. Cody demanded Bella drop her weapons. Bella told him to police the camp. She shot the grill when Cody advanced on her. I took watch."

"Thank you, Debbie," Skull said. "Succinct, clear, good job."

"Thank you, boss."

"Suck up," Ed growled.

"Cody?" Skull prompted.

Cody had time by now to reflect on whether he really wanted to complain to Skull about Bella in front of Debbie and Ed. "I withdraw the question, boss. You called us?"

"Yes," Skull said. "I'm going to re-arrange your schedule. You need Bella for your business meetings near Detroit. I'm moving those to tomorrow. Then I need Bella back in Hudson."

Cody asked, "Where do we take her in Hudson?"

"I was unclear," Skull said. "Bella is returning to Rochester. The rest of you will continue without her in Ohio. She might rejoin you later."

"Boss?" Bella asked. "How?" *Why?*

"I'll text you details separately. And we'll talk once you're back in Hudson."

Ava grabbed the map tablet. Her memory was correct. Rochester was past the opposite end of the nearby Great Lake, then on to the middle of the next one.

Skull continued, "The main point is, I want you to proceed directly to what we had scheduled for Sunday night." It was now Wednesday. "Go to your hotel in Grosse Pointe. Prepare for your meetings. Complete those tomorrow. Then drop Bella off at the Detroit River bridge into Canada."

Bella checked her phone for instructions. Yes, that was one way from Detroit to Rochester – follow the north side of Lake Erie through Ontario. Grosse Pointe was a northern suburb of Detroit, hopefully outside the slum radius.

Her questions were many. But first things first. "Boss? Do I have enough cash for these meetings?"

"Good point," Skull said. "Probably not. I'll follow up on that. Anything else?"

"I think I'm the only one with a business suit. Know any good rush tailors in Detroit?"

Skull laughed without humor. "Spend as little time as possible in Detroit. Weapons visible at all times."

"Got it," Bella agreed. "Can do."

"Thank you, Bella. I'll get back to you about the finances." Skull disconnected.

"What the –" Cody began.

But Bella was already opening the car door. "It's like five hours drive to Grosse Pointe. Let's get breakfast and full workouts first. Plenty of time to talk on the road. Cheer up, Cody. I won't be around to challenge your authority for a while. Careful what you ask for." She grinned at him.

The ex-SEAL had the grace to look daunted. He had no idea how to run the business meetings in Grosse Pointe. Acquire astronomical sums of money. Visit a tailor. Or even how he'd deliver Bella safely to the Detroit River.

To Bella's mind, that's what made the death angel job so much fun. Always a fresh new challenge.

~

An hour out from Grosse Pointe, Ava Panic clambered into Rosa's cargo space as Bella. She emerged as Caitlyn Dominici. She'd been upgrading her wardrobe for just such an occasion.

Even dressed down for her travel comfort, Caitlyn would never arrive at an upscale hotel looking like a street tramp. She did not own high-top red sneakers. Her running shoes were low, particolored, and of a conspicuous brand name. Her designer sports bra was worn only to the gym or out for a jog. Her pretty panties matched her casual bra, which might play a bit of peek-a-boo due to the plunging neckline on her cap-sleeved skin-tight brilliant white T-shirt. The businesswoman liked to flaunt the rewards of her workouts. A decade later, she kept the toned body of a nubile 18-year-old. The day was cool, below 70, so she wore a fun and light asymmetric-cut jacket, in piecework stripes over tight bleached-blue jeans.

The trainee Debbie, seated behind the driver, observed her transformation with interest.

Michigan offered some of the worst roads Caitlyn had met on her travels. This was frost-heave and snow-plow country. Clearly the heaves were still scraped open regularly, like shaved acne pimples. The resulting crumbling holes spread like leprosy. The pavement hadn't been repaired in years.

"Excuse me – Dan, was it?" she inquired of her driver, recently Cody.

"Uh, OK," Dan-KT agreed gamely.

"And your last name was…?"

"I get a last name this time, huh? Um, Eddington."

Ava-Caitlyn prompted Debbie and Ed the same way.

"Rosa, record note. In Detroit for business, I am Caitlyn Dominici, assistant Dan Eddington. Our guards today are Ellie and Fabio. Rosa, end. Eddington, could I trouble you to pull over for a moment?"

KT-cum-Dan Eddington slowed and pulled onto the highway's breakdown lane.

Caitlyn ousted Fabio from the navigator seat and flipped down her visor-mounted make-up mirror to apply eye-liner. "It's just impossible with the car bouncing."

"Christ, Bella," Fabio-Ed erupted. "We stop for you to fucking put on makeup?"

Caitlyn tilted her mirror to meet his eye. She pouted her lips in disapproval. "Fabio, I find your language inappropriate. While you work for me, you will mind your manners." She readjusted her mirror to its proper angle and applied three more deft lines of sable, the near-black extending into cat's-eyes. "Ellie, could I trouble you to pass me up the vinegar?"

A few swipes of vinegar to get rid of natural skin oils, followed by wax strips, both shaped her brows and irritated the skin around them. This added a helpfully aging bit of puffiness. She caked on moisturizer she didn't need, and thick makeup, sniffing in distaste at the smell. She spritzed her hair with a grapefruit-scented 'body mist,' about the strongest perfume she could stand. Maroon lip-liner pencil and too-brown shiny lipstick added fullness to her narrow lips. Harsh slashes of darker and lighter blush restored color that the makeup had removed, and added contour where it didn't quite belong.

She gazed at Dan, then Ellie, with an arched eyebrow. "What do you think? Too heavy for afternoon?"

"Lovely, boss," Dan quipped from the driver seat. "You don't look a day over twenty-five."

"That's amazing," Ellie said, shaking her head slightly. "Could you show me how to do that tonight?"

"Perhaps another time?" Caitlyn offered apologetically. "Gang–Group. Sometimes it's enough to use a different name. Assume a different hometown. But basically you're the same person. Ellie and Fabio, you're not really so different from yesterday. But Dan and I are successful nouveau riche –"

"Nuva-what?" Fabio interjected.

"New money. Nouveau riche," Caitlyn supplied. "We have prospered in the post-Calm shadow economy. I have extensive business experience, and part of an M.B.A. from Wharton. I'm twenty-nine again this year." She winked. "Caitlyn Dominici is not just a new name. I'm a different person. You don't treat me the same way. For instance, Ellie, you wouldn't expect me to act like a girlfriend and swap makeup tips. You're a teenager. I'm Dan's age. I need your help to stay in character. Clear?"

"Does she carry an M4 carbine?" Ellie inquired.

"No," Caitlyn replied. The very idea reminded her to buff and polish her nails, which she started on next. "Dan and I carry Glocks. Concealed carry in my case. And Fabio? I do not carry luggage. You do."

Fabio chuckled. "I hope that means we get beds tonight."

"Of course. What, you think I'd sleep in a car?" She was quite pleased with herself for how the *perish-the-thought* expression came out in the mirror. "Convincing, Dan?" she asked hopefully.

He rocked his head so-so. "Don't overdo it. You're a businesswoman, not the terror of your country club. But you're small and look too young. So you'd overcompensate, be a bit pushy. And twenty-six. Max."

"Caitlyn is a stretch for me," she agreed. "Maybe you could touch me, like my elbow, or scratch your ear, if I'm coming on too strong." She tilted her head to indicate Ellie and Fabio in the back seats. "Keep them in line, OK? Better I stay in character twenty-four seven until we're done at the hotel. Managing the hired muscle is Dan's job."

They shared a smile.

"Am I dressed OK?" Dan asked.

Caitlyn considered him. He wore jeans these days, but still favored his comfortable SEAL pullover shirts, khaki quarter-zip jersey with camouflage raglan sleeves. Minus insignia, of course. Her eyes naturally drifted to his unbound blond curls.

"What do you think?" Caitlyn asked. "Who are you being?"

He flipped down the visor. He thoughtfully brushed his stubble beard with his finger tips. "Company hired an ex-SEAL on security. My KT persona works as Dan. Got a hair tie?"

"Good call." She handed one over. As Dan pulled back into the scant highway traffic, she started experimenting on her own hair.

"Burned out houses all the time now," Ellie murmured.

Michigan was swampy compared to Ohio, with stands of deciduous trees sporadic but surprisingly tall. Caitlyn remembered Minnesota had been like that. How short the trees seemed in Texas when her family moved south. This looked like farmland. Except it was nearly June and half the land seemed overgrown and untended, the buildings falling down or burned out, as Ellie said.

"Getting close to Detroit," Dan agreed with a sigh.

~

"EVERYTHING IS PREP WITH YOU," FABIO COMPLAINED. HE DROPPED HIS sheaf of paperwork to the coffee table and rubbed tired eyes.

The quartet studied after supper. Their vast and tasteful two-bedroom suite was at the castle-like Grosse Pointe Lawn & Racquet Club, perched among emerald-green manicured lawns and gardens and tennis courts. Below, Lake St. Clair reflected the lowering steel-grey sky. The property security forces were many but tactful, constantly prowling the periphery. Canada beckoned across the water a few miles to the right, south of them from here.

Caitlyn-Ava winced in sympathy. It wasn't that Fabio couldn't read. He wasn't in her league, but he was smart enough. The challenge was the legal vocabulary. Caitlyn had to look up words on every page, and ask Dan-KT to explain when the definitions didn't help. Her Serbian family had been well-educated and tried to speak English at home. Fabio's family had alternated between Brooklyn and San Juan. His neighborhood and gang were Puerto Rican. He didn't have enough English to read this stuff. Ellie, she noted in envy, didn't reach for the tablet with its dictionary. But she was no more adept at business contracts than Caitlyn.

Their list of questions for Skull grew.

"Want to go wash the car?" Dan suggested.

Maybe Dan intended it as a joke. But Fabio pounced on the excuse. He snatched the key fob and escaped out to enjoy the palatial grounds as their diligent chauffeur.

"You can take a break too, if you want, Ellie," Caitlyn offered. Only

Caitlyn and Dan had to be conversant in all these contract terms. "You don't play a speaking part tomorrow."

Ellie stretched thoughtfully. Caitlyn wasn't sure what mix of races formed the girl's light brown features, almond eyes and wavy dark hair. Her eyes were a bit too small, looking almost crossed and faintly surprised over a spray of large freckles across a small nose. Her features were cute, but fell short of pretty.

"I'd rather stay here," Ellie decided. "Help if I can. I think I understand this one." She tapped her printout. "Harassing attacks on small lead-contaminated communities," she explained in distaste. "Encourage them to vacate. Old-style militants are the contractors. The last one specialized in inciting race warfare inside Detroit."

"Charming," Dan said. Caitlyn silenced him with a raised eyebrow.

Skull had emailed Caitlyn the appointment schedule and related documents. With duplicate copies, they had over a hundred pages of stapled contracts strewn across the leather-upholstered sitting area. Dan and Fabio got to practice the knack of refilling their cranky printer's ink cartridges with a syringe. Modern printers and their cartridges were meant for planned obsolescence, not to last for years. Theirs would soon reach the point of no return.

Ellie added, "My turn with Skull is in twenty minutes."

Dan automatically looked to the door. "Oops. Should I fetch Fabio back?"

"No, just me."

A courier arrived with a briefcase of currency, Buckeye and Canadian dollars plus a sheaf of Pennsylvania Liberty dollars.

Caitlyn and Ellie had seen the guy at West Point, but hadn't spoken to him before. He didn't even provide a false name now. He just handed over the briefcase, tapped a foot while Caitlyn and Dan inventoried it, then vanished.

Caitlyn taught Dan the job she'd done during her last and only time holding these high-level meetings in Philadelphia. He had to count out the correct mixed currency needed for each appointment – there would be seven – and apportion it into marked envelopes. Additional envelopes were pre-counted into handy quantities. They wanted to unload almost all the foreign scrip, except to fund Caitlyn's trip across

Ontario. Unless negotiations went badly tomorrow, they should have enough Buckeye left over to fund the rest of Dan's Ohio tour.

"Dan, Skull's ready for you in ten," Ellie reported, emerging from the bedroom where she'd finished her private video consult. "Caitlyn's last."

"Go OK?" Caitlyn asked.

"Fine."

Caitlyn left it at that. She debriefed Ellie instead on questions for Skull about the two militant contracts Ellie reviewed for her. Caitlyn also explained to her what they were doing with the money because the other girl was interested. But she didn't help. The fewer people who touched the money, the better.

Dan emerged from the bedroom looking solemn. "Caitlyn."

"Something wrong?"

He shook his head slightly, not meeting her eye. "Your turn."

Caitlyn-Ava collected her things, stepped into the master bedroom and closed the door behind her. She sat on the end of the bed before the generously sized TV. Dan's phone was acting as their video camera. It dangled by its charging cord at the top of the screen. Skull was tapping away at his keyboard. He glanced into his webcam and raised a wait finger.

Despite the dramatic nickname, Skull was one of the blandest-looking human beings Ava-Caitlyn had ever met. His major's uniform was impeccable despite what was probably the fourteenth hour of his workday. A tumbler of whiskey sat at his elbow. He clearly wanted to knock off for bed.

"You work too hard, boss," Caitlyn murmured. "Thank you."

He looked up with a surprised smile. "You're good." He glanced back down at his screen and performed a final click. "OK, sorry, I'm with you now."

"Great. Dan and Ellie looked browned off. Something I should know?"

4

Interesting fact: Detroit's peak population reached 1.8 million in 1950. When it filed for bankruptcy in 2013, the New York Times *described it as a city of "700,000 people, [and] tens of thousands of abandoned buildings, vacant lots and unlit streets."*

Skull sighed and took a sip of his whiskey. "Why do women always ask about other people? Is your own job so straightforward? You look great, by the way. Older. Professional. Ready for tomorrow?"

Shot down, Ava-Caitlyn flapped her note sheet. "I have questions."

"Good. But you're right, we need to talk about personnel issues. Ellie will be returning with you to Hudson."

"Why?"

"She's had enough. Doesn't want to stay in Ohio without you, be the only woman on the mission."

Caitlyn considered everything else she needed to accomplish tonight, like a full night's sleep to make up for the broken night before. "I can try to talk her out of it."

"Please don't. You can ask her once you're back in Hudson. But I agreed to let her leave. That dismayed KT. Um, Dan." He referred to a crib sheet in annoyance at his slip on the name. "I gather he felt a boys versus girls dynamic had emerged. And that it was his fault. Was it?"

"I'm surprised Ellie is leaving," Caitlyn pointed out. "We had a rough night last night. Issues happen. You work through it. That's what I'd tell her."

"And him?"

"Not my top issue with Dan tonight," Caitlyn hedged. If there was a boy-girl schism on the team, she feared she caused it, not KT-Dan. But in her experience, you'd need to fight 24/7 against human nature to keep that from happening, and why bother.

"What's your complaint against Dan?"

Caitlyn recoiled. "None!"

Skull took a bigger swig of his whiskey. "Caitlyn, I appreciate the way you defend your team. I do. But reading between the lines, I wonder if Dan has a problem with some of your interviews tomorrow. Like, he disapproves."

"Yeah," Caitlyn admitted. "Yeah, that's a problem."

She glanced over the agenda. Four of the contracts to be discussed held nothing to twinge the conscience. But three of them clearly bothered Dan. "And with him sitting next to me, it's so hard to get grownups to take me seriously, you know? They talk to him. So I end up feeding him lines."

Skull shook his head. "Different level this time, Caitlyn. Dan is better with idiots, granted. But tomorrow you talk to the bosses, not the peons. If they talk to Dan, raise a hand, interrupt, tap the contract. Say 'I'm the one with signature authority here, gentlemen. Not Dan. Please speak to me.' And if Dan can't leave his moral qualms outside, he needs to leave the room."

The teenager blanched. "Dan's my only ally in the room. I kick him out?"

Skull smiled sympathetically. "You just turned into an eighteen-year-old again, Ava. Maybe you have that conversation with Dan tonight, not at the meeting. Which discussions he can't handle. You just glanced at your schedule. Which ones should we mark ND – no Dan?"

"Three, four, and six," she admitted. She reluctantly penciled in ND on those, as Skull did on his hard copy.

"And you?" Skull asked. "Do you have qualms about those?"

"Not really. I used to. I got over it."

"Good. Tell Dan how you got over it. Ask him to leave for those three appointments. Maybe together you can reduce it to two."

She bit her lip, then recalled that Caitlyn wouldn't do that.

"On my authority, Caitlyn," Skull encouraged gently. "This isn't you against Dan. It's him learning the job."

So he can become my boss, Ava-Caitlyn thought sourly.

"What was that?" Skull asked.

Dammit, Skull doesn't miss a beat. "Maybe I have other issues with Dan. And you still haven't told me why I'm being recalled to Hudson. Did he complain about me?"

"OK. Look, Ava. You and I are overdue to spend some quality, quantity time together. We'll get that chance once you're back in Hudson. For now, you can assume that I think you're doing a great job. And so is Dan. You are on a training mission. Everybody is learning. Perfect. Got it?"

"Is it the truth?"

"It's the thirty second version of the truth. And that's all we have time for. Can we move on to your contract questions?"

"Well, there's how to get through Detroit to that bridge."

"I don't know. But my courier made it to you with the cash. So it's possible."

Caitlyn frowned. "Your courier. That's a job I didn't know you had."

"Ava, we could talk for hours. And we will. Soon. Right now, I need sleep, and you need to debug Dan. Contract questions, please?"

"Right. Sorry. Meeting three. Before we sic militants on civilians, I think we need rules of engagement –"

~

"Colonel Eck, so good to meet you," Caitlyn Dominici rose to greet her next appointment in the hushed solarium overlooking the vibrant green grounds. Caitlyn offered her hand to shake first, before Dan could rise from his seat.

Apple tomboy Ava Panic detested shaking hands. Caitlyn had a firm dry grasp, with freshly moisturized, well-manicured finger tips. She had a surprisingly powerful grip for such a petite woman. Her expensive dark red coat-dress exuded class.

She waved to her companion. "My assistant, Dan Eddington." She allowed the two burly camouflage-clad men to exchange manly shakes and eye contact before adding, "Dan, could you check on those ROE documents?"

"Of course, Ms. Dominici. Excuse me, Colonel Eck." Dan left the hushed room of wicker and floral.

"Please help yourself to tea," Caitlyn invited smoothly with a wave. She made no move to pour for him. A brilliantly colored and expensive tray of treats, crystal water decanter and goblets, gold-chased hors d'oeuvre plates and napkins and tasteful silverware also stood at the ready on the side table, and passed without comment. If you want it, serve yourself, was clear. Caitlyn's papers on the coffee table were already flanked by teacup and delicacies. The waiter knew to bus the table and refresh only between clients.

Nonplussed, Colonel Eck availed himself of a water glass, deviled eggs, and hothouse strawberries before sinking into the floral cushions of the wicker armchair to her right. "Will Eddington be long?"

"We don't need to wait for him," Caitlyn assured Eck.

Eck frowned. "What happened to Ryder?"

Ryder was agent Weyland's alias on this beat. "I'm afraid Mr. Ryder is dead. He was on assignment in West Virginia. Killed by hillbillies when he stopped for gas." This was all true. Caitlyn took a regretful sip of tea. "I'm recently of the Pennsylvania branch of the company, filling in for the moment."

"You. Not Eddington."

"That's right." Caitlyn allowed herself an edged smile. "Don't worry. I know I look young. But I'm more experienced with the company's urban operations than you might expect."

Actually Ava Panic was shooting the last time, in North Jersey, though she'd been on the opposing force to the company. Even at the time, she suspected there was no more right or wrong side to the conflict than red and blue teams in a live fire exercise. But Caitlyn Dominici had no military experience.

Eck scowled. "Hmm."

Caitlyn picked up the contracts, and handed him a copy. The table bore no trace of anyone else's business, only a blank legal pad and pens, and Eck's paperwork.

"I think you'll find most of this language was covered with Ryder." She picked up phrases like 'this language' while Cade played this role in Philadelphia. Years of backing up Cade in the gang trained her to ape his word choices for greatest impact. Skull had reinforced the lingo last night, too.

She continued, "This is straightforward. The company will hire your militia –" Outfits like Eck's still styled themselves militia, even though the Army had co-opted that term for duly sworn forces. "–To, um, 'instigate' disturbances in Detroit, Cincinnati, and Toledo, on July 4th. Ohio calls that Independence Day, right?"

Eck glowered and shook his head in disgust.

She added, "For your information, there will be other demonstrations that day in cities outside your range."

"Where?" Eck demanded. He clicked his pen ready to make a note in the margins.

"I can't share details," Caitlyn replied. "But they will be significant, distracting, and divide the Army's forces."

"I need details."

"I don't have them. I can inquire."

"Hell yes."

Caitlyn made a note on her legal pad. "If you turn to pages three through five, you'll see maps of the cities of interest. We've marked the neighborhoods, by block, for your demonstrations to target."

"Black neighborhoods. Fucking immigrants." Eck approved.

Almost certainly, Caitlyn agreed. "The marked neighborhoods. The key point is that we need to contain the violence within those areas."

Eck snorted. "Christ, lady, you don't understand. These are mob riots."

Caitlyn smiled. "Yes, Colonel, I do understand. Riots are hard to steer. But the company requires you to exert yourself. For the contract, we will be adding rules of engagement –"

"*What!?* Christ, woman, my guys want to waste this scum! You expect me to tell them to mind their manners?"

Caitlyn put up a hand. "Colonel, we understand that some, on all sides, will exceed the ROE. But following the ROE will limit loss of life and property."

"The whole fucking point is loss of life and ghetto property!"

Caitlyn shrugged and flipped back to page two. "Those are listed in goals 1-e through 1-j." Page one was an opaquely worded table of contents.

As she'd hoped, Eck also hunched forward and referred to page two. He unconsciously nodded, finding statements of purpose he agreed with.

Caitlyn donned a pair of reading glasses, the weakest she'd found in Philly, 1.25 magnification. She was too young to need reading glasses. Ergo, she hoped that wearing them made her look older. "The ROE puts some curbs on damage inside the marked blocks. But the main point is containment, *of your guys.* And some effort to control the natives. We don't expect you to risk your lives for them. But if you keep your personnel and property inside the zone, you will lose less of *yours.*"

"How the hell you gonna manage that?"

"The company prefers not to say. Colonel, deniability is in everyone's best interest."

The self-styled colonel thoughtfully sat back in his chair and stared at her. "You should get your eyes fixed. I had it done. Laser surgery."

Metaphor? Or alligator, or whatever that word was? "My eyesight was fine before the Calm. Since then, what doctor would you trust with your eyes?" She took a delicate bite of deviled egg, and washed it down with some chamomile tea.

"Hell, not here," Eck said. "I had it done in Windsor. Canada. Just last fall. They'll accept pharmaceuticals as payment."

Maybe not a metaphor. Maybe just trying to step back a moment. He is their negotiator. Cool. "Interesting! I'm new here. I do have business across the river soon. Is it difficult to reach the bridge safely?"

"Oh, I use a service. It's a gang. Gnarly bunch. But they'll escort you through safely. It's a business. Want their number?"

"Thank you very much," Caitlyn agreed.

He consulted his phone, and wrote the gang's name and number on the corner of her notepad, in tidy block capitals. He crossed his sevens.

Eck said, "If the ROE limits who my guys are up against, I'm all for it. But as a contract matter, I don't want payment docked if things get out of hand."

"Which they surely will. I think we agree, Colonel," Caitlyn assured him. "Leaders on all sides understand that there will be bad actors. But we ask for good leaders to make a good faith attempt to follow the ROE. Your personnel transports for instance. Color inside the lines, safe. Or just locals to defend against. Outside the zone, ka-boom. Your survivability goes down, drastically."

"So this is not a discussion of penalties."

Caitlyn shrugged. "There is no penalty language." *Because I should have thought of that, and didn't, when adding the ROE.* She picked up the contract again and adjusted her glasses. "I have another appointment coming. Perhaps we should read this through."

When Dan reappeared with the ROE document, Caitlyn asked him to add another two envelopes of extra cash to Eck's payment. Last night, she'd intended to squeeze him, only offer an extra 25% instead of 30% to allow for skyrocketing costs. But after the first awkwardness, the militia leader had proven himself negotiable. She'd have to remember that trick of changing the subject. His conversational gambit on laser surgery was smart, very smart. He brought his temperature down, and hers, and put them on the same side of a small win.

Dan hesitated, but only as anyone in charge of the money would pause to calculate whether the numbers worked. Besides, Eck was busy skimming the rules of engagement. No one was offended.

They shook hands at the door and bid Eck good-bye with assurances of mutual esteem.

Back at the coffee table, Caitlyn tore the top sheet off her legal pad. "Dan. Eck gave me a lead on a gang that escorts people to the bridge. Maybe you could check it out during the next appointment."

The elderly black waiter apologetically arrived to collect the snack service. He would remove it to the kitchens to be restored to pristine perfection, then bring it back.

"I called Cade," Dan admitted. "Had a good talk. I'm not sure about meeting six. But I'd like to stay for number four."

"Good," she agreed. She waited a moment for the waiter to bow himself out the door. "Dan, the key for me? Skull rigs these things so everyone is a volunteer."

"Not everyone," the ex-SEAL quibbled.

"You do any tours in the Middle East?" Caitlyn inquired pointedly. Given the dozen years he'd served in the Navy, that was a given.

Dan snorted sadly. "Yeah."

"We added the ROE," Caitlyn said. "Best we could do. Now we move on."

~

AVA-CAITLYN WAS CAUTIOUS. BUT KT-DAN CHECKED OUT THE MOJITO gang escort service pretty thoroughly. He asked for references and called them. He cross-checked the reference's phone number with an Internet search on their establishment, if it was legitimate. Several business owners said they'd used the gang repeatedly, and wouldn't dare step foot in Detroit without them.

Apparently the young entrepreneurs had found a good racket. Ava made a mental note to recommend the concept to Maz back home in Manhattan. Maybe her old gang could carve out such a niche. God knew there were enough tourist ghouls visiting the Apple. Some might enjoy a guided trek to the dark side. Some righteous types as well – for instance, the CDC might value a native escort to inspect the slums.

The Mojitos offered to let Dan just drop his women off with them. Thankfully Dan opted to keep his people in his own car to the border, and use the gang as outriders. The Mojitos were happy to oblige, since it doubled their fee.

Ava survived the Starve in the Apple. In the Army she fought in North Jersey in an engagement like Colonel Eck's planned three-city carnage. She'd sloshed through the decay of D.C., and added to it.

Fabio and Ellie were in more-or-less the same boat. Still Detroit was a shock, most of all to Dan. Detroit wasn't in good shape before the Calm. Now it was a complete wreck.

Block after block, they passed boarded-up and burned-out wood-frame housing. No one had removed the cars from the streets. They set them on their sides and riddled them with bullets, and burned those too. Grass hadn't been mown in years, or cropped for livestock either. Tree boughs stayed where they fell. Broken glass was everywhere. Several blocks appeared to have been leveled by a tornado. The roads were an obstacle course.

Dan slowed to steer around three toilets planted in mid-street. The bowl was shattered on one of them. He shook his head in disbelief. "Why?"

"Low self-esteem, that's for sure," Fabio said. "Not many people."

"But why stay here?" Dan returned.

A spate of gunfire erupted on their left, across a broken play-ground. As per instructions, Dan halted the SUV to wait for the all-clear. A Mojito in muscle shirt and kerchief, tied to give himself bunny ears on top, pounded the fender to give them the go-ahead. Rosa's car alarm went nuts. The gang kid found that hilarious.

"What are they saying?" Caitlyn asked Fabio.

The team still used the same aliases, but didn't act the parts. After a relaxing evening of hot tubs, fine food, jogging by the lakefront, and luxurious mattresses at the Lawn & Racquet, Caitlyn Dominici was slumming it this morning to slip across the border.

"Only catching half of it," the Puerto Rican replied. "Sorta kinda Spanish. Central American. Trash talk. Friendly insults."

A few more blocks along, they emerged into a more industrial sector, surrounded by derelict factories in brick. Their close-in guide stepped next to the driver and tapped the door, a gleam in his eye. But Dan already disarmed the alarm.

"This part's tricky," bunny-ears warned. "I go like this." He chopped both arms left in a large, half-body gesture. "You break that way, one block. Same on the right. Drive fast. Go three blocks, then back to this street. Got it?"

That sounded ominous. "Hey, Mojito!" Caitlyn called across Dan. "Can we shoot too? Or can't tell you apart?"

"Mojito got ears." He grinned and twiddled his bandanna flaps with a finger. "Anybody else, sure, waste 'em."

Ellie and Dan appeared dubious about this evolution. Fabio and Caitlyn eagerly reached for their M4 carbines. Fabio rolled down his window behind Caitlyn, then switched seats with Ellie to cover Dan's side of the car.

As he rolled on, Dan muttered, "Rules of engagement for this?"

"Sure," Caitlyn-Ava replied. "Self-defense."

"Works for me," Fabio agreed with relish.

5

Interesting fact: Windsor Ontario lies on the south side of the Detroit River, which flows from Lake St. Clair into Lake Erie. Windsor anchors one end of the 'Quebec City – Windsor Corridor,' which contained over half the population of Canada.

Exiting the SUV, Ava-Caitlyn happily bopped fists with their Mojito outrider in farewell. He slunk away to await Dan and Fabio down the bridge, so as not to annoy the border guards. Under the generous machine gun emplacements, and devoid of traffic, Ava felt as safe as she had since she entered Ohio.

Canadians were so polite. An unarmed border guard waited with crossed arms by his little booth, a hundred yards away, ready to interview them. But he waved for them to take their time. Hudsons were rude, Ava reflected, remembering her entry into Jersey across the Delaware a few weeks ago.

The guys climbed out, helping the girls extract their luggage. Most of their weapons would need to stay with the SUV. But they still had two duffels apiece of their wardrobe and what-not.

"You think I should trust these Mojitos, huh?" Dan asked Ava, scratching his nose. "Now you're going, little one, I wish I'd asked more questions while I had you."

"Yes. You should have." Ellie slammed her door and scowled at him.

Ava shook her head and frowned quellingly at Ellie. She turned back to Dan with a big smile and open arms. "Impressed as hell, as always. See you soon, big guy! Be safe." Enfolded in his hug, she added in his ear, "Don't worry about her. You're doing great."

Dan broke the clutch with a grateful smile. Ava repeated the exchange with Fabio, to the Puerto Rican's touched surprise. "Happy to team with you any time, gang rat. No lie."

"You too," he returned. "I screw up. But I learn."

"You sure do," she agreed. They both grinned at the implicit *both.*

They all glanced to Ellie. She remained standoffish to the last. She nodded cool respect to them, then started walking to the border guard.

"Hey, Ellie, hold up!" Ava called, annoyed. She turned back to Dan, rolling her eyes. "Rude. Hey, wait a few to make sure we're through, OK?"

"Will do," Dan agreed, with a final light bop to her shoulder.

Ava strolled to where Ellie stood with duffels dumped, half way to the border guard. "Rude," Ava repeated. "What were you thinking? Team is family."

Ellie shrugged, unrepentant.

"We need to talk," Ava continued. "But not in Canada. Til we reach Buffalo, we chat about the weather. Listen with our eyes."

"Obvious." Ellie picked up her duffels from the pavement.

Ava shook her head in disgust and resumed a slow walk. "We use our legal names. Ava Pawic. How do you do."

Ellie didn't reciprocate until they reached the border interview. Apparently her legal name was Kelly Troubadour. Ava thought it sounded like a porn screen name, and fit the girl beside her not at all.

The Canadian nodded blandly, and inquired, "And your real names? Before those Hudson legal aliases. And where you're from." His shirt label named him Miller. A welcome break from the ubiquitous American forest camouflage, Canada Border Services wore navy blue cop-like uniform, with matching bulletproof vest.

"Ava Panic," Ava supplied. "Or pronounced Panitch. I lived in the Apple until recently. New York City."

"Kaylee Prak, Princeton New Jersey." She spelled it for him.

Miller the border guard accepted Kelly's answer, but not Ava's. "Born in New York, Ms. Panic?"

"Serbia. Moved to America before kindergarten. Lived all over."

"Such as?"

"Minnesota two years. Where the children are all above average," she quipped in the round-mouthed Minnesotan vestige of Scandinavia. Then she switched to a drawl. "Couple years near Austin, Texas. Gig 'em. Everywhere else one year. Moved to the Apple when I was twelve." On that last, she finally conceded a slight New York accent. She'd never admired the raucous accents of the city.

"Documented immigrant?" Miller pressed.

"No. My parents had critical skills visas. Nurses. They died." Ava didn't find this amusing anymore. "Look, I'm a Hudson citizen now. Sir. Sorry."

If Miller was offended, he didn't show it. "Place your bags on the table for inspection."

Another two border guards rifled the bags while Miller observed their reactions. Not a thread of underwear went un-inspected. The bags were dumped, then the sides squeezed for sewn-in items. The girls were not manhandled. They were X-rayed, however, minus their sneakers, which were examined separately.

"That's a great deal of currency, eh?" Miller observed mildly.

Ava wondered if their Glocks would be allowed to travel with them. She doubted it. "I wasn't sure how much to allow for travel. Sir."

"A hundred dollars each. Max fifty for souvenirs. Make sure the rest of that cash reaches the border with you at Buffalo. Pharmaceuticals are not permitted as souvenirs. They will be confiscated."

"Yes, sir. And how do we reach the border at Buffalo? For a hundred Canadian."

Miller didn't respond until the bags were repacked. Ava was given a receipt for the pistols and ammo, apparently convertible back into weaponry at Buffalo. She imagined a Canadian gun stockpile at these border crossings. Fortunately, they decided she could keep her knives and stabbing chopstick. Another receipt detailed their currency holdings and spending limits in Canada. It didn't specify what would happen if she arrived in Buffalo without the cash.

"Are we in, sir?" Ava inquired. The guys were still waiting in the SUV.

"They can go," Miller said, with a wave to their ride.

Ava gave Dan a big thumb's up and wave. Kelly kept her eyes on Windsor across the bridge. Another ten minutes of red tape supplied Ava with a loaner phone bearing maps, compatible with the local cell towers, and the gist of how to catch a bus to Hamilton at the foot of Lake Ontario. They'd change there for Buffalo.

Miller remained cool and courteous to the last. If he wondered why these two teenage girls were allowed through the border when no one else was, he saved his questions for his chain of command.

He handed Ava the last of her walking papers. "Officer Miller?" Ava said tentatively. "I saw on the news, Canada took our most damaged kids. Early in Project Reunion. Just want you to know. I appreciate that. My gang protected hundreds of kids through the Starve."

Miller held her eye impassively for a moment, then nodded once.

Dismissed, at last Ava was free to trudge across the arch of the broad suspension bridge into Windsor. Fortunately, her heavy duffel had wheels. The lighter one had straps to carry on her back. Kelly was stuck carrying both of hers.

"How can the company get us into Canada?" Kelly asked.

"Chilly breeze off the lakes, eh?" Ava returned. Late May was not warm here.

Kelly lapsed into silence.

Stepping into Windsor at first seemed like turning back the clock six years. As though Ava had never moved to New York. The American collapse had never happened here. The waterfront boasted well-groomed public parks, replete with the weirdly tall trees. Houses looked in good repair. Traffic remained light, but far from the nearly deserted roads Ava had grown accustomed to. Windsor fixed its potholes. Only after they caught a city bus a few blocks in from the bridge did signs of stress become apparent.

Windsor used to be a busy crossroads for entry from the States. Now it was a dead end. Many of the storefronts along the broad University Avenue were empty. The ones open for business looked strange compared to a similar modest city in the States, featuring Chinese and Somali businesses. Signs were subtitled in French. Ava imagined most of the middle-class bus riders would have used cars a few years ago.

At a red light, Kelly's gaze grew fixed on a health clinic. "Dad…"

Ava poked her. But Kelly couldn't take her eyes off the clinic until the bus pulled away. Her face remained set in stone.

The bus turned left to deposit them at the Windsor International Transit Terminal. The Greyhound bus depot was once-conveniently located near the closed Detroit-Windsor Tunnel under the river. Ava supposed it was cheaper to keep the 'International' title than replace the sign.

A flurry of industriousness yielded them bus tickets to Hamilton, departing at noon. In a district devoted to hotels and parking garages, they had over an hour to kill.

"You watch the stuff, while I take a walk to the park?" Ava suggested to Kelly. "I'll be back in a half hour."

"You're not my boss, Ava. We were hired the same day."

Ava pursed her lips at the girl. "Do you have a better suggestion?"

Kelly looked away. Ava kept her lighter pack on her back, with all the cash and tickets and paperwork, and simply left. Once out the door, it occurred to her that a nicer person would have left the other girl a Canadian twenty to use at the combination news stand and snack shop. But Kelly was too rude this morning to inspire her to turn around now.

After one boring hotel block, Ava found a nice riverfront park to stretch her legs, before being cooped up in a bus for three hours. Freed of the inhibiting influence of Kelly, she exulted in actually being in a foreign country. Well, more foreign than Ohio, anyway. Time was, she never expected to survive to escape New York City. She stared up the improbable height of a tree. She took selfies at a statue to send to Cade and other friends in the company. In her imagination at least, she was even free to tell her old squad mates from West Point about what Canada was like these days.

Not that she'd been able to divine much yet about Canada. It was in far better shape than anyplace she'd seen in the ex-United States. She kicked herself on the way back on a different block. The Windsor Aquatic Club and mostly-indoor family water park were still open for business. Though she supposed an hour wasn't long enough to enjoy it, anyway.

Treating her travel companion as she wished to be treated, Ava made it back into the bus terminal with a couple minutes to spare. The small throng had grown slightly larger as the departure for Hamilton loomed. Her steps slowed as she neared the seats where she left Kelly. Her wheeled duffel hadn't moved.

Kelly was gone.

Her thoughts slowed to a crawl. The short girl stepped onto a seat to look around. *No. She must be in the bathroom or something. Hiding, in a huff? In the news stand?*

Miller at the border hadn't specified what happened if they should veer from their approved trajectory. He did make clear that they were expected to proceed directly to Buffalo, and exit Canada within 24 hours, though their visa expired in 72 hours. Ava held the visas. Their boss Skull certainly hadn't mentioned what would happen if they were to disobey orders.

Ava blew out slowly. *Cool it. She'll be back for the bus. At which point I should joke about it, not tear her head off. I save that for Buffalo.*

An executive type, in a khaki trench coat over business suit, walked toward her. Ava belatedly noticed that she was attracting disapproving stares for having climbed on the furniture. She stepped down sheepishly, and sat on the chair to think.

The man didn't divert. "Ms. Pawic? Or Ms. Troubadour?" he inquired.

Ava stared up at him. "I'm Pawic. And you are?"

The man took a seat next to hers, and placed his briefcase across his knees. "Mr. Clark. And where is Ms. Troubadour?"

Ava was afraid of that. "Good question. I went for a walk. I came back. I don't see her."

"Ms. Pawic, you are guests in this country," Clark said reprovingly. He reminded her of Skull, younger middle aged and of surpassing blandness. Just being himself was disguise enough.

"Yes, Mr. Clark. But I don't know where she is. I can tell you she has no money, no ticket, no paperwork, no weapons. She has her clothes. This wasn't the plan. I'm hoping she reappears before the bus." But Ava had a sinking feeling about this. "I could check the ladies' room."

"You will wait here," Clark directed. "You will not move until your bus is called. Then you will board the bus to Hamilton." He rose and walked toward an employee's-only door near the ticket counter.

Ava unhappily settled down to people-watch. An affronted glance reminded her that it was impolite to stare. She limited herself to fleeting peeks. She made faces with a four-year-old until his mother scolded him. Compared to the teens in the terminal dressed in Goth and piercings, Ava thought she looked fairly respectable. But adults edged away from her uneasily, perhaps sensing that the diminutive girl was more dangerous than they could explain.

The bus to Hamilton was called. Ava claimed a good window seat. As she half-expected, Mr. Clark boarded the bus. There was still no sign of Kelly. Ava pulled her knapsack off the seat so he could sit beside her.

Clark whispered in her ear. "You will stay on this bus to Hamilton. You will be met at Hamilton by a driver to Buffalo. You will make no detours. Give me your unused tickets."

Ava wordlessly surrendered Kelly's ticket to Hamilton, and both tickets from someplace named Grimsby to Fort Erie, across another bridge from Buffalo. She'd planned to find a taxi to take them from Hamilton to Grimsby. To catch connecting buses the whole way, they would have needed to go clear to Toronto, find someplace to sleep overnight, then loop back the next day through Grimsby. Yet Grimsby was only five or ten miles from Hamilton.

She didn't even consider defending herself or Kelly to Mr. Clark. Ava Panic did not expect an adult to think well of her.

Once he tucked the tickets into his raincoat, Mr. Clark disembarked, with no further word of explanation. Apparently he had better things to do this afternoon than cross southern Ontario.

A billboard on the highway out of Windsor caught Ava's eye, and imagination. *Canada's Century,* it proclaimed, *Le Siècle du Canada.* A patriotic photo montage showed a waving field of ripe grain, looking rather more impressive than the tender young corn field behind the billboard. Air force jets. Scenic Canadian Rockies. City skyscrapers. Oil derricks. The Maritime coast. A hill aflame with red maple.

It probably is Canada's century, Ava conceded. *And the whole Northern League.* She wondered if Hudson could join. If the Northern League held power over the death angels, she supposed she was part of it, either way. The thought was a bit gut-wrenching.

No, I'm not, she decided. *I'm a Hudson. I'll make Sergeant Calderon proud of me for serving Hudson, like I promised. Whether I can ever tell him or not.*

Not much farther, another billboard showed a middle-class family offering hot food to an obviously destitute white guy shivering in the snow. This public service message advised that of course it's only right to feed them. But you must call the authorities and report the vagrant. *Safety first. La sécurité d'abord.*

How politely condescending, Ava thought. She wondered what the authorities did with the vagrant after he was reported. She wondered if Kelly was headed for the same treatment.

Aside from being in better repair, with more traffic, this northern side of Lake Erie looked a great deal like the southern side. Ava napped through most of it.

~

HAMILTON ONTARIO CAME AS A BIT OF A SHOCK. IN WINDSOR, AVA HAD more or less assumed that Canada was better off than Hudson, but still hurting from climate change. Coming into Hamilton, she reflected that was because Windsor had transitioned from a gateway into a dead end. Hamilton was thriving.

There was no graffiti. She saw no empty storefronts or boarded-up buildings. The streets were packed with lively people who relied on public transportation and bicycles. Their cars, if any, were outside the city center. Only public service vehicles shared the street with Ava's bus. Corner bus stations were roofed with solar panels, and featured clean transparent walls.

Apparently Hamilton city bus stops were heated in winter.

At a red light, Ava studied a storefront advertisement for the latest ouiPhone. The battery lasted a month, and the storage was incredible. 'Ditch the computer' was its motto. Why bother when you could do it all from your phone? The ad touted its ability to photograph any document or hand-writing and store it as electronic text, and take dictation in English, French, and Chinese. The model was brand-new, proudly manufactured in Canada.

Ava guessed a ouiPhone cost significantly more than fifty Canadian dollars. But she suddenly wanted very much to acquire one. Not for herself – even in high school, she and her boyfriend Cade disdained classmates who showed off their latest, greatest phones. Ava's family wouldn't waste that kind of money. Cade's father could afford to give him any phone he wanted, but Cade chose to use his parents' castoffs instead. Ava wanted to buy the phone for Daneel, the company hacker from her cohort of new agents.

Hudson didn't have the capacity to fabricate consumer microelectronics. Most of that industry moved to Asia long ago. One of Hudson's top industries was recycling phones to eke out a few more years of diminishing returns on their lifespan. And because they had plenty to salvage, Hudson electronics were way ahead of the collapsed American neighbors. If Canada could produce something like this for ordinary citizens, its electronics could knock Hudson's exports flat.

If anybody had anything to trade to Canada for those electronics, anyway. If anyone could afford them. *Wow...* Ava thought.

She wanted to study all the advertisements at leisure. She wanted to jump out and talk to these people, and ask them how life had been in Canada these past few years. She suddenly regretted deeply that she'd kept to herself, lest she let on to her fellow passengers that she was a foreigner in their tidily ordered land.

But in retrospect, she wouldn't have done that part differently. Her instructions were to keep her head down, and pass through without attracting notice.

As she alighted from the bus at the lovely Hamilton terminal, her handler was waiting inside the door with a sign for 'Ms. Pawic.' He gestured for her to collect her bag from the under-bus storage first.

When she joined him, even before introducing herself, she blurted out, "Excuse me, but could we stop and buy a ouiPhone?"

"Non. Je ne parle pas anglais." At a guess, that meant, *No, I don't speak English.* Which seemed highly unlikely here in Ontario. But Ava got the drift. They would not be conversing on the way to Buffalo.

He took charge of her heavy bag. She followed him to a roomy dark sedan. He installed her in the back seat, on the far side from himself.

He plugged a flashy new phone – not a ouiPhone – into the dashboard. After a brief conversation with it in French, the car drove itself out of Hamilton.

6

Interesting fact: Hudson's experiment in limited direct democracy was 9 months old at this point. Hudsons could vote in local democratic town meetings, and sign national petitions. A voter test gauged competence.

"Hey, how was the trip?" Skull greeted Ava at the Hudson border. No, he was Major K. Sullivan, Hudson Army Resco, in this context. Ava still didn't know what the K stood for. "Where's Kelly?" he asked.

Unlike Detroit, Canada still conducted trade in Buffalo. Ava's chauffeur from Hamilton, driving the car himself at this point, crossed the Peace Bridge across the Niagara River and deposited her at a special lane for pedestrian drop-offs. The familiar Canada Border Service uniform ruled here, though the facility was on the Buffalo side. Some Hudson soldiers milled around. If they were supposed to double-check their Canadian counterparts, they didn't bother.

Ava's paperwork, belongings, currency, and person were scrutinized again with care. She'd 'spent' a few hundred dollars she hadn't expected. Kelly must have pick-pocketed her back in Windsor.

Ava was issued a replacement Glock and ammo, and released.

Skull matter-of-factly took her heavier duffel and led her to his car, parked nearby in the reserved-for-VIPs section.

"Um, the trip was fascinating," Ava said awkwardly. "More in the car."

"That good, huh?" When they were buckling their seat belts, he asked again, "Where's Kelly?"

Ava swallowed. She'd had a lot of time to reflect on her shortcomings as a training agent on her long ride through Ontario. "She split. I went for a walk in Windsor while we waited for the bus. I got back, she was gone."

Skull eased them onto I-90 east-bound toward Rochester as Ava dumped her tale of woe. She told him about the mystifying Mr. Clark. She dissected her relationship with Kelly, and what she might have done to cause the girl to run away. That led to her problems with the ex-SEAL KT, and vying for leadership, though she didn't detail any complaints against KT or 'Fabio.' She accused and condemned herself for not being a better training agent.

As she ran down, she realized that she talked too much. Cade warned her about that. His theory was that you looked smarter when you kept your mouth shut. "Um, sorry for dumping all that."

Skull shrugged. "It's OK. We have another hour to kill before Rochester. I hope you weren't this talkative in Canada?" The officer was bemused. Before now, Ava had tended toward diffident and reserved with him.

"No."

"Good. So. What do you think of KT and Cerveza? As agents." Fabio's street name was Cerveza. "Please think it through first, OK? Otherwise you're telling me more about you, than about them."

She thought it through, trying to leave herself out of it for once. "Huh. They're both coming along well. KT struggles with the ethics. But he's working at it. You know, really grappling with it. Cerveza isn't used to responsibility. But he's trying, and willing. Kelly… I guess it doesn't matter how Kelly was doing."

Skull didn't respond to that for a while. "No," he murmured. "I guess not."

"Do you know anything about her dad?" Ava asked. "In Windsor, she stared at a health clinic, and said 'Dad,' like she was heart-broken or something."

Skull said, "No idea what that was about."

Most Apple parents were deceased. And apparently the event was a dead end for insight.

Skull continued, "So you think KT and Cerveza are OK in Ohio without you?"

"They'll get into trouble," she replied. "They'll find their way out again. Probably. I'd keep them out of West Virginia."

Skull grinned. "Good. So back to my original question. How was Canada?"

To Ava's surprise, Skull hadn't been across the border. He knew little more than she did yesterday, about Canada since the Calm. This time she got to babble up a storm with no regrets.

Skull was as riveted by the latest-model ouiPhone as she was. "I bet they wouldn't let you take it across the border."

"We can't make the microchips for that, can we?" Ava asked.

"No. You know a lot about tech."

"I wanted to be an engineer," Ava said. "My parents wanted me to be a doctor." Medicine didn't appeal to Ava. Too much empathy was involved. She didn't want to be a cold and uncaring sort of doctor. But she didn't want to listen to people whine all day, either. And to hear her parents tell it, the medical pecking order was a misery. She hated hospitals.

"Huh. No, we don't have a 'wafer fab,'" Skull said. "The kind of lab to make microchips. I don't know much about the tech. Cameron does, the Long Island lead Resco. Oh, you met Cam in Brooklyn. He says it's really prohibitive. Specialized tech to make the tech that makes the tech, or something. Cost billions before the Calm. And the people who knew how, weren't in Hudson, because we had no wafer fab. A few, but not enough."

"So is Canada doing it?" Ava asked.

"That's a great question," Skull agreed. "Tomorrow we visit a great guy to ask."

"What are we doing in Rochester?"

"You know your presentation? The one you didn't get to deliver in

Brooklyn? Now's your chance. You present to Tony Nasser tomorrow. My boss."

Colonel Tony Nasser, lead Resco of Finger Lakes, or western Hudson, was Skull's commanding officer. He was also national head honcho of physical infrastructure in general, and fuel and electrical power in particular.

"You mean, Cade's going to present to him. Right?"

Skull shot her a crooked smile. "I had two agents in Virginia. No need to drag both of you to Rochester."

Ava studied him, perplexed. "You dragged me back from Ohio to present to Tony Nasser. When you had Cade already in Up Finger? Why?"

"Cade's benched. He can present inside Hudson. But I might send you to Schwabacher and Gantry. That's Ohio and Ken–Tenn. Depends on how talks go in Hudson. Tony can kill my proposal with a word. But he won't."

Ava looked horrified. Her part of that pitch outlined their mission into Virginia. As team leader, Cade was supposed to present that part in Brooklyn right after the mission. But General Pete Hoffman, top Resco of Hudson, canceled the meeting because he wanted his people focused on the imminent invasion of Delaware. Ava was to present Skull's addition, a proposal for Hudson to fund an expanded death angel service. Basically, he was asking to come out of the shadows and be funded directly, if clandestinely, by the states he served, instead of only reporting through the shadowy Northern League and the 'General' Ava met in West Virginia.

Skull chuckled. "Truly, Ava. Don't worry. Tony's the nicest Resco in Hudson. You'll like him." His expression grew sad. "He didn't know about me and the death angels until a couple weeks ago."

Conversation lapsed with that beguiling thought. The miles flew by as the late spring sun set behind them.

"What do you think will happen to Kelly?" Ava asked eventually.

Skull's face grew blander. "Never betray the company, Ava."

"Are you? With the funding request?"

He shot her a sharp glance. "No. And you're just a messenger."

Ava wondered if she could get a fuller explanation if she asked outside of the car with its spying dashcam. She decided probably not. She wouldn't want it anyway. She could try to be a friend to Skull. But as an ally, she had little to offer. Messenger was a safer role. She could imagine what Cade would stay.

Stay out of it, little one. Skull's out of your league.

They took rooms that night at a dormitory at the sprawling red-brick campus of the Rochester Institute of Technology. Tony Nasser ran the next-generation nuclear power initiative there, like a latter-day Manhattan Project. West Point had more spacious dorm rooms, but at least Ava got one to herself.

~

COLONEL TONY NASSER REALLY WAS A NICE GUY. HE WAS ALSO ARMY Corps of Engineers. The aspects of Ava's presentation she expected to fascinate the Rescos in Brooklyn, mostly left him cold. Ohio's military advance was devoid of technical interest. Their army drove in on roads. Even ancient Rome used roads.

Instead, Tony was riveted by the condition of Greater Virginia's infrastructure.

Ava stopped talking altogether as Tony advanced frame by frame through video clips of the bootleg oil refinery in West Virginia, and the Chesapeake Bay Bridge. The gas main fires in D.C. left him livid, likewise the plan to resettle D.C.'s underemployed near the Calvert Hills nuclear disaster.

Tony sat back and absorbed Ava's financial pitch in silence, where Skull asked Hudson for increased funding, though Ava showed the slides and did the talking. The pages portrayed a company reformed under new management – Skull's. He ran a professionally managed death angel force, with expanded staffing. He'd added new intelligence and black ops capability, such as Ava and Cade, who sprang the Resco of Delmarva from imprisonment near the Pentagon.

Ava hadn't thought about it before, but this was about Skull's half year mark running the company. This amounted to a six month performance review. Ava could barely imagine being grown up enough to accomplish all that.

Tony sighed at last. "So I was the last to know, huh? I knew you existed. I just didn't know it was you. Though I never did buy your story, Sully. Devastated by your divorce, you needed an easier slot than Albany. Christ, you had Albany running like clockwork."

"Thank you, sir."

"What I wanted was to promote you to light colonel. Have you take over as lead Resco for Up Finger. I understand the theory. I should keep my hand in and manage civilians. Don't I deal with civilians enough as power czar?"

Tony ruled energy for the whole Northeast. He was weaning the populace off centralized power generation and fossil fuels. Ava imagined he got an earful from civilians.

Skull agreed, "I should think Rochester would be practice enough, sir. I'm developing Ava's partner Cade as an assistant. And this SEAL they brought back from Virginia. Too much to do myself."

Tony nodded. "And I'm not going to let you off the hook for any of it. In fact, when Pennsylvania comes on board, you can damned well take its northern tier, too."

Skull shrugged. "Already am, unofficially. Sir? I enjoy working for you. I've worked for Ash Margolis, and he's a pain in my ass. But."

Tony smiled. "Ash isn't so bad. Yeah. Your covert empire needs to answer to him. As CO, I have nothing to offer you there. But you're still mine on Up Finger. Ava, I enjoyed meeting you." He paused to gaze at her quizzically. "I don't understand your generation downstate."

"The Rescos in Brooklyn said the same thing, sir," Ava assured him.

Tony nodded. "Well, major, I'm not one of you fancy social engineers. But I'd say that generation gap is a structural fault."

"Yes, sir," Skull agreed. "We're working the problem."

Tony nodded again thoughtfully, then studied a chipped fingernail. "Kyle, did you know the tsunami was coming?"

Kyle. Ava was momentarily distracted by finding out Skull's first name.

"No, sir," Skull said firmly. "I did not. Tony?" He waited for his superior to meet his eye. "Hell, I've got two kids. I would have let the death angels kill them. Because I serve my country. I would have warned Hudson if I knew. There is nothing – *nothing* – they can threaten me with, that would have kept me from telling you."

Ava was stunned. That was how the death angels controlled Skull? They'd murder his kids if he crossed them? She was almost more surprised that he would sacrifice his kids rather than betray Hudson, at least in some cases.

Tony nodded slowly, then caught Ava's wide eyes on Skull. "Let's walk outside and talk." The two left to stroll without her.

Ava believed Skull about the tsunami. He wasn't warm. But she liked him. Like herself and Cade, he drew the line in a nonstandard location. But he drew the line.

She packed away the laptop in satisfaction. No, she wasn't as smooth at public speaking as Cade. But she handled today just as well as he could have. Her boyfriend would be proud of her.

She returned their electronics to the car, and nosed around the labs to the extent people allowed her in.

~

TO AVA'S SURPRISE, THE OFFICERS RETURNED TO COLLECT HER TO WALK with them through the forest of brick buildings, where no eavesdropping devices could listen in.

Skull showed little sign of stress. Whatever the men spoke of one on one, it must have gone well.

"Ava, Kyle tells me you passed through Canada," Tony opened. "Tell me about that."

Ava didn't repeat her babbling mistake to a full colonel, two ranks higher than Skull. She waited for specific questions, and answered them carefully. They weren't the sort of information she would have babbled, anyway. Tony was even more intrigued than she was by the new phones, and their implied microchip production capability. He sought to form a picture of Canada's adaptation to changing times, and its technological advances since last he was there.

"When were you last there, sir?" Skull asked.

"Dawn of the Calm," Tony replied. "Three years ago."

"Wasn't that already off-limits?"

"I cut and ran. Brought Bettina and the kids home to our parents in Buffalo. My brother took me across in an outboard. Tried to claim asylum. But Canada sent me back."

Astonished, Skull took a seat on a bit of decorative wall. "You deserted? Really?"

"Hell, yeah," Tony agreed. He propped a booted foot on the brick wall beside Skull. "I was ordered to secure the Apple Zone. Build the 'epidemic control borders.'" He supplied air quotes. "The specs were clear as day, Kyle. The greater New York ghetto for efficient slaughter. Made the Warsaw Ghetto and Auschwitz look like amateur hour. I wouldn't do it. Told the authorities in Canada I was given a highly illegal order. I didn't tell them what order."

Ava knew she shouldn't be hearing this. She nearly held her breath to remain unnoticed.

Skull prompted, "And they handed you back?"

Tony nodded. "To Sean Cullen. He'd just yanked Pete Hoffman out of jail –"

Ava's eyes widened still further. Sean Cullen was now Governor-General of Hudson, their head of state. General Pete Hoffman was Tony's CO, top Resco of all Hudson.

"No way!" Skull said. "Pete, too?"

"Oh, we're a regular band of fuck-ups," Tony agreed. "The 'top leadership' of Hudson. You not included, Kyle. You were a Resco from the start. Pete was ordered to command the slaughterhouse walls they ordered me to build, the Jersey expanse. And Sean to lead all of New York–New Jersey through the culling. Ash Margolis, too. Hell, he grew up in Manhattan. Half Israeli – could have had relatives gassed at Auschwitz. And they ordered him to command the Apple Zone's border with Connecticut. You know, that garrison that went insane?"

"None of you were originally tapped for Resco?" Skull asked. *"Pete Hoffman?"*

"Nope. Pete wanted to run for Canada, too. Patty, his wife, made him turn himself in. Then she and the girls could visit him. Pete pointed out they might shoot him. Patty said then they'd visit his grave."

The men laughed out loud. "Big of her," Skull said.

"Patty's great," Tony agreed. "Your ex... Kyle, you need a wife like Patty or Bettina to survive the upper ranks. The Army is insane."

"I know it. But she wanted to split for California. You could see the writing on that wall. So I stayed married to control where my kids went. They're safely stuck in Hudson now. No need to pretend marriage anymore."

"Cold," Tony said. "But effective."

"And Sean, in this meeting?"

"Oh, yeah. We spent a day at his camp Upstate. Brainstormed what we could do. He told us about the Resco program. Some other deep dark secrets. He'd been seeded some Rescos. You looked good, but a couple others we decided to kick onto the walls. Anyway, that's where I came up with the 'power czar' job description. That I was willing to do. Pete agreed to run South Jersey instead of border command. Ash wasn't with us that day, but he fell in line."

"Wow. Had no idea you were such a rebel, sir."

"Yeah, well, this heroic crap is overrated. Hell to live through. How'd they get you to take death angel?"

Skull took his time answering. "It needs to be done, sir. Nobody gave it to me. After my predecessor offed himself, the proposal among...interested parties...was for each super-state to maintain its own death angel markers. Emmett nominated himself for Hudson and PA. I said no way. He wasn't suited to it."

"No," Tony agreed softly. "That's just another suicide waiting to happen."

"Right. So I took it instead. Cleaned house, got the operation organized. Canber hired some crazy ugly people. Upgraded my staffing. Grew from there."

"You wanted it?" Tony asked.

"I wanted more scope," Skull allowed. "When Cameron got promoted to light colonel, him and MacLaren heroes of Hudson, and me still a major, babysitting Albany... Yeah."

"You were in on this from the get-go," Tony concluded.

"Yeah. That I was."

"These death angel superiors," Tony said. "Who are they?"

"Couldn't say. Tony, I can't tell you what I know. Pete and Sean maybe, if they asked. But you're no part of this."

"No," Tony agreed. "But Canada is."

Skull stilled.

"Thought so," Tony concluded. "Friend or foe?"

"We can't afford them as a foe, sir."

"Right." Tony held out his hand for a shake. "I'll let you go."

Skull stood and grasped his hand. "With your approval?"

"You represent me in Brooklyn. Let me know how I vote."

As they walked away, Ava inquired, "Brooklyn?"

"Our next stop," Skull confirmed. "Cade will meet us there."

"Sir," Ava asked, while they were still outside the spying eyes inside the car. "What are the seven countries of the Northern League? We got five of them. In West Virginia."

Skull didn't answer immediately. He didn't pause in his stride. "Germany and Poland. Were the two you missed."

Ava was relieved to complete her set – U.S., Canada, Russia, UK, Norway, Germany, and Poland. That open question had niggled at her. "But there is no U.S. anymore, sir."

"No comment. That's final, Ava."

Ava accepted that. She hadn't expected him to answer the first question, after he refused to discuss it with Tony. "What happened to Serbia, sir?"

"That's right, you were Serbian. I'm sorry, Ava. I don't know. Southern Europe…it's not good." He let it go with a brief grimace of sympathy.

Ava let it go, too. She didn't really remember the land of her birth. She was too small when they left. Serbia was a back garden full of flowers, with a hedgehog, and tales from her grandfather. *Sorry, Deda.*

7

Interesting fact: Voter participation differed between urban and non-urban Hudsons. In the cities, especially the Apple, apathy ruled, with few voters showing up for meetings. Country life offered few entertainments, and New England in particular had a history of democratic town meetings. Voter turnout there and western Hudson was high.

Cade met Ava at the door of the Brooklyn Prospect Resco Mansion, as ecstatic to see her as she could wish. A loud thump just before the door opened, and his flushed face, suggested he slid down the staircase banister to reach her.

She was delighted herself to hug her boyfriend again. He felt great. He looked great, dark blond and buffed and tan, dressed in adult casual chinos and half-zip light sweater. Last time they were here, a few weeks ago after that hell-ride through Virginia, Cade looked strung out and extremely dangerous. The forced rest at HQ had done him good. No doubt at camp the control freak suffered no interference with his disciplined ways.

Cade took the opportunity to whisper a quick warning in her ear. "You don't know Skull."

"I caught that part," she agreed, frowning. Skull had dropped her on the Manhattan side of the Brooklyn Bridge. After seven hours in the car from Rochester, she had to walk the final mile and a half with her luggage.

"Flowers. For me?" Cade quipped, sniffing the bouquet of snapdragons and ferns she held. "Aw, baby, you shouldn't have." He grinned.

"It's a hostess gift."

"Ava! Welcome back!" Emmett MacLaren greeted her, arriving late to his front door, which Cade had taken the liberty of opening for him. "For me? Thank you!" He accepted the flowers, smelled them, and sneezed. "No hostess tonight. Dee and Gladys are in Connecticut. You'll be the only woman. But I like flowers. Make yourself at home."

"I'll carry that for you," Cade offered with a flashing grin, and swooped to snatch her heavy bag. He started trotting up the gleaming oaken stairs to the top floor. "Same bedroom, same neighbor."

"But I don't say hi to them first," Ava observed with a laugh. She shed her army boots to follow him. Emmett's glossy hardwood floors were a shoe-free zone.

"Dinner is soon," Cade said. "Say hi then."

The moment he closed their bedroom door behind them, he clutched her tight, pressing into her from calf to lips for a deep kiss. When he broke that off, he pressed her cheek against his. He breathed deeply as their bodies sighed into each other. *Home.* "Hi."

She chuckled. "Hi. Miss me?" Talking long distance just wasn't the same.

"And how."

"Are we holding up dinner? If we, um."

He eagerly pulled off his shirt. "We can hide a half hour."

"Excellent."

~

"AVA, I HOPE YOUR TRIP IN WAS PLEASANT," CAM CAMERON SAID, martial ruler of Long Island, passing the salad.

Ava and Cade contributed the salad, made from colorful vegetables picked in the sumptuous indoor garden in the room across their walk-through bathroom. Cade loved to cook. The rest of dinner was a casserole left by the absent housekeeper. Emmett only had to heat it.

"Long," Ava replied to Cameron, mentally reviewing the rules of disclosure. Skull said they should answer any question the Rescos asked. "But fascinating. I was in Detroit, um, yesterday morning."

"Detroit was fascinating?" Ash Margolis asked. Ash was now leader of eastern Upstate. He'd run Manhattan when Ava left for West Point. As first in line on the Hudson succession, he was in effect their lieutenant governor. But the half-Israeli didn't lord it over the other Rescos at the table, much.

"No, Detroit was a bombed-out wreck," Ava confirmed. "But I took a shortcut home through Ontario. That was like stepping back in time. And then forward again."

Cam had only intended casual dinner conversation. Now the four officers at the table paused in their eating to stare at her past the snapdragons. The generals hadn't arrived from their hotel yet, just the men housed at Emmett's.

"How so?" Cam followed up.

Having already related this tale to two Rescos, Skull and Tony Nasser, Ava managed to be fairly succinct, zeroing in on the parts the 'resource coordinators' found most fascinating. She omitted mention of the missing Kelly. Skull – Major Kyle Sullivan tonight – managed to look riveted through his third retelling.

"They've got new microchips," Cam pointed out to the table. The other men nodded, trading glances. They all caught that. "Ava, your company operates in Canada?"

Ava shrugged. "They let me cross Ontario. That's all I know." A change in topic was overdue. "Did you drive down today, Cade?"

She winced internally after saying it. Surely the location of their HQ wasn't something to divulge unless pressed. On the other hand, more than half of Hudson was north of the Apple. And 'down' could mean anything, really. She was safe.

"Yesterday," Cade said. "Took a day off to visit Maz. My best friend. He runs our old gang in Chelsea now," he elaborated for Kyle's benefit, who already knew that. "Everyone else met Maz last time we were here."

"How's he doing?" Emmett asked.

"Great. His girlfriend is agitating for him to 'reclaim his past.' I brought him a couple pictures. From before Ebola. Ava has more that I haven't seen. We should pick through those tonight." Cade took a slow drink of water. He wanted to help Maz. But he wasn't sure reopening such memories here and now was a good idea.

Ava missed the hint. She'd brought her waist-pack down for dinner, her usual surrogate for purse and pockets. She kept her memory stick of family photographs in there, one of the scant things she'd salvaged from home. Now she fished out a couple printed photos. During their jaunt to Virginia, she had the geeks laminate these for her. They had the equipment for faking IDs. She handed the pictures around.

One showed Ava and Cade smiling with Maz and some unremembered girl on a skating date at Rockefeller Center. The famous Christmas tree was lit, just a week or so before Ebola broke out. The other photo showed Ava and Cade ten months ago, escaping the July heat on the Staten Island Ferry, each savoring a strawberry. Every time she saw that picture, the kids in it looked thinner and wilder. They hadn't felt that way at the time. They were on top of the world, on the mend, getting stronger and healthier every day, and delighted at the sea breeze and free treats.

"I was there that day," Emmett said in surprise, studying the ferry photo. He wasn't in the picture. But the strawberries were shared from a big wedding for a couple of Coast Guard officers.

"Twice," Ava agreed. "At Project Reunion Thanksgiving, we were at Chelsea Pier, and you were on the ferry. We didn't see you, though."

"I asked Dee to move in with me that day," Emmett shared with a smile. "I hope it worked well for you too, Cade."

Cade smiled and nodded. "It was a good day. We had no idea how rough we looked."

Ava gave an exaggerated nod. "We thought we looked great."

"Compared to a few months before, we did look great. You looked great," Cade said. "I love that photo."

"I want a copy of that one you have, of you and Maz with Sergeant Zurk."

Cade frowned, then figured out which she meant. "Oh, summer before high school. Quaffing beer and shooting with the right-wing militia in New Hampshire." He laughed and shook his head. "We thought we were so cool."

"You were in high school in that picture? I thought you were like twelve."

Cade shrugged. "Fourteen."

"Sergeant Zurk?" Skull inquired.

"Maz's dad," Cade clarified. "Marine sergeant Mazurkiewicz, retired. Medical discharge, PTSD." He shook his head. "My dad was horrified. But they shared us every summer after Maz and I met. First thing, when I told Dad I got into Yale? He said he'd call Maz's dad to see when he could come down to celebrate. Ebola happened first though."

Ash Margolis stared at him, arrested. "You got into Yale. Wow."

"We're in college now," Ava said defensively. "Distance ed. The company pays."

The photos had made it around the table back to Cade. He stared at them. He'd been so proud to leave copies of those for her, when he left the city last Thanksgiving.

She took them back from his hand with a caress. "I love these photos, Cade. Thank you. We'll find more for you and Maz."

It was the right thing to say. His lip quirked up in a grateful smile.

"So we present after dinner?" Ava asked Emmett. "I should change into my suit."

"Nah," Cam said. "We saw your suits last time. Kyle, we were impressed."

"OK, I'm impressed," Skull agreed. Though he would rather have seen Ava in her suit. She wore camouflage for Tony.

"Not sure what Pete wants to do," Emmett answered her question. "General Pete Hoffman. Cam has a proposal. Plus you guys. One will have to be tomorrow morning."

"Should we split during Cam's proposal?" Cade offered. "If it's tonight."

"You can watch me present if you want," Cam told him. "No big secrets, just Resco training. Kyle might want to split. You realize you should be handling half of this, right, Kyle?"

Kyle-Skull confided to Ava, "Cam and I trained the original Rescos for the Northeast, with Niedermeyer. Emmett took South Central. Yeah, I should do more," he conceded to Cam. "How do you figure half, though? Where's Niedermeyer?"

"The admiral? Off the Carolina coast, I think."

Kyle chuckled. "OK, maybe I owe you a third of the work. Emmett's here now. I might second you someone."

"There's an idea," Emmett murmured hopefully.

"Too much confidential material in the training" Cam hedged. "Need someone who can handle the deep dark secrets."

"I've got someone in mind," Kyle promised.

Cam pointed at Ash Margolis. "You're not off the hook, either."

"Never doubted it," Ash agreed. They all laughed.

AFTER DINNER, AS THEY FILED INTO THE LIVING ROOM TO SIFT THROUGH Ava's family photos, Skull sidled up to her.

"Are you sure you want to share this with all of us?" he asked, and added pointedly, "Now? Seems rather personal."

Ava shot a glance at Cade, assuming Skull's concern was not to set off Cade's PTSD a second time, right before an important presentation. "It's fine. These are my family photos, not Cade's. Our karate meets and stuff."

Skull squinted disagreement, but let it go. Kyle Sullivan wouldn't press the issue.

Ava plugged her memory stick into the tablet and started rummaging. She got fairly adept at Emmett's – his wife's, really – living room big screen and controller the last time she was here, while editing a video montage of their Virginia trip.

Cade sank into the couch beside her. But she turned a cold shoulder on him. "I'll put up on the monitor what I want to show you. No looking at my baby pictures."

He affably rose to wait by the screen.

"Found it. Karate meet." She tossed an image onto the screen. Their dojo team posed with sensei before the competitions. She and Cade and Maz didn't stand together. As junior instructors, each of them, plus her friend Kat, squatted grinning at the front, one knee down, surrounded by their top student hopefuls for the day.

The crowded picture had looked harmless on the tablet. On the huge screen, sensei was half life-size. The photo quality was excellent. Ava could almost see the pores on Kat's face. The emotional impact was like a gut punch.

Ebola took sensei, their karate master. Kat died of typhus. Some of the younger kids joined their gang. A few made it to the end, almost unrecognizable. They handed the survivors under twelve to the Navy over a year ago for quarantine and adoption. Ava thought a couple of the older ones were still in Chelsea, now in their teens.

"I'd like that one," Cade said.

Ava swallowed and nodded. She created a new folder to copy photos for Cade and Maz. There was a followup picture of the student instructors with sensei. She copied that directly into the folder, along with images of Maz and Cade with their dads. The shell-shocked ex-Marine wore desert militia camouflage. Cade's father, the suave blond president of a high-tech investment firm, was overdressed for his kid's karate meet. Maz was wealthier, but all the money was on his mother's side.

Ava posed with her grandfather. She put that on the big screen on automatic.

And she froze, staring at Deda, the man who raised her while her parents were at work. This was a closeup, not a group shot. The flushed and excited 15-year-old smiled from ear to ear. Deda looked proud of her, grateful to be included. They wore the same smile. Funny, the girl had never seen the strong resemblance while he lived. Now that both faces were strangers, Ava could see the young teen had the same eyes, same lips, same smile. Different nose and ears, thank God.

"Deda," she breathed.

"Panic," Cade said. "You OK?" He watched her, not the screen. The officers also gazed at her in concern, especially Skull.

"You haven't changed a bit," Skull lied.

She blew out. "Yeah. Sorry." She got back on task, dragging a few more photos into the folder without showing them. "Oh, hey, I've got video."

She played one of Cade's matches for everyone. Cade stood front and center to watch his younger self in his proud black water tiger *gi,* facing off against a challenger.

"Damn you're good," Ash Margolis said.

"What an idiot," Cade commented.

"He's not so bad," Ash countered.

"No, I meant me. I could take that me down in seconds."

"We've practiced, Cade," Ava said. "We got better. It's harder when you can't hurt them. We barely use karate in a street fight."

"Still," Cade quibbled. "Even you could take that me down."

Ava replayed the clip, then chuckled. "Yeah. Drop and spin."

Cade stepped into an open stretch of the sparse living room, and beckoned her with his fingers and a fey grin. "Bring it. Don't break me."

"Well…" Ava said, leisurely setting aside the control tablet, and thus setting the expected speed of the encounter. Then in a flash she hopped backward off the couch. She rolled across the floor. She carried the momentum up to throw a cross-punch never intended to land. She fell to her hands instead and swung her legs at knee height. Cade jumped back just in time, laughing, and caught her feet in self-defense, a move he only risked because her toes were already at maximum reach without shifting her pivot.

He yanked to slide her toward him. Then he dropped her legs and extended a hand to help her up. And then deftly blocked the kick to his head. "Done yet, darling?" he inquired, with both of her knees secured on his thighs.

"Mm, yeah," Ava agreed.

"Don't you kick me after I let go your legs. Vixen."

She let him pull her up. Then she flounced back into her seat on the couch, feeling much better. "It's hard to watch karate video without playing along," she quipped to their audience with a grin.

"Damn, girl," Ash said.

"She's hella fast," Cameron commented. Emmett was answering the doorbell.

"Yeah," Cade told Cam proudly. "She's small, but she makes it work for her." He waved at the monitor. "Her formal matches don't show it. But street-fighting, she's like this giant alley cat landing on your face, with claws."

"Tougher than you look," Skull said, looking at her thoughtfully. He stepped over and pointed to the background of the frozen video. "Is that what you're doing back here? Tiger paws?"

Ava peered at the image, then laughed. She and Kat stood on the far side of the mats, leading the younger kids to cheer Cade on. "Speed bag, cross, I think," she said, demonstrating with her hands. Then she stuck her tongue out, just the tip, and daintily lapped her 'paw.' "Tiger works, too."

"Do that again," Cade invited.

"No! No, I shouldn't have done it at all," Ava said, as her face advanced from flushed to burning.

"Get a room, Cade," Cam advised, echoing her thoughts.

"Don't let us interrupt," General Pete Hoffman said, interrupting. General Ivan Link, once Governor-General of New England before it merged with Hudson a few months ago, stood alongside. Pete looked amused, Ivan not so much.

"Good to see you again," Pete continued. He waved down Skull's tentative offering of a salute. The others were frequent guests at these summit meetings, strictly first-name and sock-footed. "If you're ready, gentlemen. Cam tonight, Cade and Ava in the morning."

"If I could, sir," Cade spoke up, "I'd like to watch Cam's presentation. He suggested it might be OK."

Ivan frowned. Pete reflexively glanced at Skull, and corrected that to the karate match on the wall. "Can't see why not," he agreed.

"Thank you, sir."

Cade bent over Ava to unnecessarily help her 'put away' one memory dongle and turn off the TV. He kissed her cheek. "I'm here on assignment," he murmured.

"Me too," Ava whispered back, puzzled.

"Different one." He straightened. "Babe, you don't need to join the meeting. Long travel day for you. Head up to bed early if you want."

"Sure," Emmett confirmed. "Or step out if you'd rather. Standard curfew here, but the gardens are fair game."

"Well, I'd like to use the hot tub again," Ava hazarded. The merest eye-flick from Cade confirmed her choice. "Thank you for offering, Cam. I'm sure it's brilliantly Resco-ish."

She made sure to be out of the hot-tub and up to bed before their meeting broke up, as requested. Cade and Cam stayed downstairs talking over beers in the living room, while the others found their own beds. She heard them down there singing along to *Let Her Go* over the living room sound system.

Only know you love her when you let her go.

Ava scowled as she recognized the mournful song. *Cade, what the hell are you doing?* Surely he wasn't on assignment to seduce the gay lead Resco. *Skull wouldn't ask that of him. Would he? And…why?*

But what bugged her most was him doing it right in front of her. *Clod.*

At least imagining Cade with Cameron distracted her from the faces of Kat and Deda. Her conviction that *he wouldn't!* freed her imagination to wander in erotic directions as she drifted into sleep.

8

Interesting fact: Voter participation in Long Island was the exception to the rule. Lt. Col. Cameron of Long Island was responsible for developing the Hudson Constitution, a work in progress. He claimed that Hudson forbade representative democracy, and this meant the few could not pass laws for the many. Many issues, including taxation and punishment, required a quorum of direct votes to pass. Systems evolved to make it possible, if cumbersome, to gather the quorum. In practice, LI rules favored 'initiatives' over laws – gather a group of like minds and do what you want. Just don't try to foist it on others.

"Cam, you don't need to stay for this," Pete Hoffman invited in the morning.

"Wouldn't miss it," Cameron assured him, taking a seat. The handsome blond officer, youngest of the Rescos, smiled encouragement at Cade and Ava. They stood at the front of Emmett's office, ready to present.

Cade smiled back, warmly. Frosty the Snowman was not ordinarily warm. Ava's smile was somewhat wan, but anyone could chalk that up to nerves.

She swallowed and started her trip video playing on the second monitor. In slow motion, it showed highlights, and lowlights, of their swing through what was once West Virginia, Virginia, and Maryland. The bootleg gas refinery in a blackened Appalachian hollow held a special horrifying fascination, and the lights of the National Mall sinking into the swollen Potomac. She was proud of how the video turned out.

Pete took a seat. "This morning we have two presentations. First, these young people will describe their prison break mission to retrieve Lieutenant Colonel Jack Ekstrom for us. The second is a funding proposal from their company." He paused. "Mission team leader, special agent Cade Snowdon, and his partner Ava Panic. With the death angel branch of the Resco service."

Cade involuntarily shot Pete an edged look. He stepped gamely toward the laptop holding the presentation Ava developed.

Pete held up a finger to bid him wait. He gave it a couple beats, then turned. "Cam?"

"Pete." Cam looked shocked. He hadn't reached angry yet. But that's where he was headed.

"Do you need to leave?" Pete invited. "These young people did us a great service. They deserve every courtesy."

"These young people are cute as kittens," Cam agreed. He didn't smile at them anymore, though. "My comments are directed entirely to you, sir. Since when are the death angels part of the Resco service?"

"The beginning," Pete said. "The death angels have always been part of the Resco service."

"I would be astonished if my commanding officer Colonel Mora was aware of that," Cam returned. "Or my previous CO, Colonel Nasser. Or myself. Though I have been in the Resco service. From the very beginning. Before you, I believe. Sir."

"I don't think Carlos can handle it," Pete replied. "The Apple destroyed his family. Tony knew in the abstract. He has recently been briefed at a deeper level. If you remain in this room, you will also be in the know."

Cam sat back. "Understood, sir. Cade, Ava, my apologies for my outburst."

Ava tried to read his eyes, easier for her because the young colonel was staring at Cade. *Hurt? Betrayed? Pitying?* Her best guess was all of those, plus anger. But if she had to choose, she'd describe his look as calculating.

"For what it's worth, Cam," Cade said, poking at the laptop, "I love my job. My career prospects were limited. As gang royalty, we're tagged in the Hudson database for organized crime. The company is a leader in my field."

"Ava had a way out through the army," Cam returned.

"And I encouraged her. As I told you. But I signed up months before that." Cade met Cam's eye, cool as ice. "Cam, last summer I was locked in this city. Never free to leave. Without my gang, I'm a dead man here. The company was a way out. I took it."

"Your experience makes you uniquely qualified, Cade," Pete interrupted. He glanced at Cam again, and apparently was satisfied with his progress digesting his shock. "Let's begin."

"Thank you. Does everyone have a copy?" Cade said.

"They do…now," Ivan Link confirmed, tapping a key on his laptop from beside Pete.

"Ava developed these slides with our boss. You did a great job, Ava. But I'll present out of order." With a light pointer, he circled page number 5, which showed a timeline and overview map. "This is an outline of our mission. Monday night, team assembled in Erie, PA. Tuesday a.m., crossed into Ohio – West Virginia – near Morgantown. The following night, we made rendezvous too far south into West Virginia. That's why we needed to visit the gas station from hell on the video."

"Your gas mileage sucks, Cade," Ash Margolis quipped.

Cade smiled crookedly. "I was hauling a ten foot trailer. The rendezvous was inconvenient. But not really of interest to this group."

"What was in the trailer?"

By the rules they were given, this question merited a direct and truthful answer. Those instructions visibly stuck in Cade's craw.

"Munitions," Ava volunteered. "For another branch of the company."

"Contractors?" Ash pressed.

"No," Ava said. "Gran caravan."

Ash's eyebrows flew up and he nodded, fascinated. Of this group, Ash kept tabs on the Hudson intelligence community.

Cade pushed on. "We convoyed with the gran caravan through a mountain pass Thursday a.m., to follow the Ohio Army advance up the Shenandoah Valley. We reached our first objective, Mount Weather, Thursday p.m. Preparations overnight, then infiltrated Mount Weather Friday."

"How did you infiltrate Mount Weather?" Pete asked.

"And why?" Ivan added.

"We can cover that," Cade said smoothly. "I wanted to give an overview first. Two objectives. That was number one. Friday night we handed off one of the two specialists we brought for Mount Weather. The other chose to continue with Ava and myself. We rendezvoused with a SEAL team to get through the Ohio line halfway to D.C. Contractors," he added for Ash's benefit.

Cade continued, "Please note, everything to this point was in Pennsylvania and Ohio. Friendly allied powers."

Ava was impressed. After that initial awkwardness, Cade was relaxed and polished in his presentation. And if she read him right, he was setting up to suggest that everything that happened before they met up with the SEALs was of no concern to Hudson. *Neat trick!*

"Objective two was for Hudson. Infiltrating Greater Virginia to free the Resco of Delmarva," Cade continued. "Saturday we scoped out the prison where he was held in Arlington. Ava posed as Ekstrom's illegitimate daughter to make contact." He smiled at Ava.

"Midnight, jailbreak. Hide and seek with a drone. Thanks to Emmett, for getting that drone off our tails. Five a.m. Sunday, across the sunken Chesapeake Bay Bridge. Late morning reached the Delaware River, returned to Hudson. About four p.m. delivered Ekstrom here, Brooklyn Resco Mansion. Elapsed time just under six days."

"Wow," said Ash.

"We're not going to skip Mount Weather," Pete informed Cade.

"Very well," Cade agreed. He took that as tacit approval to skip everything up to Mount Weather, and presented it succinctly. "Questions?"

"What did you catch?" Ash asked. "Intel."

Cade punted. "Ava, that comes later?" Ava nodded. "Note that Ava and I aren't hackers. Or intelligence analysts. Our job was to protect our specialists, and get them there." He optimistically clicked forward to the next slide, on the prison breakout challenge.

The Rescos weren't having it. They had questions on the Ohio invasion into Virginia, how they handled the locals, resistance, and the general condition of western Virginia. Cade triaged and passed most questions to Ava to answer. She was more fluent in army-speak, and had asked more questions at the time.

Intimidated by the generals sitting front and center, at first Ava took refuge in Cade buffering the questions. Cade encouraged her, and drew out more detail before the scary dudes could pounce, or signaled her that was enough. After the first few questions, though, she forgot to be nervous, stepped forward, and started flipping back and forth through the presentation herself. On a question where Tony had brought up a related point in Rochester, she volunteered the information.

"You presented this to Tony Nasser?" Cam interrupted.

"Yesterday morning," Ava agreed. She added with a self-deprecating smile, "Tony was more interested in the bridges than the refugee camps."

Cade smiled perfunctorily, and said to Pete, "Half time, sir. And still in Ohio. In the interest of time?"

"You're right," Pete agreed. "Last question on Ohio. How was it getting through their line?"

"We hired Navy SEALs. They bombed us an opening. No casualties. It was awesome." That earned Cade a chuckle from the audience.

He resolutely skipped forward to the prison breakout, and pressed through the slides in order until the team reached the eastern side of Chesapeake Bay. "Let's stop here to discuss the condition of Greater Virginia. Because that's a concern for you." He drilled into one of Ava's backup slides, titled *Virginia*. "Ava?"

Ava stepped forward again, gaining confidence in this dance. "I've numbered these concerns in order. Number one is the meltdown of the Calvert Hills nuclear reactor within the fallout radius of D.C." She continued to a rapt audience. Much of what was left of Virginia was a radioactive toxic waste dump. D.C. itself was half-flooded from sea level rise. The city was literally exploding with leaking gas lines. The populace was systematically lied to, and clueless as to their true and dire situation. The currency was worthless. The inner cities were bottled in and violent. Even with SEAL backup, they didn't dare head north past Baltimore. Refugees from the coast were everywhere. The thin facade of law and order died at sunset. Virginia was a living hell.

"Tony Nasser recommends blowing the Chesapeake Bay Bridge as soon as practical," Ava concluded. "Plus the bridges across the Potomac in D.C. For Delmarva's security."

"We might need those bridges to clean up that crap," Pete said to his people. "Thoughts?"

"If I could, sir," Ava got in first. "Tony's point was that the bridges are unsafe for army trucks and tanks. But viable for refugees. A risk without advantage."

Cade backed her up. "We can vouch for the Bay Bridge. We degraded the bridge with just a few Humvees and an SUV. Better to blow it. The Potomac bridges seemed sound, but I can't see how. They're footed in mud. Would I take a car across them? Yeah, I'd chance it again. Mount a military operation, put trucks across them? No. You'd need to route overland. I'd also suggest shutting off their natural gas lines."

Ava corrected him. "Ohio took care of that last week. All fuel and power lines are dead into rump-Virginia. From Carolina and PA and Ken–Tenn, too."

Cam said, "We're doing the Apple again."

"We are never doing the Apple again," Pete said firmly.

"We kinda are, Pete," Emmett said. "This status quo is the Apple again."

"Minus Ebola," Ash quibbled.

"Typhus came by itself," Ava pointed out. "Starvation, and the rest."

"Fuck." Pete allowed himself the one word, then rallied. "Ava, thank you for the succinct summary. Let's move on."

Ava was furious. *How dare they blow this off?*

Perhaps Cade could see the steam coming out of her ears. He touched her elbow and took over at the laptop. "Delmarva was straightforward. You have better intel there now." The fairly friendly Hudson invasion was going well. "To us, it looked like the survivors adapted. There weren't very many of them."

"We're seeing a lot of people at low elevation," Pete countered. The tsunami waves hit 23 feet high at Delmarva, then sea level rose nearly 9 feet in mere days. Everything less than 20 feet elevation over sea level was supposed to be off limits, condemned.

Cade replied, "With respect, sir, they may be running from your troops. When we passed through, it looked like the locals shunned the lowlands."

Ash volunteered, "He's right, Pete. Ekstrom had no trouble winning compliance on that one. Nobody flocked back to their homes after the tsunami. If they lived there, they'd already drowned."

"No greenhouse construction that I saw," Cade added. "Few fields under cultivation yet. Not enough rain to rinse out the salt. Looked shell-shocked. But you know all that."

"We do," Pete confirmed. "Jersey, Long Island, Narragansett. We are familiar with the problem."

Ava started to ask what they intended to do about that problem. Hudson just acquired another large peninsula, full of hungry people and fields sown with salt. *What the hell do you plan to do about it?*

Cade tapped her elbow again. She turned furious eyes on him, met by a raised brow over ice blue eyes. "Of course, sir," Cade said to Pete, and shrugged disarmingly. He flipped the slide, and completed his remarks. "That's all we had for before the break. We have five minutes for questions. Unless Pete wishes to extend the time."

"Pete does not," Pete confirmed. "Gentlemen, recall that there is a second inning after the break."

That inhibited his subordinates to carefully weigh their questions. Ivan Link, the general in charge of Boston and Narragansett, spoke up first. "How would you gauge the mood in Virginia?"

"Deluded," Ava said angrily. "Cooperative with the lies they've been told."

"Maybe in the suburbs," Cade differed. "Middle class wishful thinking. The inner cities are feral. Like Boston and Detroit. That'll spread when the burbs realize they've been had. Black market thriving. Migrant laborers sell themselves south into slavery."

Ivan's look was incredulous and pained. "OK, I'll bite. Why sell yourself into slavery?"

"To be taken care of," Cade replied neutrally. He shrugged. "I've seen slaves everywhere. Most start out voluntary."

Skull – Kyle Sullivan – chimed in. "It's rough at the bottom of the heap. Too easy to scapegoat. Justify stealing from the ones just below you on the economic ladder. I provide armed security to protect the farm laborers."

"Charming," Ivan replied in distaste, rubbing his face.

Cameron sighed and made a note. "I'll add it to the tricks for Resco training."

They closed the mission presentation to a standing ovation. As they drifted out for refreshments, Ava noticed Pete hung back with Skull for a minute in the office.

~

"BOTTOM LINE," AVA SAID, ON HER FINAL SLIDE. "DEMAND IS HIGH AND rising for company services. Costs are skyrocketing. We're under new management and professionally run. We've added staff and developed new capabilities, like our missions in Virginia. The company seeks this funding to meet this year's challenges."

She pointed to the astronomical number, cast in Hudson dollars. "We suggest Hudson's share at thirty percent. We also seek Hudson's blessing to approach other stakeholders with the same request, prorated by size of nation. For instance, another thirty percent from Ohio. And so forth."

Justification of the numbers, staffing, and details on the capabilities came earlier. This was just the summary page. Pete ordered at the outset for everyone to hold questions to the end for this segment. He would handle questions, not Ava.

Cade sat in the front. Since he wasn't presenting, he had only skimmed Skull's pitch. Now he looked daunted. So was Ava. The projected food shortfalls from the disastrous spring were the stuff of nightmares. Hudson managed to save more people from the culling than they were supposed to. Now it was overpopulated. Without a miracle, the death angels would have to resume culling to meet quota.

"Thank you, Ava," Pete acknowledged. "First, I'm very sorry to hear of your losses in West Virginia."

"Thank you, sir," Ava said. "Cade was friends with the senior field agent."

Cade nodded, face cool. "Weyland and I joined the company at the same time. He led a gang in Yonkers through the Starve."

Without fuss, they observed a moment of silence for Skull's dead agents.

"This was clever," Pete resumed. "Pairing a demonstration of new capabilities with a funding request. And regardless of what we choose here, Ava, Cade, I'm deeply impressed. Please know that. Believe that. This conversation could get messy. That is no reflection on you."

Ava gulped. "Yes, sir."

"I have a question," Cam Cameron said, before Pete could open the floor. "Is the death angel in the room? The head of this 'company?'"

"Are you going to be difficult?" Pete countered.

"If it's Emmett, I might need to leave the room." Cam was best man at Emmett's wedding, and his room-mate during the formulation of the Calm Act. If the death angel was Emmett, he should have told Cam long ago. "But Kyle is too damned good for Resco of Elmira. So I'm guessing it's Kyle."

Pete glanced to Skull.

"Good guess," Skull, Kyle Sullivan, confirmed. "I'm the company's new management in Hudson."

"Just Hudson?" Cam asked. "Or all these countries?"

Ava flipped back to her company range map stretching across eight of the original Calm Act super-states, from Carolina to Indiana–Michigan, encompassing the whole Northeast region, and dipping to the Georgia border.

"All of them," Skull clarified. "I – Never mind."

"Go on," Pete encouraged.

Skull said, "I volunteered for Hudson, just New York–New Jersey and Pennsylvania. But we know the reward for a job well done."

"Pete," Cameron continued, "I recommend Hudson fund one hundred percent. Not the thirty percent figure."

Pete's brow flew up, and he turned in his seat to stare at his youngest officer present. "Forgive me, Cam. I'm not buying the Damascus Road conversion. You're not a fan."

"No, Pete," Ash interjected. "What Cam's saying is we should take ownership of our death angel. Full control. I don't agree, quite. I mean I like it, Cam, but only to fifty-one percent. These other countries need ownership, too. I want buy-in from Ohio."

"I suspect Ohio would feel the same way," Skull suggested hesitantly.

"How much external funding, Kyle?" Ivan asked, the once-ruler of New England. "How much are you getting from outside these countries of your, um, service area?"

"We will not discuss that," Kyle-Skull said with finality.

"But there is external backing?" Ash demanded. "That's news to me."

Kyle sat silent. Ivan and Pete traded a glance.

Pete stated, "We will not discuss that. So. Only this number is under discussion at this time. And we cannot – will not – disturb the…externalities."

"I trust these 'externalities' have effing *big* guns?" Ash demanded, irate. "Hudson is not a podunk little country anymore, gang."

"Good guess," Skull murmured.

"Oh, hell," Ash said. Judging from his face, Ash now knew exactly what 'externalities' they were talking about.

Ava had a good guess herself – the 'Northern League,' which included Canada. A few weeks ago, she might have assumed Hudson and Ohio together could stand up to little Canada. After seeing Ontario, she wasn't so sure. The Northeast had warm bodies in plenty, more than Canada, for cannon fodder. But they didn't project enough food to feed them. And the Northern League alliance included Russia. Canada had major backing.

After a thoughtful pause, Emmett said, "I like controlling the majority of that which we can control. Ash's suggestion, fifty-one percent of the ask. And seek to increase control later. Decrease externalities. Tactfully."

"And when Ohio says, screw you?" Kyle inquired. "Demands equal standing with Hudson?"

"Ohio is welcome to establish their own death service," Pete said mildly. "Yet they're using you, Kyle. Probably because you're better at it than their guy. Even if they're not willing to split the difference with Ken–Tenn and Carolina, though, Ohio should still pony up for Virginia."

There was further discussion, but that was the verdict.

And Ava had to deliver it to Ohio.

9

Interesting fact: Though Indiana–Michigan was one of the original Calm Act super-states, they merged into Ohio separately. Indiana joined voluntarily, then helped conquer lower Michigan. Canada also helped, in exchange for the Michigan UP (Upper Peninsula). The neighbors were fed up with raids from the failed state.

Ava took a train back to Ohio. Or rather, she took several trains. The first was standing room only from the Apple to Philadelphia. Fortunately, the troops disgorged there to continue south into Delmarva.

It felt strange that the tsunami-ravaged peninsula was no longer her concern. She'd done her bit part, and was off to the next thing. During training, Cade advised her not to get attached. She shrugged that off, as more Cade's cool personality than a job requirement.

But it was neither, she began to realize. For everyone around them, the world had grown smaller. People they met expected them to be as deeply invested in their local dramas as they were themselves. But Cade was used to the fact that he was only passing through. His horizons were wider. The local dramas of today's acquaintance would be gone tomorrow.

Ava managed to exchange a few quick mesh texts with her old squad from Basic while she was in range. They hadn't been sent south. Doc said they were urban pacification specialists in North Jersey now. She replied vaguely that she was busy, and getting more responsibility.

She wasn't sure that was true. Messenger to the stars seemed less important than training field agent. More visible, but responsible for nothing. These men were important. She wasn't.

She wondered how much longer she'd keep in touch with her friends from West Point, when she couldn't tell them anything about her life. Lying to Doc and Cookie and Puño hurt too much to do it often. She'd already given up texting Fox. The Jersey girl demanded answers Ava couldn't give. At least the guys were glad to hear from her on her own terms.

She was glad she carried official diplomatic paperwork from the top Resco of Hudson to sanction her travel. The Pennsylvania border was locked tight against Jersey. But as a courier to Ohio, she wasn't even subjected to a luggage search. They just told her not to exit the train stations while in PA.

Most of the vast and echoing terminal in Philadelphia was unlit. She tried to explore to kill time, but the place gave her the creeps. After that, she mostly waited in the main concourse, where at least the ticket cashier and cops were around.

Midnight Philadelphia to Pittsburgh was a less popular train, with only two passenger cars among the freight. Ava managed to evade a woman threatening maternal concern for a young girl traveling alone. She claimed a three-seat bench for herself for the night, plenty for a short girl to lie down on her side. Unfortunately, the track was far from smooth, and her bed was slippery vinyl. She anchored herself in place by leaning her bigger duffel against the middle. A balled-up sweatshirt served as pillow, keeping the torn upholstery off her face. The car smelled of spilled milk and unwashed bodies, with brown crud buildup around every seam in seat and floor.

I've been living the high life too much lately, Ava reflected, *if body odor and rotten food bother me.* The Apple smelled far worse during the Starve. *Yeah, and I hated it even then.* Still, the Grosse Pointe Lawn &

Racquet, and Emmett MacLaren's Resco Mansion with its gleaming sock-sliding floors, were not her native habitat. *Just passing through.*

She flopped onto her back, knees up. A couple shifts right and left didn't help, so she moved the pillow sweatshirt to cover the largest tear in the seat, a big vinyl triangle curling up. On the Resco Raj priority list, she imagined train upholstery ranked up there with cat toys. Civilians were not encouraged to travel. A jerk of the train wheels nearly crowned her on the steel armrest. She hoped train safety and maintaining the rails rated high on the martial to-do list.

Probably. Trains move troops and rations.

Her parting with Cade was highly unsatisfactory. After the meeting he swooped in to whisper in her ear, "Remember I love you. And I'm on assignment." He gave her a quick kiss, and added perfunctorily, "You did great, baby." He turned to trot up the stairs and pack. Skull held Ava back to congratulate her on her performance, and offer some constructive feedback. By the time she could follow Cade up to the bedroom, he was headed down with his overnight bag. "Following Cam to Ronkonkoma. I've been seconded. See ya!"

See ya.

She never did ask whether he was trying to seduce Cam Cameron. Of course she didn't. She could never ask that, because it was ridiculous.

Wondering about him all the way to Cleveland is ridiculous.

She had no information. She had no viable communications. She didn't need Cade to tell her that chatting on the train was a bad idea. People expected to talk about who they were, where they were from, where they were going. All natural conversation was off limits. She should make up somebody to be, to cover small-talk on the way to the ghastly lavatory.

Inventing a persona kept her diverted for a few minutes. *Patty,* she decided, the kind of girl who would grow up to tell Pete Hoffman to turn himself in so she could visit him in prison. Or bring their daughters to visit his grave if he got shot for treason. Patty was flexible. Ava could identify with this Patty. The idea of being the kind of woman who could boss General Pete around made her feel better.

I did OK presenting. Skull and Cade said so.

Of course, Skull also told her to beware of getting invested in her message. She was supposed to deliver it, dispassionately like Cade did. Not get fierce and demand the Rescos do something. It was a whole lot easier to demand that, than for them to mobilize and manipulate millions of people. If they didn't care to discuss the problem with her, that was only natural. She was a young girl who could describe the problems, but had no valid input on the solutions. She had no right to get angry at the Rescos. And yes, Skull saw the steam coming from her ears just as readily as Cade did.

Emmett's advice was different. "Relax and be yourself. You're a likable person. You've got great material, don't worry about that. If you worry about advanced public speaking tips – be that, don't say this, stand up straight – you tie yourself in knots and end up looking shifty. As a beginner, just try to relax."

Ash Margolis was standing with them at the time, and agreed whole-heartedly. They remembered what it was like, giving their first presentations. Like her, and unlike Cade, they weren't naturals at it. They learned to put all their worries into preparing the best materials they could. Then when it came time to present, they tried to relax and connect with the audience. "You get better at it with practice. Like everything else."

She picked over the meetings again, reviewing her performance line by line, as she jounced the slow and steel-screeching, curving miles across Pennsylvania. She finally fell asleep and her subconscious took over, presenting to camouflage-clad officers in her dreams.

AVA APPROVED OF CLEVELAND. THE LOCAL SIGNATURE DISHES WERE Central European, rich in stuffed cabbage and kielbasa, close to the flavors of her childhood. Already late afternoon when she arrived, thoroughly browned off after 28 hours transit from Brooklyn, she was vastly relieved to be met at the terminal. The efficient and incurious Buckeye soldier dropped her at a hotel near the city's West Side Market.

He promised she would be notified of her appointment by morning. Ava got the impression he had no idea what her errand might be. She was no more than a simple driving assignment to him, and he liked it that way.

The front desk clerk was mildly scandalized that a young girl was traveling in the big city alone. When pressed, he allowed that the streets were safe enough until curfew at 8 p.m., and gave her directions to the Market. She was exhausted, but eager for fresh air, and exercise unleashed from her luggage.

She fended off offers of employment from a couple pimps with ease. One required a punch and a roundhouse kick to the kneecap, followed by a sprint into the Market beyond the security of uniformed militia. Nothing she couldn't handle, and she wanted exercise, after all.

Evening wasn't the time of choice for a food market. She tried not to dwell on memories of fun times with Cade in the Pennsylvania farm markets, and just focus on the here and now. About ten stands were open at this hour, looking lost and a bit forlorn under the high barrel-vaulted ceiling. Fortunately they lit the stalls brightly to compensate for the dim mood-lighting far above.

She bought stuffed cabbage. She wondered where KT and 'Fabio' – Cerveza – were now. She bought a draft beer, and visited every stall. Cade would have finished his first full day in his new job in Ronkonkoma working for Cam Cameron. She wondered if Cam had a big house with guest rooms, or if Cade got an apartment somewhere. He'd like the former better. Temporary housing wouldn't include cooking facilities these days, and Cade got squirrelly being alone. She picked up dried fruit and cheese and hard rolls to keep on hand.

She emerged from the old brick market to find the hookers and pimps had swarmed. Nearing the summer solstice, curfew would arrive in broad daylight. Black market commerce always looked so tawdry in sunlight, especially the bling and gaudy makeup. Ava paused near the police to contemplate the tableau.

That pimp she accosted might want payback.

She transfered the heavier items into her waist pack, then tied the plastic bag of hard rolls to it, to keep her hands free. Then she launched into full urban workout mode, kick-boxing her way down the center of the street. People stopped and stared, clapped or jeered or hooted. She was supposed to be inconspicuous here. But no one cared what the street people thought. She moved fast. Her flinging punches and kicks encouraged a wide margin. She made it back to the dreary hotel without a single pimp approaching her this time.

"Welcome back, Miss Pawic." The front door clerk beamed at her. "I hope you enjoyed your outing? You have a message." He handed her a folded slip of paper. Apparently the message wasn't secret.

She glanced at it. Car pickup, 11 a.m. Hurry up and wait some more. She sighed. "Ms. Pawic."

"Pardon me?"

"It's Ms. Pawic. Or Ava." Due to her travel documents, she was forced to use her legal name here. That fact made her shoulder blades itch. But she didn't have to put up with anybody calling her *Miss*.

"Excuse me. *Ms.* Pawic," the desk clerk said coldly. "Sleep well."

I played that wrong, Ava realized, as she climbed alone to her boring and musty room. *I could have been friendly. Let him call me 'Miss' by local custom. Chatted about Cleveland. Got pointers for what to do with myself all morning.*

Ava Panic was alone in the world again. It wasn't the first time. She'd been alone and friendless for the most part for months in Soho Ville after she walked out on Frosty. After work, at least. When she wasn't visiting with Guzman, the ville chief. No, she hadn't been so thoroughly alone in Soho Ville, or ever, really.

But what she most remembered about Soho Ville was that she didn't like being alone. *Losers,* they called them in the Apple. Kids who survived without backup were losers.

Run, rabbit, run.

She hoped after Cleveland, Skull would send KT to pick her up to drive to Ken–Tenn. Camping out with her own tribe in an SUV sounded heavenly.

Ava, armored in her custom woolen coat dress and laptop, was ushered into a library-like office. She would be joined in a few minutes, she was informed.

The walls full of books were real, as were the heavy draperies. The room should have smelled musty. It did not. The marble floor was waxed to perfection. The fine rug under the claw-foot oaken desk was perfectly groomed, its colors vivid. The few items on the desktop squared perfectly. The woodwork had that flawless low gleam that spoke of wax and elbow grease. The hush was profound, despite the clamorous army headquarters outside.

She ran a finger along the back of a beautiful deep red armchair parked before the desk. *Real leather.* Ava couldn't imagine how a room furnished like this could smell clean and fresh. Except for the obvious – its owner must demand it. A brief frown of concern flitted across her brow.

She couldn't imagine the likes of top Resco Pete Hoffman in this room.

"Good heavens," a deep voice murmured from the door. Ava wheeled as the younger of two men closed the door on this inner sanctum. He was a Major Porta, Ava easily read from his uniform, of similar age to Skull.

The one who spoke looked to be over sixty, almost as old as Deda. Four gold stars adorned his collar. Ava regretted *wheeling* and vowed not to do it again. Her palms started to sweat. *General Schwabacher,* ruler of Ohio.

Unlike his peers, Charles Schwabacher didn't style himself Governor-General or wear business suits. Ohio was under martial law, Schwabacher was a general, and that was that. To the extent that he had peers – Hudson's familiar Governor Sean Cullen, and her more recent acquaintance Ivan Link of New England, were younger. Sean was perhaps in his fifties. Ivan's hair was still more black than grey. From the news, Governor Taibbi of Pennsylvania and O'Hara of Virginia appeared similar to Ivan in age.

Another general flashed to Ava's mind, from the very different surroundings of a field HQ in a children's classroom in West Virginia. That no-name general, Skull's Northern League minder, still wore an American flag and three gold stars. 'The general' looked about the age of this one.

Schwabacher looked like a kindly professorial grandfather. And he probably was that. He was also the most unabashedly militant of the martial governors.

He graciously waived his guests to seats, and took his own. Ava automatically slid back to reach the backrest, then realized her feet wouldn't reach the floor that way. Next to her, Major Porta sat ramrod straight in his seat, feet square on the floor, his back a good six inches from the upholstery.

Ava scooted forward, straightened her back, planted her feet, and kept her laptop on her lap, squared like Porta's.

With elegant formality, Schwabacher handled the introductions. Major Porta was explained as 'an aide.' "We had not expected someone so young and lovely," Schwabacher concluded with a gentle smile.

"The Hudson Rescos," Ava paused to clear her throat, "said the messenger was part of the message." The quip wasn't funny in this hushed library.

But Schwabacher smiled politely. He also pushed a button behind his desk and murmured, "Tea service, I think. Let's wait a moment."

He and Porta waited silently, and Ava perforce did the same. In only a moment, the door opened where Ava was too short to see it through the chair back. Another aide – a female captain this time – carried in a tea service. Ava was no connoisseur, but at a guess the platter and flatware were actual, hand-polished silver, and the china authentic porcelain, chased with delicate flowers. The captain, a stratospheric rank above her at West Point, poured Ava a dainty cup, and offered sugar. The woman also left glasses of water on the desk before she retreated with the tray.

"Impressive," Schwabacher said, eyeing Ava across the teacup. "You have manners. I was told you were a 'gang rat' from the streets of Manhattan."

Ava raised her chin, straightened her spine and met him straight in the eye. "I am. And proud of it. I am also a graduate of Hudson Basic Training at West Point."

Schwabacher smiled, broadly this time, and nodded. He pushed other buttons unseen behind his desk. A huge monitor slid smoothly down from the ceiling to their right. Shades slid over the windows to their left. Recessed lighting dimmed except on the desk itself and a spotlight beside the big screen.

"My electronic copy of your presentation, please, Ms. Panic?" Schwabacher invited. Porta was the one who held out his hand for the dongle, though. "With respect for your organization's hacking ability, you won't be using your laptop here."

Porta took her laptop and briefcase, and stowed them on a shelf. He also rearranged their guest chairs to the left of the desk, to face the monitors, and offered her the farther seat from Schwabacher, and a laser pointer. On Porta's laptop, touched only by the major's hands, Ava explained the three files. Porta pursed his lips at the concept of playing the video alongside the main presentation.

"No," Schwabacher agreed. "Play the video first." Porta plugged an Ethernet cable into his laptop and started the video playing. He made copies of Ava's files, then placed the memory stick in front of Schwabacher's seat.

"Speed it up," Schwabacher instructed, from where he stood now before the monitor to study the images. "Ms. Panic, join me." He looked around as though surprised to not find her already at his right elbow.

She corrected her error promptly. As always in the Army, she offered nothing. She replied when spoken to. She instantly obeyed his slightest hand gesture to indicate that was enough. He looked unutterably sad, and older, at the cheesy lighting on the Capitol building, and the more dignified lamps of the National Mall marching to sink into the broad Potomac.

When the video ended, the old man sighed and said, "My, my." He resumed his chair while Porta put the mission presentation up on the screen.

"Please. Begin," Schwabacher invited.

Ava didn't dare play games with the order of the slides. She also had no say in which backup pages were shown. Porta showed every one, in order. If she so much as skipped a bullet point, Porta helpfully highlighted it for her.

And she thought Cade was a control freak.

There were no questions during her presentation, only poker faces.

Occasionally Schwabacher smiled encouragement when she flagged. Porta looked grim, and made sure her water glass was within easy reach.

There was a brief bathroom break before the second set of slides, Skull's pitch for funding. Other than that, they held discussion to the end.

10

Interesting fact: General Charles Schwabacher commanded the small group of officers who vetted the Calm Act at Fort Leavenworth, Kansas. The Resco system was devised under him. The original legislation provided only for armed population control borders. Internal matters were left to the states. The war-gamers argued that the states were ill prepared to succeed at that.

"The company asks that the remaining forty-nine percent be split between Ohio, Carolina, and Ken–Tenn," Ava concluded. "Twenty-five, twelve, twelve."

"That is unacceptable," Schwabacher observed mildly. "Porta, let's begin with Pete Hoffman."

"Sir." The major rose from his seat while the general was still speaking, and closed the door softly behind him.

Schwabacher pulled Porta's laptop in front of him, and backed up a few slides to review numbers. He paused the longest at a slide that outlined the new capabilities of the death angels developed under Skull's management.

Ava stood sweating in the spotlight to the right of the monitor. During her delivery, a few times she'd moved out of her assigned circle. The officers pointed her back. Now, she had not been invited to sit. So she perforce studied whatever slide the big man read, hands clasped before her. She nearly jumped when Schwabacher finally asked a question.

"Whose idea was it for Hudson to claim majority ownership of our death angel?"

Ava swallowed. "If you're about to speak with Pete Hoffman, sir…"

The general smiled in a grandfatherly way. "Let me rephrase. Was this your boss's suggestion?"

Ava wasn't sure she was on any safer ground. But she said, "My boss proposed a proportional split between the nation-states. That, um, changed. In discussions. Sir."

"And were you present during these discussions?"

"Yes, sir. They were confidential. Sir."

"Yes, quite." Ava was relieved that he didn't seem angry at her for that response. Unfortunately, he continued fishing. "You survived the Apple. How do you feel about Virginia?"

"I obey orders, sir."

"I'm sure you do."

Fortunately Ava was saved by the reappearance of Porta, who said Pete Hoffman could make himself available in a few minutes. He was regrettably engaged in a combat operation and needed some time for a hand-off.

Schwabacher recoiled. "I trust you made clear this isn't so urgent as that."

"Yes, sir," Porta hastily assured him. "He said Hudson does it all the time." He rigged a camera between Schwabacher and the big screen on a delicate boom arm, for a video conference.

Schwabacher looked even more offended. "Hand off command during combat?"

"Ah, excuse me, sir," Ava hazarded. "In Hudson, a Resco supervises the regular army when they deploy against civilians. Command wouldn't change. Just a different Resco making the judgment calls."

"Ah." The full force of his attention fell now on her. "They taught you that in Basic Training?"

"Yes, sir. I was deployed for a police action in North Jersey. An attack on a food hub. Wrote a report for the Resco after. Um, Lieutenant Colonel MacLaren."

"The messenger is indeed the message," the general mused.

"I have General Hoffman for you now, sir," Porta reported.

At Schwabacher's nod, Pete came on screen, his face an alarming three times life size. Ava's pinkie could fit through one of his pores. She couldn't help but recoil out of her spotlight. Porta beckoned her back to her seat.

"Pete, good of you to take my call," Schwabacher greeted the casually disheveled giant. "Your young emissary was just explaining your Resco oversight system in civilian combat."

"Unexpected depths," Pete acknowledged. "Ava is in the room?"

"Ava, my aide, and myself," Schwabacher agreed. "Hudson's claim of majority ownership in the...company...is not acceptable. Is why I called."

Pete nodded a fair-enough. "On the other hand, the head of the company reports to me. He is a rare and precious commodity. Who would otherwise be a lead Resco, running all of western New York state and a big chunk of Penn. Instead, he turned his substantial talents to overhaul and significantly enhance the capabilities of the company."

"Ohio did not request these enhancements."

Pete shrugged. "I approve them. He's my guy. So there we are. We did anticipate Ohio's objection. But Ohio could opt out and run its own operation. I believe that was the arrangement when our guy took over. If Ohio split off, we would still need to cooperate closely in Virginia."

"Take it or leave it?" Schwabacher asked, eyebrows raised. "Pete, do not mistake yourself for holding all the cards."

Pete sat back and looked into the camera, and then the ceiling. "I prefer a pie analogy. We can squabble over limited pieces. Or we can make a bigger pie. The essence of this proposal is that the super-states self-fund to make a larger, more effective pie."

"Pie."

"There was a proposal for Hudson to take ownership outright," Pete said. "We decided regional buy-in was more important."

"You're playing with fire."

"I'm not playing at all." Pete leaned forward again, arms crossed on the desk before him. "I'm facing another Apple. On the *other* side of Jersey this time. I own this problem, Charles. Ohio can't buy its way into owning more blood than I do."

Schwabacher retreated into dispassion. He tapped a finger. "Four nations carved up Virginia. We agreed to divide the rest after a pause for digestion."

Pete replied, "I'm claiming there was no company like this until Hudson created one. Because we need it. We're offering to share nearly half with the other stakeholders. Remember, Charles, it isn't each other we're stealing the pie from. I'm responsible for the 'civilian capital' of Hudson. I need this control to do that job. So I'm going to claim it. Fortunately, you have another option, setting up your own company."

"Which won't be as capable as your company."

"It is in our mutual best interest to cooperate." Pete sat back again, arm over his chair back. "I see real possibilities, Charles. My guy is creative. You see the caliber of people he's developing."

"The presentation was effective," the general allowed. "Please convey my admiration to 'your guy.' You could have asked permission and safe conduct through Ohio."

Ava had wondered about that. She'd asked whether she should re-edit everything to downplay anything that might seem critical of Ohio. Skull told her it was more important that all the principals viewed the exact same presentation. Only the tail sheet was to be updated to reflect funding commitments made.

Pete shrugged. His phone beeped at him. He read a text and acknowledged it with a finger-stab. "Sorry, Charles, I need to go. The natives are getting creative today. Let's meet tomorrow. In the meantime, I suggest you ask Ava about Ontario."

"Ontario."

"Unicorn sighting. Charles." Pete nodded respect, and cut the video feed.

"Unicorn," Schwabacher echoed to the blanked video screen. "Thank you, that will be all, Porta. Please send Becky with more tea."

"Yes, sir. You have that appointment at fifteen hundred."

Schwabacher flicked his fingers to dismiss that concern, and Porta.

Ava was not dismissed. She unhappily sat, back erect, hands folded in her lap. These discussions on high had nothing to do with her. Why was she still in the room? *What unicorn?*

But Schwabacher remained silent until Captain Becky came and went. He studied something on a small tablet computer he drew from his keyboard drawer. Finally he sipped his tea, and invited, "Ms. Panic. Tell me about Ontario."

Ava sighed. "The most interesting thing I saw in Ontario was an ad for a new ouiPhone." *After I lost my trainee.*

"Back up. You visited Ontario?"

Back at her hotel, Ava did the needful. Her custom-tailored coat dress, grown whiffy with stress sweat, would be returned dry-cleaned with all her laundry by morning, with her continental breakfast, the front desk vowed. She washed her own underwear and stockings and hung them to dry in the bathroom. She got another great workout, with a shower before and after.

It was too early to go find dinner. That was her only entertainment for the night, so she intended to hoard it.

By 5:30 p.m., she was climbing the walls. After wringing every last detail out of her about Ontario, Schwabacher had kindly requested that she remain in Cleveland. He would consider, and confer with Pete Hoffman again, and get back to her. He didn't actually specify *tomorrow.*

Skull's instructions were that he would contact her when she was done in Cleveland. In the meantime, she should stay away from communications. Anything she said would be monitored by Ohio, guaranteed.

What would Cade do? she wondered mournfully, gazing around her cage of wallpapered walls. She wondered why hotels wallpapered their walls so much, when normal people preferred paint. At least this paper had a ridged yellowish texture instead of little flowers or something. A flowered pattern on the wall might inspire her to take out a pen and play connect-the-dots. And that would be bad.

Cade would do his Western Civ homework for school. She was hoarding that for after dinner.

Cade, where are you? What are you doing?

In anxious desperation, she grabbed her phone and called home, HQ in Elmira. She wasn't supposed to. But field agents could always call a handler in an emergency.

"What is the nature of your emergency?" a cool voice answered. *Not Cade. Not Skull.* Ava didn't recognize the voice.

"I was hoping to speak to Cade," she said. "Can you patch me through?"

"No. Is there an emergency?"

"Well, no. Daneel? Could I speak to Daneel?"

"Checking." Dead silence on the line. "Transferring."

"What's what?" Daneel answered, her goofball hacker friend from West Point. Next to Cade, he was her closest friend in the company.

"I'm going insane from boredom," Ava said. "Save me."

Daneel laughed. "You'd be surprised how many calls like that we get from couriers."

"I wouldn't be surprised at all," Ava assured him, heart-felt. "This job sucks."

"Well, I can't talk long. Work to do. How's the weather?"

"Slightly overcast. Cool for May. Like every other day."

"Turned June today, girlfriend."

"Oh. Time flies. How's Cade?"

"Not here. You saw him since I did. I got my bedroom back with the old man."

Ava took that to mean Daneel wasn't at the HQ campground anymore, but back in Binghamton studying the hacker arts under Ike. No, Ike's real name was Art Walsh. "Say hi to him for me. Good to be together again?"

"Sure. Can't complain. There's almost nightlife in this town. Band at the bar on weekends. Today isn't weekend. Work is fun."

"Did it go OK, you living with Cade?"

"Yeah. There was a suggestion that we were becoming codependent. Or some psycho-babble. He's working through a ton of crap. You know. All these little ice cubes with his emotions frozen away in them. Dripping out everywhere. We got close."

"How close?" Ava asked, with an edge. Daneel was bi, and adventurous. He'd flirt with anybody, and if they showed interest, he was game.

"I'm not trying to steal your guy," Daneel crooned.

"Can you patch me in to talk to him? Cade."

There was a pause on the line. "Contraindicated."

"That would break his cover?"

More silence. "Give him space. You turning up unexpected was an issue. He didn't expect to see you for weeks."

Ava froze, heart pounding. "Are you saying he doesn't want to talk to me?"

"No. Hell. I shouldn't have said anything."

"Daneel! You did! So tell me!"

"It's nothing, OK? When you left him last year, it hurt. Bad. But he wants you back, so he can't tell you how angry he is. So he froze it with the rest of the ice cubes. Guy's head is like a beer cooler. But he wants to be close to you. So he has to thaw it out and deal with it. With you away, he was taking the opportunity to do that. And then bam, you were back. Just give him a little space, OK?"

"Is he thinking of breaking up with me?"

"How in hell did you get that out of what I just said?" Daneel demanded. "Look. My opinion? Neither of you can let go of the other. Ever. But you have to. Which drives both of you kind of nuts. And you know? It's really uncomfortable to stand next to, let alone be caught in the middle. So leave me out of it. OK?"

"Sorry," Ava whispered. "Yeah, that's not fair. Sorry." Back in the gang, Frosty's best friend Maz absolutely froze her out, when it came to talking about Frosty. Cade. She detected a pattern. No one in their right mind wanted to get between her and Cade. "Daneel, you're still my friend, right? Not just his?"

"Yeah, Panic. I'm your friend. Just let's not talk about him any more."

After that, their conversation got lively. Daneel made her laugh as usual. They'd developed the system on their way through Virginia.

Since they couldn't talk about what they were really doing on this connection, they made up ridiculous stories, each topping the other, until tears came, she was laughing so hard.

"Feeling better? I ought to get back to work."

"Yeah. Thanks."

"Any time," Daneel said. "That's a lie. You are so busted."

She laughed. "Yeah. Thanks, though. I needed that."

It helped. That connection to Daneel, that she wasn't a citizen of nowhere cast adrift in Cleveland among unfriendly strangers, was like a lifeline. After that, she could buckle down and do constructive things. Extra homework. Watch the Ohio evening news, which was different and interesting, just like Virginia's had been. Mostly living out of KT's SUV, they hadn't caught the news.

The assimilation of western Virginia was a hot topic, along with further violence in Michigan. Ohio was big on targets and quotas, and making sure the populace understood their roles in the annual and five-year plans. Continued challenging agricultural conditions were acknowledged, but not dwelt on. The anchor's face lit up when he'd covered all the notices and could turn to sports. Hudson had only recently resorted to sports again, since the tsunami. Judging from the many teams and rivalries, Ohio may never have let sports lapse.

Well, the country was well-run. She'd give them that. In her travels, the average Buckeye seemed to live a well-ordered life of quiet desperation, confident that trouble-makers would be punished. They seemed eager to toe the line. Having spent the afternoon with Charles Schwabacher, that surprised Ava not at all.

~

"Ms. Panic. Thank you for coming. Please." Major Porta waved her to a seat in his own office late the next afternoon.

The modest room looked like what Ava expected for a mid-level officer, with a small bookcase, and off-white painted walls. Plenty of clutter and two screens on the desk in addition to the laptop, and a few touches of color to brighten the place. Pictures made clear that he married young. They had three kids, probably all still in the nest. The oldest looked about fourteen.

The only thing strange about Porta's office was the profound hush and clean smell. In those, his office matched Schwabacher's.

"General Schwabacher is occupied," Porta apologized. "He asked me to explain your next assignment. Sorry, let's back up. That... percentage...issue was resolved. There will be no need for you to visit Ken–Tenn. Instead, you've been seconded to us for a special mission."

11

Interesting fact: Washington–Oregon was remarkably isolated. Communications with the West Coast degenerated over time. California went dark after the earthquakes, just a couple months after Ebola broke out in the Apple.

Porta smiled a warm welcome aboard. Well, compared to his stone-faced demeanor of yesterday, it was practically gushing. In absolute terms, it was the pinched smile of a shy and unhappy man trying to be friendly.

Ava managed to contain her delight at the news that she was seconded to these scary dudes in Ohio. "I…expect to hear from my boss. Sir."

"Of course. I'm sure he'll confirm what I tell you now." Apparently Porta was so certain that he didn't pause in briefing her. He reached into his desk and produced a small black box. "You will be our courier. You will travel, across Canada, to the Pacific Northwest. And deliver this to the top Resco there. Or as far up the command chain as you can reach."

Ava accept the black box in slow motion disbelief. It was made of steel, and rattled. One oblong object was inside, judging from the sound effects.

The box was locked. He hadn't given her a key.

Ava pursed her lips to formulate a question, but her mind moved like molasses. *How the hell am I supposed to do that?* was the gist of what she wanted to know. But with officers, she was well trained not to speak until invited. Her training held, her mouth arrested in a purse-lipped *Oh.*

"The box isn't actually that important," Porta continued. "But as our courier, that's your cover mission. To deliver the box. What you will actually deliver is instructions on how to contact us securely for negotiations regarding what's in the box. Those you need to memorize." He detached a stapled two-page sheaf from the top of a pile of paperwork, and handed her that as well.

She glanced at the top sheet.

```
Good
00:06 011 878 277 549 211
03:17 011 870 433 309 158
```

The second page offered different numbers, formatted the same, under the title *"Compromised."* Her discerning eye noticed the colons, and that the second group of digits was always 011. Other than that it was gibberish.

Porta looked concerned. "We were told that you would be able to memorize this?"

"Ah, I guess," Ava said. It couldn't be much worse than memorizing reactions for chemistry or biology, she supposed. Her poor track record at memorizing dates in history gave her pause, however. "I don't know."

"I'll coach you through it," Porta promised.

Or he threatened, depending on how you looked at it. Fortunately he didn't notice Ava's look of alarm.

"Those are satellite phone numbers," Major Porta continued, "paired with the time of day to call them. Greenwich Mean Time. The 'good' numbers are to be used if someone can speak securely. The 'compromised' numbers will still be picked up, and a conversation will be held. But both parties will be aware that something is wrong, and speak carefully. Calling each number at the wrong time of day will not result in a connection."

"Am I to use these numbers?" Ava asked. She couldn't help blurting it out.

Fortunately, Porta didn't seem to mind. "No, the numbers are for delivery in Washington–Oregon. With the box."

"To?"

"Ah, you'll need to memorize that, too, I'm afraid," Porta said. He reached for Ava's pages, and wrote a name on each page, *Good,* and *Bad.* "Those were both classmates of Skull and mine at Leavenworth –"

"You know Skull?" Ava interrupted in surprise.

"Yes." Porta didn't elaborate. "Marcus Wetherby is most likely a lieutenant colonel now, but possibly still a major. He should be a Resco in good standing. Whatever they call a Resco in Washo. He can help you reach the top Resco there, the local equivalent of Pete Hoffman. But we don't know who that is, or what their table of organization might look like. For instance, here in Ohio, General Schwabacher is his own top Resco. In that role, he speaks on an equal basis with Hudson's Pete Hoffman. As head of state, he speaks on an even footing with your Governor General, Sean Cullen. Pete's boss."

"So Marcus Wetherby is not my target?"

"Probably not. But he's a safe person to ask. He was assigned to Seattle, which makes him easy to reach. Easier. And he knows Charles Schwabacher, Arturo Porta, and Kyle Sullivan. Among others."

"And Pete Hoffman?" Ava suggested.

"Maybe not Pete," Porta said. He flipped to the *Compromised* page. "This second name, Deke Fowler, also knows us. He was the death angel for the West Coast."

"Like Skull."

Porta inclined his head in reservation. "More like Canton Bertovich, I would expect. Canber. Skull's predecessor. Canton was a nice guy. Fowler killed more people. He wasn't a nice guy in the first place. Anyway. I'm giving you the name. I'm not at all sure you want to use it. If all goes well, you want to avoid him." He scribbled *Vulture* under the second name. "His nickname. Fowler. Bird most foul. Vulture." He flipped back and added a nickname for Wetherby, *Goonie.*

"Do you have a nickname, too?" Ava asked wanly.

On the *Good* page, Porta added *Arturo Porta, Deck.* "I doubt anyone out west would know that Skull or I was ever a death angel."

"You were a death angel?" Ava asked.

"Briefly." Porta's lips pressed together. He didn't want to talk about it.

Ava hazarded, "Did Skull tell you, I don't really drive?"

"You don't know how to drive?"

"No, I just… I don't get a car until I've been driving six months. It's only been a few weeks." No, Skull never said that. But it would be a reasonable decision on his part, she decided.

Porta shrugged. "Well, he wasn't concerned about that part."

"Do I get a key for the box?"

"No. It's thin steel. Easy enough to cut open. If you had a key, someone could peek inside."

"What is inside?"

"Microchip designs on a memory stick. And that's our second memorization task." He handed another sheet to a despairing Ava. "The vegetable names are in alphabetical order," he pointed out helpfully.

They were, in fact. All 22 vegetable names were in alphabetical order. Each vegetable was paired with gibberish like 'MP87A 6-axis Gyroscope and Accelerometer Combo' and 'BCM7986 Touchscreen Controller.'

"Those are the names of microchips," Porta explained. "When we speak via satellite phone, we'll use those code names. Availability of beets. And so forth."

"I can't memorize all this."

"I'm not worried about that," Porta said. "Here." He took out another sheet of the same vegetable table, and a scissors. He cut out the list of chip names. "You can carry this parts list. You only have to memorize twenty-two vegetable names in alphabetical order."

Ava had to concede that sounded easier, if only because 22 sounded close to the number of vegetables she could name. "And if I'm caught?"

"Skull says the authorities in Canada will be aware of your surface mission, to deliver the box to Vancouver. I'm hazy on which authorities in Canada. As for the list of chips," he shrugged. "As a courier, you're not expected to know what any of it means, Ms. Panic. A courier is discreet. Your job is to hand-carry that box. Probably to Seattle. And carry back a response. That's all. Ideally, if you're in trouble, it would be better to destroy the chip list. You can chew that and swallow it, burn it, whatever. The list of chips is on a file inside the box, in the same order. It's really only the list of vegetables you need to memorize."

"So. You want me to travel across Canada to the West Coast, then south to Seattle. I figure out who the top Resco of Washo is. I give him a box, and stuff I memorized. Do we know that he's in Seattle?"

"No. We're not sure that Washo uses the Resco system, either. Or even what they call Washington–Oregon these days. If this works, it will be very exciting for us."

"And if it doesn't work?"

"We're fairly sure the Canadians will give you back to us."

"Fairly sure," Ava echoed faintly.

"You are not a spy, Ms. Panic. You are a courier. Of course, we're eager to see your pictures and hear all about your trip. Camera! You need a high quality camera and data cable. Be right back."

Ava watched him scurry away. She wondered why anyone in their right mind ever thought Arturo Porta could cut it as a death angel. No wonder Skull got Ohio back.

~

"OH, MY GOD!" RUSHING OUT OF THE CAR FROM CLEVELAND HIGH Command, Ava ran into KT's arms. Cerveza stood beaming beside him. He relieved her of her laptop and briefcase and gave her a half-hug, too.

"I am so glad to see you guys!" And she was. To her astonishment, she was nearly in tears.

"You know these men, ma'am?" her driver verified unnecessarily. He was dropping her back at the hotel from her long hours with Porta, memorizing gobbledygook.

"Yes! Yes, thank you for the ride, private. I'm fine."

"Yes, ma'am."

"Caitlyn Dominici?" KT whispered in her ear. "Cody and Ed here."

She remembered. "Ava Pawic," she whispered back.

KT-Cody let that go with a quick raised eyebrow. "I'm told you're ready to check out of your hotel. Oh." He pulled her back for another bear hug and access to her ear. "Don't tell us anything. Especially not in the car. Where you've been, what you're doing, where you're going. Treat us as just another driver."

"Got it." Ava sighed. Bitching to KT-Cody and Cerveza-Ed would have been wonderful after the days she'd had. She longed to complain. But even the prospect of being with them, and out of this damned suit, was a sudden oasis of joy in the dreary work of Cleveland. *Back with my own kind!* she exulted.

If only for a little while.

West Point recruits learned to shower and change and pack in minutes. The Ohio Army footed the tab for the hotel, so she only had to drop the key at the front desk. Soon, they were back on the open road, sprawled in Cody's luxury SUV, wind blowing through their hair from open windows. Ava was back in jeans and a T-shirt and her high-top red sneakers. She felt real again.

"You're going to love our next assignment, Ava," KT-Cody shared. "Grosse Pointe Lawn and Racquet for two nights R and R. How awesome is that?"

"Yes!" Ed yelled from the back. They traded high-fives all around.

"I have to play Caitlyn Dominici again," Ava realized sadly.

"That bitch got style," Cerveza-Ed consoled her. "Attitude. Owns the place." He approved. He only had to act as her lowly hired goon. That was easy. A goon got a full-size bed, full gym privileges, and no speaking part.

"I guess we're waiting on something at the luxury hotel," Cody continued. "Then we visit our pals at the bridge again." He eyed her quizzically, but asked nothing.

"Where's Debbie?" Ed asked. That was Kelly's name when Cerveza was Ed.

After a brief silence, Ava replied, "Not here." She reached over and pressed Cody's hand. "Two nights. I'm glad."

Surprised, Cody squeezed her hand back. "We got your back, girl. No worries."

"I'M STILL TRYING TO FIGURE OUT HOW TO USE YOU," SKULL ADMITTED TO Ava by video that night. "Some girls – female men – are happy enough in admin roles. You, that'd be a crying shame. You're too good in the field. But getting men to take you seriously, that's a puzzle."

"You don't think Schwabacher took me seriously?"

Skull barked a bitter laugh. "Ava, Schwabacher doesn't take me seriously. To him, you amounted to a curious choice of stationery. At first. Then he saw possibilities. Or maybe he just won a round, bought a new toy, and demanded his turn to try it out."

"Won a round?"

"Hudson claimed fifty-one percent ownership of the company's new capabilities. Ohio took forty-nine. Carolina and Ken–Tenn only get the old markers. Or whatever Hudson and Ohio choose to give them." Skull rallied. "Ava, it's not your concern. They overruled me, too. It's what generals do."

Ava's heart fell. "You're not behind this mission?" It was bad enough to be sent solo to the other side of the continent, under unknown conditions, to find someone they didn't even have a name for. If the company didn't back her, she was out on a limb with the wood starting to crack.

"Oh, as a Resco, I love it," Skull assured her. "But as a death angel? Not really my department."

"Why send me instead of a GI?" Surely any soldier would do. Ava tended to forget her class at West Point was the best and brightest, if flawed.

Skull shook his head. "Don't sell yourself short, Ava. I tried sending Weyland into Quebec. Lasted maybe three hours before the Canadians dumped him back. Promised jail if he tried it again. Kelly defected. You have advantages. A Minnesota accent when you want one, for instance. You can pass as a new Canadian. And that disadvantage – men have trouble taking you seriously – becomes an advantage. The Canadians can't see you as a threat. Even after Kelly went AWOL, they still let you pass. That's huge. You're smart, cunning, deadly. Yet you look like a harmless young girl."

Ava didn't consider that a compliment. "I don't know how to do this, boss."

Skull studied her face a moment. "You take a train to Vancouver. You find a way to visit Seattle. You take the train back. You can do this." He nodded, apparently reassured by what he saw in her face. "You're not racing a clock. Take a couple days in Vancouver to learn about conditions in Washington–Oregon before you make your move."

"I could always call for advice before," Ava complained. "And I wasn't –"

"Wasn't what?"

"Alone." She swallowed.

Skull nodded slowly. "We'll just have to get you a phone, then. And find a way for you to reach us. I'll put Art and Daneel on it."

"Thank you!" Ava breathed. "And – can I talk to Cade before I go?"

Skull scowled. "Oh, yeah. That reminds me. You broke operational security. To drag Daneel into your relationship insecurities. With another agent. Ava? Grow up."

Ava pursed her lips, and blinked furious tears under control. "Yes, sir. Sorry, sir," she growled.

"Apology accepted. But do not let it happen again. Recite your memorized material for me, please."

She did so, flawlessly she thought.

Skull frowned. "I think one of those digits is off. I'll get back to you on that. But be sure to mentally review your material three times a day. That's how short-term memory becomes long-term."

"Damn. Sorry."

"No trouble, Ava. But that's why I'm holding you at Grosse Pointe an extra day. Emotionally regroup. Get your memory straight. Ah –

yes, I've got your corrected digit." He rattled off a corrected phone number.

Ava could have sworn she had it right before. *Damn!* She wrote the new number down. She needed to memorize it visually. But she could *see* it with the original digit.

Skull gave her a moment to start re-memorizing. When she nodded, he said, "I'll see about getting you a video date with Cade. It won't be secure, Ava. You can't tell him about your mission or ask about his. No promises. But I'll try."

"Thank you," Ava breathed. "Boss...did you send him to seduce Cam Cameron?"

Skull laughed out loud. "OK, Ava. You have to promise not to ask Cade that. Promise?"

Ava's face burned. "Promise."

"OK. One: *Why?* Two: No. Three: You just tried to drag me into your relationship with Cade again. Four: Don't. Clear?"

"Clear, sir," Ava grumbled.

"Ava, I'm gonna let you in on a secret about men. You've met Cameron's husband, Dwayne. Cute, compact, dancer's build, bouncy, goofball. Half-black or so. Sound like anyone you know?"

"Daneel?"

"That's what Cameron is attracted to, physically. Now describe Cameron. Blond, athletic, brainy, sincere, intense, oozes authority. Hm, who does that remind you of?"

"Cade."

"If I wanted Cameron seduced sexually, I'd send Daneel. Cameron sees Cade, he sees *himself*. Not a sex object. Got it?"

Ava frowned, puzzled. "What good does that do you?"

"Cameron is deeply offended by the company's existence. He wants to take us down. His boss is worse. But when you visited before, Cam identified with Cade. Just by being himself, and struggling with his inner demons, Cade makes Cameron more tolerant of the company. Because Cade is committed to the company. But the main thing – and Ava, this is important."

"Yeah?"

"Cameron thinks I owe him half the work to revise his Resco training material." Skull grinned.

"Better Cade than you?" Ava guessed, breaking into a smile.

"Bingo. Cameron is a self-righteous perfectionist prick. We drive each other up a wall. But Cade admires him. May they have joy of each other. Satisfied?"

Ava nodded sheepishly.

"Good. When you talk to Cade, your assignments are off limits. And you get your head in the game. You have a tough job ahead. Trust Cade to me. He's fine, Ava. Or he will be. He's going through some tough stuff. Hold on loosely and all that."

AS THE VIDEO WINDOW CLOSED, KYLE SULLIVAN'S CONSCIENCE TWINGED. Time was, he couldn't have used kids like this. But he consoled himself that if they knew, they'd be all for it, anything they could do to stick it to the Northern League. Cade, at least, wanted payback for all the lives he'd lost in the Apple.

Skull wasn't so sure about Ava. He'd made a good start gaining the girl's confidence in the past few days. Time well spent. She still surprised him.

Seduce Cam Cameron, indeed. He grinned.

This game Skull and Cameron were playing was far too dangerous to let the kids know their role.

Steeling himself against further youthful romantic angst, he gave Cade a call.

12

Interesting fact: Continental communication land lines broke down across the Dust Bowl before the Calm Act. Those were bypassed through the Southwest until Southern California was lost. The surviving cables passed through Canada, which blocked American Internet traffic.

Standing on the bridge again from Detroit to Windsor Ontario, Ava clung to Cerveza first. "You listen to him, alright? Work on that impulse control. Stay safe."

"Yeah, teach your grandma to suck eggs."

"Good American idiom," she agreed with a grin. "Us foreigners got to stick together, right?"

"You know it."

Ava turned to KT for a bigger hug. "God, I'll miss you guys. Wish I was staying."

KT murmured, "What are you up to, little one? Don't answer that." He'd seen Ava in action in Pennsylvania and Virginia. He found it hard to imagine what assignment had the girl spooked now.

"No," Ava agreed, breaking the hug. "Don't wait this time. I'll wave good-bye from here." She glanced over her shoulder at the border facilities. Miller would be her border guard again this morning. Mr. Clark, whatever he was, stood by. *Good.*

"You're sure?" KT scratched his jaw and contemplated the cop and the suit. "OK, boss." KT kissed the top of her head. They jumped back into the SUV and left.

Ava watched them, hand in the air for a final wave, until they disappeared into the wreckage of Detroit. She let her arm drop, and took a deep breath.

Detroit smelled awful. Her home and future lay in the opposite direction. She resolutely picked up her ruck and turned to wheel her big duffel southeast into Canada.

"Hello again, Mr. Miller," she said with a brave smile. "Mr. Clark. Is that a new ouiPhone?"

She hadn't realized what it was until now. The trench coated Clark bore a stylish ouiPhone box, shiny new and shrink-wrapped, as though fresh from a big box electronics store Before. Hudson phones hadn't been sold in slick consumer packaging for a long time. She should know. They salvaged the things by the millions in the Apple.

"For you," Clark agreed, and held it out.

"I'll take your things first," the border guard Miller interjected, and relieved her of ruck, duffel, and waist-pack. He carried them to the inspection table, as Ava accepted the electronics box. It bore a yellow post-it note with two phone numbers, both Canadian.

Clark and Sullivan. Sweet! Ava's grin was delighted and genuine. "What a wonderful gift! Thank you!"

I can do this! If forced to be logical, she'd have to admit that a phone to call home was a pretty flimsy weapon. But it made her feel better. Her belief in the factory-new shrink-wrapping was nonexistent. Whoever Clark worked for, she'd bet anything they installed surveillance on the phone, then replaced the shrink-wrapping. *Fine by me.*

Clark reached into his trench coat for an envelope and passed that to her as well. "Canadian ID. Additional currency. The phone has a good camera."

Ava's eyebrows flew up as she studied the envelope contents. The Canadian ID carried her own name, as Ava Panic, at her childhood address in St. Paul, twin city to Minneapolis. "Happy memories," she murmured in a rusty Minnesota accent.

She wasn't sure how much the cash was worth. At a guess, after a quick riffle with her thumb, it was enough to buy a quality used car. A card seemed to provide phone minutes. She'd forgotten people ever paid for phone service.

Skull hadn't mentioned any of this. He'd sent along more Canadian currency by the same courier as last time. He said he was still working on the phone.

Clark frowned slightly. "You're going to Buffalo again?"

Maybe Clark wasn't in on this. She nodded. "Through Toronto this time." She imagined she'd re-enter Hudson through Buffalo eventually. Or maybe Quebec. She'd heard Montreal was nice. That would be up to her, she realized. She mentally grasped the opportunity to feel in charge of her own destiny.

Miller interrupted. "Miss, where's the key to the box?"

"The recipient has the key," she replied. "It's a memory dongle."

"Containing?"

Porta had furnished her with an answer to this. "Intellectual property. Engineering schematics."

Miller looked dubious. "You're entering the country for technical discussions?"

"I just carry the stuff, sir. I don't even have a high school diploma."

"Right. Shoes."

Clark twitched his nose in distaste. "Perhaps you could buy new runners in Toronto."

'Runners,' check, not sneakers or trainers. "They are ragged, aren't they?" Ava agreed, shedding her signature red high-tops. "But they're my favorites." Her best break dancing inspired fighting moves required a well broken in shoe. "Will you be escorting me to the bus, Mr. Clark? I won't bolt, you know. Did you ever find Kelly? Kaylee?"

"No. I'll drop you by the transit terminal."

"Oh, thank you."

"Three days again," Miller said, "for the visa."

"Oh. No, I'll need to wait around," Ava said. "For something to carry back. Could be days, or weeks. I work for PIAGO Power." That was Tony Nasser's big project for next-generation nuclear. Canada was keenly interested and invested. It cheered Ava to think of something poor Hudson still had to offer. Her boss's boss Tony Nasser was respected, even in Canada.

Miller frowned at his paperwork.

"Do it," Clark told him. "It counts as technical discussions."

Miller completed a 90-day visa, the standard for technical discussions, and handed it to her. Given the length and nature of the visa, he could hardly limit her from spending cash this time around. The Glock was non-negotiable, of course. He tore off a receipt for that.

"She's free to go, sir," Miller told Clark.

Ava thoughtfully repacked her bags, then smiled at Clark. As she hoped, he took the more scenic route to the terminal, along the river park.

She shook his hand after he gallantly unloaded her bags for her at the curb. "Thank you so much for your help, Mr. Clark. You've been delightful."

Had she heard someone say that once, as a kid in St. Paul? She couldn't imagine the words had ever fallen from her lips before, but perhaps. Her family never spoke English that well. The comment was too effeminate for Cade or Maz.

Pursing his lips in distrust, Clark nodded and drove off.

Ava blew out slowly between her lips. *So far so good.* She headed in to buy a bus ticket northeast to Toronto. She saved unwrapping her new phone for the eleven-hour bus ride. In the meantime, she cherished her freedom of motion as much as possible with her luggage as an anchor.

Don't let the future gang up on you, Panic. That was Cade's advice during their video chat. He could see she was worried about her mission. *Just focus on one step at a time. Sometimes only five minutes at a time. One damned thing after another. But take one at a time. I believe in you, baby. The boss does too. He wouldn't send you if you couldn't handle it.*

~

CADE GOT A *FORD EXPEDITION*, AVA GROUSED MENTALLY.

The bus had escaped the conurbation of Windsor by now. The cows took over the landscape. Cows. Corn and soy fields to feed the cows. The corn was a week taller than last time she crossed southern Ontario. Scattered little white buildings housed the cow servants. People did other things here, too. Greenhouses aplenty glinted in the hazy sun.

But the land belonged to the cows, for a thousand miles. Staring out the window was dull.

In a rallying spurt of mental fairness, Ava allowed that Cade didn't get his SUV Darcy his first month on the job, or his second. When he started with the company, he still lived with the gang in Chelsea, without electricity or running water. He found his own phone and solar chargers to power it. He got poisoned drugs to distribute, or an assignment of violence to instigate by a skinhead visitor now and then. He worked his way up by sheer talent and force of personality.

Looked at this way, it was unfair that Ava leapfrogged her crop of new hires as Cade's girlfriend. Time to earn it.

Cade worked his way up by exceeding expectations. He made the most of what he was given.

Ava was given a phone. And an all-expenses paid deluxe trip to Vancouver. Come to think of it, she wasn't entirely sure 'Darcy' started out as a car. When Cade said 'Darcy' he was actually speaking to his phone, and the SUV by extension. Looked at that way, this modest shrink-wrapped package was her first Darcy.

Cade named his digital sidekick after the girl he lost his virginity to. Or maybe he just liked Darcy more than the previous liaisons – she was hazy on his girlfriend history. Well, she wasn't about to name her phone after Cade, by any of his aliases, because she was still involved with the real one. Daneel was off limits.

She toyed with naming her new partner Milan, after her father. But her parents would always be part of her life as themselves, not a dinky phone.

"Jana," she decided, murmuring the name aloud as Deda pronounced it, *Zha-nah.* It was Ava's middle name, for her grandmother who died when Tata was a teenager. She took a swig of her water bottle and dripped some water on the shrink-wrapping to christen the phone. There, now Jana the phone was dedicated to her family's patron Saint John.

A man seated across the aisle from her burbled a laugh. "Do you christen a phone? She looks like a baptism." Clearly French-Canadian from his speech, he gestured broadly and grinned wide, a distinct contrast to the courteous and reserved Anglos Ava had mostly spoken with here. Maybe in his forties, he had a curly mop of dark brown hair, an expressive lean body and face, and an infectious smile.

Ava smiled back bashfully. "It was a very nice present."

His eyebrows rose in amusement. *"Mais oui!"*

"What exactly does that mean? 'May we.'" Ava asked. As soon as the words were out of her mouth, she reflected that anyone from Ontario probably already knew that. But she was from Minnesota, so that was OK. But she needed to watch her accent.

"Mm, the words mean, 'but yes.' Together it means 'of course yes!' An idiom."

She smiled and nodded thanks, but decided she should quit getting chummy with the locals. She at last slit the plastic wrap with a fingernail and started inspecting the contents of her box. She lay out the items on her empty aisle seat carefully, slipping off plastic sleeves and taking inventory. *We sure used a lot of packaging. They still do.*

The phone itself was gorgeous, in pink gold, rather large for her small hand. She inspected it closely, but could see no obvious signs of tampering. Of course, that could have been electronic.

"You are a generous receiver of gifts!" the man across the aisle said with a laugh, still watching her. "I am Jean-Claude. En route to Toronto."

Oh, great, we'll be chummy for ten hours. "Ava. Also Toronto." She pointedly studied the quick start guide more closely than it deserved. Basically, it told her to turn on the device and follow the prompts. A pull-off plastic tab already told her as much.

"Ava! A beautiful name. It suits you!"

She smiled politely. She pressed the power switch and waved the phone to excuse herself.

"Yes, yes!" Jean-Claude cried, holding up his hands in surrender.

"Do not let me disturb you! You are bonding! With *'Jana.'*" He caressed the phone's name like a lover.

Ava couldn't help laughing silently along with him. "It's a long ride to Toronto," she excused herself. "Jana is my time-killing project. I have hours to savor this."

Jean-Claude leaned toward her theatrically. "Enjoy!" he exhorted. He sat back and turned still grinning to his window to leave her in peace.

Ava made it through the ouiPhone onboarding experience with ease and increasing delight. At each step, she was given an option to speed through activation, and save the tutorials for later. She opted for the slow route, and performed all the exercises. Along the way she sent glowing thank you notes to Mr. Clark and Skull, and received her first texts in return.

She explored the phone's ability to communicate with anything in the neighborhood via near field communications. She paged through the cameras on other devices on the bus, staring into other people's noses. She promptly found the setting to disable anyone else's ability to inspect her own nose hair. She experimented to find how quietly she could give dictation and have the phone hear her accurately. She mastered the cameras, for still shots, closeups, landscapes, videos from front and back of the phone. She practiced until she could snap a clear photo of a cow through the moving bus window.

She saved digital pictures of her Minnesota ID, her visa, and her post-it phone numbers for Skull and Clark. Using a makeup mirror, she managed to capture photos of Jana herself, front and back.

Ava set up cloud storage to automatically back up her images, and shared that storage with Skull. She finessed the settings, so that images would only be sent after an hour, giving her time to mark them private, or phone-only, or to delete them.

The tutorial on the voice-controlled database functions was a tantalizing demonstration, but not a how-to. Her first to-do list collected the tantalizing accessories she wanted to buy for Jana in Toronto if she had the chance. Her databases and lists and applications could also be synchronized to her cloud storage, both shared and private. She decided to create a starred storage as well, for things shared and recommended for Skull's attention. She set starred items to back up to the cloud as soon as possible.

Then she dug into the user manual in earnest.

Somewhere during her study of voice-controlled relational database design with AI assist, she got another text from Skull.

Boss: A+! Don't spend it all in Toronto.

Panic: Clark doubled my allowance. I wanna selfie tripod.

Boss: LOL!

Jana alerted her to a change in her to-buy list. Skull had separated selfie tripod into separate entries for selfie stick and tripod. He added a max capacity memory chip and added '2X' to that and 'external charging battery.' Before her eyes, her clip-on lens kit became two entries as well, adding a telephoto lens. *Neat trick, boss!* And good ideas.

The last addition from Skull was 'Faraday case.'

"Jana, ask Boss, what's a Faraday case?" As instructed, Jana composed the text and sent it to Skull.

Boss: Put phone in case, go dark.

Ava acknowledged by moving 'Faraday case' to item 1 on her shopping list.

Boss: A++. Be good in Toronto.

Later, when boss wasn't chatting, Jana showed her two more new entries. A ouiPhone for Daneel, and back up the user guide. She grinned and copied up the manual for him to drool over.

~

Toronto was the largest city in Canada at six million souls, bigger even than Los Angeles before the earthquakes. Jana was getting pretty good at supplying such details by now.

By the time they rolled in, most of the city was dark. Aircraft warning lights still blinked atop skyscrapers, though no aircraft flew. Rare business offices were lit, but not whole floors. At ground level, the only streetlights were blinking red at intersections, or low blue emergency lights, like the rape lights once strewn across American college campuses. The streets were remarkably deserted downtown.

Ava studied one of the blue-light installations as the bus paused at a four-way blinking stop light. Apparently you hit a big red help button, and stood in view of a video camera. If your attacker kept after you, at least it would be on camera. She made a mental note to avoid those cameras when taking down an assailant.

Doesn't matter. I'll be out of here on the first train.

As they disembarked at Union Station, they were penned in by orange sawhorses supervised by police. She and Jean-Claude retrieved their bigger bags from under the bus, and queued up for release into the station.

"After curfew," Jean-Claude guessed. "Past my bed-time." He grinned.

She grinned back, and ducked behind him in line so he wouldn't overhear her interview with the cop. Though no one seemed to get very far. After check-in, the disembarking passengers remained huddled just past the sawhorses in several groups.

Eavesdropping supplied her the options before her turn came. The ticket counters were closed for the night, as was Union Station, and Toronto was indeed past curfew. Transfer would be provided gratis to one of three overnight facilities. She had a choice of a ten dollar bunk in a transient dormitory, a fifty dollar room for up to two at an inexpensive hotel, or rooms from eighty to two hundred dollars at the Hotel Nouveautel nearby. Vagrancy was not permitted.

"Nouveautel, please," she said promptly when her turn came. Jean-Claude had selected the same. "When do the ticket counters open tomorrow?"

"Seven a.m. That way."

Ava was growing jaded to luxury. When she arrived, the

Nouveautel proved comfortable, but it wasn't the Grosse Pointe Lawn & Racquet. Her room was on the 26th floor. She punched the elevator button in a trance, her face carefully schooled. She tried and failed to suppress the memory of her last trip above the sixth floor of a building. Six months ago she climbed to the sixteenth story in Greenwich Village to retrieve her parents' wedding bands, and one small photo stick holding the family memories.

Her hotel room door had an electronic lock. She blinked with the lock as the LED turned green. She pushed the door open. A rocker switch turned on every light in the room and bath. She dumped her bags without a thought.

Still trance-like, she drifted to the window wall and drew the tall curtains to gaze onto the city view. She checked Jana. Yes, the phone could turn off the room lights for her. In the dark, Ava slowly and carefully photographed the Toronto night skyline.

"Jana, record caption. Toronto after curfew, from twenty-sixth floor Hotel Nouveautel." Jana transcribed her comment clean and sanitized, without the husky emotion and catch in her voice.

Toronto. Montreal. Vancouver.

The Apple. Lost Angeles. Chicago that was. Drowned Houston. Parched Phoenix.

Canada's great cities lived. America's cities, like Ava's, died.

The tears ran silently down her face as Ava hated Canada with a yawning ache that reached deep inside her gut and wrenched.

13

Interesting fact: Air travel was grounded by international treaty. Canada and Colorado enforced that ban, even against fighting wildfires, a painful sacrifice for Canada. The Naval Republic of Hawaii – the ex-U.S. Pacific Fleet – destroyed the Panama Canal, effectively divorcing itself from the Atlantic Fleet. Eastern nuclear subs still prowled the globe, but they avoided port cities.

"Sunday," Ava repeated blankly at the Toronto Union Station ticket counter. Today was Saturday.

"Be sure to bring your medical clearance," the counterman added, handing her a freshly printed form with her name and train. "They won't let you board without it."

"My… Where do I get that?" Ava inquired.

He pointed to the A-frame sign board sitting next to the ticket counter. Since there was no one in line when she strolled up, Ava hadn't paused to read it. She stepped back and did so now. Apparently medical clearance was required to travel beyond Winnipeg, and a survival kit.

"Do you want to add the survival kit? For Saskatchewan. It's easier."

"Easier," Ava echoed.

"The steward provides your survival supplies. Hands them out at the proper time."

"Yes, fine," Ava agreed faintly. She had no idea what he was talking about.

"Sleeping in your seat? Economy class."

"My other options?"

The ticket seller unfolded a brochure to show her pictures. The top class looked elegant, with an entire cabin to herself, day and night, and her own in-cabin bathroom facilities. It also cost $12,000. Ava selected business class. That offered wireless Internet when available, freedom to use all the train amenities, and a bottom bunk berth, bedding included. Ordinarily she'd prefer a top bunk, but in this case, the bottom bunk got the window. In any case, the top bunks were taken.

That was a mere $3000. She thoughtfully tucked away the brochure.

"And when do I reach Vancouver?" Ava finally thought to inquire.

"Three and half days minimum. Lately, it's been running six and a half days. Could be longer."

"I see." She didn't.

"And yes, you have permission. That could change," the counterman cautioned her. "Refundable, of course."

"OK." Ava had no idea how he came to the conclusion that she had 'permission,' or under what conditions that permission might be revoked. "And this medical form, where do I get it filled out?"

He shrugged. "Any health clinic." The sixties-ish man shot her a quick glance of disapproval, quickly masked in courtesy again.

Ava decided not to give him the satisfaction of asking again. He knew she was American, or new Canadian at least, from her ID. He disapproved. Screw him.

"Credit card?" he requested.

"Cash. Will you excuse me a moment? I'll be right back," Ava promised.

She ducked into the restroom – washroom in Canadian – and into a stall to count out the money from beneath the false bottom of her waist pack. She'd only kept out $1000 in ready cash. She never dreamed she'd need more than that for train fare. Just as she never imagined the train didn't run every day.

With what dignity she could muster, she returned and paid the man, and received her sheaf of travel documents.

A random policeman in the concourse directed her to a health clinic.

~

THE NURSE PRICKED AVA'S FINGER AND BLOTTED HER BLOOD ONTO A test strip.

"What is this test for?" Ava asked.

The woman, Gillian, a comfortably padded fifty or so, frowned at the plastic scrap. "Verifying your birth control status, dear." Her accent spoke more of Minnesota than Toronto. "Where is your implant?"

Ava stared at her in disbelief. This was not her expected script for this checkup. But, as it happened, she did have a birth control implant, courtesy of the Hudson Army. She pointed to her left upper arm.

"Oh!" Gillian said, in apparent revelation. "American. When were you implanted?"

"Um, January, I think," Ava hazarded.

Gillian nodded. "That explains it." She selected a different test strip and stabbed Ava again for more blood. She also poked around Ava's arm to verify the implant by feel. She checked off a box in satisfaction, and entered the expected expiration date of the implant. "All in order. You're a little off the usual schedule, is all."

"I see," Ava said. She didn't.

"And how are you doing with the smoke, dear?"

The air in Toronto was surprisingly smoky. Her eyes were irritated, and she was coughing after her outdoor run this morning. The city lay under a brown cloud, the sunlight reddish. She described her symptoms honestly.

Gillian clucked sympathy. "Any history of asthma? Pneumonia?"

Ava started to deny asthma, then stopped. "I've had pneumonia," she allowed. She wasn't prepared to divulge her full medical history. Surviving Ebola, typhus, cholera, and starvation – these things would be hard to explain in St. Paul. Her last medical treatment was for worms. But pneumonia seemed harmless.

"Controlled with antibiotics, or…?"

"It ran its course," Ava said. "Took a few months." More like half a year. "But no asthma."

"Let's have a listen." Gillian groped with her stethoscope inside Ava's T-shirt, lips pursed in concern. "Well, you'll need a nebulizer. But I'll pass you for travel. You be careful in Saskatchewan. Would you mind if I give you a Moo Cow? It's just, with the smoke like this, demand for nebulizers is through the roof. They're cute. See? The men won't take them."

Gillian pulled a children's toy package out of a drawer and handed it to Ava. According to the photos on the box, the friendly plastic cow nebulizer was housed in a red barn soft-sider case. Handy velcro pockets on the barn secured the albuterol bottles to fuel the breathing treatments. Ava was wholly diverted for a moment. In the meantime, Gillian had already made a note on her medical clearance.

"Wait, no! Gillian, I've never needed a nebulizer! I don't have asthma. Really." Ava defied anyone to pass Sergeant Calderon's gimlet eye and five-mile runs with undetected asthma. She tried to return the Moo Cow.

Gillian got that steely medical glint in her eye. She rapped her form sharply. "Anyone with a history of pneumonia gets one for Saskatchewan. No exceptions. And you, young lady, need one even in Toronto while the peat fires are burning."

"Peat fires?"

Gillian shook her head. "Such a shame. Keeps setting the forest back on fire."

"What's burning?"

"You just left Minnesota recently, eh? No worries, ducks." Gillian patted Ava's thigh. "This is a judgment free zone. Everything is confidential."

Ava hoped not to take her up on that. "But what's burning?"

"The boreal forest, dear. Northern Ontario, Quebec. Clear to Hudson Bay sometimes. But it set the peat burning this time. No help for that until winter, eh?"

"You mean the ground is on fire?"

"Smoldering. Bad enough with the forest fires. At least they can clear cut around that and contain it. But the peat fires burn deep. They thought they had it contained last month. It just broke out again somewhere else. Now, with summer coming…"

That sounded horrific. "For months?"

"Years, sweetie. May keep burning til it's all gone. Russia, too. Such a shame. And are you sexually active?"

God. "I'm in a committed relationship. We use condoms. Every time." Ava attempted to look virtuous.

"That's a smart girl. Now let's teach you to use Moo Cow."

The damned thing was net weight 1.5 kg, or over 3 pounds. Just what Ava needed to add to her luggage. And it used a power plug instead of a battery. And yes, it was cute, in a preschooler sort of way.

Finally Ava escaped the kind Gillian with her conditional medical clearance. She paused at a poster in the waiting room, entitled *Birth Control.* It hadn't occurred to her earlier that there might be something she didn't know about that topic.

While she waited to see Gillian, she'd read other posters. Vaccines were available now for six different cancers, though Ava wasn't a candidate for the new ones. She took a photo. She'd also made a mental note that the names for races were different here. Native Americans were First Nations. 'Visible minority' was the Canadian term for non-white. Having come from the Apple, she was surprised to read that Canada had more immigrants than the ex-U.S., over 1 in 5. *More than the U.S. as a whole,* she quibbled. No one beat the Apple's foreign-born density, at nearly half, or so she thought.

Now she took another poster snapshot. Like all official pronouncements, English and French sides were provided. Three-year birth control implants were mandatory from age 14, repeated at 17. Apparently after age 20, one could apply for a waiver to permit pregnancy. The conditions included a marriage of at least two years' standing, plus financial solvency and medical clearance. Dangerous occupations required a two-year waiting period after separation from employment. After giving birth, there was another mandatory 3-year birth control implant.

The Canadians didn't limit the number of children directly. But they sure slowed it down. The friendly waiting room poster didn't specify penalties for non-compliance. Nor did it cover religious objections.

As Ava turned away from the poster, she caught a glaring eye on her. A dark-skinned woman in dark turquoise head-scarf clutched a two-year-old. Ava smiled at her. The mother looked away in anger.

Ava blew out and approached the last hurdle, the front desk for payment. She handed a younger man her slip from Gillian, and a prescription for albuterol to feed Moo Cow. After Ava's initial resistance, she'd changed her mind and decided to cadge extra drugs from the nurse, on the theory that controlled substances might come in handy in Washo. And she had a legal excuse to carry these.

"Health card?" came the inevitable request.

"I don't have one," Ava admitted. "I can pay." She'd already been through this on check-in. Minnesota wasn't on board with national health care yet.

The guy – his name tag said Peter – recoiled. "I am sorry. Well, that will be forty dollars for the visit, twenty for the nebulizer, and twelve for extra albuterol. Seventy-two dollars, miss. Credit card?"

"Cash," Ava said, bemused. She'd mentally allowed five hundred for the doctor's visit. She expected the surprise medical equipment and prescription drugs to add a few hundred more.

"Ah," Peter said, taking her eighty dollars in distaste. "I don't believe we have change. I'm sorry, everyone uses…their health card. Or a credit card. You really should find a way to get insurance, miss. Then you can avoid these big surprise expenses. No one needs extra stress when they're ill."

"Keep the change, Peter." He looked offended, so she added, "Give it to another patient who needs help. My job is paying for this."

"Oh! Well, thank you very much, then, Miss Panic."

"Peter, where might I buy a credit card?"

"Well, if you buy it, it would be a debit card, eh?"

"Right! A debit card." It sure beat ducking into the lavatory to hide how much cash she carried. *Washroom.*

"Perhaps the bank next door, eh?" Peter suggested slowly, as though to the dim-witted. "Now don't forget your meds."

Her extra twelve dollars bought four remarkably generous bottles of albuterol. She only had her usual pocket shopping bag with her, so she stopped back at the hotel to unload. She posed Moo Cow and her drug haul on the bed for another portrait.

"Jana, caption. Doctor's visit, purchased nebulizer, spare albuterol, cost seventy-two dollars total. Cash is a problem here, will buy debit cards. Jana, starred photo." Ava was proud of herself for training Jana to complete a transcription or message without being explicitly told, after three seconds of silence. She starred and captioned her poster shots, too, for Skull's edification. Or her own, really – she imagined there was another trip report in her future. Hopefully without all the road trips to present it in person this time.

Ava hated writing.

Skull noticed her additions, apparently. Jana served her a text.

Boss: You have asthma?

Ava sighed and decided on a voice call to explain the rich educational experience that was Toronto. Along the way, Skull confirmed that Cade was doing great things on assignment. Cade had never under-delivered yet, and Ava was shaping up to be just as good. Impressed as hell, as he put it, the company standard attagirl.

Bottom line, Skull loved what she was doing with the annotated photos and data sharing. Keep it up. Write more, and often.

In other words, she had to sit and write up everything she'd called him to avoid writing. Fortunately, Jana took dictation. Ava started ongoing starred note files on birth control, environmental issues, and how-to Canadian medicine, money, and travel. She photographed all her travel documents and medical forms, too.

While she was polishing up, Jana informed her that Boss had edited her birth control document.

AP – Add details on enforcement and public acceptance. – CS

CS? Ava wondered. *Oh, no…* Charles Schwabacher. Skull must have shared access with him. Whose idea was it to have a phone to call home? *Mine.*

Fortunately, Jana made child's play of finding the requested details on the Internet, as released to the public. Ava didn't read them, beyond the unsurprising approval rate of the birth control policy on polling – just under 60%. Ava simply saved the web pages to her starred folder, and referenced them in her notes.

If she were a little more honest, she might have admitted that she loved the attention. The part of this trip that made her heart quail was being cut off and alone. *Loser.*

~

SHOPPING FOR PET TOYS FOR JANA WAS EVERY BIT AS FUN AS AVA expected. And yes, she bought a second ouiPhone for Daneel. That cost an extra $100 under the table to hopscotch the waiting list.

There were supply issues. Color her astonished.

Most of her wads of currency were converted into a convenient deck of debit cards, as well. The ouiPhone bribe served to corroborate her choice to reserve twelve grand in cash, with a thousand ready to hand. She could always buy more debit cards later.

Content that her to-do list for Toronto was done at last, she struck out toward the University of Toronto campus for a detour on the walk back to the Nouveautel. The green and yellow and brown of unfurling tree leaves beckoned like an oasis among the downtown skyscrapers in the lowering smoky orange sunlight.

Maybe I could use new 'runners,' she mused. She couldn't wish for more broken-in soles, but that meant they didn't cushion well for this all-day pavement pounding.

Like a flash, a punk ran out of some shrubbery and snatched her shopping bag.

Ava shrieked, "Thief!" She was walking in the opposite direction, of course. An accomplished street thief herself, she knew that was the way to do it. She had to halt her momentum, spin, and run after him, which won him a 10 yard head start. He darted, desperately seeking to lose himself in the foot traffic before she caught up. Pedestrians stopped and stared, impeding him.

Ava hit him with a flying tackle at the 25 yard point. Her thousand dollar bag of consumer electronics scattered to the pavement. She got him in a head lock between her thighs and rolled twice. For good measure, she slammed his skull into the pavement one extra time, and stomped his gut on her way up.

Ava was a firm believer in discouraging repeat offenders. It wasn't enough to win. Pain and humiliation, that was the ticket.

The skinny guy didn't fight worth a damn. If he were any good he could have grabbed her leg. He just lay there mewling for breath. Pathetic. A passing workman had already begun gathering strewn items back into her bag.

"That was unnecessary violence!" a woman shrilled, pointing at Ava. A skinny senile, she pointed a manicured fingernail and clutched her carpet bag in self-defense.

Like you'd know, Ava thought. But she quickly stooped to her bag. "Thank you, sir, I've got it."

"Drug addicts, up from the States," he muttered.

Ava glanced up sharply, then realized he was referring to the punk. "We're not all that way," she attempted, putting extra oomph into her Minnesota accent.

"Where'd you learn to fight like that?" he returned.

"Uh, karate competitions," Ava said, with a quick smile. She slapped her palm down to capture the fluttering receipt. She rushed to verify she'd found all the items. *No, dammit.* "There should be a memory slip. Anyone seen it?"

The audience checked around. "Oh, aye," a senile said, a man this time. In extra-slow motion, he started to bend down to get it.

The punk, still on the ground, grabbed for it first. Ava stomped on his hand. "Stay down, idiot." She swooped down to collect the memory. "Thank you so much, sir."

She turned to run as police sirens approached.

The workman yelled behind her, "Eh, you can't leave! You have to wait for the police! They'll want a statement!"

Ava sure didn't want to make one. She ducked, she dodged, she dove between people. She made it half a block.

Then she ducked straight into a cop. She froze as her eyes climbed his uniform to his face.

"Ah, afternoon, officer."

"I imagine you're from that ruckus down the block," he replied. "Let's go see, eh?"

14

Interesting fact: The Canadian health system enforced the new birth control strictures, as both carrot and stick. Non-compliant women were ineligible for health care, as were their families. Restoring the family to health care after an off-schedule birth required sterilization, and surrendering the child to the province. Few considered their objections worth the risk.

"But I have a train ticket Sunday," Ava wailed at the police station. "It cost over three thousand dollars! Give me my waist pack, I'll show you. They won't refund my money if I'm in jail waiting for a Monday morning court hearing."

"They might," suggested the desk sergeant.

Ava coughed. The air quality really was terrible in Toronto today. Running and the fight made her gulp in the smoke, too. "And I need my inhaler. In my hotel room." She coughed again theatrically. But reflexes took over to send her into a real coughing fit.

When she regained control, she croaked, "I've got a receipt for that too. In my purse. Went to the doctor today. No, come on, don't search my purse! Look, I didn't do anything wrong! I was the victim here!"

"Witness claims you used unnecessary force on the thief," the sergeant reiterated.

"How would she know?" Ava demanded. "Has she ever taken out a mugger? It doesn't pay to be gentle." She was talking at New York speed. She needed to slow down and channel Minnesota, she reminded herself.

He looked pointedly at her arm, which was dripping blood a little.

She looked too. She spat on her elbow and rubbed off the blood. She inspected her palms, too. One of them needed some spit.

The sergeant recoiled in disgust.

Ava was getting damned tired of that reaction from Canadians. "Come on, sarge. Always gonna be a few scrapes when you tackle on pavement."

"Miss Panic, that's called assault, eh?"

"That's how we do it in Minnesota! 'Course I wouldn't have to if you let me carry a Glock. Just shoot him." She wasn't speaking any slower.

"Miss Panic, you're not helping your case."

"Don't I get a phone call? I've got a police contact. He's important. I don't know the number. It's on my phone. In my pack there."

The desk sergeant relented and gave her the phone. She texted first, copy Skull, asking Mr. Clark of Windsor to call her back because she was in jail in Toronto. Then she called him instead of waiting. As she recounted her tale of woe, she wondered if Skull was monitoring the conversation. She bet Art and Daneel had time to figure that out by now.

"You're going to Vancouver. Not Toronto," Mr. Clark concluded.

Oops. "Yes, of course, Mr. Clark. I thought you knew. We just weren't sharing with Mr. Miller. I mean, that's why, um, the money."

"You have to obey Canadian law, Miss Panic."

"What, I was supposed to let a thief get away with a thousand dollars worth of stuff? What kind of law is that? I tackled a punk. He deserved it."

"You're supposed to let the authorities – Never mind. I'm not sure this is going to work."

"Mr. Clark," Ava said. "If I were a nice, well-adjusted, middle-class Canadian girl – would you send me to Vancouver?"

He snorted. Ava imagined Skull laughing.

"Right?" she pressed. "The job needs a nice girl who can defend herself. Against rapists, and pickpockets, and stuff. I'm just doing my job here, Mr. Clark. And my attacker was probably American. If he was a polite Canadian mugger? I wouldn't use nearly as much force." Yup, all those words flew out in a New York minute.

"And Mr. Clark? Consider the consequences. If I can't get a refund on my train ticket, think of the paperwork." Yes, Skull would definitely be laughing.

Clark groaned. "Enough. Hand me to the desk sergeant."

Ava couldn't tell what Clark told the man. On her end, the cop used raised eyebrows, monosyllables, and head-shaking. After a couple minutes, he ended the call and pushed phone and waist pack to her. He reached under the desk to return her shopping bag, one of a matched pair she picked up for herself and Cade. The bag pictured two alley cats on a wall, gazing romantically at the full moon. The caption read, *If I had two dead rats, I'd give you one.* Ava loved it.

She blew out in relief. She extracted the receipt, and took inventory again. She also quickly verified the top contents of the waist pack, though that never left her sight.

Ava looked up brightly. "All set. I'm free to go?"

"You're free to return to the Hotel Nouveautel. Where you will consider yourself under house arrest, Miss Panic. Until your train."

"Fair," she agreed.

Jana pinged a message on her walk back to the Nouveautel. Evening was advancing, so she waited until the lobby to draw out her pricey phone again.

Boss: LMAO. D+

Well, D was a passing grade. And she'd guessed right about him laughing his ass off.

THE TRAIN WAS FOUR HOURS LATE BOARDING. AVA FIGURED THAT WAS NO surprise, since they couldn't say whether the trip would take three days or six.

The train had arrived already. It was on the platform being cleaned, while passengers from points east left to stretch their legs. A corner of the cavernous Union Station concourse was roped off to keep them organized.

Ava was glad she paid extra for business class. The concourse was gorgeous, its stone floor gleaming, but it offered nowhere to sit. One of the business class perks was a seat in the lounge. The many economy passengers stood packed like sardines, amid tottering piles of luggage. Ava's lounge was practically deserted. Business class was advised to return twenty minutes before departure. But she was chained there by her parole.

It was a shame, too. From gossip she overheard, an epic protest march was passing a few blocks away. She would have liked to take pictures of what riled the polite Canadians. She could hear the roaring, but no content.

"What's it about, then?" she asked a cop by the doors, on one of her luggage-toting constitutionals around the station. She remembered to pronounce 'about' as 'a boot' this time. "The ruckus?"

"Oh, the usual," he replied. "Birth control, taxes, jobs, economy. French separatists. Justice to the First Nations. Demand Ottawa fix the climate. Foolishness."

"First Nations?" Ava asked.

"They demand recompense for losing their forests. Lost livelihood. They're not the only ones, though, eh?"

"No," she agreed. "How many protesters?"

"More all the time." The cop shook his head and wandered away on his rounds.

Ava dutifully entered a note via Jana, but her lack of detail made it vapid. A half hour later, she expanded her note as the business lounge started to fill early. The buzz said the cops resorted to tear gas outside to disperse the marchers. No one was surprised by this. Passengers from Montreal and Ottawa said the marches were getting worse all the time at home. The new Toronto passengers remarked that they never heard that on the news. They thought it was just Toronto.

Ava counted back. She guessed it was about six years ago that she became aware of the weekly American demonstrations, spreading to every city. And that the news didn't match reality. Of course, she was only twelve then. It was Deda and her parents who remarked on the media coverage when they moved from Austin, Texas to New York. Ava only remembered because she was startled, that her parents thought the news was lying to cover up how bad the protests were.

Maybe Canada hadn't dodged the bullet.

Ava eavesdropped avidly. But she didn't join the conversation as the Ontario and Quebec and Maritime contingents compared notes. As the throng grew, it became clear that she was an anomaly in business class. Everyone under thirty-five belonged in economy. And no one else under twenty was in either group, that she could see.

Most in business class looked the part, even on a Sunday. A man who looked like Mr. Clark's spiritual twin, including the trench coat on an early summer day, glanced at her surreptitiously now and then. His luggage consisted of a single briefcase. The two other women were over forty and wore neutral-colored skirts and pumps. Most wore a jacket as a simple expedient to carry it rumple-free.

In contrast, many out in steerage wore practical stretchy outfits to sleep in, and hugged their pillows and blankets. Some even toted paired gallons of water, yoked together in a wire carrier. There were young women out there, but not many, and usually as part of a couple. More commonly, a woman came with a man, kissed him good-bye at length, then left him there. The train would carry mostly men.

"Allo, allo!" Jean-Claude boomed to her. He arrived to dump his luggage at her feet. "We meet again! I am not stalking you! Promise!" He laughed.

Ava was beginning to think that was exactly what Jean-Claude was doing. But perhaps not.

"Ah! Excuse me," he said. "A colleague. Dr. Devereaux!"

Dr. Devereaux – Alain – a tweedy older man, walked over to join Jean-Claude in front of Ava, neither bothering to move their copious luggage. By the conversation, both men were doctors. Devereaux was moving to Saskatoon, and Jean-Claude was going through to Vancouver, facts that inspired mutual pretend condolences between the doctors. Both actually seemed enthusiastic and committed to their chosen destinations. They expected to stay indefinitely and practice medicine.

Devereaux returned to his pile of belongings when a conductor announced business class boarding would begin shortly. First class didn't tarry in the station at all, free to leave and board at whim.

"Are you both from Montreal?" Ava asked Jean-Claude, as they stood and shifted their stuff to head for the platform for boarding.

"Ah, no. We are with Médecins Sans Frontières. Doctors Without Borders. Alain is from Quebec City, I think? I am from France. But I will never return." He smiled to soften the statement. "I was in Haiti, when the planes stop to fly. Now I am stateless." He laughed. "I apply for Quebec citizenship."

"Do Doctors Without Borders cross the border into America?"

"Sh!" he said theatrically, with a wide-eyed grin.

The train was full. Ava and Jean-Claude had assigned sleeping berths and seats together, perhaps not such a surprise since they arrived from Windsor at the same time. The berths were closed for daytime. Day configuration gave each a wide bench seat facing one another across the window. The compartment was open to the corridor and the berthing pair across the aisle, but fairly private. The Mr. Clark-alike was installed in a one-man cabin ahead of them.

The conductor urged everyone to stay put while luggage was stowed. That process was mostly complete for their business class sleeper car by the time they rolled out of the station, but was expected to take a while in economy.

Ava stroked the flawless vinyl upholstery of her bench. She noted everything was clean and fresh. Even the screws and the seam where wall met floor were spotless, no brownish cruft. The window was squeaky clean on the inside, though regrettably scratched on the outside. She'd entered Toronto at night, so drank up the sights as they left, phone at the ready to try out her new clip-on lenses.

"This is wonderful!" Jean-Claude said. "You have such joy of your phone!"

"Jana is a great toy!" Ava happily showed off the accessories she picked up in Toronto.

Jean-Claude had a seemingly boundless supply of good humor. They stuck Jana on the selfie stick and extended it in every direction, to see how many of the passengers in the car they could spy on – not many. Ava invented a life story for each of them. They set up the tripod and recorded a deadpan video regarding the cows.

Jean-Claude took the role of an alien visitor reporting back on the structure of Earthian society as he'd seen it so far. Ava played along saying no, he had it all wrong. Humans were the preeminent species on Earth.

"Non! Clearly the dominant life forms are the trees and grasses, vying for supremacy! The cows, and their human servants, belong to the grass alliance!"

A conductor stopped by, labeled Macdonald. "You're having fun here, eh?"

Jean-Claude gestured expansively to Jana on her tripod. "Ah, would you too like to report to home planet?"

"No, thanks. Just getting to know everyone. I'm your host for this car through to Winnipeg. If you need anything, let me know. Feel free to explore the train now. Our turn at the dining car is at seven-thirty." He turned to the passengers across the aisle.

Ava promptly tore down the tripod.

"Everyone will do that now," Jean-Claude warned her.

"I'm very agile," Ava assured him.

He laughed, of course. Jean-Claude bubbled up laughter at everything.

Ava's plan had been to stick to herself and make no connections with her fellow passengers. Jean-Claude scotched that plan before they set foot on the train. But she couldn't regret it. He was fun.

She smiled sunnily at the awkward berthing couple across from them. They averted their gazes. The uptight older woman and middle-aged man seemed determined not to know each other, or Ava and Jean-Claude, in defiance of their obvious joint destiny for days.

Yeah, she was lucky to have Jean-Claude.

AVA EXPLORED BACKWARD FROM THEIR SLEEPER CAR FIRST, BECAUSE THEY were closer to that end. The train was enormous, with 26 cars plus the engine. The next was a troop car, configured like an America commuter cabin, with seats three to one side and two to the other of the aisle. Gear overflowed from racks above and in some of the seats.

A couple privates close to her age leaned across the aisle playing cards. They flirted with her as a toll for her to pass. She was game to flirt back, but their sergeant shut them down sharply and apologized to her. As she passed on, the sarge yelled at his charges to keep the walkway clear at all times. If he caught anyone else fraternizing with a civilian, there'd be hell to pay.

Ava grinned, remembering her tour of duty in Brooklyn after the tsunami. Her sergeant was the first to bolt for civilian companionship when the day's work was done, as she recalled. Granted, the civilians weren't forced to walk through their troop bus in Brooklyn. Guys grabbing at her each time she passed could get old. She didn't envy them sleeping in those seats. But it sure beat her school bus in Brooklyn.

The following three cars were economy, with only four seats across. The seats reclined fairly flat at night, leaving plenty of leg room in day configuration. Which was just as well, since every seat was full, and often wedged with bedding and luggage. Plenty of people were up and on the prowl, exploring as she was. She was finally grateful for the Canadian tendency to gently correct lapses of courtesy in others. Traffic flowed to the right, and holdups were soon prodded to clear the aisle.

The washroom lines were already forming in those cars. Ava imagined the lines were permanent.

Then she finally reached the bar car. No wonder most of the traffic was headed this way. A conductor encouraged the standing-room-only crowd to finish their purchases and head back to their seats. The wait at the bar was long.

The train tracks were smooth – smooth as glass compared to Jersey and Pennsylvania – but not smooth enough for pitchers of beer. Most of the steerage-dominated crowd bought bottles, and shrink-wrapped snack boxes.

The intriguing feature of the bar car was a staircase to the second level. The car had an observation bubble on top, with windows that arced overhead to a central steel beam. Ava joined a queue waiting for their turn to look around up there. A sign limited their stay in the dome to 10 minutes today, so everyone could get a chance.

Ava overheard a man complain that he'd lost phone service. His buddies joshed him that phones would only work in the towns from here on. She pulled out Jana to check. She still had a good signal. She ought to use it before it ran out. But not jostled in line at a bar. People were giving her oh-so-expensive phone funny looks, too. This bar was dominated by economy-class workmen.

She was in line for the stairs only a few minutes before the bouncer decided that no one had descended lately. He jogged up and kicked out a flock.

And suddenly, Ava had a seat, on top of the world. The view really was much better up here. Between the height of the train, and tracks raised above the winter snows and spring thaws, she could see past the woods most of the time. She feasted her eyes for a few moments.

In the distance, one of the Great Lakes shone calm and grey-blue, with no farther shore in sight. They'd left Canada's population corridor by now. Signs of human habitation were sparse, or even agriculture. There were grasslands, unusually brown and short for early summer. These mingled with fragmented boreal stands, evergreens mixed with birch and red maple. The woods were far shorter than the amazing tall trees of Michigan. Like most boreal forests, this was recent growth, bare dead trees poking out regularly.

Ava dutifully drew Jana out of her waist pack.

"Jana, record message to boss. Just checking in before I lose service," she told Jana to transcribe. "My train left Toronto late, a couple hours ago –"

The phone vibrated. Skull was calling her.

"Hi, Ava. Great pictures. About your berth-buddy –"

"He's great! Jean-Claude. I'm lucky."

"Ava." He paused to make sure she listened this time. "Jean-Claude is a known agent. Travels with the gran caravans."

Skull's boss, 'the General,' traveled with the gran caravans. Not his nice boss, Tony Nasser, lead Resco of Hudson's Up Finger region. Skull had another boss and controller from the Northern League. The 'externalities.'

Ava replied, heart sinking, "He told me he was with Doctors Without Borders. He implied he'd been to America."

"He certainly has," Skull confirmed. "And his cover is legit. He really is with Médecins Sans Frontières. He really is a doctor. What else he is, I'm not so sure. Canadian Intelligence, we think."

"So I've been suckered."

"Not necessarily. We're doing something novel. They're curious what we're up to. So this Jean-Claude takes a trip with you to Vancouver. And his cover works all the way."

All the way to Seattle, Ava supplied mentally. "I think I'm stuck with him, boss. The train is full."

Chock-full, in fact, she now realized. And this wasn't exactly a spur-of-the-moment kind of trip. People planned ahead to take this week-long train, and packed carefully. They needed to save a pile of money for it, too. Canadian travel wasn't as difficult as American. But clearly travel between the large provinces had grown unusual.

So how did she waltz up and get her choice of accommodations the day before departure?

Maybe that's what the 'permission' business was about at the ticket counter. She bounced someone off the train. And then Jean-Claude did, too, and matched her choice of berthing. She bet he was relieved when she didn't choose economy. Or maybe they just made sure she had the funds to opt for comfort.

"Not a problem, Ava," Skull said. "Just be aware of it. Remember, you're a courier. Stick to your mission. If you stick your nose where it doesn't belong, then you might have a problem. But your mission was approved. And Jean-Claude works for a friendly power."

Both Skull and Jean-Claude answered to 'the General,' plus someone else. In theory, at least, Hudson and Canada were friendly as well. This was so far out of her league.

Ava asked, "Should I tell him I know who he is?"

"Up to you. I'd wait."

15

Interesting fact: Ontario is big. Toronto is toward its southeast corner. From Toronto to Sioux Lookout is 1,100 miles, then 200 miles further to cross into Manitoba (2,000 km combined).

Dinner with the doctors was surprisingly fun. Ava didn't have anyone else to eat with. Her ticket included deluxe meals on the linen-napped tables in the exclusive dining car. No riff-raff allowed. The wait staff were the only people in view under thirty.

So dining with seniles it was.

At least they were interesting and cheerful seniles. Dr. Alain Devereaux shared a sleeper cabin with an older woman named Madison Lusk. Clearly the pair had bonded since Quebec.

Madison was an avid bird watcher headed for Winnipeg. There she planned to turn due north several hundred miles. She wore light binoculars strung on a chain around her neck, the way the elderly librarian back in Soho Village wore her reading glasses. She frequently broke off conversation or eating to peer at something out the window.

More grassland with sporadic scrubby woods and ponds flashed past. Birds weren't especially plentiful, as the sun was setting. Madison hoped to spot bats, though.

Continued smoke in the air made the sunset spectacularly red. The diners' eyes were fairly red as well.

"Bats," Ava repeated. She'd forgotten that, from the Minnesota summers. "Is it very buggy?" Those summers explained why Minnesotans preferred winter. The land of 10,000 lakes was no exaggeration. The biting gnats traveled in black clouds.

"Oh, yes!" Madison agreed. "Though less so than it used to be. So little rain." She shook her head sadly.

Ava checked Jana for a map. Her phone service was gone for now, but the train wireless Internet was working, if slow. The map showed her that the notoriously frigid Winnipeg was actually not far north of the Minnesota–North Dakota line. Manitoba stretched north from there to the western shores of Hudson Bay. Like Ontario, the prairie province had a sea coast. It also put Minnesota's mere 10,000 lakes to shame. Manitoba boasted 110,000. Lake Winnipeg rivaled the Great Lakes for size.

"How does it have so many lakes if there's no rain?" Ava asked.

"Ground water," Madison supplied eagerly. "When the glaciers receded, they melted into a lake that covered, oh, all of Manitoba. The water is gradually receding. But the glaciers scratched holes in the land, and the water seeps into them."

"So there's no water shortage in Manitoba?" Ava asked. North Dakota was part of the Dust Bowl.

"We reach the Dust Bowl after Portage la Prairie," Jean-Claude told Ava. "After Winnipeg."

Alain laughed. "Days from now."

The train wheels screeched a bit, and there was a jog to the right that sloshed their glasses. The train slowed.

Ava frowned. "It can't be that far."

Alain shook his head. "They held us at Toronto to let the freight trains pass. It's been a few hours now. We're overdue."

"Speak of the devil," Madison agreed with a sigh.

Ava looked at Jean-Claude in question. He sat back to explain. "We just, ah, shunted? Onto, hmm." His English was short of fluent.

"A siding," Madison supplied. To Ava, she added, "We park here on a side rail next to the main track while the freight trains pass. We have to share the track. Freight has priority. And troop trains."

"And trains coming the other way," Alain added.

"So we only go forward half the time?" Ava asked, aghast.

"Maybe," Alain confirmed.

"They should add another track," Jean-Claude said.

"National priorities, localize, they say," Alain said with a Gallic shrug.

Madison threw up her hands. "No politics, please!"

The seniles laughed. Jean-Claude poured more wine around for everyone but Ava. She was of legal drinking age here, years past it in Hudson, but their bottle of red didn't go with her quiche and salad.

They were still parked on the siding when Macdonald reconfigured their berths for bed at 10:00 p.m. The freight trains were immense.

Ava climbed into her bunk, heavily curtained from the corridor. She was glad she opted for the window. Jean-Claude's bunk above hers was claustrophobic indeed. Her throat was scratchy from the day's smoke load, so she took a couple pulls of breathing treatment from Moo Cow. She verified that her black box was still safe and sound in her smaller ruck.

She dutifully clasped her hands as if in prayer. She reviewed everything she'd memorized. *Still perfect.*

She roused slightly when they started moving again, but then drifted into much deeper sleep, rocked by the train's movement. Their first station stop, Sudbury Junction, came and went with the sunrise at 4:30 a.m. Aside from being a modest settlement in the swampy countryside, it didn't strike the sleepy teen as interesting enough to stay awake for. She rolled over to ignore the sun for a couple more hours.

Trouble boarded the train at Sudbury Junction. Ava just didn't know it yet.

"AVA! WELCOME BACK!" JEAN-CLAUDE GREETED HER, AS SHE SLID BACK into her spot by the window. Her berth mate briefly raised his legs to let her by, then replaced them on her rucksack. They used each other's bench as a footrest.

She'd been out exploring forward of the dining car this morning. Their berths were in the last of the premium cars. The next eight cars forward were likewise elite. Then economy, bar, and troop cars filled to the front of the train. Ava thought their exclusive panorama car was very cool, with glass walls curving up to the ceiling. Not quite as much sky as in the second-floor domes on the bar cars, but an immersive experience, at one with the landscape. Minus the swarms of midges, which were out in full force. They'd crossed fully into the land of lakes. The panorama car wasn't full like the economy-class bar cars, so no one enforced a time limit.

Jean-Claude surprised her by leaning forward, and crooked a conspiratorial finger. She leaned forward, ear toward his mouth.

"I took a shower," he told her. "When I came back, a girl your age was rifling your bag." He pointed to the rucksack. "She claimed she was a friend of yours."

Ava immediately pulled her ruck to Jean-Claude's seat in front of her, and dug in for inventory. The black box was still there, thank God. "She knew my name?"

"No, she said 'your seat-mate.' But she knew that bag was yours."

Ava glanced around their seats and stuff management arrangements. Jean-Claude kept a laptop messenger bag on the bench beside him, rather masculine for a teenage girl. There wasn't much feminine about Ava's tough olive nylon ruck, either. But it bore a four-inch patch embroidered with the Project Reunion logo, a broken heart enveloping the Apple. Tourist stalls sold them by the thousands near the salvage clearinghouses at the downtown end of Central Park. She'd even seen the logo merchandise for sale at a farm market in Pennsylvania. She'd sewn them onto both her bags to mark them as hers.

Cade wasn't worried about the patches being too revealing. But then, traveling with Cade, her bags were piled with other stuff in the back of an SUV. And she wasn't this far from the Apple then. A Minnesota girl bearing that logo was harder to explain.

"My age," Ava repeated. There were precious few women on this train, and she hadn't seen any as young as herself. A horrible thought occurred to her. "Multi-racial? Little bit Asian?"

"Yes," Jean-Claude confirmed. "She left quickly." He pointed backward in the train, past the expensive cars. "I waited to speak to you before telling Macdonald." Jean-Claude's accent lightened considerably when he was serious.

"Thanks." Jana's user manual was missing. And Ava had folded that scrap of paper in it, with the list of microchips. And the post-it note of phone numbers. Were those labeled? Yes, Clark and Sullivan. Everything else was accounted for, so far as she could tell. She cursed herself for trading the black box for Porta's camera in her waist pack. She swapped them back.

"Friend?" Jean-Claude inquired.

"Not exactly."

"From...Minnesota?"

"Something like that." She sat back and stared out the window to think.

"I expected you to go after her," Jean-Claude commented. "And do what, I don't know."

"That's the problem," Ava agreed. She pulled out Jana and checked. Still no phone, but she had Internet.

She could place a file on her starred storage to ask Skull's advice.

But she wasn't sure she wanted to ask him anything. Sure, she was pissed at Kelly for running off. Stealing money from Ava's bags, and going AWOL in Windsor, were way out of line. So was rifling her ruck and lifting her things on the train.

Then again, Kelly was a fellow Apple survivor. Ava didn't know her very well. They spent days together camping across Ohio. But Kelly didn't say much. Maybe she really was that desperate to escape Hudson. Who was Ava to say she was wrong? Ava might feel the same way if it weren't for Cade.

Her gang during the Starve was livable, even family. That was Cade. She ranked high in the gang, royalty instead of bullied and brutalized. That was Cade too. Canada was in far better shape than Hudson. Seattle and Washo might be even better. Yet Skull needn't worry about Ava defecting. He held Cade. So far as Skull knew, Ava might defect, but she'd return for Cade first.

It wasn't true. Ava was a Hudson patriot, far more so than Cade. The Project Reunion logo meant a lot to her. But Skull might not know her that well yet. She wasn't sure even Cade knew that about her. Ava couldn't really explain it, except that she'd hate to let down Sergeant Calderon and her squad mates from the Point, or her friends back in the Apple. Hudson was her people. Hudson granted her citizenship. Ava took a proprietary pride in her fledgling country.

If the company knew where Kelly was, would they kill her? Return her to Hudson? What would Hudson do to her? Kelly had worked for the company for well over a month. She wasn't on probation. She was under contract.

Ava didn't like Kelly. But a death sentence was a bit much. Worse, as the only company agent on the scene, it might be *her* responsibility to kill the girl. Which Ava would surely do, if Skull ordered it.

Maybe.

Also, she realized, it was quite possible that Mr. Clark, and whoever he worked for, would see any note that she left on her cloud storage for Skull.

That was more of an excuse than a bar to communication, she decided. There was always a subtle way to communicate past eavesdroppers. She knew Skull better than Clark's people did. She could even write something only Daneel or Cade, or KT and Cerveza, could decode. Skull didn't miss a trick. If she was cryptic, she could count on Skull to figure it out.

She just wasn't ready to tell him. Yet.

She sighed. So then the question became how to decide what to tell Skull. And how to make sure Kelly didn't screw up Ava's mission. She wanted her list of microchips back. She'd only managed to memorize some of those yet. There was a backup copy inside the black box. But there was good reason to have backup.

Good point. She rummaged for a scrap of paper. She wrote out 22 numbers, and jotted down all the chip names she could remember. She was fairly confident of numbers 21 and 22, and certain of the first 8. Number 9 she knew the letters but had little confidence in her digits.

That's where her list bogged down into four different model numbers of 'PMIC,' whatever that was. Maybe she'd remember more later.

She tucked her new list away in her bulging waist pack, and rose. She couldn't carry the rucksack around the train. It was too easy to pickpocket in the jam-packed economy and bar cars.

"If she comes back?" Jean-Claude inquired.

"Tell her I'm looking for her."

He nodded. Then he smiled crookedly. "No unnecessary force?"

She'd told him about her misadventure with Toronto's finest over the thief. "No promises. Thanks, Jean-Claude." She squeezed his shoulder in passing.

Her first stop was Macdonald, the car steward. She explained the incident, described Kelly to him, and asked him to keep an eye out for her. She didn't belong in this car.

"I'll contact security at once," Macdonald said grimly.

"Could you not, please?" Ava wheedled. "I mean, I'm concerned. I wanted to let you know. But I'd like to talk to her first. Maybe there's an explanation."

"She can explain herself to the authorities, eh?"

"Well, if I can't find her," Ava hedged. "Let me try first?"

"Alright. I'm about to make an announcement, though. Could you return to your seat, please, and wait a few minutes?"

Ava returned to her seat and updated Jean-Claude on her lack of progress. Fidgety, she stared out the window. The sunlight was dimming and growing yellower. Were those snowflakes amid the gnat clouds? Surely not. Perhaps they were some sort of predator moth.

Soon Macdonald got on the loudspeaker to explain what she was seeing. "Attention, everyone. We're heading rather close to a wildfire. The air filters are struggling a bit. I'll hand out masks in a moment, and eye drops, for passengers who – Ah, all passengers in this car bought the survival kit package, right."

Ashes, not snowflakes. Ava and Jean-Claude stared at each other, eyes wide.

"If you have your own nebulizer," Macdonald pressed on, "I suggest using it now. I have a backup for anyone who doesn't have one."

Ava and her berth-mate rummaged in their bags to draw out their nebulizers. Jean-Claude's was a dolphin, which looked way cooler than Moo Cow. They grinned at each other's equipment and set up to take a quick treatment.

"At this point," Macdonald continued, "the wildfire hasn't reached the tracks."

Ava boggled. She'd assumed when he said nearby, he meant like 20 miles or something. Not actually threatening the train tracks.

"That could change," the steward said. "But our next siding is beyond the fire. We are instructed not to stop here and tie up the rail. I'm sure that will change if it gets too dangerous. But this could get a little exciting.

"Any time we experience, um, exciting, we ask that you remain in the berthing car as much as possible. If you do need to exit the car, please check in with me first. Thank you. And I'll distribute your masks as quickly as possible."

Macdonald's den was at the far end of the car. Ava pulled out one of the silk scarves that she painted at the Pennsylvania farm market near the company HQ. She twined it over her mouth and around her neck. It surprised her not at all when Jean-Claude pulled out a scarf whose pattern could have been marbled in the same water trough.

"Great minds think alike!" he said, eyes crinkled in a smile above the particolored moire scarf.

"I like your nebulizer," Ava returned. "I would have picked a dolphin if they offered me one."

"No grown man would be caught dead sucking on an udder in public."

Ava stifled a giggle. "I see your point."

By now, Kelly could be anywhere in the train, or at least anywhere rear of Ava's car. Any advantage of hurrying after her was lost. Grudgingly, Ava bided her time and waited for Macdonald. The steward was taking lunch orders, as well, to be served in their seats, as breakfast had been. The dining car capacity was strained to its limit. Only first class passengers had the option to eat at its tables every meal. Business class only rated supper in there, though the dining car's hard-working kitchen produced them three excellent meals a day.

At last Ava was issued her breath mask and bottle of eye drops, and entered her choice of split pea soup with ketchup chips for lunch. Jean-Claude assured her he'd eat the chips if she didn't like them. Ava smiled wanly and told him she wasn't a picky eater. Compared to cockroaches, and rat soup made without benefit of boiling water, she was confident pea soup with ketchup-flavored potato chips would be glorious.

She didn't mention that part.

She meekly promised Macdonald she would return to home base if the fire situation outside got scary.

With that, she was off to hunt Kelly. Or Kaylee. Debbie. Whatever the hell her name might be today.

16

Interesting fact: Fire is part of the natural forest renewal cycle. Several boreal tree species, such as lodgepole and jack pine, even require fire to reproduce. Fire unlocks their pine cones to free the seeds. Fire also opens up the canopy so the sun can reach young trees, and recycles nutrients in the forest floor.

Ava darted back through the cars quickly. She didn't ask questions in the troop car. She kept her head down and sped through.

In the following three economy cars, a steward waylaid her to earnestly advise that she'd be safer in her seat. But she had her silk scarf over her mouth, and the breath mask hanging from her neck. She solemnly promised that she'd return to her seat just as soon as she finished her errand.

She asked if they'd seen a girl about her age in their car. One said yes. A girl was headed toward the rear, probably not long after Jean-Claude saw her. Yes, she was a visible minority, probably not First Nation.

The other stewards said they didn't have such a girl, and saw entirely too much foot traffic to notice one. Ava checked all the seats anyway, but didn't spot Kelly.

She paused at the near-empty bar car, and sank sideways into a seat to stare. The seats here ringed the walls, facing a hollow interior. For the first time she had a view of both sides of the train through the windows. The air was noticeably browner since she left her own seat. But the smoke was thicker to the right, opposite her berthing side. The swarms of gnats had evaporated. Scraps of grey and white ash spiraled through the air, propelled by winds unseen.

It was the damnedest thing. The train was passing through swamp country. Small to medium swaths of lake glinted regularly. The grass was short from the long winter, but greening. No signs of human habitation crowded the tracks. Being near a train meant noise and smokestacks, and silverware-rattling vibration. The trains didn't stop here. So people and their livestock gave the tracks a wide margin. If there were any people around here.

The little stands of woods they passed weren't burning. But something sure was.

Ava shook off her reverie. She needed to find Kelly quickly and get back to her own car. The bar car was closed, no barkeeper or steward on duty. A big sign ordered passengers not to linger here, although of course several did anyway. A young couple were getting busy under blankets. Ava pursed her lips and didn't bother them, for now. The body bits that stuck out were inconclusive. Kelly could be shacking up.

Ava snorted. That didn't sound like Kelly.

She jogged past the *Closed!* sign, and up into the dome. She paused at the top of the stairs to look around. To her surprise, it was deserted. *Why didn't they climb up here to shack up?* Ava wondered. It was more romantic than the bar pass-through.

She started back down the steps, then stopped. Did she just hear something up there? She waited and listened, but didn't hear it again. She turned and padded back up softly.

Just as Ava took the last step up to cross the threshold into the dome, Kelly dove into her feet. That would send most people sprawling out of control.

Ava wasn't most people. She landed on her knees, one jabbing into Kelly's lower spine, and one on the floor beside her hip. Her hands quickly pinned Kelly's shins, just in case.

"What the fuck, Kelly?" she demanded.

"Let me up!"

"Talk first," Ava demanded. With the other girl firmly immobilized, she scooted around to sit on Kelly's butt, facing her head now. "My stuff. Give it back."

"You need to let me up first," Kelly insisted. "I can explain!"

"I let you up, you go backward in the dome car. Or you have a very unpleasant accident on the stairs. Broken bones."

"Yeah, fine. Bitch."

Ava twisted one of Kelly's arms behind her. She held onto it for leverage as Kelly clambered off the floor. Once she was on her feet, Ava shoved her into a double seat. Ava blocked her exit to the aisle, anchored to handholds on the seat backs.

Kelly had seen Ava fight. They practiced in camp in Ohio, and back at HQ. She'd take the hint.

"I need money," Kelly demanded.

Ava stared at her in disbelief. "You thought you'd steal from me? *Again?*"

"No, look, I was just trying to get your attention." Kelly dug into a cargo pocket on her army camouflage pants and pulled out the ouiPhone manual.

Ava took it and leafed through. "The papers that were stuck in here. Now!"

Kelly grimaced and dug into another pocket. "I forgot about those. What the hell is this, anyway? Looks like a parts list for a mobile device."

Ava blinked, reflecting that she really didn't know Kelly at all. What kind of nineteen year old Army recruit would recognize a list of microchips? "What are you?"

"I'm your backup!"

Ava huffed a laugh. "Try again."

"I needed to make sure you'd come look for me."

"Next time leave a note," Ava suggested.

"How would I know that?" Kelly returned. "I don't know who your seat-mate is. He could be one of them."

"Them who?"

"I don't know!"

"Good work, Kelly. Now everyone in the train knows about you. They know I'm looking for you, too. Start over. You deserted."

"Shit, shit, shit…" Kelly whispered. "Look. I'm here on assignment. Sk– The boss told me to leave you in Windsor. But dammit, you should have split the money with me!"

"How the hell did you get here then?" Ava demanded. Even the cheap seats on this train cost hundreds of dollars. Did she steal enough from Ava in Windsor? Ava didn't think so.

Kelly's gaze was arrested past her ear, though. "Ava…"

"You want me to look behind me?" As though Ava would fall for that.

"Fire," Kelly squeaked.

Ava glanced up at the window beyond the other girl's head. She didn't see fire on that side. She did see scraps of grass in the air with glowing embers, though. The general haze of smoke had thickened.

Cautiously she backed up toward the stairs, holding onto bars on the seat backs to keep blocking Kelly's escape. She finally dared a glance at the window wall on the other side.

Kelly wasn't lying. The smoke on that side now came at them in thick brown billows. After a few seconds, Ava caught a glimpse of flame at mid-tree height, not a hundred feet from the tracks.

"We're not done, Kelly. Where's your seat?"

"Next car back."

"You stay rear of this car until I come find you," Ava hissed.

"You're not my boss, bitch!"

The girls glared at each other in open dislike. "Stay back here in economy," Ava demanded. "Cross my car again, and you'll be caught as a thief."

"Dammit!" Kelly conceded. "Go!"

Ava wheeled and pounded down the stairs. A pair of troopers were downstairs now in the bar, clearing out the loiterers. Kelly scampered rearward into her car, but Ava faced the troops.

"Excuse me, I need to get back to my seat," she hazarded.

"Where?" the corporal demanded. "Haven't seen you back here before."

"I'm in the last sleeper car."

"Too far," he declared. "You're with us."

His sidekick took a quick turn up through the dome to make sure it was empty, and came back brandishing an ID. "This your friend's?"

Ava promptly took custody of it, and shoved it into a pocket unexamined. "I'll get it back to her later."

"Alright, come on," said the corporal, labeled Mogadishu. 'Visibly non-white' by Canadian standards, Ava pegged him as a son of African immigrants. The name Mogadishu sounded vaguely familiar.

With Mogadishu ahead setting the pace, and Ava bracketed between him and his henchmen, they rushed rearward through an economy car, past Kelly, and into the final troop car. The corporal dragged her to a sergeant, who rolled his eyes at Mogadishu's choice to adopt a civilian girl during an emergency.

"Couldn't you stow her in economy?"

"No open seats."

Ava interrupted. "Please, sergeant, could you contact my car steward? Let him know where I am. Macdonald."

This accomplished, the sergeant awarded Ava with Corporal Mogadishu's aisle seat and sought to ignore her. He had plenty else to occupy his attention. Some of the troops were donning protective overalls. All were being issued gas masks. Ava herself pulled her breath mask on top of her scarf, over her nose and mouth.

"What are you doing?" Ava asked the pair of privates she blocked from the aisle.

"We pull off on the next siding," he explained. "The troops will get out and hose down the tracks. Maybe fire-fighting."

"You've done that before?" Ava asked.

They snorted. "Lots."

Ava turned and tugged on Mogadishu's uniform. "Let me help. I can work the relief station. Or fight the fire if you have gear small enough for me."

"Miss, we don't need untrained –"

"I am trained. I can administer oxygen and breathing treatments, get them lying down on their sides, hang IV fluids. I can triage the symptoms for the doctors. There are doctors on the train. My seat mate is with Doctors Without Borders. We ate dinner last night with another. Jean-Claude Alarie and Alain Devereaux. Ask for volunteers."

Corporal Mogadishu considered the suggestion. The smoke was lightening on both sides of the train now, though embers still flew on burning scraps of leaf and grass. The air was getting pretty murky inside the car too, despite excellent seals, proof against the Canadian deep winter cold.

The corporal nodded in decision and left to confer with his sergeant again.

The private beside her held out a fist and nodded respect. "Get some, girl!"

Ava bopped his fist back, and the other private past him. "Get some!" she agreed happily. She'd asked Sergeant Calderon once, 'Get some what?' 'Adrenaline,' he told her – grab whatever action you could.

Soon the announcement came over the loudspeakers, asking for medical volunteers as a precaution. Please proceed to the troop car at the rear of the train as soon as they stopped moving. All stewards to remain on station in their assigned cars.

Ava was issued an upgraded gas mask with goggles and fireproof gloves. The smaller of the privates she sat with donated a spare uniform, which was considerably more fireproof than her T-shirt and skinny jeans, and roomy enough to pull on over her clothes.

Soon the smoke cleared still further. The train gave the familiar screech and jolts and brakes of shifting onto a siding.

When they stopped, Ava told the sergeant her first task was to roll an extension cord out as far back from the train as it would reach, to plug in nebulizers. Sure enough, Jean-Claude arrived soon after. Ava grinned. He brandished her Moo Cow and combat boots in triumph.

Jean-Claude donned a gas mask while Ava laced up her boots. He stepped out with her to look over her arrangements so far and declared them good. But he collared a medic and sent him and his partner packing to fetch more drinking water to Ava's forward position. He told her she and the medics should stay here for triage, but he'd keep the doctors inside the troop car. If anyone was in trouble, their main need would be oxygen. That was too flammable to deploy outdoors.

He quickly reviewed her understanding of first aid for burns and smoke, and declared it good enough. "But don't get cocky, yes? The medics have experience with forest fire. You follow their lead. Stay safe. I'll be inside!"

Ava started another trip to the train to help fetch water jugs. But the platoon lieutenant told her to stay on station. Anything that needed carrying, his men could do that. Indeed, the two of them drew back out of the way as a group jockeyed out a pump and another reel of extension cord. The hose bearers had already passed from one of the forward troop cars, seeking a convenient scrap of lake closer to the fire front. Ava was surprised the train carried fire hoses. This scenario must have cropped up before.

The medics returned carrying a surprisingly large collection of gallon water jugs on top of a folding banquet table. Setting up, Ava felt like they were opening a lemonade stand.

The troops were fresh and happy to move a muscle. The aid station had some waiting to do. They faced away from the train, into the smoke. They didn't talk much. Occasionally wildlife darted their way, unconcerned by them or each other. Lynx and hare fled the fire in brotherhood, plus deer and all manner of rodents. Ava hadn't been to a zoo in years. But seeing truly wild animals run for their lives was different. She could see the intelligent desperation in their eyes.

One of the medics, George, kept a pistol at the ready just in case. But the last thing the wildlife wanted to do was stop here. The clutch of humans was merely an obstacle to flow around. A lynx darted by only a few arm spans from Ava, beautiful, strong, and divinely indifferent to her.

A lemonade stand wasn't a bad idea. It was hot out there, over 90 degrees. That was over 30 degrees to the Canadians. The northern plains had been baking under the midsummer sun for 8 hours already today, and would get another 9 hours before sunset. Ava hadn't been truly hot since last October, except in a tub. She broke open the first water jug for herself and her companions.

At last their first customers stumbled back from the lines, some local firefighters. George ran to greet them first. He checked their breathing with a stethoscope. Reassured, he and the other medic helped them back to settle behind the table, on their sides. Ava served out cups of water, and helped remove their protective gear to cool off. They seemed to suffer nothing worse than heat exhaustion, though one man requested a turn on the nebulizer.

After another brief lull, the returning traffic of soldiers grew steadier. At one point, the train stewards sent out a huge tray of cut fruit and cheese. The business class and first class passengers volunteered their lunch desserts to the firefighters. That was a big hit with everyone who stopped back for a break.

The medics left Ava alone to hold the fort while they ran to fetch a man with burns to the doctors. It got hectic, but nothing she couldn't handle. The soldiers were happy to lend a hand if she needed one. One suggested a shade awning from his troop car up the train. That she accepted, but only if he rested 15 minutes first. She wanted them to lie down and cool off. More water poured onto heads than down throats.

Since she handled her first solo stretch without difficulty, George and his fellow medic decided to wait at a more forward position from then on. What they could give didn't rely on Ava's extension cord. Anyone who needed help breathing, could also use help to reach the equipment. They brought sufferers back to her, or passed her on the way to the doctors, more frequently as the afternoon temperature soared and the soldiers wore out.

The next big excitement came in late afternoon. At last another train came through, headed east. Ava and the men around her stood and stared as car after car of fuel oil and coal passed not a hundred yards from them.

"Won't it burn?" Ava asked a professional fire fighter nearby.

He stood tiredly to pull his gear back on. "Nah. We'll hose it down going through," he explained. "To be on the safe side. That's what we're here for. Protect the trains."

Ava handed him a last cup of water. "Take care."

"Will do. Nice break area you have here. Don't usually get that, eh?" With that, he turned to plod back to the fire lines.

The fossil fuel trains were heavy. A single engine could only pull so many cars. Four trains passed headed east, spaced 20 minutes apart. After another hour's lull, a couple trains of freight and empties, much longer, passed westward. That was the last of the traffic they were waiting for. But their troops still labored to control the fire well back from the crucial rails.

By 8:30 p.m., with the lowering sun deep orange, the powers that be declared they'd helped enough. Local pros could contain the fire from here. The medics gave Ava their thanks, and told her to just carry in her nebulizers. They'd handle the rest.

Ava and Jean-Claude returned to their sleeper car to a standing ovation from their home car. They got dibs on use of the shower. Macdonald reheated Jean-Claude's supper, and Ava's missed lunch of congealed pea soup. She assured him she didn't need any more than that, just bed. The ketchup chips tasted fabulous. While Macdonald converted their berths early, Ava and Jean-Claude sat with the previously unfriendly neighbors across the aisle to eat, and explained their roles in the firefight.

Morris and Camille weren't bad sorts after all. They even thawed toward each other.

Ava fell asleep the instant she crawled into the bunk. She didn't mentally recite the material she'd memorized. She forgot all about Kelly and the ID in her pocket. She didn't spare a thought for what Skull might think of her all-day silence.

17

Interesting fact: In the town name of Sioux Lookout, Ontario, it was the Ojibwa people who used a local mountain to watch for enemy Sioux crossing a nearby rapids. The modern town population was about 5,300, over a third First Nation.

Ava's phone was incapable of waking her. Morris from across the corridor did that, very apologetically. But her phone buzzing was keeping everyone awake except for her and Jean-Claude. Could he trouble her to power it off?

Ava apologized abjectly, and told him of course he was right to disturb her. *Fussy senile,* was a reaction she kept strictly to herself.

It was midnight. Skull's latest text said, *FUCKING CHECK IN NOW!* Leafing back, he'd built up to that through 15 hours of texts.

Good, she had a signal. She muffled herself into a corner with pillow and blankets, and mumbled. "Hey, I was asleep. What's up?"

"Report," Skull demanded.

"Mm, could we do this in the morning? People are sleeping."

"You can type. Or you can talk. But you do it now."

"I spent the afternoon firefighting."

"Meaning?"

"There was a fire? Outside. I volunteered to help. Kind of an aid station?"

"A literal fire?"

"Yeah, you know, like burning trees and stuff."

Skull sighed. "Ava, we need to work on your reports."

Ava yawned. "Uh-huh."

"Anything else you'd like to share?"

There was something? Oh, yeah. Kelly. "It can wait."

"Kelly is on your train," Skull prompted.

Damn. Who told him? "I'm handling that. Well, I will. Can't right now."

"Ava, did you know she planned to run in Windsor?"

"What? No!" Ava cringed and brought her voice back down to a mumble. "No, I told you. She claims you sent her. As my backup."

"Now? Untrue. And Ava? She went AWOL a week before your mission was hatched."

"I figured. She stole some stuff from my bag." Ava had to break off for a huge yawn again. "I got it back. Then a fire attacked the train. Oh, there's that." She sat up and rifled through her jeans, in a wad at her feet. One of the advantages of being short was storage space at the foot of the bed.

"Really need to work on your reporting skills…"

Ava could picture him pinching the bridge of his nose. "Yeah, bite me. She dropped an ID, and I have it. Yet another spelling of Caillee, Brougham." She spelled it out for him. "Sault Ste. Marie, Ontario. Oh, wait. That doesn't matter if it's a fake ID, does it."

"Probably not. What did she steal from you?"

"The manual to my ouiPhone. I had some papers in it. She said she didn't know that before she took it. That I believe. She knew what the list was, though."

"What list? What papers?"

"Parts list. And phone numbers for Clark and Sullivan. Those were the papers. Stuck in the manual. She gave it all back."

"Alright. What's your plan?"

"Been kinda busy since then. And then, you know, sleeping."

"That's why you didn't report in? It was more important for you, as a civilian train passenger, to help fight a wildfire?"

Ava pursed her lips and glowered at herself in the dark window inches from her face. The image was ghostly and one-sided in the slight light leaking from Jana.

Skull had asked point blank. Cade's strategy for boss management was to tell him exactly what he asked for, if Skull guessed well enough to ask. Whether the boss would like the answer or not. Cade got away withit.

"I was afraid...what the punishment might be. I wanted to hear her side first. But she lied. But so would I. She wants money. I could spare her some for food. I don't know."

Skull snorted. "Truth."

"Yeah. I still haven't heard her side. Except lies. If they're lies."

"I sent her with you to Buffalo."

"Did she like her next assignment? She looked kinda sour."

Skull sighed. "No idea. I can't read her."

"I can relate. Can I go back to sleep?"

"Ava, you can satisfy your curiosity. But you are to do nothing about Kelly. Except in self-defense. Let the Canadians deal with her."

"Deal with her how?" Ava asked.

"That's not up to us."

Silence.

"Panic? Acknowledge your orders."

"I hear you."

Skull snorted again. "Don't help her. Don't hurt her except in self-defense. Don't allow her to interfere with your mission. It's not smart to interfere with the Canadian authorities. Which part of that can't you agree to?"

"Maybe if I knew what she was running from. Or to. I don't know squat."

"You know you have orders. You are a courier. You arc to proceed from point A, to point B. Deliver your package. You are a guest in Canada, as an extraordinary favor. You are not a spy. You do not piss off Canadians. Any clearer?"

"Well, I'm glad."

"Glad?"

"That she's not my problem. To, um."

"Oh. No," Skull said slowly. "That's not your job."

"Good. I still want to know what the fuck she thinks she's doing."

"Was she forthcoming on that topic?"

Now it was Ava's turn to snort. "No."

"Has she been forthcoming on *any* topic? Your training agent," Skull meant Cade, "informs me you're absolutely reliable in a firefight. No one he'd rather have at his back. Clever as hell. But you're a tad gullible. Don't be. Kelly has already conned both of us."

Ava hadn't considered that. Skull screened his prospective new hires with a fine-toothed comb. He watched Ava for weeks before confirming her contract. Skull wasn't the tiniest bit gullible. And Kelly burned him. What chance did Ava have to see through her act? "Yes, sir."

But I'm here, and Skull isn't, her reservations spoke a moment after her mouth stopped. *It might not be that simple.*

Skull accepted her agreement as close enough, and signed off. Ava sat up and stared at her bottom-lit, bluish reflection in the window for a moment. She covered the phone with her pillow for pitch blackness in the berth. But the view outside didn't resolve into more than a procession of black humps under a starless sable sky.

She reviewed her memorized material before falling back to sleep. She also checked her written-from-memory microchip list against the master strip of printout. She'd written two errors in the half she remembered at all. She corrected and completed her hand copy and tucked it deep within her Western Civilization textbook, a tome that weighed as much as the Moo Cow nebulizer.

I'll review it all four times a day, she vowed as she turned to sleep. Her self-belief in this was frustrated by the fact that she hadn't studied Western Civ since her visit to Grosse Pointe – the first time.

Irritating as Cade's rituals could be, his discipline reliably got things done. She needed to be a grown-up about her chores.

~

With a 5-hour layover in Sioux Lookout, Ontario, Ava was eager to escape the train at mid-morning to nose around. Train life didn't offer enough exercise. And she'd never been so far north. Boreal forest sounded interesting. And considering how small the town was, a nice run ought to carry her out to the forest.

Jean-Claude said he might stretch his legs for an hour. But if so, he'd get Morris or Camille to watch their stuff. Go have fun. His dubious glance through the window at the broad flat rail yards of Sioux Lookout made plain what excitements he expected from the place. Train traffic headed southeast was in full swing, car after car of oil and coal and lumber.

Ava didn't share his pessimism. Jana informed her that Sioux Lookout offered a town beach. She carried her bathing suit rolled in a towel.

The train station was impressive. New and large, it looked vaguely Tudor, with brown wooden beams on a white facade. It was also nearly deserted. Train passengers simply passed through to reach the warm early summer day.

An impromptu market gathered on the lawn between the station and the main drag. She strolled through, snapping pictures with Jana as she went. The locals were preparing for a big Walleye Tournament next weekend. Walleye was a fish. The whole town occupied a headland jutting into Pelican Lake. Fishing was big here. They also looked forward to Canada Day on July 1st, and a Blueberry Festival in August.

She kept an eye out for Kelly. She'd considered hunting the girl down before the train stopped. But she wasn't sure how she felt about letting the Canadians handle it. Maybe it was best to just avoid her.

She stopped and inquired at one table what a 'turpentine conversion' was. The native explained that his business was converting cars to run on turpentine derived from local pines. Aside from the forestry industry, no one here merited a gas ration. Which meant bargain rentals on summer vacation properties, because few tourists made the trip. He offered turpentine converted cars for rent to reach those no-electricity camps. Or for a reasonable rate, he'd provide a driver. Ava thanked him for his time, and walked away.

Ava recognized this place now. It was like any small town in backwoods Pennsylvania. Add more severe seasons, subtract the agriculture. Ava had seen no crops, no livestock. They'd left the southern Ontario dairy lands behind long since. The town itself probably hadn't changed much from Before. But they were nearly cut off from the rest of the world. The train visits every few days were a big deal.

Perhaps for the First Nations, that wasn't such a bad thing. They lived where their ancestors had long since. Native lifestyles seemed to be enjoying a renaissance. The native Ojibwa crafts were interesting. The birch bark baskets, and ones decorated with porcupine quills, were pretty, as were the dream-catchers and gaudy beaded moccasins. She wasn't set up to carry souvenirs. Maybe on the way back.

Ava set off onto the street at a jog.

Prosperity for the North! a sign announced. Ontario had a plan once to improve the livelihoods here. The sign was old and faded. There was no traffic. A few latecomers still converged toward the train station, merchant groups carrying their tables and wares on handcarts. The street was broad, soon sloping down toward the basin of the lake. There were a few trees, rather small and deciduous in town.

It was hot out, almost as hot as yesterday by the fire lines, warmer than Jana said it ever got here. Ava was used to that, though. Historical temperatures meant little anymore.

"Tail Panic!" a voice called out.

Ava spun and stared. No one had called her that since she left the gang nearly a year ago. Panic, yes. But not Tail. Cade thought the nickname was sexist and demeaning.

A boy about 13, open-mouthed, tried to grin at her. The grin only reached one side of his face, then drooped. Dark eyes under a fishing visor flashed wild and lost. One of his legs was fitted with a running blade prosthetic. "You don't recognize me."

"Germy," she whispered at last. "Of course I do." Recollecting herself, she stepped closer to him. "Ah, I'm Ava Panic here. From Minnesota."

"Jeremy Hodgins," he returned. "Quebec City. My new parents brought us here for the summer. Thought it might help." He spaced out for a moment, then rallied. "Is Frosty here?"

"No. He's back home. He's fine. Maz runs White Supreme now. Frosty and I moved on. Wow. In all the time since you left us, you're the first kid I've seen again." Ava's eyes teared up involuntarily. "They been good to you?"

"Yeah, I guess." Jeremy's focus drifted away again, up the street. "Screwing with my leg was bad."

Ava never wanted to cause anyone such pain again, as the day they cut off Germy's foot. She chickened out, couldn't do the cut. Maz stepped in with an ax to do that. Ava cauterized it, while Frosty held her for emotional support.

Germy was too old, when the gang turned over the young ones for quarantine and relocation. But he couldn't make it in the city. The Navy ratings let it slide about his age. They understood, and took him anyway.

"Do you love them?" Ava asked. "The Hodgins?" She didn't remember his original surname, but he was Italian. The Hodgins must have adopted him. That was why the Raj drew the line at 11-year-olds. Older kids weren't adoptable. They were too old to bond right with new parents.

Jeremy cocked his head and considered the question. "I don't remember how, I guess. To love them. Too bad. I don't remember my own anymore. What they looked like."

"I do," said Ava. "I was going to find the beach. Is that too far for you?"

"I'll walk with you," Jeremy said. "Our camp is that way." He fell in beside her. His gait was pretty smooth on the blade. "Really? You remember my parents?"

"Sure!" Ava said. Jeremy was the youngest founding member of White Supreme. He'd been one of Ava's students from the dojo, Before. Frosty and Kat tutored the youngest kids. Maz taught sparring. Ava coached the middle-schoolers. The boys were hopeless at dealing with an older girl, always bragging about grabbing a tit when they fought her. Having Frosty keep them in line might have made more sense. But teaching was his only playtime of the day, and he loved tumbling with the little ones. Sensei insisted that Ava's crop of young barbarians learn to be gentlemen. That Ava learned to stand up for herself was an added bonus, in his view.

"Your parents had dark hair, like you," Ava told him. His little sister hadn't survived Ebola. Best not to mention her. "Hey, did you go to that last karate meet with us? Just before the epidemic."

"I dunno."

"I have pictures from that meet. I'll look."

Jeremy stopped and stood stock-still. He started to cry.

Ava folded him in her arms. "I can go run the other way. If you want. It's OK if you don't want to see me."

"Not that," Jeremy said, holding onto her for dear life. "I wanna go home. The Hodgins are nice. But I miss you. And Frosty and Maz and everybody. I can't be what they want me to be here."

"I'm sorry I can't take you home, Germy," Ava murmured. "It's not my home anymore, either. I'm headed the other way."

"I know. And I should be grateful. They're…kind." He pulled away and mopped his face with a bare arm.

A couple kids Jeremy's age rode by on bikes. They made fun of him for crying, and for his prosthetic foot. He pulled out a generous-sized knife to brandish at them. They wheeled on their bikes and rode away fast. "Dumb-asses."

"Made friends here yet?"

He resumed walking. Eventually he replied. "Not in Quebec, either. They shouldn't have taken me. They were right. I was too old."

Ava suspected that was true. But she shook her head vehemently. "You're never too old for a second chance. And Jeremy? The Hodgins wouldn't have adopted you, unless they loved you. If they love you hard enough, you'll love them back."

She walked with him to his house, to meet his parents. Their 'camp' was a nice little one-story wood frame house right on Pelican Lake. Jeremy took her out in his canoe. He was surprised that the girl from the city already knew how to paddle.

When they came back, Ava caught Mrs. Hodgins alone in the kitchen making lunch. Ava asked his new mom whether she thought it would be a good idea to show Jeremy pictures from Before.

"I cried when I saw them," Ava admitted.

Mrs. Hodgins stared out the kitchen sink window at the lake. "We brought them here hoping nature would help," she said. There was a girl, too, maybe 10, who didn't speak. She sat in the living room, rocking to soothe herself. The girl hadn't acknowledged Ava's existence. From family photos, the Hodgins raised three of their own first, before adopting two more into their hearts. They had grandchildren.

"If you have pictures of Jeremy, he should have them," Mrs. Hodgins said. "Thank you. I'm afraid he won't take it well, though."

After lunch, the mom brought a laptop computer to the dinner table, for Ava to show pictures from her memory stick. First she showed Jeremy her hard copy photos, of her and Frosty with Maz and the unknown girl, skating at Rockefeller Center before the epidemic. And Panic and Frosty eating strawberries on the ferry a year ago.

Jeremy loved those, and demanded copies.

Mrs. Hodgins was the first to start crying. "Oh, for heaven's sakes! You poor thing." She enveloped Ava in a hug.

"We were OK, ma'am," Ava denied, muffled in her embrace. "It was over by then. We were getting better." But her eyes pricked with tears against her will.

Jeremy looked steely at her. "They looked way worse when I left the city, Mom."

"Hey, don't ask where these pictures are from, but I'll give you some others of me and Frosty. Oh, I've got a couple others, too." Ava fished out her old phone and transfered photos of Ava and Butch, Frosty and Maz and Elon goofing around at the Resco Mansion. Ava and Frosty at their cabin in Elmira, and at a Renaissance Fair weekend in Pennsylvania.

"We're OK, Jeremy," she told him. "The gang's OK. It was hell the day you left us. Frosty and I cried a river."

"Frosty would never cry!"

"He cried like a baby. Me, too," Ava insisted. "You kids held the gang together. We weren't just monsters. We were protecting you. You saved us. Frosty was terrified what we'd be without you."

"You're making it up."

Ava shook her head. "Truth. Ready for karate meet photos? They made Frosty cry too."

He gazed at her with fearful brown eyes. If the Frost King couldn't take it, he knew he couldn't.

Ava found the first picture, all of them with sensei before the meet. "Let's see if you're in here first." She full-screened the photo. She started to zoom in on her group, but Jeremy put a hand over hers to stop her. He was still looking at sensei and others. "Mom."

"Yes, darling?" Mrs. Hodgins said, squeezing his shoulder.

"No. That's Mom." Jeremy put a finger on a fuzzy person off to the left, standing past the dojo group. "That's me." His image was also blurred because he was moving just behind Ava. Laughing and cringing away, the photo caught him clowning around with another middle-school kid.

"Oh, my," Mrs. Hodgins said.

Jeremy let Ava zoom in on both. There wasn't much detail of his mother, but it was something. He made her zoom in on sensei as well.

Ava glanced at the time. "I better run back to the train soon. I haven't looked through all these. I can copy all the pictures I have from karate meets, and you can check? You know, slowly. Maybe you'll find more. I don't know. But I need a picture of you with your new mom, OK? For Frosty and Maz."

"All of us!" Mrs. Hodgins insisted. "I have a selfie stick!"

It took a few tries. But Jana captured them by the deck railing in front of the lake. Jeremy aped for the camera, his blade foot folded up to his chest. Mrs. Hodgins made him do it again simply smiling. Ava got her phone number and sent her the photos.

"Thank you, Mrs. Hodgins. It was a beautiful thing you did, adopting Jeremy. He's a great kid."

"For heaven's sakes. Thank you, Ava, for protecting him in New York. I can't imagine what he would have done without you. You're a hero. You know that, eh?"

"I didn't feel like a hero when we cut off his leg."

"Sh. You saved my son's life. Thank you. God bless you."

Ava shared a last big hug with Jeremy and kissed him on the cheek. "I meant it, Germy. You kids saved us during the Starve. We remember, always. Love you!"

Ava ran full-out to make it back to the train in time.

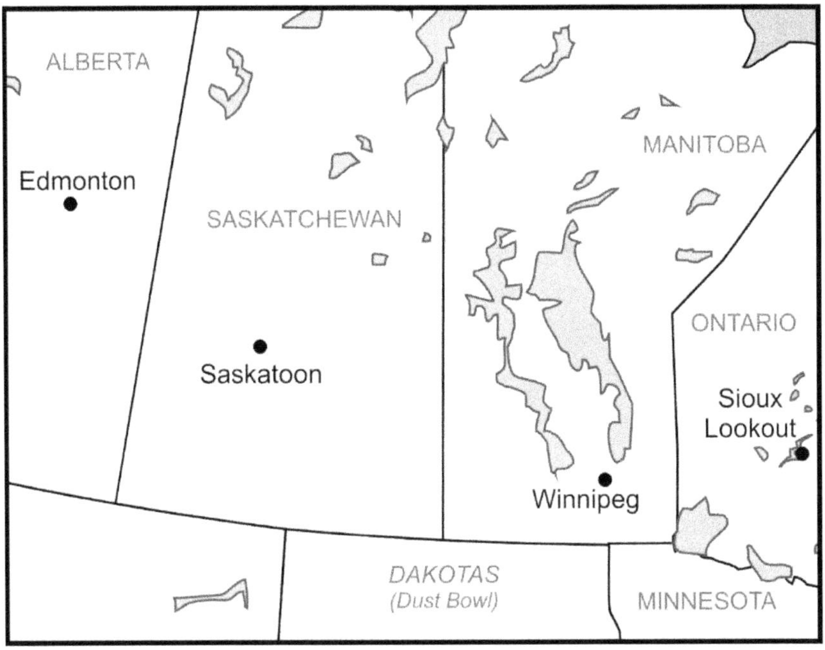
ALBERTA
Edmonton
SASKATCHEWAN
Saskatoon
MANITOBA
Winnipeg
ONTARIO
Sioux Lookout
DAKOTAS
(Dust Bowl)
MINNESOTA

18

Interesting fact: Peat fires weren't limited to boreal landscapes. Indonesia, originally a tropical rain forest, had severe peat fires. Their carbon emissions sometimes rivaled industrial India and the U.S. One study claimed the smoke caused 100,000 premature deaths in 2015.

"Buy you a beer," Ava announced after dinner.

She found Kelly in her aisle seat in economy, poking at the remains of a bag lunch she picked up in Sioux Lookout. The train box meals cost more. The guy beside her slept against the window, though the sun was still shining.

Kelly rose grudgingly. Ava guarded her waist-pack with her arm. The black box had lived in there since Kelly rifled her luggage, as well as all her cash and debit cards. Ava jutted her chin toward the bar car.

"What did you get for dinner?" Kelly grumbled.

"Walleye, poached in butter, with new potatoes," Ava said. "Nice salad. Glass of wine. Strawberry tart. Excellent conversation with quality seniles." That last word was all the sop to Kelly's ego that Ava was willing to offer.

Her emotions were wrung out from visiting Jeremy. She cried on and off for an hour as the train got back underway. 'I ran into a boy I used to know,' was all she told Jean-Claude. He was kind, and hugged her a couple times, and eventually made her laugh.

Ava fetched them two beers to nurse. Neither girl was much of a drinker. They'd watched too many go down the drug road to take it casually. The bar car was emptying as the sun set, and would close soon. Kelly selected seats private enough if they spoke quietly and didn't act out.

"You dropped your ID," Ava said, handing it over.

"Took you long enough to give it back."

"Busy," Ava returned. "Spoke to the boss. Someone told him you're here. Not me. You're no part of my mission." Telling Kelly that much might be interfering with the Canadians, she supposed. She didn't care.

Kelly's eyes burned into hers in fury. "What will he do to me?"

Ava shook her head. "Why'd you run?"

"Spur of the moment," Kelly claimed, and took a swig.

"Bullshit."

"I can help you," Kelly said. "Earn my keep."

"Win your way back into their good graces?" Ava mused. "You didn't answer my question."

"Supervisor was a pig, with the handlers," Kelly whispered. "I was afraid the boss would put me back there. KT told him he couldn't get a read on me. I wasn't meshing with the team."

Ava considered that. That the death angels had pigs among the supervisors, who would abuse underlings, didn't surprise her. She shrugged though. "You should have told me. We could have talked it through with him in – Where we were going."

Kelly snorted. "Like he'd protect me."

"Hey, Kelly? I protect myself. Do I lose? Sometimes. But I make damned sure my opponent hurts, too. You're trained. As for the boss, I spent hours on the road with him after you left. He would have listened. Him, Frosty, our crew. We're making the company better."

"You're right," Kelly said. "I should have talked to you. I want back in."

"Not up to me." Ava knew this ought to be her final word. She should stand right now and stalk out of here. But she ran a gang once as queen bee. Kelly had made a dumb choice. But it was far from unforgivable.

Kelly saw her hesitation and seized on it. "I can help."

"You don't know that." Ava was recalling that she didn't actually like or trust Kelly. She needed Kelly on her team like she needed a hole in the head. But she didn't like being on her own in Canada. On her guard all the time, especially against Jean-Claude. Ava liked Jean-Claude.

"I'm a geek," Kelly insisted. "Not in Daneel's league. Hardware. Dad was an engineer at Princeton. He taught me. You don't even know what you're carrying. And I got this far, didn't I? Money, ID, train ticket. I'd be useful."

"How did you do that?" Ava asked, diverted. So far as she knew, Ava only made it onto the train because Canadian…whatever…set her up. They even provided her a fake ID, fistfuls of cash, and a waiting-list-only pretty phone.

"Not going to tell you that in a bar," Kelly said.

That was fair enough. *But.* "Non-interference," Ava said. "You don't screw with me. I don't screw with you."

"I'll show you," Kelly promised.

"Stay back here," Ava insisted. "You can't show me squat if I don't see you. And that's how it's going to be." She rose and left.

But, as she reflected on her way back to her own berth, that didn't cover what happened off the train during stops. She'd better watch her stuff in Winnipeg in the morning.

~

THE RAILROAD AGREED WITH HER ASSESSMENT. AVA NEEDED TO WATCH HER stuff in Winnipeg.

Macdonald roused everyone from their berths at 4 a.m. for an early cold breakfast before they pulled in at 5 a.m. Winnipeg looked normal enough on the way in, if asleep. It was bigger than Ava expected. She read up using Jana. At about 800,000 people, the city lay 100 miles north of the Minnesota–North Dakota line. Ava already knew it had a reputation for the coldest winters of the big Canadian cities.

Macdonald got on the loudspeaker, and said this was good-bye. He would spend time here with his family, then head back east on another train. They would reconfigure the cars here, so everyone needed to exit the train. Their car would continue to Vancouver. But he strongly cautioned them to take all their luggage with them off the train, and stay with it in the terminal.

"Winnipeg has mushroomed lately with refugees. Desperate people do bad things. Be safe. And enjoy the rest of your trip on Canada Rail! Expect to leave Winnipeg in about six hours."

Ava stared at Jana's screen regarding Winnipeg. Like so much of the Internet, the encyclopedia page was out of date. "What refugees?" she asked Jean-Claude.

"Ah, from Minnesota? North Dakota. Saskatchewan."

"Saskatchewan? That's the province, right?"

"Yes. The Dust Bowl doesn't stop at the Canadian border, Ava. Not as bad here, but..."

They piled out and were directed to wait in a concourse Ava didn't much like. Its proportions, wide and low, with walls and pillars curving into ceiling, reminded her of the bigger subway station caverns in New York, except brightly lit and painted a glaring white. She didn't mind subways as a teenager commuting on them to school. During the Starve was a different story. Some gangs holed up in them for warmth. Hers stayed out of the subways except for a fight, or to bypass another gang.

She and Jean-Claude teamed up with Camille and Morris from across the aisle, and made an impressive pile of luggage. Madison, the naturalist from their dinner table, spotted them in the side gallery. She came to hug them good-bye again. Alain Devereaux rolled copious luggage in her wake, and parked it with them while he gallantly helped Madison navigate her things to the exit from this huge station.

With six hours to kill, Ava would have liked to see some of the city. But between her little Kelly problem, and Macdonald's strong warnings, she decided to try behaving for a change. She settled with Jana to catch up on adding captions and notes to her pictures from the past couple days. She wanted to do that first, put her best effort into writing succinct, well-organized reports. And then she'd try to talk Skull into forwarding pictures and a letter to Cade, about her meeting up with Jeremy.

She didn't get far before Skull called her. "Can you talk?"

"Not really," she acknowledged. "Can barely hear you." She described where she was and why.

"Then stick mostly to yes and no," Skull directed. With that, awkwardly, he grilled her about her progress on the Kelly front. Except it took more than yes and no to tell him much. A bout of ground-rumbling yet incomprehensible announcements, repeated in French, interrupted for minutes. He agreed she'd just have to text him a report, or call later.

"What was that?" she asked Jean-Claude, pointing to the ceiling.

He stood peering down the middle of the concourse. They were in a seating section off to the side. "Train arriving from Saskatchewan." Camille and Morris looked likewise solemn.

The walking wounded came first.

Grey and worn, in filthy work clothes, they trudged up the concourse dragging duffels and gear. They smelled as unwashed as they looked. Dirt seemed embedded in their skin, their faces old and wrinkled. Most bore one of those wire braces of water gallons, empty, slung over a shoulder.

"Excuse me," Jean-Claude said, touching her elbow. "Watch my stuff."

"Of course," Ava agreed.

"Doctor!" he called out, striding into the stream. "Anyone need a doctor?"

Others among the waiting passengers conferred to arrange luggage watch, then waded in to offer help carrying bags, or a shoulder to lean on. Ava and Morris consulted briefly, and Morris left to help. Ava didn't dare risk her luggage. But she could defend it against all comers. Camille looked perturbed, but she wasn't strong enough to be much use.

"What happened to them?" Ava asked her.

"Hm? I imagine they're coming off their shifts in Saskatchewan."

Ava took a moment to digest that. "They work in the Dust Bowl?"

She nodded. "I will, too. I'm headed to Saskatoon. I'm with the

Ministry for Natural Resources." Camille pursed her lips grimly. "They work for us now."

"Why send such old men?"

Camille broke a surprised smile. "Ava, none of those men are over forty. It's the dust. They work three weeks on, two weeks off. They're only allowed two years. Most don't last that long. After their time off, a doctor has to recertify them, or they lose their jobs."

"And you find people willing to do that?"

"Here? By the thousands. Tens of thousands. We hire Canadians, of course," Camille added apologetically. "The American refugees are in desperate straits."

"I didn't think you allowed in American refugees. Except for the states Canada accepted." Maine, Minnesota, Alaska, and that northern scrap of Michigan were Canadian now, or transitioning at least.

"We don't. But they keep coming. It's a long border, Ava. We can't defend it all. Not out here." She turned back to her reading.

Ava watched the next wave come from the Saskatchewan train. They sent out the walking first to clear room for the wheelchairs and stretchers. "What do they do in there that's so important?" Ava demanded.

"Oil, coal, mining," Camille replied patiently. "Takes an army of them to keep the auto-trucks running."

"Auto-trucks?"

"Self-driving." Camille frowned at Ava, then shrugged. Who could account for what Canada's new immigrants knew? "The AI's get puzzled – the artificial intelligence driving the car. Then someone has to go untangle them. Or a tire blows out, or they jack-knife or something. There's only so much a computer can solve. Some problems take muscle and a mechanic."

"Canada still trucks things across the continent?"

"Some. Critical goods, minerals and fuel. Not as much as before."

Ava let her be. She took some pictures, then bent her head to Jana, to compose her reports in earnest.

General Schwabacher added requests for clarification and elaboration. Skull intervened to request that the general let his courier collect her thoughts. He reminded him – and Ava – that intelligence was not her mission. These were sightseeing notes. Schwabacher conceded the point. He thanked her for her fascinating snapshots and captions, and let her be.

THE TRAIN WAS CERTAINLY 'RECONFIGURED.' THERE COULD BE NO MISTAKE – their group was escorted from the concourse to this new train. But the distinctive dome and panorama cars were missing. The familiar Corporal Mogadishu, and the medic George, stood by the doors to their sleeper car. Ava noted the soldiers were armed with pistols. The pair greeted Ava and Jean-Claude warmly, the other passengers coolly. They checked every ticket and ID.

It was truly hot on the platform, maybe 90 degrees, 30-odd Celsius, and bone dry. And it was still morning. The sky had turned a brassy yellow.

Boarding took a long time. No one traipsed through their car en route to another. Mogadishu and George made sure of that. After Ava squared her stuff away, she joined George at the door to chat while they waited. The central, high-priced cars were mostly loaded by then, so the middle platform was clear. But he pointed out the slow lines loading into new cars on the economy ends. "Workers for Saskatchewan."

"Where's our steward?" Ava asked.

"That's us to Edmonton. Rules are different through the Dust Bowl. More safety concerns. Mogadishu will read the announcements." He grinned at her expression. "What, I don't look like a waiter?"

"You really don't," Ava agreed.

"Thank you!" They bopped fists. "You better go in. We're supposed to be strict. Passengers belong in their assigned seats and crap."

"This is your job? You protect trains?"

"Hell, no. My unit's transferring to Edmonton. Beats taking a troop train, though. More to do."

Ava detoured to the washroom at the front of the car. The Mr. Clark-alike was missing. She stared a moment too long at his replacement. A burly older man nodded to her politely and returned to reading his tablet.

She wondered whether Kelly was still on the train, and whether economy passengers even kept the same seats.

The train got rolling again around 11:15. Ava's stomach was growling for lunch. Mogadishu got on the speakers promptly, as promised, and introduced himself and George. After announcements, they would distribute the emergency survival supplies. From there, he switched to reading from a prepared script.

"For passenger safety, Canada Rail has special rules for the Dust Bowl corridor from Winnipeg to Edmonton. Passengers will remain at all times in their assigned car. There are no bar cars or panorama cars on this train. The dining car prepares meals for passengers to eat in their seats. Troops provide security. You will clear the aisle immediately to allow soldiers speedy freedom of movement through your car. These troops are here for your protection. Do not interrupt them in their duties. Wait for announcements before asking questions.

"In addition, Canada Rail observes Canadian law regarding the Dust Bowl Territory, which includes Saskatchewan and portions of Manitoba and Alberta. Persons entering the Territory will carry the following. Two gallons of water. Four face masks. Safety goggles. First aid kit. Survival multi-tool. Rations for four days. One flashlight, extra batteries. Four emergency heat blankets. Four flares. One hundred feet of rope. A two-way radio with unique electronic ID. A printed survival manual. 'Carry' means that these supplies must remain with you at all times."

Mogadishu broke from the script to clarify, "Yeah, in practice, we'll let you leave the gear at your seat when you visit the washroom. Just keep it brief."

He resumed the canned spiel. "You'll be interested to hear that Canada has a history of such requirements when entering dangerous areas. During the Yukon Gold Rush of 1898, prospective prospectors," he stumbled over that phrasing, "were required to bring one year's worth of supplies, including 200 pounds of bacon, 400 pounds of flour, 8 pounds baking powder, 5 bars of soap, etc., etc. Yeah, I've got the whole list. I'll pass it around. You get the point.

"You are entering a large and dangerous territory. Canada Rail sincerely hopes that your train ride proceeds smoothly and safely without incident. But in case you need to exit the train, you must be prepared to survive until help can reach you. When you receive your survival manual, you are expected to read it, in its entirety. There will be a quiz. Yada, yada. Right. We'll serve lunch after we hand out the supplies."

George got started lugging two-gallon braces of drinking water, while poor Mogadishu attempted to repeat all that in French. Ava gathered that he butchered it. Jean-Claude frowned in disbelief, then cracked up laughing. He swung his way to the steward station end of the car to volunteer. Though he was technically breaking the new rules, the Francophone passengers cheered when his voice took over on the loudspeaker. Mogadishu got busy doling out the survival kit backpacks.

Ava stared out the window, and took a lot of pictures. Winnipeg didn't look so normal anymore. The yellow sky and scorching light looked ominous. There was little traffic except for pedestrians and buses. A lot of people on the streets appeared aimless, hanging around instead of pursuing a busy workday. She noticed that many windows had criss-crossed masking tape, as though to ward against flying glass. As they reached the outskirts of Winnipeg that was, the refugee camps began, spreading toward the high plains.

According to Jana's encyclopedia entry, Winnipeg was the seventh largest city in Canada. Ava wondered if that was still true, with all these squatters. Jana also reported the average January temperature here was 3°F, with 13 days a year below -22°, and the same above 86° in summer. Ava was confident that part was out of date. Judging by Hudson, the cold got colder, the hot got hotter, and predictability was out the window.

She sure wouldn't want to face a Winnipeg winter in the seemingly endless rows of emergency trailer homes she watched flash by. Then apparently they ran out of those. The outermost rows were tents. Beyond that, the tents were no longer official emergency-management style quality, but whatever people could cobble together. She watched as some kind of distribution truck, with troop carriers for backup, got mobbed by raggedy thin people. Shots were fired before they fell behind the train out of view.

Ava figured these were American refugees. She tried to be offended on their behalf. But she imagined Canada was treating them better than the ex-U.S. had. Like New York City, the Dust Bowl stack of states was penned in to die. Ava could relate.

I survived. Hang in there.

19

Interesting fact: Dust Bowl storms reached far beyond the drought zone. In May 1934, a 'black blizzard' carried 350 million tons of silt from the northern Great Plains to the eastern seaboard, and beyond. Ships 300 miles into the Atlantic reported dust on their decks.

Ava tried to concentrate on her Western Civ text. But a brown wall across the sky approached faster than the train's motion could account for.

She already wore a wetted silk scarf across her nose and mouth, plus a face mask, and her goggles. There wasn't a lot else she could do about riding into a wall of airborne prairie soil.

The Internet died a couple hours back. She took Mogadishu's official advice to power off all electronics for safekeeping. Dust motes floated through the cabin in a haze. She brushed a layer of dirt off the page before her.

The sky behind the train was already a browner shade of yellow. But the lowering sun was beyond the dust wall, and little light passed. The scratches in her window filled with dirt. Not that there was much to see. The land was brown dust drifts, and not much else. Granted, in the murk, visibility was low. But the landscape looked like something sent back from a Mars Rover. Occasionally some structure, or abandoned vehicle, or a canted telephone pole or fallen tree, served to seed a drift of dirt.

As the storm loomed closer, she could see lightning flicker in the brown wall.

Ava was in awe.

She'd looked for someone to blame for the Apple. The rage in her heart demanded revenge for her dead, for her agony. But the tsunami in February opened a crack of doubt. When she learned of the Northern League, her resolve rebounded. Canada was the enemy!

She should be so lucky. The only enemy here was vast and implacable, impervious to the puny weapons of men.

The lights in the cabin flickered a few times, and died. Mogadishu and George waded along the aisle to remind the passengers that they expected that. The cabin power might well remain out to Saskatoon.

Even Jean-Claude looked worried. Ava reached a hand across to shake. He held it a moment, and smiled. He half-rose to shake hands with Morris and Camille as well. Ava, with her shorter arms, had stepped into the aisle to reach them when the first buffet of wind hit the train. She staggered into Camille's bench and held on.

Ava waited for the car's wobble to steady. Braking slowed the train. Then she extended her hand again to Camille, and Morris. Her smile behind the mask reached her eyes, as did theirs. They all nodded respect. Ava slid back into her proper place as the next buffet hit.

George had no seat at the back of the car. He slid in beside her. Jean-Claude shifted to the middle of his bench to give them all a place to brace their feet.

The yellow behind them died as they were enveloped in billowing dark brown. Lightning flashed closer. The train slowed to a crawl. The gust buffets continued, and grew constant, jouncing them side to side. A hiss of dirt in the air grew to a shushing roar, with odd keening. Grumbles of thunder erupted into peals. But the background sound of megatons of dirt particles rubbing together nearly drowned the thunder. No one even tried to talk. Or perhaps they screamed, and Ava couldn't hear them.

Jean-Claude reached a hand across to brush her mask, and George's as well. *Point taken.* The dirt built up quickly across their mouths. George dutifully stepped over to remind Camille and Morris, and fell on Camille. After a minute he disappeared from Ava's world, working his way to the next berths forward.

Ava endured alone wonderingly in the midst of hell for a while. Strangely, she was exhilarated, not afraid. Time stopped. She was one with the storm.

Perhaps Jean-Claude wasn't as calm. He reached across again to capture her hand with both of his. He started tapping on her palm. It took her a moment to catch on that it was Morse Code. She did remember it, though.

Dinner, he tapped.

She laughed out loud. *La* – she began, intending to tap *Late.* Instead she slid forward, slamming her hand into his chest, as the train jerked to a sudden dead stop.

Ava assumed they'd stay stopped. But after a while, the train reversed for a minute. It pushed forward again, and slammed to another stop. For the next attempt, the engineer backed up longer, then sped up to build momentum. That time they managed to push through. They continued.

Ava had no real way to gauge how fast they went. The car was dark inside, and she saw only swirling dark dust through the window. She couldn't see the ground.

After a seemingly endless time, she groped to find Jean-Claude's leg. She tapped out, *Sun.*

A dim disk of glowing brown showed to the west, and grew brighter. They'd passed through the storm.

A COUPLE HOURS LATER, THE TRAIN LURCHED TO A STOP AGAIN. JUST A FEW minutes before, Ava heard and felt the clanks and sideways jerks of shunting onto a side-rail. They needed to wait out another train passing. So she didn't think much of this event. She expected more of the same.

She was wrong.

Mogadishu got on a megaphone. "Emergency evacuation. Everyone into the aisle. Bring your full survival kit and water. Leave everything else. We will exit the car. Emergency evacuation."

Stunned, Ava and Jean-Claude stared at each other. Both dove into their bags to grab last-minute items to carry on their persons. Ava chose to fish out her camera from Porta in Ohio and shove it into a pocket. No way would she risk Jana in the dust. Jean-Claude took a medical bag. Then they slid into the aisle, facing forward, survival packs slung on their backs.

The backpacks were convenient. The brace of water gallons was not. Ava would have done better with one gallon in each fist to balance the load. But at least she could carry it that way. Camille couldn't. Ava hurriedly helped the old woman to break out one gallon to hold in her other hand, then picked up her own set again.

The car door opened behind them, ushering in a gust of fresh air and blowing dirt. "Exit this way for the back of the car," George called, once he got the door propped open securely.

Ava pushed in front of Camille to take first in line to the rear. She was glad of the two-gallon carrier stepping out of the train, because it gave her a hand free to hold the railing. The three steps down were tall for her. At the bottom, she sank nearly to her ankles in fresh fluffy dust, unleashing a cloud. She turned to reach up and take a water bottle from Camille, then steady her on her way out. Camille lost her dignified leather pump to the dust on her first step on the ground. Ava pushed her onward to clear the exit, and retrieved the pump.

"Do you have more practical shoes?" Ava demanded of Camille, as their male berth-mates clambered out.

"I have runners," Camille admitted. "In my luggage."

Ava prodded for further details about how to find the sneakers. "For now you don't wear shoes." She opened the woman's backpack and shoved in the pump she still carried, then held out a hand to demand the other one.

Camille grudgingly complied. "But why are we out of the train? This is insane."

This was the topic of the moment as nearly twenty people collected outside the rear car door. A troop car was the next door down, only a few yards from their own. Ava had elected to step up-train from there, to keep out of their way. Everyone else followed her lead, taking formation beside Camille and sticking by their car for further instructions. The disgorged soldiers headed back toward the economy cars, which had far more people to extract. Those were forming into lines stretching perpendicular to the train.

As George started to disembark last, Ava pushed forward to tell him of the shoe problem. Annoyed, he took her water carrier, and told her to hurry.

Ava was good at hurry. Without the bulky water, she scampered up the high steps in a flash, and bounded to Camille's luggage. The suitcase was exactly where Camille told her. She found the sneakers with ease.

Beneath them was a folio bearing the frosted cabbage logo of the Northern League. *I don't have time for this. And it's none of my business.*

She bit her lip, then pulled out Major Porta's camera. She snapped quick photos of the first few pages inside the folder, trying to block the flash with a blanket hurriedly thrown over her shoulders. She remembered to grab some socks, since Camille was wearing pantyhose. George hollered for her. She closed the suitcase and ran out.

Ava knelt to get socks and sneakers onto Camille while Morris and Jean-Claude held the woman upright.

Finally George had them all together to explain what was going on. East-bound trains were expected through in half an hour. And they'd only managed to shunt half the train off the main line before they ran into a dirt drift covering the side rails. They needed to dig the tracks out to clear the right of way. In the meantime, half the train was in danger of a collision. Communications were down.

Camille erupted, "Surely you don't expect us to dig in the dust!"

"Not you, ma'am," George agreed. "Everyone willing to help, step forward."

Ava wasn't done tying shoes, but she held up an arm and called, "Me!" Damned if she'd be stuck senile-sitting. *Northern League bitch.* She pulled the laces too tight and Camille whimpered. Ava figured Camille could solve that for herself later. She hopped up and grabbed her water bottles.

Volunteers from the front of the car were already on the move away from them. Ava's group followed their lead. Each placed one hand on the shoulder of the person ahead of them to trudge along. The greatest danger in a dust storm was getting lost with no visibility. The survival guide had hammered on that point. That was why they carried rope. It wasn't storming now. But plenty of dust was still in the air. Simply walking billowed up more. Breaths of breeze stirred up little pocket dirt dervishes around them. The sun would soon set, bringing twilight to dim the scene still further.

Sinking a few inches with every step, and walking as a chain, it took ten minutes to even reach the front of the train. Meanwhile, the train inched forward beside them as each car-length stretch of track was cleared. As they passed the engine, a squad of soldiers cleared everyone off the track for the engine to scoot up again. Then the soldiers evicted the passengers working ahead of them and took their place, to finish clearing the length of track they'd started on. The troops had industrial grade snow blowers and shovels. The passengers labored with the small entrenching tool configuration on their 'multi-purpose survival tool.' The tool wasn't a tenth as effective. But there were hundreds working, including a couple platoons of soldiers in peak condition.

Ava's group had to pass hundreds to find fresh dirt to clear.

The dust drift was several feet deep over the rail. Ava waded across to the far side. She took out her camera to capture the drama of the train's dilemma. The laboring passengers. The glowing red orb of sun angling down toward the flat horizon. A dancing dust devil. Jean-Claude and Morris digging through their packs for their tools. She got out her own and photographed it closed, and opened as a shovel, with her small hand showing how inadequate the tool was to the scope of the task.

Then she brushed the dust off her face mask once more, and dug in. Dust billowed and slithered at every stab.

News trickled up the line as they labored. No one feared a train collision anymore. Job one after they stopped was to dispatch soldiers up and down the line to erect warnings. No ropes for them – they just ran, with their signaling gear. Another team walked the main tracks, parallel to the side-rail, and found them likewise drifted over with dust. Laborers returning to Saskatoon were diverted to dig over there, a couple stone throws from where Ava battled the dust.

Blisters rose as the sun set. She soon wished she'd grabbed for her gloves, or fighting hand-wraps, instead of a camera. Word passed up the line to conserve the flares until it was too dark to work.

Blisters broke as the twilight died. An east-bound train pulled in to work on the main tracks beside them. That brought more blowers to the party, in addition to the plow and raw horsepower of the engine itself. The second train was short, but massive, with bucket cars piled with coal and minerals. Ava saw that the crews over there worked farther apart, simply making cuts in the dust so that the train could muscle through with the plow.

Their own engine pulled closer before their first flare burned out. They kept working under its powerful head-beam.

The soldiers displaced Ava's gang and told them to rest a bit. She and Jean-Claude and Morris stepped well back and ate. Inside her scarf, Ava unwrapped an energy bar and ate, standing because the dust in the air was thinner above waist level. The food still smelled and tasted of dust. But she was too hungry to care. They told her in Toronto that the survival kit was a rental, unless she needed to use it. Her inadequate shovel was nicked and dented, the food broken into, and ointment and blood oozed through gauze bandages.

That was OK. The company paid for the handy little survival kit, not her. And she certainly didn't regret the gallon of water she'd used and no longer had to carry. She drank some. But sprinkling water on the dust made it easier to work with.

Another passing soldier suggested that when they were done with their break, they could shift to the other track. They worked there until Morris spotted their car pulling up beside them by the light of the flares.

They were done in by then. They packed up their tools and walked back to George. He brushed them down outside and sent them back to their seats. Camille was already asleep on her bench. No ovations, nor bunks that night. Mogadishu apologetically told them earlier that they would not reconfigure the berthing until they were out of the Dust

Bowl. They needed to be able to mobilize quickly in case of emergency.

At the time, Ava assumed the emergency preparedness measures were excessive. Now she was amazed that Canada still pushed trains through here at all.

She and Jean-Claude changed into fresh face masks, brushed a layer of dirt off their bench seats, and fell asleep. The early midsummer dawn had no power to wake them.

20

Interesting fact: The northernmost stop on this route was well south of the Arctic Circle at 53°32′ N in Edmonton, Alberta. This is about the same latitude as Hamburg and Liverpool. The longest day of the year is 17 hours. In contrast, Midsummer Day in Seattle sees 16 hours of sun, Toronto 15.5, and the Apple 15 [New York City].

Ava woke in the throes of a full-blown panic attack, heart pounding, hands sweating. Something had terrified her in her dreams. She yanked upright on her bench seat. Jean-Claude was still dead to the world, wedged facing away from her.

"Ow…" She had a sudden vivid memory of Sergeant Calderon back at boot camp, chewing her out for straining her hamstrings. *Life sucks when your hamstrings hurt.*

Yeah, sarge, and it sucks when your back hurts. And your hands… Hours of stoop labor with a toy shovel yesterday had exacted a price. Blistering her hands wasn't smart either. She hadn't even stopped to wash the broken blisters with soap before falling asleep on a bench seat. *Ow…*

That wasn't what woke her in a heart-pounding sweat, though. She looked out at the early morning Dust Bowl. Visibility was better, and the sky hadn't turned to brass yet. Signs of human industry taunted from the distance, kicking up dust. She didn't bother to reach for her camera for a closer look.

What was I dreaming about? Numbers. Sitting for her final GED exam, to pass the English part of her high school diploma, only to realize she'd left home in her underwear. Her class-mates pointed fingers and cackled at her. She fled down locker-lined high school hallways, seeking somewhere to hide her shame.

Oh, hell! She hadn't reviewed her memorized material yesterday!

She opened her blistered hands and decided to visit the washroom first. Wincing, she collected her first aid kit and toiletry bag and did the needful. After seeing how caked with dust her scarf and mask were, she replaced those when she got back to her seat.

Before anything else could happen, she sank forward, elbows on her knees, and clasped gauze-clad hands as though in prayer.

Twenty-two vegetables, in alphabetical order. She liked to start each session with the easy one. She had a bad minute with one of the satellite phone numbers, sure she'd lost it. Her heart started to pound again.

She blew out slowly. *Just breathe out. Your body breathes in by itself.* Cade's voice, cool and dispassionate. Once upon a time, she believed in his Frosty act. She was as taken in as the rest, that he really didn't give a damn what was happening. *He cared. He hurt. He got afraid, too. He was only teaching me what he did to control his own nerves.* She breathed out slowly. She mentally recited 22 vegetables, in order. That she could do.

The problem phone number was the one Skull corrected her on, during a video call at Grosse Point Lawn & Racquet. She recalled his voice, how he looked on the screen. She reviewed what else he said, and – yes, the correction, and how she wrote it down. Her fingernails were freshly lacquered as Caitlyn Dominici, and the numerals she wrote were – *Got it.*

In penance, hands still clasped in prayer, she took it from the top, and reviewed all her material three more times. Still shaking from how close she'd come to losing one of the phone numbers, she decided to skip the microchip list for today. Today she would dedicate to reciting her phone numbers and times flawlessly, over and over, until they were so rock-solid in her mind that she could never falter again.

And – *ow* – she would do penance for abusing her body yesterday.

You know better than that, Panic, Sergeant Calderon reminded her in her head.

In cautious slow motion, she retrieved her World Civ textbook, and did penance some more until breakfast. She read about the medieval Champagne Fairs in France, where the northern and middle and southern trade routes met and cross-fertilized. *That's what Detroit and Windsor could be…*

~

JEAN-CLAUDE AND MORRIS AND AVA WAVED CAMILLE GOOD-BYE AT Saskatoon. They didn't offer to help carry her bags. But George kicked the threesome out onto the platform while the ear-splitting industrial vacuum cleaners went in to suck dust from their car.

Saskatoon had become a company town. The sole employer was the Ministry for Natural Resources. Continuing passengers were not welcome to leave the platform.

They returned to their seats the moment they could. As did the dust. George set up some air filters in the aisles. They drew the air through water. Ava noted that the water looked like sludgy coffee when he changed it after an hour. It didn't look much better after a half hour, the next time he changed it.

Mogadishu confiscated all their used breath masks and issued fresh ones. He reminded the passengers hourly to use their nebulizers if they needed to. Near Saskatoon station, at least, they had power again.

Ava still wasn't risking Jana in the dust. She took some photos with Porta's camera. But her own electronics stayed powered off and safely swaddled in their cases.

She cautiously carried out a stretching routine in the aisle. She taught her older men friends to do the same, more gingerly still. Jean-Claude made the rounds with a bowl of hydrogen peroxide solution, to make sure everyone's blisters were clean.

Before departure, they loaded the car's sole new passenger. A nicely built blond guy a few years older than Cade took Camille's place. Laurent was far cleaner than everyone else, and freshly barbered around the edges of his haircut. He wore a summery suit, though he promptly stowed his tie and jacket. When asked, he self-effacingly answered that he 'worked for the government.' He smiled extra hard at Ava.

She'd just been musing on Skull's comment about men's taste. How if he wanted to bait Cam Cameron, he should choose Daneel, who looked like Cam's husband. *Women aren't like that.* Or she wasn't, at any rate. Though a man might assume so.

"Ava," she said with a smile, not bothering to offer a handshake. Morris had already explained to the newcomer how they came to have blistered hands and sore backs today. "I'm a courier. Headed to Vancouver."

Laurent broke into a huge smile. "Oh, good! We'll be together a while then!"

Ava nodded tiredly. "What day is it?" she asked Jean-Claude.

"Thursday. We're past the halfway point!"

She gave an exaggerated nod, and they both laughed.

"I just came from Vancouver a few days ago," Laurent offered. "It's a nice ride. Except for Saskatchewan."

Indeed, things seemed to be looking up. No fires or dust storms attacked them that afternoon. Dust gradually gave way to grass, then stands of aspen trees. Between Ava's determined tutelage in flexibility exercises, and their turns in the shower, they felt better by supper. George's air filters made steady progress removing the dust from the air. They even removed their masks to eat.

Huge cheers broke out when cabin power was restored, and cheers again when the Internet returned.

Ava decided she could risk Jana again. The clever phone figured out how to extract her photos from Porta's camera without wiring. Ava blocked the images from Camille's Northern League folder, but let the rest transfer. She happily settled in to add captions and star the best shots.

Boss: Jesus. Glad you're OK.

Panic: 3 days to Vanc. :)

After an hour happy bonding with Jana again, Ava curled up for a long nap. Edmonton arrived at 2 a.m., and they would be evicted again while the train reconfigured back to sightseeing mode.

At the appointed hour, after Mogadishu's final announcements, the passengers awarded their temporary stewards a standing ovation for their service. Ava shook George's hand on her way out and wished him well.

A small army of civilian entrepreneurs awaited them on the concourse, offering hand vacuum cleaners for rent to rid themselves and their luggage of the dust. The berthing foursome happily took them up on it. Ava's lady vendor held up a blanket to shield her while she vacuumed out her bra and other creases. Working together, they vacuumed their way through all of Ava's duffels and clothes. Ava made absolutely sure her inventory was intact. No help was offered or accepted while she cleaned out her overstuffed waist pack.

The pre-dawn air of Edmonton was blessedly fresh and cool. The local entrepreneurial spirit extended to making sure everyone on the train had the option of a seat, luggage space, and a great meal, at a range of high prices. Ava was pleased to see that the soldiers received a welcome banner and reception area. Ava's group splurged on the deluxe breakfast buffet. After dawn, they took turns minding the stuff and walking the empty but prosperous streets, breathing deep.

Ava took great pictures of fighter jets flying by.

One damn plane and I could have crossed the continent in a few hours. But no, these days only the air force reached the sky. She wondered whose.

RETURNING TO RE-BOARD THE RECONFIGURED TRAIN, AVA DROPPED HER bags suddenly by a group of troops in the concourse, hanging around with their duffels and gear. It looked like about a company's worth.

Jean-Claude, Morris, and Laurent turned back. "Do you need help with your luggage, Ava?" Laurent offered hopefully.

"No, go on ahead," Ava said. "I'll be a minute."

These troops wore American camouflage, the same print Ava had at West Point. Except where Hudson troops wore an Apple patch, and Ohio troops a buckeye, they wore the U.S. flag and a frosted cabbage. *Northern League troops.*

Morris and Laurent, the latter looking crestfallen, started walking again. Jean-Claude remained planted. He didn't step over to Ava, just dropped his luggage and watched, arms crossed. His head tilted and brows lowered in amused curiosity. *What are you up to?*

Cade and Maz had told Ava about this one time in a train when they visited Japan. She wondered if it would work. She kicked her luggage toward Jean-Claude, and pulled out Jana. She strode up to the troops.

"Hey, guys! Great to see Americans like me! Any of you from Minnesota?" She exaggerated the round-mouthed Scandinavian pronunciation, as though puckering for a kiss.

A single arm rose. "Me!"

Ava snapped a picture. She set Jana to take caption dictation, too. "Yay, Minnesota! You know what, though, I lived for a while in Austin, Texas. Anybody here from *Texas and the Southwest?"*

ROAR! A good half of the soldiers cheered for Texas and the Southwest. "Yay, Southwest!" Ava cheered them on, capturing them and the caption with Jana. "Gulf? Let's hear it for the Gulf states!"

Roar! Fewer than the Southwest. "Southeast? How about the mountain states?" Plenty of them. "California? Pacific Northwest!" Only a couple of those, she noted with profound interest. "Midwest! Northeast!" She captured them all.

"Ten-hut!" a sergeant bellowed.

A captain strode beside him. He called out, "Men, we do not fraternize with Canadians!"

"But Cap, she's American!"

The captain glared at Ava. She stowed Jana quickly. "I'm from Minnesota," she said, with a childish wave. "Saint Pauli girl."

"You don't look like no Saint Pauli girl!" a soldier yelled.

"No?" Ava asked her pocket audience. She put her hands on her hips. "So what's a Saint Pauli girl supposed to look like?" As though she didn't know. The buxom blonde barmaid, multiple overflowing beer steins in each fist, appeared on classic beer labels.

The troops, already riled up, lovingly called out features of the ideal Saint Pauli girl. Tiny, trim, and Slavic, Ava was a far cry from the busty German ideal.

"Can it, idiots!" the sergeant reminded them.

The captain glowered at her, and his men. "A Minnesotan is a Canadian. We do not fraternize with Canadians." He shot her a look of poison.

Ava didn't care for his attitude. "Yeah, Cap, I was fifteen when the Calm Act came down. I didn't choose this world. You seniles stuck me with it."

The captain predictably ignored her and turned away, pivoting precisely on the stick up his butt. He strode away.

"Saddle up!" the sergeant yelled in his wake. He called out additional instructions, unnecessary at this juncture, just to capture their attention. Apparently they were boarding Ava's train.

As the soldiers shuffled to comply, a couple sidled out toward her. "Hola, chica, you forgot Puerto Rico!"

Ava pulled out Jana and snapped their picture, grinning. "Yay, Puerto Rico!" she whisper-cheered. They grinned and bopped fists with her.

"Morales, get your ass over here!" the sergeant beckoned.

"Never forget, chiquita," Morales urged her.

"Never forget," she agreed ardently.

Ava wasn't entirely sure what he meant by that. The sentiment didn't require accurate translation, though. She raised her fist in solidarity to the soldiers as they passed, and netted grins and raised fists in return salute.

"And did we have fun?" Jean-Claude inquired, as she retrieved her bags to board with him.

"I had a blast," Ava said. "You?"

"It was fascinating," he assured her, eyes twinkling.

THE BREATHTAKING SCENERY OF THE CANADIAN ROCKIES WAS ALMOST worth a week on the train. A couple hours west of Edmonton, they reached forest at last, and turned southwest to climb into the mountains.

Ava soon jettisoned her attempt to catch up on Western Civ. She couldn't take her eyes off the window.

Morris guarded their possessions while Ava, Jean-Claude, and Laurent moved to the panorama cars. Laurent had passed through only a few days before on his way to Saskatoon. He made sure they didn't miss the most gorgeously sweeping views, following the course of the Athabasca River.

Just gazing at them, Ava felt her heart fly up the forest-clad mountains. An eagle soared the air currents above. The river was in full spate, its highest of the year. They passed fields of wildflowers, brilliant purple spikes against emerald green. They rode through a rain shower, with sunny peaks still visible in the distance, a double rainbow in between. She spotted a black bear and cub, and deer and elk.

Laurent said moose and caribou used to roam here, but they'd disappeared lately. He claimed snow should still cap the highest peaks into June, but they didn't spot any. Maybe that time was gone forever. Unlike the East, it had been an unusually warm spring for the West and the Rockies.

Ava drank in beauty and it filled her soul, sending the rage in her heart to rest. Jean-Claude seemed just as entranced.

They reached their Rockies train station at Jasper near 3 p.m., in a broad valley surrounded by majestic peaks. Laurent insisted they bring hats and sweaters and warm jackets, though they exited the train into shirtsleeve weather with a warm breeze blowing. He broke into a grin and pointed to a gathering group at a board advertising the Jasper Sky Tram – guaranteed return in time for train departure. This excursion offered gondola rides up the side of a mountain, for a cloud's-eye view.

Ava suspected Laurent wished it would be just the two of them. But Jean-Claude stuck to them like glue. She almost regretted that. The doctor was great fun clowning around on the gondola, and on the trails above. Ava caught him and Laurent on video at the platform above, ad-libbing stand-up comedy. Ava's cheeks began to ache from grinning so hard and long. But without the doctor, it would have been romantic, just the two of them, Laurent so intent on flirting with her.

Not that she'd let things get beyond flirting. But it was fun to imagine. Cade was far away. And this day was too big, too gorgeous, for anything but right here and now.

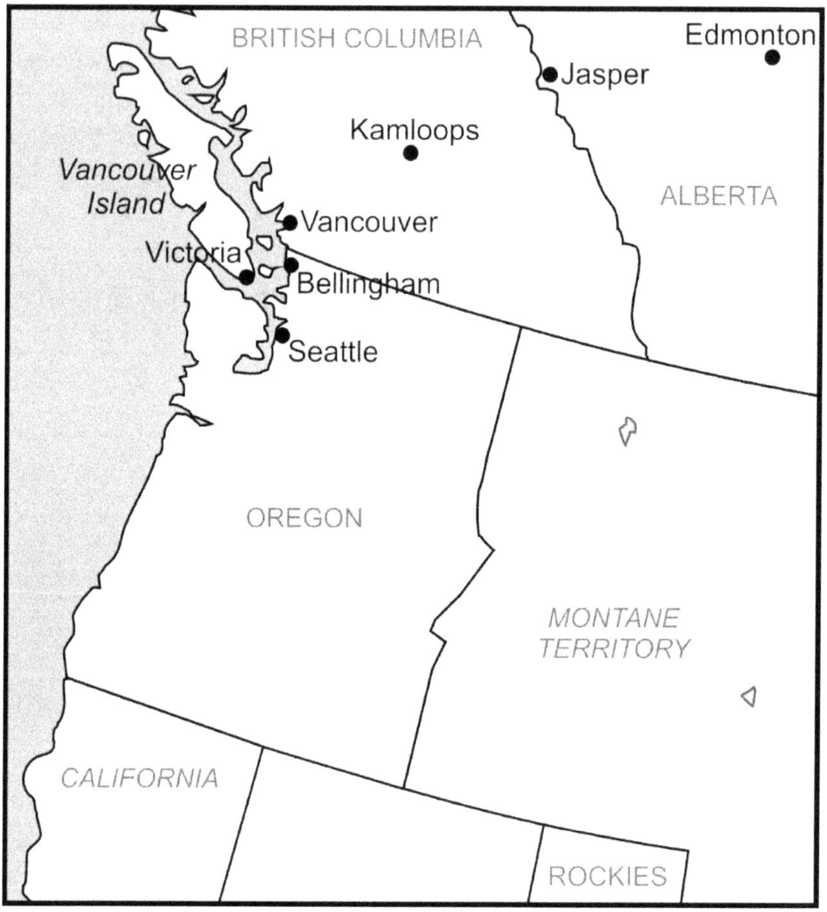
BRITISH COLUMBIA
Edmonton
Jasper
Kamloops
ALBERTA
Vancouver
Island
Vancouver
Victoria
Bellingham
Seattle
OREGON
MONTANE
TERRITORY
CALIFORNIA
ROCKIES

21

Interesting fact: Semi-arid Kamloops, British Columbia, was warm for Canada, with hot days and cool nights in summer, and winter daytime temperatures usually hovering around freezing.

"They won't let me visit the bar car," Ava complained to the clan, flouncing back into her seat. This was the last evening of their train trek. They'd left scorching hot Kamloops about 3 p.m., and were on the final leg to Vancouver at last.

"They who?" Morris asked. He was the least inclined to migrate between cars. Before the Dust Bowl, he and Camille even skipped seatings in the dining car. He'd eaten with them tonight, though, an early shift.

"The American troops in the next car," Ava said. "Said no traffic between the upper class and economy. But economy has the dome cars." The late evening scenery was pretty through the rugged desert.

Laurent shook his head. "Business class has access to all train amenities. I'll help you push through." He looked hopeful.

Jean-Claude was skeptical. "Looking for your friend again?"

Laurent deflated.

"I think she left in Winnipeg," Ava replied vaguely. Laurent brightened again. That man was too easy. Ava might not be a native New Yorker. But for a guy to wear his heart on his sleeve like that was just embarrassing.

"You kids have fun," Jean-Claude proclaimed, and settled back to digest his supper and medical journals. He had a seemingly endless supply to catch up on.

Ava hadn't wanted company. As Jean-Claude guessed, she wanted to verify that Kelly was history. But she rallied and stood. "OK, then, if you're willing to help."

Laurent beamed. He paused to pull on his tie and suit jacket over his crisp button-down tattersall and jeans. Ava assured him he looked very professional. Privately she thought he looked less sophisticated than Cade did in his St. Ignatius high school uniform, before the Starve. But she conceded the comparison was unfair.

It isn't possible to look dignified while hauling open inter-car train doors. But Laurent persevered, doing his gentlemanly best to hold open both doors for Ava to waltz through, a gesture he hadn't bothered with up til now. Based on his contortions, she concluded she was stronger. But she rewarded his efforts with a smile.

The same corporal rose to kick her out again. But Laurent stepped in front of her. He chastised the soldier for speaking that way to his lady friend. He threw his weight around 'with the Ministry.' He cited Canada Rail perquisites of business class. He demanded they be allowed right of way.

Ava resisted the temptation to stick her tongue out and say, "Nyah!"

Laurent wore the corporal down, who let them through to be rid of them. Past the door guard, Ava grinned at the soldiers and high-fived and fist-bopped her way down the aisle to calls of 'Hey! Minnesota! Saint Pauli girl!' A sergeant followed in their wake to remind his men that they were idiots.

Never forget.

The car wasn't full. The seats all had stuff on them, but several rows were missing an occupant. The captain had three seats to himself at the far end of the car. He pointedly ignored Ava and glared a hole into the tablet he was reading. That man truly had an issue with the states that joined Canada.

Ava considered the frosted cabbage patch far more traitorous than Minnesota. She bet New York would have gladly ditched the rest of the Northeast for a chance to swap allegiance like Maine and Minnesota. But New York was far too strange and large an elephant for little Canada to swallow.

Between cars, Laurent awkwardly proved that he didn't know how to properly high-five or fist-bop. Ava taught him. She grudgingly admitted this was almost romantic again, each of them standing on a bit of different car in the private vestibule, bathed in the crisp evening mountain air. He certainly grinned in triumph.

After three more economy cars for practice, Laurent was growing almost suave at holding the train doors for her. Ava kept an eye out, but so far no Kelly. She expected the Canadians took her into custody in Winnipeg. Or Kelly might have run. Ava did warn her. But then again, before Winnipeg, her ex-colleague lived beyond the dome car.

They burst into the bar car in the middle of an American soldier klatch. A half dozen held the seats near the door where they entered, with a few more at the bar fetching beers.

"Hey, Minnesota!" Morales called from the bar, holding up a beer bottle in question. She nodded enthusiastically. Laurent swallowed his disappointment as Morales added beers for both of them. He accepted Morales' seat, as the soldier took a knee. Ava perched on a low cocktail table between chairs.

"They let you guys out to fraternize?" she asked the group in delight. "I gotta get a picture! OK, names and home towns!" She snapped a picture of Laurent as well to include him in the game. He was from a tiny town on Vancouver Island. This was apparently separate from Vancouver the city, which lay on the mainland.

Morales left Puerto Rico after the hurricanes, and graduated high school in Philadelphia. His family went home once he was old enough to fend for himself. Others supplied origins in Missouri, Arizona, Nebraska, Montana, Hawaii, and North Carolina. "Our brigade's from all over," Morales summarized.

Brigade. Ava knew that was 1,500 to 3,000 troops, probably led by a colonel. But the girl she pretended to be wouldn't catch that.

Morales continued, "We were at Lewis-McChord before Edmonton. That's on Puget Sound, south of Seattle. Before it all went to crap."

"And you're based in Edmonton?" Ava asked. "Where are you headed?"

"Summer exercises, Vancouver Island," Arizona grumbled to Laurent. "If you can call it summer."

Laurent grinned and pointed at the ceiling. "The sun is higher in summer."

"What sun?" The ensuing conversation made clear that this would not be the first summer they endured in the chilly rain forest of Vancouver Island. Nor their first field exercises with Russian and Norwegian troops, and Canadian of course. They talked too much. Canadians shunned them. They were happy to tell a sympathetic American girl anything.

"I'll buy the next round!" Ava announced to cheers. She laid her hand on Laurent's on his thigh, and winked at him. He forgave her instantly.

The bartender was arranging her beers in a carrier when a light hand touched her shoulder.

"Introduce me," Kelly asked. She plucked a beer for herself out of the carrier. Ava automatically grabbed to guard her waist pack.

~

AVA DEPOSITED THE BEERS WITH THE GUYS. SHE BEGGED OFF TO LAURENT with a 'wait' finger, "Be right back." She drew Kelly into the vestibule between train cars. Not romantic in the slightest, but between cars was as private as the train offered.

"I thought you left in Winnipeg," Ava hissed.

"Because you turned me in. Bitch."

"I didn't," Ava said. "I told you. Why didn't you run?"

"I applied for asylum," Kelly said, fiddling with her beer bottle. "I have a hearing in Vancouver." She took a swig.

"Why do I bother to talk to you," Ava mused, "when I don't believe anything you say?"

Kelly shrugged that off. "I can help you with these guys. Find out where they're from. About their unit. Stuff like that."

"Already did. What, were you listening?"

"No," Kelly said, defeated. "Look, I can still help you."

"Why?"

"I want to go home. Make it up to the company."

Ava shook her head. "How stupid do you think I am? Look, Kelly, you burned me. You burned Skull. I can't trust you."

Kelly pursed her lips. "I see you already got yourself a new boy toy. What if I tell Cade?"

Ava snorted. "Cade? My boy toy? He'd enjoy that." She should just go back in, and not listen to her anymore. She did still want to know, though. "How did you get on this train?"

Kelly shrugged. "Turned some tricks, the usual. You know how to get money."

"Took more than money to get on this train," Ava insisted. She also doubted Kelly could earn that kind of cash on her back.

"Ticket counter guy. Made his day," Kelly said bitterly. "Older guy. Had to spin him a fantasy about getting a blow job at the counter –"

"Stop!" Ava laughed. "Look. Promise me you didn't kill anybody."

"I promise," Kelly intoned. "Not that you believe me anyway."

"I don't know why you did it," Ava insisted. "Why you're on my train. Why you bolted in Windsor in the first place."

"I saw the health clinic," Kelly blurted. "It just – I wanted to live in a country where my life mattered. They're not playing musical chairs here. Too bad, bang, you're dead. But there's no life here for an American. You see how they treat us."

Ava had seen prejudice against Americans, sure. But the average Canadian was more polite than anything else. Canada even erected billboards to remind its citizens to report a desperate vagrant after feeding him supper. Hudson didn't need those billboards. Hudsons were naturally hostile to strangers.

"You said 'Dad' when you saw the health clinic," Ava reminded her.

The other girl shook her head. "They didn't have health insurance. Mom got cancer. Racked up hundreds of thousands in debt. She died anyway. Dad was never the same. The debt ruined him. Collection agencies banging at the door. Lawsuits to garnish his wages. Lived in a dump. Landlord always trying to evict us. Big honking family issue."

"I'm sorry. Is he still alive?"

"No. But Dad always said if I had a chance to move to Canada, jump at it. Never mind. Anyway, then the company contacted me. Said you'd be on this train. Not Skull. Somebody else. Told me to be your backup. Win back my life. Or they'd terminate me. Finish your mission if you couldn't. But they wouldn't tell me what the damned mission was."

"Give me your contact info," Ava insisted. "For whoever told you this."

"Can't contact him again. Report at a wireless dead drop in Vancouver."

Ava drew out a scrap of paper. "Write it down. Everything."

"It won't work for you," Kelly objected.

"Doesn't matter. It's for Skull." When Kelly still hesitated, Ava pushed harder. "You say you want to earn back his good graces. So communicate with him. Like you should have in the first place." She held out pen and paper to Kelly again.

Kelly wrote an address and time in Vancouver, 15:00 hours. She gave Ava her phone number too. "The drop is a tea room. I'm supposed to go at that time, order tea, and power up my phone to deliver my report. The phone knows how to hook up, I don't. Stupid thing doesn't take dictation like yours, either."

"OK. I want to see what reports you send," Ava said.

"Bite me," Kelly returned.

Ava shook her head. "Hook up however you want. But you're not doing it for me." She yanked open the the door back into the bar car.

"I will," Kelly agreed. She was all smiles heading for the the guys. "Americans! Any of you from Hudson?"

Grudgingly, Ava had to concede that Kelly extracted interesting stuff from the GIs. The soldiers had only the haziest notion of what

Hudson was, and Ohio. They were also surprisingly ignorant of the Apple culling.

Morales said, "Sarge says the Apple is just a wild rumor."

Kelly and Ava shook their heads. Laurent corroborated the story. "Something like fifteen million died in the Apple Zone. It was on the news. You don't get Canadian news?"

"We get what our command chain shovels at us," Arizona griped.

Morales nodded. "We're stuck on the reservation around the ark."

Montana jabbed him in the side for that slip of the tongue.

Ava suspected it wasn't a slip. Morales may have suspected all along he was being lied to.

"Ark?" Laurent asked.

"Nothing," Morales said.

Kelly twirled a lock of hair. "You don't get out to socialize? Must get lonely."

"All the women troops are hooked up by now, if they want it," Montana said. "Some import a mail order bride from the Winnipeg refugees. American."

Most rolled their eyes at that. One looked furtive. Ava suspected he had a bride on order.

"They're pretty desperate," Morales said. "One guy in our company got an Okie. Blew all his savings. Showed up like sticks and bones, her lungs full of dust. They didn't hit it off. Now he's stuck with a dependent who coughs up mud all the time."

"From Oklahoma?" Kelly asked.

"Nah, eastern Montana," the Montanan replied. He took a thoughtful swig of beer.

Laurent didn't like all this talk of hooking up. He touched Ava's leg hopefully. "We wanted to visit the dome? The sun is setting." The steward would start converting the berths for bed soon.

Ava was torn. She was far more interested in what these traitor troops knew than Laurent. No, not traitors – grunts obeyed orders. It was their officers who answered to the Northern League. But Laurent might be useful in Vancouver. And she had dragged him here with the lure of a private drink in the bar car dome.

She rose. "Great getting to know you all, if I don't see you again!"

She met Kelly's eye and exchanged a nod. She made no promises. But she had no doubt Kelly would extract more from the lonely soldiers.

Laurent claimed Ava's elbow and propelled her toward the dome stairs. "How do you know Kelly?"

"I've been on this train all week," Ava said. "She's the only other woman my age."

A couple guys vacated a seat for them up top, volunteering that they'd been there more than 20 minutes, the posted limit. Laurent bowed Ava into the window seat. The red sun was just sinking into the mountain range off to their right, the sun line receding from them across the desert to the left. Laurent laid his arm across the back of the seat.

Ava didn't choose to object to that just yet. She drank in the rugged sagebrush beauty until the last arc of sun blinked out behind a wooded mountain. "That was worth seeing. Thank you."

Laurent pulled out his phone. As an added plus, he had to retract his arm from behind Ava to do it. "Give me your number? I don't have work tomorrow. You'll want to check into your hotel. But maybe tomorrow afternoon I can show you around Vancouver?"

Again with the offer Ava couldn't refuse. Her plans for her first day in Vancouver were orientation, anyway. She already had Jana out to capture the scenery. They exchanged numbers. But she'd probably led him along far enough.

"Laurent. I have a boyfriend back East. We're…" What? She and Cade hadn't put a label on their relationship since they got back together. They'd never discussed monogamy. They were a couple, but not bound. "Pretty serious."

He flashed a disappointed smile. "Just friends. And who knows, maybe you'll decide to stay. I haven't been to Ontario for years. But you'll like Vancouver. It's booming."

She smiled back politely. He was the youngest man in business class, sure. But he was a university graduate with some kind of salary man job with the government. Whatever this was to him, she figured it was a fling. There was no basis for a girl at least five years younger to move in with him.

Her phone vibrated with an incoming text.

Boss: text me on arrival Vanc. Will set up videoconc.

"Problem?" Laurent asked, as she spent a few strokes to text back a quick OK.

"Just my boss."

"You like your job?

"It's orgasmic," Ava automatically parroted Cade. She chuckled at Laurent's expression. "Sorry. Kind of an inside joke. Yeah. I love my job. Travel. Freedom. At my age it's hard to get a job with so much..." She couldn't think of the word.

"Autonomy?" Laurent suggested. "Seems like a lot for someone so young."

"Yeah! Yeah, they trust me. Give me responsibility, let me make decisions. Treat me like a grown up."

"Nice. I wish my job were more like that," Laurent lamented.

She took him up on the tour. She and Jean-Claude had already taken his advice for which hotel to book. And she'd been so worried she'd be alone in Canada. The way things were going, her first challenge in Vancouver would be how to evade her devoted chaperones.

22

Interesting fact: Vancouver at this point had a population of about 750,000 in the city, and 2.8 million in the metropolitan area, called the 'Lower Mainland.' In the city, 52% had a first language other than English, and 51% were of a visible minority, mostly Asian. Nearly 30% of the city was Chinese, 6% South Asian, especially Punjabi, and 5% Filipino.

Ava completed an arcane series of steps in her new hotel abode in Vancouver. Laurent did them a good turn with the hotel. Her mini-suite was full of rich reds and golds and browns, decorated with architectural wood slats on walls and ceiling. First Nations totem pole style artwork of fish and funny faces festooned head-board and wall, for an overall funky modern look. The rooms were trapezoidal instead of rectangular, which added to the playful ambiance of the space. She even had a cute mini-kitchen and a deluxe safe. Jana easily interfaced with the appliances.

Back in Grosse Pointe, the last courier package included printed instructions for how to set up a 'videconc,' as per Skull's text. She needed to memorize that, too, but at least Daneel supplied easy mnemonics. Hopefully this video conference was more secure than any conversation she'd had since entering Canada.

"Hi, boss!" she greeted him, on the appointed hour, 11:00 a.m. her time, 2 p.m. back home. "Slumming it?"

Skull was in jeans and T-shirt for a change. His officer's posture and bearing shone right through the flimsy attempt to dress down.

"I have the kids here," he explained. "I do the Dad today."

Ava knew from Cade that Skull's kids were a young teenage girl and middle-school sized boy. All Skull had ever mentioned in front of Ava was that the Northern League held him in check with death threats to them.

"Have fun," she said. "All summer?"

Skull waved that away. "Babysitters and camps are lined up. So. Your photo albums and notes are great. The train was inhibiting for conversation. So this is a chance for you to speak openly." He clicked the Record option alive on the video connection. "More openly, anyway. Anything we need to cherry-pick the audience, save it til you get home. Unless it matters. Sort of thing."

Well, that was ambivalent. "It can wait," she agreed. She'd shared just one photo of American Northern League troops in Edmonton. The Southwest troopers were roaring in that shot. But intelligence on the frosted cabbage corps was not her mission, just her burning question.

Skull nodded. "Not many pictures in Edmonton."

Ava took that to mean he got the message. She nodded back. "Well, we pulled into Edmonton at oh two hundred. I was sleepy. Why recording?"

"Vancouver is where you walk the tightrope without a net. If you go dark too long, I might have to send someone in to follow a cold trail. They'll need all the clues they can get. You're not tempted to stay Canadian, are you?"

Ava blinked. The thought that she might be speaking from the grave on this video was intimidating. She blew out to soothe rising jitters. "Skull, I'm a patriot. I'd die for Hudson. Ohio, not so much. But if it's humanly possible, I will come home."

Skull smiled, pleased and surprised. "It shouldn't come to that on this mission. Think 'mail carrier,' not 'Rambo.' Or do kids know Rambo these days? Mine say I'm out of touch."

Ava shrugged. "Never saw the movie. Means macho gonzo, right? So I should channel more Art or Daneel, than Cade and KT."

"Not as flamboyant as any of them, I hope. I'd prefer a nice boring pizza delivery. Ava, there may be a fine line between sightseeing and spying. Stick to sightseeing. Avoid spying. Avoid the appearance of spying. That's an order. Especially in Washo. At least Canada would tell me if they threw you in jail."

"Yes, sir." He made a good point, Ava conceded.

"So what's the plan of attack?" he asked.

"A friend from the train is showing me around Vancouver this afternoon," Ava said. "Sort of a Sunday off concept."

"What friend?"

"Laurent. He's the young blond man in my photos. We did the Jasper Sky Tram together."

"The honey trap. Check. Did you bite?" He smiled crookedly.

Ava scowled at him. She figured the most likely person to follow any cold trail was Cade. "Cynic. I told Laurent I have a boyfriend back East. Pretty serious."

Skull nodded. "So you kept your options open."

"I suppose," Ava conceded. "Anyway, that should give me an overview of the city. I may feel him out on how people reach Seattle. Mostly I'll just keep my eyes open. Tomorrow seek out friends in low places. Oh, speaking of which, Kelly is still shadowing me." She hadn't spotted the other girl when they disembarked.

"Whoa, back up," Skull replied. "First, keep notes. Everywhere you go. See if you can get your fancy phone to map your trail with timestamps, and automatically upload it in real time."

Ava dictated a quick note to Jana to remind her.

"Next, why start with low places instead of high? You waltzed into Canada with their blessing."

Ava frowned. "I thought I had permission to visit Vancouver. Not Seattle."

Skull shrugged. "You arrived. You're on the wrong side of the continent. You looked. Oops, the addressee skedaddled to Seattle. You need to follow to complete the delivery. You've come this far. And so forth."

Ava considered that approach, head tilted. "It's a backup plan. But what if they say no? They can make that stick, plonk me onto the next train eastbound. Better to start low and work my way up, I think. If I can't find a good free market option."

Skull waved an open hand. "I think you're right. Methods are up to you. Just wanted to make sure you considered the high road."

Ava nodded. "Kelly?"

"Please."

"She claims someone in the company, not you, ordered her to be my backup. There's a wireless dead drop active at fifteen hundred hours every day at a tearoom." She rattled off the address. "And that's all she's got for a contact. Aside from me. I saw her last night. I left her chatting up the troops who boarded at Edmonton."

Ava looked straight into the camera and blinked deliberately, to underline that the troops from Edmonton were important. Important to Ava, anyway.

Skull's turn to purse his lips. "Nothing you just said reassures me."

"Sorry, boss," she said unrepentant. "Oh, there was one other thing. Few days ago. She was afraid you were going to put her back with the handlers. And her supervisor was a pig. When she ran."

Skull shook his head. "Saundra? Middle-aged, three kids. Used to work for the FBI. Ava, Kelly fed you more lies in a sympathy play. Even if it were true, she should have talked to me, or you, or KT. Run? That's pure b.s."

"I could see myself running on a bad impulse," Ava quibbled. "Instead of talking. But you can't see this Saundra as a 'pig'?"

Skull scowled. "She's overweight."

Ava covered an involuntary giggle with a fist. When she got herself back in control, she said, "Boss? Some apples have a problem with fat people."

"Yeah? Get over it."

"Yes, sir."

"Have you figured out Jean-Claude yet?"

"No." Ava made another note on Jana.

Skull tapped a finger on his desk. "No spying. No Kelly. Ava, from here, focus on your goal. Avoid distractions. Clear?"

"Clear. Boss… Am I doing a good job?"

"Yes," he said, brow lowering. "Why?"

"I was wondering what my role is, in the company. I thought I was training to be a field agent, like Cade. But I wasn't very good at it in Ohio, was I. Is this my job now? Just a courier?"

"KT didn't complain of your performance in Ohio. You two had an authority conflict. That's natural. The customers didn't take you seriously. That's just who we deal with."

He paused and looked thoughtful a moment. "Ava, it's true that I have an issue with sending a woman into our assignments. You're tough. But in the field, those men, Sixers and rogue militia – they manage women with rape and battery. You're only suited to work with a male agent. Cade wanted you, and he's entitled. I allow agents to recruit their own backup. But he's benched at the moment, and this came up. It's a rare assignment. Up to now, I wasn't worried about your physical safety. That equation changes now. Be careful out there, Ava."

"So I'm not a real agent. Just Cade's sidekick. Because I'm a girl."

"Ava? Cade is doing desk work. You're across the continent on a solo. You're my best agent for this assignment. I admit, I'm still trying to figure out how to make the best use of my new female operatives. You're trail-blazing. Just don't prove it the wrong way. OK?"

"What's the wrong way?"

"By getting raped and brutalized. You'd survive. We know that, because you already have," he said gently.

"Yeah." She breathed out. "Been there. Done that."

"Stay safe. Remember that high road. You can ask the Canadians for help."

"I do want to prove myself," she admitted.

"Do that by completing your delivery. Not by risking yourself and the mission. I'm glad you asked, Ava. I'm sorry it's hard to talk about."

"Yeah. Thanks."

"Ava, you're not less than. You're different. I hired a bunch of different with your cohort. It gives me options."

"I'm not less than Cade?" Ava asked sourly.

"That's a high bar. Cade's one of my best. But you know why? He's creative, and good at so many different things. You are, too. In different ways. Your goal isn't to be a second-rate Cade. Be a first-rate Ava. OK?"

"OK." With the conversation drifting to Cade, she couldn't resist. "Did you give him my note and pictures from Sioux Lookout? About seeing Jeremy from the gang?"

"No. Cade's dealing with a lot now emotionally. Wait and share that in person, OK?"

"OK," she whispered. She'd really wanted to touch Cade. But Skull had made clear that he had a low tolerance for playing go-between. And in truth, if hearing about Jeremy brought Cade to tears, she should be there for him to cry on.

"And just so you know," Skull said, "you and – I guess you knew her as 'Rahema.' The one you picked up through West Virginia. So far, the two of you are the best new hires from your cohort. Both women."

"Really?"

Skull smiled slightly. "Don't let it go to your head. Stay safe. And the guys all have potential, too. They just haven't caught the mission where they shine yet."

"Thanks."

After they signed off, Ava took a few minutes to bask in the praise.

~

AVA POSED, DRAPED IN A DARK RUBBERY LEAF BIGGER THAN SHE WAS. SHE attempted a sultry smile. Hands modestly crossed her crotch and breast. She'd just used Jana to check the right stance from the painting.

"Perfect!" cried Laurent, snapping the photo a few times with Jana. "Venus on a half shell!" He switched to his own phone to capture the moment again for himself. "Sort of."

Venus stood naked on the giant clamshell, not inside a clam standing on edge, fully clothed. Laurent was the one who'd come up with the idea. Ava had never heard of the old masterpiece.

"What is this thing, anyway?" she asked, emerging from her giant green clam. She jostled it on the way, unleashing a cup of water onto her neck, bypassing her red rain poncho. "Ach! And does it ever stop raining here?"

Laurent consulted a little bronze plant marker stuck in the ground. "It's called an elephant ear. And yeah, cloud failure happens."

"'Cloud failure.' Love it. Jana told me summer was the dry season," Ava complained. "Rain one day in five or something."

"Yeah, not any more," Laurent said apologetically. He wore a dignified trench coat over jeans. He handed back her phone and the hotel loaner umbrella. "I caught the news. As of today, it's rained for forty days and forty nights straight. Plenty of Noah's ark jokes."

Ava laughed. "I bet. Does it get any warmer with cloud failure?" She started strolling again through the beautiful Chinese garden, a hushed oasis walled into the middle of downtown. Jana reported it was almost 60 degrees, or 15 Celsius. It felt chillier when wet. On the bright side, it smelled absolutely fresh and salty, without a speck of dust in the air. The St. Pauli girl might not have felt at home, but the New Yorker did.

"Maybe twenty-five degrees max," Laurent supplied. "We have a long growing season. Milder than most of Canada. Not warm, but not cold."

Ava let Jana do the math. That was still below 80 degrees. What a clammy town.

She posed Laurent for a portrait with a squat Buddha in front of the pagoda. The concrete Buddha needed a shave on the green algae beard he was growing. But on the whole, the gardens seemed immaculately well kept. Laurent perched on the wall beside the statue in lotus position, staring down toward his navel, eyebrows raised quizzically.

"Enough with the garden?" he asked, accepting his phone and umbrella back.

"Yeah. I want to see the drowned waterfront," Ava requested. They'd arrived at the train station in a fairly drowned section, less than a mile from here. Apparently the locals chose to raise the rail yard in situ while they developed a new station outside the downtown buildup. Downtown was a peninsula jutting into Vancouver Harbor, ending in the famous Stanley Park.

"Want to eat dim sum before we leave Chinatown?" he offered.

Ava cocked a skeptical eyebrow at him. "Vancouver is short on Chinese restaurants?" The place seemed more Chinese than Anglo. Chinatown didn't seem to make much difference to the complexions on the street.

Laurent laughed. "You're right, we can catch dim sum anywhere." They passed through the walled entrance and back out to the street. Laurent checked a map on his phone. "Huh. I'm not allowed into the closest section of waterfront. My job says."

Ava peered over his arm and made a mental note of the neighborhood, for investigation tomorrow. "I'll protect you."

"I'm sure you will," he crooned. "But apparently the Triads own the Eastside and Gastown waterfronts." He lowered his voice for that. The street wasn't busy in the pouring rain. But at least half the pedestrians were Asian.

"Triads?" Ava asked. The term was familiar, but she couldn't place it.

"Chinese mafia," Laurent murmured, and took her arm. "This way."

Ava considered this news dolefully. Yes, she had heard of Triads before, in the Apple's Chinatown. In her experience, a race-centric gang did not do business with outsiders. And the Chinese were more xenophobic than most. If she dealt with them, she'd get burned. "Are there other gangs? Competing with the Triads?"

Laurent shot her a look. "Keep your voice down. No, the Triads pretty much have a monopoly now. The Punjabi Sikhs used to be a problem. But we got a new influx of Chinese just before the embargo. Then the Punjabi lost the turf war. Vancouver used to be the premier port of entry for opium into North America. The Pacific blockade has been bad for business."

"All business," Ava suggested. If she had a choice between Punjabi and Chinese, she'd pick Chinese. At least she was familiar with them. Crossing an intersection, she glimpsed the harbor water downhill, in Laurent's proscribed zone.

"Yup. Vancouver exploded in size on Chinese trade."

Something in his tone prompted Ava to ask in surprise, "And that's not gone?" Trans-Atlantic trade was truly dead, so far as she knew.

"Not really," he murmured. "We shouldn't discuss this on the street. It's not safe. Here's our SkyTrain." He led her down a subway stair.

"SkyTrain?" Ava objected. "The subway?"

"Here, yeah. Later, I hope to take you to see the University of British Columbia. My alma mater. The trains run above ground out that way."

To Ava's eyes, the subway looked beautiful and clean. Laurent muttered darkly about it getting wet and moldy down here. He started to buy her a week-long transit pass, but she insisted on paying for it herself. The colored line style of subway map, with symbolic nods to actual coastal geography, was similar to New York's, though of course less extensive.

Ava asked, "Was it hard? When the sea rose?"

"Yes and no. Vancouver had contingency plans. All the coastal cities did." A train arrived and they stepped on. Laurent resumed, "The flooding isn't so bad. The land is steep here rising out of the ocean. Only, the housing market was tight before. And we lost more housing to the water. And people keep coming. I commute an hour each way to work downtown. Best I could afford, straight out of university. Sorry, I won't offer to drag you to my apartment."

"I appreciate you giving up your weekend for me," Ava said. She could only dimly imagine a 9-5 commuter office lifestyle. She'd only seen it on TV before the Starve. "And you just back from your trip."

The next subway stop was theirs. Laurent continued the conversation after they were back up on the street, headed downhill to the harbor. "I'm delighted to show you around. And work's only four days a week. I can show you around again on Wednesday, when more places are open."

"You only work part-time?" Ava asked.

He sighed and took her arm. "You blew your cover there. Standard work week is thirty hours, usually weekends and Wednesday off. Labor's answer to increasing automation. Everyone knows that, even in Minnesota." He aped her pronunciation on the state name.

"Sure but –" Ava attempted.

"Don't bother," Laurent advised. He leaned over to whisper in her ear. "You're from Hudson. I'm guessing the Apple."

"When did you know?" Ava asked. Her conscience suspected that visit with the American troops in the dome car, when Kelly set them straight on the Apple culling. Ava had trouble biting her tongue through that. Kelly was miles away in Princeton, practically living in luxury, while Ava scrabbled for survival on the mean streets of Manhattan.

Laurent scratched his nose ruefully. "I went to Saskatoon to meet your train."

"You always knew," Ava concluded. "And before Saskatoon?"

"The Ontario agent turned back at Winnipeg," said Laurent. "No one in their right mind would bolt in the Dust Bowl. I was ordered to meet you in Edmonton. I paid for Saskatoon out of my own pocket."

"Curiosity?" Ava guessed. "And you are, what exactly?"

"RCMP. I'm a Mountie," he confided with a smile. "But I would have offered to show you around Vancouver anyway."

"You have a horse?" Ava asked. "Red uniform and fur hat?"

Laurent laughed out loud. "Sorry. Civilian side. Just business suits and a trench coat for me, I'm afraid."

"And your interest in a tiny American courier?" Ava asked.

"RCMP is responsible for border security and smuggling," Laurent replied. "But I enjoy your company."

"Ew!" Ava cried out, recoiling from a fish shop window. She pointed in horror at a tray of giant snails, over a pound apiece. Bending to look closer, the obscene wrinkly pale tan shafts had a small bivalve shell attached – not a snail. "What is that?"

"Gooey ducks," Laurent replied. "It's spelled geoduck, but we pronounce the 'geo' part 'gooey.' It's a clam." He laughed out loud at her expression. "They're tasty."

"Huh." She had to take pictures.

"There are off-color jokes about gooey ducks," Laurent suggested.

Ava laughed. "I bet!"

She let him take her arm again, still chuckling, their umbrellas overlapping, as they strode another couple blocks downhill, to where the harbor lapped quietly at the pavement. This was a marina. The floating docks were still in business, with new ramps climbing up to them from further up the street. Lamp posts stood above the water, footed on concrete plinths. Across the harbor, the north side of the city rose toward encompassing mountains, mere shadows in the rain.

The front ranks of high-rise apartments with balconies were probably condemned. Only about a block was inundated above the front step level. But the foundations were underwater. Judging by the sea wrack, it was low tide at the moment. Gazing back up the street, the high water line surprised her.

"How high are your tides here?"

"Five meters," Laurent replied. "Less than St. John, of course, on the Bay of Fundy. But yeah, it's a big swing. That made it easier to cope with the sea rise. The city wasn't built right down to the water's edge."

"Clammy place you've got here," Ava said.

"But it's home," Laurent returned with a warm smile. "Stanley Park is a lot more walking in the rain. Ready to see the university instead?"

23

Interesting fact: The geoduck clam shell ranges from 6 to 8 inches long, but the animal's protruding siphon can reach 3 feet or more. The geoduck is one of the longest lived animals in the world, up to 140 years. Its Chinese use as an aphrodisiac is likely inspired by its phallic appearance.

"I can't invite you up," Ava told Laurent bashfully in the hotel lobby. "Thank you so much for a wonderful day."

"Maybe next time," Laurent suggested. He ducked in for a kiss but got Ava's turned cheek instead. He kissed it anyway. "I'll call you."

"I'd like that," Ava said, and smiled at him as he stepped out and unfurled his umbrella again. He set off into the clammy evening murk.

"Tempted? Or leading him on?" Jean-Claude inquired.

She thought that was his head. He sat in a lobby armchair with his back to the door, forever reading his tablet. Surely he was growing tired of medical journals. She sank onto the chunky funky coffee table facing him, stretching between her knees to clasp her sneaker-clad ankles. He frowned and gestured with a couple fingers toward a proper seat.

She moved. "Who are you drinking with?" He had a bottle of wine and two glasses, only one filled.

"I was waiting for you." He poured for her and presented the wineglass with a flourish. "To hear all about your date with Laurent!"

"Wasn't a date." Ava sipped the light sweet wine. "I almost like this one." She stared at its pale rosy depths a moment more. "He says he's RCMP. A Mountie."

"I'm not surprised. There was another. He had a cabin in our car. Got off in Winnipeg."

Check. That was the Mr. Clark-alike Ava had suspected. "And you? Are you a Mountie, Jean-Claude?"

"Non. I am a doctor. I have not lied to you, Ava. Maybe told you less than everything."

"You didn't lie about France?" she challenged. "I think you're Quebecois."

"I applied for citizenship," Jean-Claude allowed. "I attended Université Laval Faculté de Médecine. Means I graduated medical school in Quebec City. Then joined MSF later – Médecins Sans Frontières. I meant to go back to France someday. Maybe not." He smiled warmly to show he didn't mind. "I like the New World very much."

Jean-Claude put his glass down decisively. "You are delivering your package tomorrow?"

"I don't have an address," Ava hedged. "I start looking tomorrow."

He leaned forward, putting lips to steepled fingers. "If you were going to, say, cross the border? I like to go with you."

"Vancouver was my destination," Ava returned. "Are you Canadian Intelligence?"

"Non. I am a doctor." He frowned slightly and met her eye. "Ava, the world, she is not simple. My work is to help people. Sometimes I tell them things because I think they need to know. Mounties. Intelligence. Rescos. MSF. Others. But I work for no one except MSF and my patients."

"Why do you want to go south?" Ava pressed.

"MSF wants to know how they do," Jean-Claude replied. "Your general wants to know what you do." He giggled conspiratorially, and shook his head. "I do not plan to tell him."

My general? Ava swallowed. "Were you in West Virginia last month?"

"Non. I stayed in Ken–Tenn. They go without me." The cheerful man looked sad. "MSF can do nothing for Virginia now, I think." He took another sip of wine. "I think you do not want your general to know what you do. Or he would already know."

"We say, 'that is above my pay grade.'" Ava shrugged lightly.

"If you go south, take me with you," Jean-Claude repeated. "I can be useful."

"Is that a threat?" Ava asked. "You'll tell the general if I leave without you?"

"No threats." Jean-Claude placed a theatrical hand across his breast. "We are friends. But you know, we travel together very well!"

"We do," Ava agreed with a grin. She stood decisively. "Thanks for the wine. I need to sleep and think."

"Mm, yes. If you leave Vancouver, do not tell Laurent."

"Good night, Jean-Claude."

~

AVA REARRANGED HER WAIST PACK THOUGHTFULLY IN THE MORNING. SHE was tempted to leave Jana behind, but Skull was right. She needed Jana to track her whereabouts. Even if she risked losing her electronic sidekick, she went nowhere without Jana.

Most of her cash and debit cards she stashed in the room safe, and the black box and papers and Porta's camera as well.

She studied the instructions on the safe for setting a personal unlock code. After three retries, the safe would jam up completely and require the hotel staff to reset it. That wouldn't prevent the police from getting in, but at least they couldn't do it secretly.

She entered a four-digit number that would not be on anyone's first three guesses – her father's birthday, in Serbian day-month order, 2803 for March 28th. She snapped a picture of the contents, and starred the photo to upload immediately.

Her weapons options were limited. She French-braided her hair and secured the pigtail end with her sharpened chopstick. A small knife slipped into her left high-top sneaker. Her lightest leather jacket would be a tad warm, but gave some protection in a fight. She tucked pre-counted bribes into each pocket of her skinny jeans. Feeling rather silly, she took a selfie before and after adding her red rain poncho over the jacket and waist pack.

"Jana, mission notebook, date stamp entry," she murmured to her phone. "Visit Chinese waterfront to seek transportation south. The area is forbidden to RCMP personnel. Too dangerous. Chinese mafia turf, Triads."

She contemplated her room for another few seconds. She couldn't think of any other protective steps.

In a few minutes, she was out in the pouring rain, walking through Chinatown toward the harbor. She crossed a larger street, East Hastings. A fair number of homeless and drug addicts were scattered about there. This seemed a hopeful sign, but she couldn't find a direction that seemed to decay from there. And East Hastings wasn't down in the forbidden waterfront.

Chinatown didn't stretch to the harbor. Another neighborhood called Gastown intervened. With brick streets and upscale tea shops, indigenous art galleries, and lower floor shops painted fresh black with gold trim, Gastown looked like a tourist mecca. The buildings were well back from the harbor waters, not affected at all by the sea rise.

Ava wondered if maybe her standards were too low. Compared to Manhattan, this whole town looked like Disney World. She happened across a rack of rental bikes and grabbed one. There was little car traffic to worry about, and few pedestrians on a Monday morning in the downpour. The bike could speed things up.

She soon realized why the streets weren't mobbed with bikes. Riding on these charming brick streets was hard on the tail bone. The slopes down to the water were steep, too. She pedaled standing up by preference. The Gastown streets dead-ended not into the harbor, but a wide rail plaza of maybe ten parallel tracks, blocked by a chain link fence. She followed the fence along some seedy alleys. But she saw nothing more challenging than more vagrants. Quite a lot of vagrants, really, and they begged for food and money.

One grabbed for her handlebars. She jerked to drive straight into him, karate-chopped his hand and rode the bike over his foot. He fell behind her easily enough.

Finally she spotted a raised road that bridged the rails, and took it. This one was smooth paved instead of cobbled, a nice reprieve. Near the top of its arc, she ran across a matched pair of Chinese lion statues flanking the nearly deserted roadway. She stopped to take pictures and enjoy the elevated view. With so much rain, the surrounding mountains were invisible. Touristy Gastown lay behind her. Below, the tracks stretched left toward the skyscrapers downtown. A waterfront park lay ahead. And to the right was a container shipping yard, vast, with maybe a dozen tall and boxy orange cranes stretching down the harbor. It was busier than she would have expected.

What could bother the Mounties about this waterfront? she wondered. It all looked –

Transportation, smuggling. Container yards, acres upon acres. *Damn.* She'd hoped for a nice decrepit drowned city block or three.

She followed her arching road further, but it turned left into a now-tidal city park instead of right toward the cranes. Only pedestrian staircases gave access down on that side. She could carry her bike down the stairs. But below was more parkland turning to mudflats, with no route into the harbor complex.

There has to be some way to drive into the loading docks, she reasoned. She turned back toward Gastown and continued east, hugging the train tracks as closely as she could. She was relieved to leave the bumpy tourist brickwork behind. The area grew more industrial, no longer painted for charm. The tea shops and galleries gave way to business establishments, often labeled in Chinese without subtitles. That looked promising.

She found another elevated road across the train tracks. A high barred steel gate blocked the way. The sign advised, 'DANGER. Heavy Industry Area. Private Road. Access for port related business only.'

That's alright, she consoled herself. *I didn't want to go in there anyway.* No, the people she wanted to talk to would be on the public side of the gates. Right about here, in fact. She rode skirting the puddles to one side of the raised road.

"Hey! You lost?" One of a quartet of middle-aged Asian men hailed her. They were loading a truck that bore a picture of a crab, captioned in Chinese characters. She doubted crab was shipped in the kind of unmarked brown cartons they loaded.

Bingo? Ava pedaled toward them, slowly. "I'm looking for transportation south," she said. "Not sure where to look for that. Any ideas?" She stopped the bike ten yards from them.

The one who'd called to her approached and stood arms crossed, sizing her up. "Where south?"

Ava didn't like the look of these guys. They were wiry and weathered. She had experience fighting this sort of compact build at West Point, not much different from her own. Hand to hand combat against her squad mate Fang was brutal. Or from another perspective, they were exactly the sort of men she was looking for.

"Border. Seattle," she replied. "No goods. Just passenger."

"Border closed."

"I noticed," Ava agreed. "Know any travel agents who can handle that? I can pay."

He waited. She selected a sixty dollar bribe from a pocket and held it on her thigh, out of view of the other men. He stepped closer and she handed it to him. He counted and glowered at her, with a wave to indicate three other men. Annoyed, she pulled out another sixty for them, but held onto it.

"I know travel agent," he allowed. He pulled out a business card and a pen, and scribbled something on the back in Chinese characters. He didn't have an address, but described a location on East Hastings Street only a couple blocks from the Sun Yat-Sen gardens and her hotel.

"A hundred twenty dollars, for an introduction to a travel agent?" Ava objected.

"For card," he replied sourly. "She no talk to you without it." He looked her up and down. "We take money anyway."

She didn't doubt they could. Sourly, she handed over the second sixty in exchange for the card. She walked the bike back a few yards the moment the card was in her hand. "Thank you."

He turned his back and walked away. She pedaled out of that block as quick as she could before the others got any ideas.

When the loading crew was safely out of view, Ava pulled the card out of her pocket to look it over. The crab logo and phone numbers were the only parts she could read. The card could say 'take this sucker for another $200' for all she knew. She pulled out Jana and marked the approximate location of the travel agent. She made a note on her mission log, and snapped photos of the card, captioned with grumbles about how much she paid for it.

Gazing around the industrial block, she dolefully decided she wasn't likely to find any better here. As that sort went, the man was unusually friendly and helpful.

She kept an eye out for anything else that looked promising, but rode back to return her bike to the tourist rack where she found it.

~

Ava stopped her Chinese waitress from turning away after delivering her lunch order. "Please, could you translate this for me?"

The Gastown dim sum place had just opened, getting ready for lunch. There were no other customers. The waitress, Catherine, took a seat across from Ava. She frowned at the card, front and back. "These no good people," she whispered.

"A friend wants to visit Seattle," Ava murmured back.

"This legal restaurant, good people," the waitress objected, trying to hand back the card.

"I'm sure," Ava agreed soothingly. "I just need to know what the card says."

The waitress shook her head minutely. "Triad company card. Shipping. Guy's name on back. Please, no involve me in this." She rose abruptly to escape. "Enjoy food, please."

The steamed shrimp dumplings tasted pretty good. Ava winced at the clangor of Cantonese drifting from the kitchen. She hated the sound of that language. She left a hundred percent tip for her reluctant translator, and noted the restaurant as one not to visit again.

~

Back in Chinatown, Ava grew paranoid. The sensation was familiar. Life on the streets had taught her to pay attention to that feeling. A trio of Chinese men were behind her on the street. That was hardly remarkable, but worth testing.

She turned at the next intersection, away from her travel agent destination. They turned, too. A block up, she turned again, a 180 from her original direction. They turned again as well. *Yeah, they're definitely following me.*

Fortunately, there were storefronts on this block. Ava selected a Chinese souvenir shop and ducked inside. From the exterior, she expected cheap red plastic toys with gold gilt. The place offered plenty of that. Dumpy little Buddhas in everything from resin to jade. Chopsticks from cheap bamboo disposables to beautifully lacquered wood. Ornately painted thin porcelain in many shapes.

Dust-catchers.

The door chimes summoned a male proprietor from the back. "Good morning! How I help you!"

"Do you have weapons?" Ava inquired. "Nunchucks?"

The diminutive old man frowned in consternation. "Ah, one minute." He ducked into the back.

Ava continued surveying the shop's overladen shelves, moving on to gaudy piles of silk pajamas and Mandarin collar pant suits. Three years after the ocean embargoes went into effect, this shop was still stocked to the brim. The silks bore none of the browned signs of long storage in a damp climate. Ava tried to work out what that meant. She doubted selling this junk could pay the rent, let alone cover years of excess inventory.

Another jangle of door chimes made her look up. Her three tails from the street ducked in out of the rain.

These guys are beginning to annoy me. She briefly considered asking the shopkeeper for help against them. She discarded the idea as unworkable. Ties ran too damned deep in a Chinese community. The shopkeeper would automatically side with fellow Chinese, because it wasn't worth it to cross them.

Once upon a time, Ava Panic tried not to be racist. That Ava died after her family moved to New York. In her experience, racial stereotypes were simplistic. Any individual could vary. But shallow stereotype was based on cultural reality.

The shopkeeper emerged from the back, bearing a stack of presentation boxes. He peered around the shop to see whether she'd left, or others came in. Ava noted he froze a little, eyes narrowing, at the three guys.

"Here, Missy," he beckoned her, subdued.

He left the boxes on the crowded counter for her, and strode forward to greet the men in Cantonese. They responded with grunts and remained blocking the door, looking around in distaste. He bowed backward and stepped away from them.

Ava tucked herself next to the counter to keep an eye on the guys. She opened her first gift box. Tacky red foam-covered safety nunchucks with gilt panda bear faces. *Pass.* The next set were chromium steel. The reflections might be an interesting effect, but on the whole, no.

On second thought, she tried them out for a couple swings. Holding one handle, she flopped the other forward on its short chain, caught it, back, caught it, forward, and off it flew, nearly missing one of the goons by the door.

"Sorry!" she called out cheerfully. "That one was defective."

"Careful, Missy!" cried the shopkeeper, wringing his hands. In an under-mutter, he added, "Red button."

Ava replaced the one-handled nunchuck in its box. She took the next, and leaned over to press the red button behind the counter. She was blocking the proprietor from the cash register.

Nice nunchucks! she finally noticed. This set was red oak, with a dragon design burned along the side of the batons. She emerged from behind the counter for more space, and experimentally twirled one free end. It swung freely and smoothly on good bearings. The shopkeeper cringed and held arms in front of his head protectively.

Ava dismissed that. She was missing him by at least six inches.

She tried the simple forward-and-back catches again – smooth as glass, and she loved the sound of the good wooden percussive *thunk* on the catch. Frosty might like these. *Cade.*

"Missy no fight in store!" the shopkeeper pleaded.

She smiled at him. "I'm just trying out the nunchucks. A gift for my boyfriend."

One of the goons stepped closer.

She stepped sideways for more space and tried a more complex routine, with back-and-forth swipes from each hand and twirling in between. The nunchucks were beautifully well balanced. She kept her eyes focused at the near distance, on the flying wood and chain steel. But of course she could still see what the goons were up to. Which was involuntarily recoil from the slapping nunchucks.

Such a showy weapon. That's why Frosty liked them. They made for a glitzy mesmerizing sort of background threat, while negotiation proceeded in measured tones. And if his opposite number said something he didn't like, he could express annoyance by slapping something loudly, without striking anyone. He used them in the dojo all the time, discussing possible punishments with a wayward gang member. Ava didn't recall him actually striking anyone with them. They amounted to a stage prop.

Nunchucks also extended the arm's reach by quite a ways. And while the opponent had his wary eye on the distracting thing, you could pivot and kick him in the nuts. Not that Ava or Cade went out to fight on the street with nunchucks stuck in a pocket. They weren't a practical carry weapon, just a toy in the dojo.

Ava stepped closer to the goons for more aisle space to her right and left. She did a quick routine she'd first seen Kat perform in a Pride parade in Greenwich Village. She lunged to the right, dropping her left knee to the floor, and spun and flipped the nunchucks. Then she rose into horse stance, knees flexed evenly, spinning the batons in the middle, then lunged left to repeat on the other side.

That was Ava's first introduction to sensei's dojo, his demo team during Pride, wearing their cool black gi, water tiger emblems flashing in the bright June sunlight. Sensei ran a highly profitable operation. He combed the Internet for novel marketing concepts. Ava dumped her old Soho dojo and joined theirs in Chelsea within the week. *Happy memories.*

She hopped a foot across the chain as though playing jump rope –

an impossibility with the short chain – then flicked the chuck down the aisle, still a good eight inches short of the nearest goon.

By then the shopkeeper was screeching in Cantonese. His clasped hands, arms guarding his head, reached heavenward. Whether to invoke the protection of the gods or to call down demons, Ava couldn't say. Chinese could be too melodramatic for her taste.

The goons had enough and stepped back out into the rain.

Ava turned to the shopkeeper. "I like these very much. Does the button summon the police?"

Apparently it did. Two uniformed beat cops wandered by to encourage the goons to move on. They stuck their heads in to make sure all was well.

The shopkeeper vented his spleen about how goons weren't allowed in Chinatown. "Bad for tourist!" He shook his fist at the window.

Ava finished selecting an unnecessary lavender silk jacket to add to her nunchucks purchase – a tip for the man's trouble, more or less – and was on her way.

24

Interesting fact: Vancouver and Seattle are 140 miles apart (230 km). Both lie on Puget Sound, a complex waterway with branching fjords between the mainland and Vancouver Island, itself 285 miles long. Both cities are on the mainland, on the east shore of the Sound.

"We're closed!" the woman called out on automatic. She didn't look up from her utilitarian grey steel desk. A few other steel chairs with grey vinyl seats lay pushed back against the window.

Ava scowled, and continued stepping inside. She let the travel agency door continue closing behind her with its coin chimes, a square hole in each golden disk. The shop's walls bore travel posters long since faded to blues, their reds and yellows leached away by years of sunlight. Considering how little sunlight Ava had seen in Vancouver, they could have been hanging there for decades.

The decor seemed designed to repel customers.

Ava stepped up to the young dragon lady at the desk. A standing name plaque read Grace Kwan. "I'd like to make a trip."

Grace didn't look up from her laptop. "Closed."

Ava slipped her ill-gotten business card onto the keyboard under Grace's nose. "To Seattle."

Grace examined the card. "Border closed."

"Yes, that's the problem. I need to cross the border. Ideally, to reach Seattle."

"Why you bother me?"

Ava crooked one eyebrow. "You're a travel agent?"

"Shipping agent."

"OK, I'm shipping a person. Me. Maybe two people."

"Illegal."

"Yes, I expect that costs extra," Ava allowed.

"Risky. Two thousand."

"For two people? How would we reach Seattle?"

"One person around border. Land north of Bellingham."

Ava pulled out Jana and found Bellingham on the map, only about 10 miles south of the Canadian border. "Land Bellingham? You mean a boat?"

"Shipping I said!" Grace spat at her.

"How would this work?" Ava asked reluctantly.

"You pay, cash up front. I tell you where meet ship."

Ava used a finger to draw the card back across the desk, and pocketed it. "Two hundred per person."

"Two thousand two person."

"Six hundred for two. Where would we land exactly?" Ava extended her map of the area on Jana.

Grace waved away Ava's phone. "Up to captain. Busy man. Deliveries to make. Tides. One thousand for two."

"One thousand for two to *Seattle,*" Ava suggested. "Not Bellingham."

Grace threw up her hands and pursed her lips at Ava. "We no go Seattle. Captain run border, not whole Puget Sound. This no ferry. Deliver Bellingham."

"I'll think about it," Ava said. She plucked up one of Grace's business cards from the holder, and turned away.

"Eight hundred for two, pay *today,*" Grace returned. "Tomorrow back to two thousand."

"When does he sail?"

"This week, couple day maybe. I tell you after pay."

"I'll think about it," Ava repeated, and left the shop. On the street, she marked the travel agent on Jana's map and dictated a note of the current terms, with a snapshot of Grace's business card.

Do I trust these people to deliver me to Bellingham? she wondered, *Or cut my throat and throw me overboard?* She splashed off through the puddles toward her hotel to dry off for a while.

Well, this was one option. She wanted a better one.

Jana pinged her with a text.

Boss: Fascinating reading. For all of us. C-

Dammit. Ava winced. The Canadians were monitoring her online storage, too.

Oh, well. She didn't like that plan anyway.

TOASTY AND DRY AFTER A LONG HOT SHOWER, AVA SAT TO BRAINSTORM IN her hip hotel room.

A way across the border wasn't all she needed. Once in Washo, she'd need food and currency as well. The high road remained an option on the other side of the border. She could always turn herself in to the authorities and request an audience with the leader of Seattle.

As in Vancouver, that was a fall back plan at best, she thought. They might take her seriously and do as she asked. They might throw her in jail, or deposit her back at the Canadian border. She had no idea who or what 'they' were or what motivated them.

That extended to the cash challenge as well. She had money. The usual approach was to convert that into some high-value commodity, carry it across the border, and sell it for another currency. But what did people need in Washo? Drugs were in high demand in the Northeast, but she shouldn't assume that here.

She also didn't have the company's lock on the pharmaceutical supply chain in Vancouver. She'd be stuck paying retail for illegal drugs of unknown quality. The company's opiates killed back home. But they killed at a carefully controlled rate, usually 6% on the opiates. The idea of pushing drugs that might kill everyone who took them made her queasy.

Hypocrite! she thought.

But then she decided it was a valid point. If she were caught pushing killer drugs like fentanyl or something, they might lock her up and throw away the key. That route violated her mission parameters, for good reason. Don't break laws if you can possibly avoid it.

OK, medical grade drugs, or none at all.

She could visit a health center and claim a refill on her albuterol. She'd only used one bottle, so nearly doubling it came to a fair bit of value for $24. She could make a case for some valium, as well. She did suffer panic attacks. That might amount to enough resale value to cover food for a few days.

Dammit, back home the company had infrastructure and a team for all this. Here she was on her own.

That thought brought her up short. When in Canada had she ever truly been alone?

~

"THE REST OF THE AFTERNOON," AVA CONCLUDED, "I SPENT IN THE Vancouver public library studying up on Washo. The reference librarian was nice." She took another big bite of bacon and mushroom pizza.

The hotel concierge had been most helpful. She reserved Ava a private back room at a New York City style brick oven pizza joint to host her little dinner party. The bacon was Canadian and more like ham, and the sauce seasonings were vaguely off. But the thin crust was perfect.

Jean-Claude nodded. "I spoke with MSF. They have sent people across before. A doctor here has a boat. He could sail us down. Near Bellingham."

Ava nodded enthusiastically. "Much better than the Triads. Kelly? What ideas did you come up with?"

"Date rape drugs," the girl grumbled. "For Laurent. Get him to drive us to the border for sight-seeing, drug him, get him to take us across..." She trailed off. "The doctor's yacht sounds better."

Ava agreed. But the first rule of brainstorming was to appreciate all suggestions. "Good thinking. Any ideas using the American troops?"

Kelly replied, "They already crossed to Vancouver Island for their exercises. They're staying in Victoria now. But those guys were grunts. No access to water vehicles."

"By land, I could rent a car," Jean-Claude suggested. "Or buy one, if you have funds?"

"I have funds," Ava agreed. "Canadian. Thanks, you can get a car more easily than I could. The land is drowned south of Vancouver. We'd have to detour east twenty miles, then head south. There aren't many roads that cross the border. And mountains in our way. But it's an option."

Ava didn't like cars, though, in strange territory. Buying gas, or recharging the batteries, could too easily become a fatal problem.

"A hiking trip," Kelly said. "Take a car south, and hike into the mountains."

All three nodded reluctantly. That could work, but no one was eager to hike in the rain, with luggage. These weren't the nicely rounded worn-out hills called mountains in Pennsylvania. They looked like serious technical climbing. Ava and Kelly were probably fit enough to manage it, but lacked experience. And Ava had her doubts about the middle-aged Jean-Claude.

"Any other ideas?" Ava asked. The other two shook their heads. Everyone liked the classy yacht idea, and other concepts dried up. "OK, Jean-Claude, could you make sure this yacht is really an option?"

"Mais oui." He beamed. "What do you learn about Washo?"

"They call themselves Oregon, for starters," Ava said. "I guess the name Washington isn't so popular anymore."

"Hell, no," Kelly agreed.

"Biggest health challenge is smoke and burn treatment, I think," Ava continued. To her surprise, her albuterol and stupid Moo Cow would be valuable.

"Forest fires?" Kelly asked, glancing dubiously at the puddles under their dripping rain gear.

"It's only wet by the coast," Ava confirmed. She pulled up a map on Jana and placed it next to the pizza for them all to see. "This mountain range east of Seattle is the Cascades. The eastern slopes are on fire. Drought and brutal heat on the other side. These mountains toward the north of the state, too."

Kelly said, "So if we hiked, we might be headed into forest fires."

"Good point," Ava allowed. "Anyway, Oregon is militant beyond anything we've seen in the East. Mandatory public service for age eighteen to thirty. Army, fire lines, public works."

Jean-Claude chuckled. "Well organized!"

Ava nodded dourly. "Very well organized. They're holding back the tide of refugees trying to flee up from California and Nevada. They're not too friendly with 'the Montane Territory,' either, their eastern neighbor. That's Idaho, Montana, and Wyoming."

"Not many people for Montane," Kelly pointed out. "Between them, that's what, less than a million? Those were big empty states."

"More like three million, Before," Ava replied. "I looked it up. Sounds like they accepted refugees from the Dust Bowl, though. Then drafted them, like Oregon."

"Oh."

"Still, you're right. Oregon is bigger," Ava continued. "Twelve million? Plus however many California refugees they couldn't keep out. Could be a lot. They just have a lot of unfriendly border. Oh, and the nation south of Montane is called Rockies. That's the Four Corners – Utah, Colorado, Arizona, and New Mexico. Only the mountains are really habitable anymore. But Utah's pretty savvy with the deserts. They're teaching the others new tricks. Not that it matters to us."

"Non," Jean-Claude agreed. He sat back and drank some wine. "I can buy drugs through MSF. I need money."

Ava nodded, wondering how much money she should fork over to a charitable organization. What if Jean-Claude just took off with it? Then again, he could probably buy quite a lot for the price of a good used car, at wholesale instead of retail. And the right drugs could buy a lot of good will on the other side. Teaming up with Jean-Claude could give her expedition stature.

Teaming up with Kelly didn't offer much. Or did it? She calculated in her head.

"Would two thousand be enough, Jean-Claude?"

He grinned. "MSF would be very grateful! I make the arrangements. Ah, could I have in advance?"

Ava handed him a quartet of debit cards.

"And Kelly? Maybe you could buy us some food," Ava suggested, and pushed another debit card on her. That card was depleted. "Should be about a hundred left on there. You know the stuff, lightweight, no refrigeration required. A variety. Cheese, fruits, crackers, energy bars. Water purifier tablets."

Kelly jotted it down on a napkin. She wouldn't have thought of the water tablets. "Can do. And deliver it where?"

Ava hadn't told her where their hotel was yet. Kelly was slumming it in an overcrowded youth hostel nearby. "I'll tell you tomorrow." She held her hands up to forestall a hot retort. "I need to hear back from Jean-Claude. Then clear my plans with the boss. Relax, Kelly. You're a key part of the team now." She tipped her head to one side. "The boss might feel otherwise. And the plan isn't solid yet. But you can trust me. Can I trust you?"

In truth, Ava had been entirely trustworthy to Kelly, since they met back at HQ before Ohio. Kelly was the one who'd broken faith. Kelly blew out softly, then nodded. "You can trust me."

Ava continued, "I won't even ask you to make a choice between Canada and Hudson. Not yet. Just do the shopping." She smiled. "Date rape drugs. Really?"

Kelly extracted a miniature baggie from her waist pouch and pushed the pills between the pizza debris. She shrugged. "A guy wouldn't expect it."

Jean-Claude said, "Because women never rape men!"

Ava returned, "Maybe guys just aren't willing to admit it." She accepted the drugs and tucked them into her waist pack. You never knew.

~

Ava emerged from the elevator at her floor, still dripping rain.

Laurent waited for her, leaning on her room door, looking grim.

She smiled at him crookedly. "I'd invite you in, but it's against hotel policy. A drink in the lobby, perhaps?"

"I'm here on official business," Laurent said quietly. "Let us in."

"Do you have a warrant?" Ava inquired.

"A private word," he said. "Nothing more."

She opened the door and let him in. "Jana, low lights. Play downtime playlist. Volume three. Open the curtains." After three seconds to conclude her orders to Jana, she added for Laurent's benefit, "The view is nice."

Like Toronto, the lights of Vancouver died at curfew at 23:00. It was too early for that. Much of the city would remain bright for another hour and a half, though office lights in the towers were growing scarce. Sunset was theoretically an hour ago, but with the rain dark, the street lights had been on for hours. Ava enjoyed the way the clouds crept between the downtown skyscrapers, lit in all different shades of grey, tinged with red from building-top warning lights.

Laurent nodded. He hung his wet trench coat with Ava's poncho on the hooks by the door, then claimed one of the two compact armchairs by the window.

"Need a beer?" Ava offered. "I'm having water."

"I'm fine, thanks," Laurent said. He waited for her to take a seat. "Ms. Panic, your trip was approved to Vancouver. Your company represented to my government that your delivery would be in Vancouver."

"Yes, and I made delivery today," Ava ad-libbed. "My company is very grateful to your government." Perhaps that was too much. Companies and governments weren't people. They were incapable of feeling anything at all.

Laurent blinked. "Then why were you – Ava, you're insane. I warned you, even as an RCMP agent, I'm not allowed into the harbor waterfront near Chinatown." His beseeching eyes looked upset, as though he was here because he was honestly worried about her. "You were making plans to pay *Triads* to *smuggle* you into Oregon. Do you have any idea how dangerous that is?"

Ava took a sip of water. "I got that vibe, yeah." That was actually kind of sweet, that he was concerned about her.

"What were you thinking?" he demanded.

"Just sightseeing," Ava said. "My company would love to know more about Oregon. And I have a week or two to kill here."

"You're not leaving right away?" Laurent looked cheered by this. "You said you made your delivery."

"The response isn't ready yet," Ava said. "It'll be another week. Could be three. I don't know. Just thought I'd look around while I was here." She smiled at him warmly.

"Don't leave Vancouver without telling me," he begged her. "I'm trying to protect you, Ava."

"You're sweet. You're also in my bedroom. I didn't exactly invite you."

Laurent rose abruptly. "Ahem. Yes. I should – Good night, Ms. Panic." Trench coat on, he paused at the door and turned back. "Maybe I could show you around Wednesday? Or next weekend? I could trade days off. We could have Friday through Sunday."

"We'll see," she said. "Good night, Laurent."

After he left, Ava turned the lights off in the room to enjoy the view better. She wondered what it would be like to stay. To live in his apartment, attend the University of British Columbia. Who knew, maybe become a doctor or engineer herself. She could go yachting on weekends and live the high life.

While her friends back in Hudson scrabbled to get by. This winter there would not be enough to eat. Just how bad it would get remained to be seen. But the early signs weren't good. Hudson didn't have the food stockpiles. Most of the spring crops had already failed. They wouldn't even attempt the long-season crops, except under glass. Of the all-important orchard crops, the peaches were already an epic fail. Doubts lingered about the grapes and apples. If the corn or potatoes failed, they were in for a world of hurt.

And there was Cade.

Laurent was sweet. It could be fun to fall in love with a gentle romantic. She'd never be in fear for her life when Laurent lost his cool. She tried to imagine him even breaking a plate in anger. That picture made her giggle. No, he was safe. A well-adjusted Canadian *consumer,* doing all the right things and reaping the economic rewards.

Consumers had screwed up Ava's planet. The Rescos might dream of making the world safe for American capitalism again, someday. Apple survivors like Ava had other ideas. And the survivors would inherit the Earth. *Consumers* would die off, by and by. Maybe not in *Canada's Century.* But in America, the consumer past was dead.

Good riddance.

She considered sleeping on the floor, in token solidarity with Hudsons who didn't have enough to eat this night. But that was dumb. For better or worse, Hudson decided not to cut rations for the growing season. They left everyone strong to give their best shot at getting harvests in, battles won, and structural hard labor accomplished. Anyone who wanted shelter and a bed could find them. That was as much consumer creature comfort as anyone needed.

It was better than she and Cade had during the Starve.

Laurent could never understand her the way Cade did. No one could.

25

Interesting fact: Navigation in Puget Sound was tricky even before the sudden sea level rise. Tides at Seattle and Vancouver ranged up to 16 feet, with asymmetric highs and lows. For instance, a day's successive tides might be 11 feet high, 7 feet low, 9 feet high, 1 foot low. 'Spring tides,' when sun and moon aligned, were more extreme. The Sound was riddled with reefs and treacherous currents. Newly flooded lowlands and current patterns were poorly mapped, and not yet stabilized.

"You finally let me see your secret lair," Kelly grumbled the next evening. "Sweet crib." She regarded the funky totem face on Ava's headboard. The totem head showed its tongue stuck out at her. "What is that supposed to be?"

"Frog. Maybe," Ava replied. "Make yourself at home. For a week or so." She dug into the bag of supplies Kelly had brought. "Good job, Kell. Water pills, check."

Kelly sank to the bed, eyes on Ava, waiting for her to elaborate.

Ava shifted the shopping bag to the top of her luggage, then joined Kelly on the bed. "I'd like you to be my backup. You stay here in Vancouver. Live in my room. Give us a head start, no one looking for us. Twenty-four hours should be enough. But try to spin it out. I don't dare leave much detail about my plans where the Canadians can find it. But if I don't come back, I want someone to come get me. Those details are with you, and on my phone. Meet Jana."

Kelly's eyebrows rose. She accepted the phone. Jana was currently set to display Ava's text history with Laurent. Kelly scrolled through it for a moment. "You're a tease."

"He knows I have a boyfriend," Ava defended. "And he's RCMP – a Mountie, assigned to watch me. But, yeah. He's decorative."

"Not my type."

"You have a type? I thought that was a guy thing."

Kelly said, "Looks is a guy thing. Personality is a girl thing. He's too…clean."

Ava chuckled. "I guess. But Cade's pretty clean, too. I never had a boyfriend besides Cade."

Kelly boggled. "You're kidding! Really?"

Ava nodded. "Sad but true. Anyway, you willing?"

Kelly frowned in thought. "I have to give up my asylum application?"

"Up to you," Ava said. "But I'll leave my Western Civ textbook with you. In case you want to keep up with the cohort."

The boss had encouraged that one college freshman class for all of their crop of new hires. He hoped it would provide a unifying experience, and a common intellectual framework and vocabulary. Some of the previous agents, like Cade and Daneel, were in the course, too. In a nation where even high school was an extreme luxury, the company offering free college distance education was a treasured perk. And it was fun to be in class together with people who had so much in common. The company recruited some highly intelligent oddballs. This novel sense of belonging and fitting in was like catnip to the recruits.

Kelly's eyes fell longingly on the hefty textbook, lying on the bed stand. Kelly had left her copy behind at HQ in Elmira, since Ava brought hers along to Ohio with them.

"It can't be that simple," Kelly whispered. "I go back to Hudson like nothing happened."

"Probably not," Ava agreed. "But this puts you one step closer to the boss's good graces. And you get a nice room in Vancouver. The artwork grows on you." She pointed to the headboard frog with attitude.

"I complete the mission if you don't?"

"No. You contact the boss. Maybe he'll ask you to come after me. Maybe he'll tell you to hang tight until he can get someone else out here. You're my lifeline."

"The boss agreed to this?" Kelly asked.

"He was grumpy," Ava allowed. "But it's my call."

Kelly blinked back a tear. "Hell, yeah. I'll do it. Thank you. But, why? I've been a real shit to you."

"You're on my team," Ava replied. How to explain this? "I feel like I let you down in Ohio. There was this poster in my doctor's office when I was a kid. 'Love is like algebra. Someone has to show you how to do it.' Respect. Trust. Teamwork. Someone has to show you. In training you guys, I was so focused on the world that I overlooked the people."

Yeah, that felt right. Skull's encouragement, that Ava and Rahema were his best so far among the West Point cohort, gave Ava confidence.

"Kelly, I think you belong with the company. And you'll never belong in Canada. At least that's how it is for me. I can't outgrow the Starve. I'll always be an apple. Back in Ohio, you were so busy playing good girl that you weren't real with us. I should have called you on that. Drawn you out. Good girl was an act. Mousy and eager to please. That wasn't you."

"You didn't do anything wrong in Ohio, Ava," Kelly said. "It was me. I didn't know how to connect. Still don't. I was a loner in high school. West Point was hell for me in the Jersey companies. Kids in my face all day and night. But I never fit in."

Ava could see that. Kelly's upbringing had more in common with the South Jersey recruits, not the inner city types. But she was Apple Zone, and survived Ebola. Yet she never ran with the urban gangs. She wouldn't relate to the North Jersey starve-lings.

"Open up," Ava advised. "Risk a little. Not too much. I think I can trust you this much. Kelly, I want to go home to Hudson. To Cade, and the boss. Be my lifeline. Make sure I get out of Oregon. Or if not, help them get closure, so they know."

"Will do."

"Oh, and Kelly? The boss is kind of squeamish about sex work. Don't lie to him, but try to underplay that. You know. Say, this man told me X. Not, I bribed him with sex to get him to tell me X."

"That's not good strategy?"

Ava shrugged. "Up to you. Just, don't tell men about it if you can avoid it."

Kelly nodded thoughtfully. "Because men don't respect whores."

"They really don't."

"They're easy to manipulate with sex," Kelly said.

"That probably bugs them, too," Ava agreed. "I'm not saying to lie. Just don't lie, don't tell, until the boss pushes for details."

She grabbed the ouiPhone manual from her luggage and belly-flopped back onto the bed. Kelly rolled beside her. The girls put their heads together. Ava taught Kelly how her data storage and communications protocols worked.

~

"IT'S PAST CURFEW, MISS PANIC," THE FRONT DESK NIGHT MAN HAILED her. Kirkman, said his name badge. At 03:00, it was more like before curfew lifted.

"Yes, I'm helping Dr. Alarie with his luggage," Ava replied. "He'll be down in a moment to check out."

The second elevator bell pinged after a few minutes. The doors opened to disgorge Jean-Claude and his suitcases, one new and filled to bursting with medical supplies for Washo, now called Oregon throughout. Ava was navigating one of his duffels and his briefcase, in addition to her own smaller duffel. The big one, containing most of her wardrobe, she left with Kelly back in the room.

Jean-Claude checked out quickly. They headed out on the dim street. He ordered an auto-cab with his own phone, to pick them up at the nearest intersection.

The taxi bore them to their rendezvous in a commuter lot beside

Canadian Highway 1 in Burnaby, a suburb southwest of downtown Vancouver.

Fortunately for their nerves, a generously sized SUV flashed its headlights once as they pulled into the parking lot. After a few false starts, Jean-Claude gave up on how to instruct the automated taxi to navigate to the SUV. They just dumped all their stuff on the wet pavement and told the thing to go away. The laden sports van pulled up to them instead.

"Donal! So good of you!" Jean-Claude greeted the driver who clambered out. He embraced the taller, rangy man. "Ava Panic, this is Dr. Donal Friesen."

"Glad to meet you, Ava," Donal replied. "My son Gordy. About your age."

Gordy stepped around the car to exchange handshakes as well, with a diffident nod. "High school?" he asked Ava.

"Just graduated," Ava replied. "Taking my first college course now, distance ed." Technically, she hadn't graduated quite yet. But she hoped to pass her final GED English exam real soon now. Work schedule permitting.

"Cool! Same," Gordy said, grabbing up the heaviest bags. "Well, college in the fall." Donal popped the hatchback for loading with his remote. They dragged the rest of their gear to pass in to Gordy for stowage.

The cargo space was well stuffed. Ava noted life vests, medical kit, maybe some navigational gear. An inflatable Kodiak-style boat, small outboard engine, and four fuel cans took up a lot of room.

"You don't store this at the marina?" Ava asked. They kept their voices low. But they seemed to be alone in the dark world, except when a chance set of headlights stabbed past on the Trans-Canada highway.

Donal said, "Our boat is in Vancouver. That's a long sail, maybe eighty kilometers each way. No, we'll rent a ten meter out of Surrey, cut the trip to thirty kilometers."

"Even sixty round trip is a lot," Gordy told Ava. "Expect a windy day."

Under the car's dome light, the boy clearly favored his dad, with a lean rangy frame not quite filled in yet. He might have another inch or two to grow. He had clear open blue eyes and splotchy freckles, with a reddish thatch of hair. Donal's hair had turned a dignified silver. But there was no question the sportsman remained fit and hale.

"Check the outboard," Donal prompted his son.

Gordy grabbed the little engine and wiggled it in demonstration. "It's secure, Da. Trust me." He shot a bashful smile at Ava.

She wasn't sure what he meant by that smile. Maybe, *'Parents, what can you do? They never believe you've grown up.'* She felt jealous that he had a dad showing him the ropes as he entered manhood.

Not that Tata, her own father, could manage more than a canoe. Ava knew more about sailing than Tata did. He used to share what he did know, though, patiently and thoroughly. He started teaching her to drive a rental car the summer before Ebola. *I miss you, Tata.* Usually it was Deda, her grandfather, she remembered, the one who spent the most time with her. It felt nice to be reminded of Tata and Mama once in a while, too.

Their luggage secured, they climbed into seats. Donal tossed the key to Gordy to drive for the next leg. Soon they were on Highway 1 headed east.

Donal turned and asked, "Jean-Claude, how much experience do you have sailing?"

"Ah, none, sorry," Jean-Claude replied from behind Gordy. "I'm happy to do whatever I'm told."

"Alright," Donal said. "Ava?"

"I took a few sailing classes," Ava said. She considered whether it was safe to elaborate. But a kid from Minnesota could have lived elsewhere beforehand, or traveled on vacation. She certainly had. So she elaborated, "I was eleven, though. And it was just a lake in Texas. Pretty different."

"Texas! Very different," Donal agreed. "Where are you from?"

"St. Paul, Minnesota," Ava replied.

Jean-Claude made a disapproving negative sound.

"Ava?" Donal prompted, eyes narrowed. "It doesn't matter what the truth is. So long as it's the truth."

The man's bearing and tone oddly reminded her more of the officers she'd met in Brooklyn than the doctors Alarie and Devereaux. Ava took Jean-Claude's point. Donal was putting his family and future on the line. He deserved some truth in return.

"My family moved around a lot," she admitted. "We left St. Paul when I was ten. Texas when I was twelve. New York since then. It's called Hudson now."

Donal glanced at his son. "New York state?"

"New York City," Ava replied. "We call it the Apple now. What's left of it. I left the city a half year ago for army boot camp. That led to my current job."

Donal paused a moment to think that over. "You were in the city when Ebola broke out?"

"Yes, sir. I survived Ebola. My boyfriend, too. Our parents didn't make it." Well, Cade's father survived. But he was remarried and living in Jersey. Cade didn't see him again for years, at the same time Ava left for boot camp.

"God bless you," Donal murmured, a stern frown on his face. "I hear the kids formed gangs in the city. Brutal ones."

"I was gang royalty, yes," Ava replied. "My boyfriend ruled the gang. I was what we called 'queen bee.' I led the girls and children."

She fished out her phone – the one she bought for Daneel. She cloned its contents and configuration from Jana, and named her Jona. Her original ouiPhone Jana stayed with Kelly as a decoy. She planned to show Donal the photo of her and Cade on the Staten Island Ferry. But on a whim, she picked the picture of herself with Jeremy in Sioux Lookout instead.

"We were brutal as the rest, sir," she said. "We had to be. But we saved over seven hundred young kids. This is one. He got adopted up to Canada. I ran into him in Sioux Lookout." She handed him the phone. "I'm not proud of all I did during the Starve, sir. But I am proud of that."

Donal studied the photo, and held the phone for his son to take a look without taking his eyes off the highway too much. This wasn't a self-driving sort of SUV. Or perhaps they just didn't choose to engage that feature.

Flashing amber lights and warning signs advised of a detour ahead.

Donal handed the phone back to her. She selected the ferry photo and handed it forward to him again.

"My boyfriend Cade and me, a year ago. We had food back in the city by then. Some, anyway. Jeremy – the boy in the last picture – the Navy took the younger kids away a few months before." She didn't remember when, except it was winter.

Donal carefully shared the picture with Gordy again. By then he was negotiating the exit onto a bypass road. Apparently the ocean cut significantly farther east than it used to. The Highway 1 bridge was out going south and east, which necessitated a 20 km detour while the Canadian government began construction on a new interstate-grade road bed to the site for a new bridge.

"Thank you for being honest with me," Donal said, handing Jona back to her. "As captain on a ship, I need to know my crew. Why are you going to Seattle?"

"I'm sorry, sir. I can't be as forthcoming about that," Ava said. "I'm a courier. My employers want me to deliver something to their counterparts in Oregon."

"Hell of a trip," Donal acknowledged. "Alright. Just so you know, I served in the Coast Guard. Did my time in MSF like Jean-Claude. Settled down to raise my family. But the world's gone to hell in the meantime. May be about time to get back in the saddle and do something about that."

Ava judged the man as nearing sixty. She didn't doubt for a minute he had more to give.

~

"Boot camp, you said," Donal murmured to Ava. "Look over those, will you? See if you think you can handle any against pirates."

At the marina, Donal dispatched Jean-Claude and Gordy to fill the gas cans. He brought Ava with him to the rental office. The side table he waved her toward bore an assortment of weapons. Donal continued to the rental counter.

"Yes, sir," Ava agreed. But first she dug into her waist pack and drew out a sheaf of currency. "I'd like to contribute."

Donal shook his head minutely. Ava stuffed the money away and turned to the guns.

The harpoons were interesting, but she didn't know how to use one. She selected an AK-47 assault rifle and ammo, a grenade launcher attachment and grenades, and a half dozen marine flares. She carried them to the counter, where the two men consulted over a nautical chart.

Donal looked over her selections and nodded. "We'll rent these, too, Brent."

"That's included if you have crew who can use them," Brent replied, a man possibly younger, but less fit. "I'll only charge you for expended rounds. So long as you keep the rest dry. And Donal, don't shoot the big junk. That comes at you, you run like hell and call the Coast Guard."

They completed a purely cash transaction while Ava waited with her armaments outside the door in the twilight. When Donal came out, she asked, "You don't know how to use these, sir?"

"I do indeed," he replied with a smile. "But if it comes to a fight, I need to focus on the boat handling." He strode toward their slip, Ava rushing to keep up with his long strides.

"Pirates?" she inquired.

"Chinese opium trade out of Vancouver," he murmured grimly.

Oh, yeah, Ava thought. That was the other reason she didn't mind working for the company. Their precisely controlled business, narcotics delivered solely under the discretion of the Rescos, beat hell out of letting black market drug cartels run amok. Canada wasn't ahead of America on every innovation these days.

They clambered aboard their rental 33-footer, the *Canada Day* out of Surrey, and prepared for departure on the tide.

~

"*Canada Day, Canada Day!* This is Canadian Coast Guard vessel *Vector*. Over," squawked the radio.

The sky was lightening with a steady rain. They'd just cut the engines to proceed under sail, after passing the last of the harbor channel buoys. With clouds dripping down to the sea, and the veiled sun barely above the horizon, the mountains and shore were rapidly disappearing from Ava's view. For the moment, Gordy had her minding the mainsail sheet as a refresher lesson on how to sail. The *'sheets'* were the lines used to control how close the aluminum *'boom'* at the bottom of the triangular sail hugged the boat's hull. *'Refresher'* was a bit optimistic. Ava had never sailed in a 33-foot yacht, let alone crewed one. And the stark wild mountain beauty of Puget Sound was a far cry from a glassy-calm man-made lake steaming below the hot Texas sun.

Jean-Claude stuck his head up from the galley, curious about the radio. He'd proven to have no sea legs. Donal had sent him below to fix brunch.

Dr. Donal, at the wheel, picked up the button-press radio mike holstered at the side of the helm. "*Vector,* this is *Canada Day.* Switch channel 68. Over." After he let go the button, he explained to Ava, "We don't tie up the hailing frequency talking."

Ava nodded, intrigued.

Meanwhile the radio confirmed, "*Vector* switching to channel 68. Over."

Donal completed the channel switch. "*Vector,* this is *Canada Day.* Good morning. What can I do for you? Over."

Donal didn't seem concerned. To Ava, he looked fey and exhilarated to be under way in the cold wind under spitting rain, cutting through sizable waves.

"*Canada Day,* this is *Vector.* Your current heading crosses into American waters in half a kilometer. What are you doing? Over."

"Understood, *Vector.* That's the only way out of the bay. Over."

"A comedian. Who are you, and where are you going, *Canada Day?* Over."

A bit of cloud shifted, and Ava spotted a red junk emerging from the mist. When Bert said 'big junk,' it hadn't occurred to her that he meant the Chinese sailboat sort of *'junk.'* In retrospect, that made sense.

An area with so many wealthy Chinese would see some choose their traditional style of boat.

She pointed toward the distinctive trapezoidal battened sails, with angled booms at top and bottom. They looked like partly spread Oriental fans. "Donal!" She snapped some quick photos with Jona.

He looked over his right shoulder where she pointed, and sized it up. He turned back and nodded reassurance to her. "*Vector,* this is Doctor Donal Friesen. My crew is my adult son Gordon."

He grinned proudly at Gordy, sitting across the boat from Ava. Gordy held up a left fist as though to show off his bicep. Ava matched his fist, and grinned back at him.

Donal continued on the radio, "I have been advised by the rental company not to give specifics over the radio about my plans. Too many ears. We're headed near Gulf Islands. There's a bit of America in the way. The boat's owner approved my plans. Over."

"*Canada Day,* understood. Be careful out there. *Vector* out."

Ava called to Gordy, sitting on the bench across from her, "The Coast Guard won't stop us crossing into America?"

Gordy shrugged and pointed toward a darkening to the right of the bay. "Point Roberts. It's American. Other side, too. We cross the 49th parallel in a few minutes." He laughed. "This is Boundary Bay."

"No other way out of the bay," she repeated. Her grin was becoming a permanent fixture on her face. This was a blast!

A raincloud lowered to swallow up the red junk behind them. Ava was fervently grateful she was on this boat, and not that one.

26

Interesting fact: The historical Oregon Territory included the old states of Oregon, Washington, Idaho, plus Montana and Wyoming west of the continental divide.

"Porpoises!" Gordy called, pointing.

Ava stood to capture photos of the frolicking pod leaping from the water, racing the flying sailboat. She'd already caught pictures of seals and a small pod of orcas, and an otter. They were miles from shore now, pyramidal waves heaving, streaked with white. Ava's lips tasted of salt from the constant fine spray.

"Ava, hold onto the boat better than that," Donal cautioned from the helm.

She grinned and sat again on the starboard bench cushions, feet braced on the opposite bench, bringing her center of gravity safely back below the rail. His point was well taken. The *Canada Day* was currently canted 20 degrees to port, running tight alongside a brisk wind at 18 kph, lurching as she broke the waves. Digital readouts mounted on the back of the cabin conveyed this information, as well as depth and wind speed and direction, helping the passengers and crew share the sailing thrills with the captain.

The rain had backed off them for the moment, the cloud cover rising. Here and there in the distance cloud and rain still reached fingers down to touch the sea and steep forested land.

Ava wished the clouds would break for a while so she could see the magnificent mountains ringing the Sound. Porpoises were an excellent consolation prize.

"Ava, put the phone away," Donal instructed. "Prepare to come about."

This evolution took place regularly, as the boat zigzagged into the wind. The mainsail needed to travel to the other side for a while. Gordy went forward to manage the adjustments to the jib, the no-boom sail in front. Ava's brief and long ago sailing lessons hadn't included a jib. No one offered to teach her now. Donal kept his passengers in the stern, behind or inside the cabin, preferably applying butts to the seat cushions, with their feet safely in the well before the wheel.

Ava carefully crouched to the other side and coiled up the tail of her main sheet line, in position to shift. "Ready!" she reported. A few moments later Gordy sang out the same from the bow.

"Coming about," Donal reported, and turned the wheel to the right, starboard, away from the mainsail.

Ava unclamped the line and ducked, pushing the mainsail boom before her across to the other side. In a race, the crew would do all this while spilling the least possible speed. In open water without a race, or a safety motorboat, they worked more carefully. But as sailors, Donal and Gordy were too good to be sloppy.

Ava stepped to starboard pushing the boom before her, to clamp off her sheet on that side. Donal reached to grab the boom and add his strength to push it across. As the boom crossed the boat's mid-line, a gust could swing the mainsail either way.

Unfortunately, it did just that. A gust slammed the sail back into Ava just as a wave rocked the boat down on her side. She stumbled back, and the line in her hand yanked her over the railing. She spun and grabbed the railing to jack-knife over the side, her whole torso overboard, hanging with her face mere inches from the heaving Sound.

Ava yelled, 'Woot!' and laughed out loud. The temptation was almost overwhelming to let go one hand to reach down into the rushing water. She'd fall in for sure if she did, though.

In two seconds, Donal grabbed the back of her life preserver and hauled her back up, still laughing.

"You'll do," he said, grinning back. "Let's try that again."

In a few minutes, Ava had the main sheet properly cleated to starboard, and shifted back to sit on the left to add her scant weight to the boat's high side. They settled onto the new tack, canted a bit less now. Gordy stayed in the bow for a bit, lying on the deck to savor the view.

The clouds finally broke. A teasing hole of blue grew and spread across the sky. The last gray ragged fingers of rain lifted up and dissipated to port. Color and clarity leeched into the dark green forested shore. As the clouds lifted still further, the sun struck a snow-capped mountain beyond. Ava's mouth hung open in awe.

"Mount Baker," Donal told her. "That's a pretty shot."

She nodded and captured the view with Jona. "How far is it?"

"Fifty kilometers maybe," he replied. He grinned at Ava's boggled reaction. "It's big, eh?"

Ava let the understatement pass with a smile. She was too busy clicking pictures. She ducked low to work her way around, trying to capture 360 degrees of the panorama. Gordy cordially rolled out of her way in the bow. She was working her way down the other side of the boat when another bank of raincloud pulled upward. There was another boat over there.

She zoomed in on the sails of a red junk, to take a better picture of it. Back near Surrey, the junk had been distant and veiled by rain, not much bigger than their own boat.

This was a different junk. As the fog thinned, and her picture improved, Ava realized this was a much bigger ship. Instead of a little cabin in the middle, this one had a cabin the size of a small house. Its raised stern was double-decker, with some kind of roofed promenade on top. It wasn't really red, just a reddish shade of brown, with gold trim. Jaunty pennons of true red and yellow danced from the top of its three masts. To her unpracticed eye, it seemed to be running parallel to them.

"Donal!" she called. "Big red junk!"

Donal raised binoculars to take a good look. Gordy clambered back from his sunspot in the bow, and Jean-Claude stuck his head up from the cabin. Ava passed Jona to them to take a look.

"How far away is that?" Ava asked.

"Few kilometers," Donal gauged, "maybe." He passed the binoculars to Gordy. "New job. Watch his bearing. If he starts closing, let me know."

"Can we track it on the radar?" Gordy asked practically.

"Radar doesn't show anything," Donal reported. "Son, that may be the gun boat supporting the local smugglers and pirates." He clapped a hand on his son's shoulder and looked him in the eye.

Gordy gulped, but nodded. Donal nodded back.

Ava tried to gauge the challenge. "Should I get the grenade launcher?"

Donal said, "No. If he closes, we run. Annoying him won't help."

"How big is that boat?" Jean-Claude inquired. Over water, it was difficult to judge size or distance. He and Ava didn't have the experience.

"Fifteen, twenty meters," Donal guessed. "Technically, it's a ship, not a boat. Small one. But it has three masts and a bowsprit."

"But radar can't see it?" Ava asked, surprised.

Donal shook his head and pointed up the mast to a large ball with folded-in concave sides, like sheet metal origami. "See that round thing? That's our radar reflector. The sea is big. We're small, and don't have a lot of metal. Same for him. We have to work at being visible to radar. He doesn't want to be seen."

"Da, he's turning," Gordy reported. "Toward us."

"Jean-Claude, stay below," Donal ordered. "Close the hatch."

Gordy said nervously, "We're caught between him and the shore, Da."

"I know where the shore is, son," Donal said. "Let's come about. Gordy, we're pulling a one-eighty."

That would send them back toward Canada. "We don't run before the wind?" Ava asked. They would go fastest that way, with the wind behind them.

"That would take us toward our friend over there," Donal said mildly. "We're aiming for behind him. And hopefully not worth his trouble."

Ava and Gordy handled the sails. They came to their backtrack heading and settled into it. Gordy returned promptly to the stern and took up binoculars again. Ava checked through Jona's zoom lens, and saw almost as well as he did, with a sinking feeling.

"He's coming about, Da," Gordy reported. He handed over the binoculars.

"I see that," Donal agreed. He sighed. "Come about again, due south this time. That's about two hundred degrees, Gordy. Let's see who's faster."

They came about again. This time, Donal micro-managed the lay of the sails. He dragged Jean-Claude back on deck to position his weight in the right spot for them to lay on the speed. Their original heading tacked into the offshore wind. Now they pushed nearly perpendicular to it, a direction Donal explained that he hoped was less than ideal for a round-bottomed junk with a wind-catching superstructure.

But this was no 18th century junk. Their opponent was a modern ship with junk-rigged sails and oriental trimming. He didn't appear to have any trouble at all heading the same direction they did, and angling toward them.

After a few minutes, the radio squawked. "Oregon Coast Guard vessel *Sea Lion* to unidentified sailboat. You seem confused. Over."

Donal snatched up the radio. Again they traded identification on the hailing channel, then switched to channel 68. "*Sea Lion,* this is *Canada Day,* a ten-meter sailboat out of Surrey. Delighted to hear from you! Where are you? Over." He eagerly checked his radar. "Gordy! Ahead of us, maybe."

Gordy searched the southern waters with his binoculars. Ava looked too, but his optics were more powerful. They were also going a lot faster on this heading, and she didn't care to leave her assigned seat, which cut into her view.

"*Sea Lion* is south of you, *Canada Day.* Is there a problem? Over."

"*Sea Lion,* a large red junk has taken an interest in us. Approximately two kilometers to our starboard, west, and closing. *Canada Day,* over."

"I see it, Da," Gordy reported. *"Sea Lion.* She's not much bigger than we are."

Apparently *Sea Lion* shared the same concern. After a long pause, they resumed, *"Canada Day,* this is *Sea Lion.* How big a red junk? Over."

Donal described the ship. The Oregon Coast Guard took even longer to get back to them this time.

"Sorry, *Canada Day,* our orders are not to engage. Advise turning for shore. Avoid Birch Bay. Shoot for halfway between Point Whitehorn and Cherry Point. There's a pier if you can get far enough south. *Sea Lion* will rendezvous. Requesting bigger guns for backup. Over."

"Roger that, *Sea Lion. Canada Day* out." Donal switched back to the hailing frequency and hung up the radio.

"Shoal water, Da," Gordy pointed out sadly.

"There goes our deposit if we're grounded," Donal agreed. "Can't be helped."

They turned as close as they could to the wind, and angled toward the shore. Directly into the wind was a direction the sailboat couldn't go except with the engine. The depth gauge looked fine at first, with 40 meters below the keel. From the water, it wasn't readily apparently why they were advised to avoid Birch Bay, a broad opening off to their left. The wooded shores and mudflats looked peaceable enough at first.

Then Ava spotted a more modest red junk in there through Jona's lens, and snapped a picture. She advised Donal, who in turn forwarded the sighting to *Sea Lion.* They responded that they were aware of smugglers in Birch Bay, but were likewise under orders not to go in there without backup. Apparently the smugglers had shore guns. No one had gotten around to clearing them out of there yet.

Yet? Ava wondered. *Or have they decided to leave it be?* There were reasons to leave a known threat in place. For one thing, a known problem spot was more manageable than a shifting target. They were sure to relocate if forced to leave. For another, the smugglers might be bringing in useful goods. Canada's smugglers might be Oregon's saviors, or vice versa. Or more likely, they were a mixed bag of good and evil to all parties.

The wooded shore of Point Whitehorn suddenly drew close off

their port side. The depth gauge jumped from 40 to 9 meters in a flash. The beach was an empty stretch of grey rocks, rising abruptly into cliffs. Ava spotted no people, nor even seals. Donal laid off the wind a little further to stay offshore and sail parallel to the deserted coast.

Ava stared fixedly at that near shore, heart thudding. The Pacific waters were icy, their currents strong. If they had to abandon ship under fire, she'd need to swim for those forbidding cliffs, her limbs growing numb. Her black box was in her waist pack, under her life vest. She didn't imagine salt water would be good for the flash drive inside. After she drove across the sunken Chesapeake Bay Bridge last month, Cade's mechanic back in Elmira had waxed sarcastic on that point. He recommended that Cade sell his beloved SUV for scrap and buy another. He warned that Darcy's microprocessors might be glitched forevermore. Jona might survive, though. The ouiPhone claimed to be waterproof.

The red junk was less than a kilometer away now. Twice as long meant eight times as big as *Canada Day.* Its red fans of sails were truly impressive. But *Sea Lion* was visible to the bare eye now. They could hope the red junk didn't want to tangle with the Coast Guard.

"The junk is coming about, Da!" Gordy called out triumphantly. "Heading out to sea, running before the wind."

Ava blew out, long and slow, and rubbed sweating hands on sea-damp jeans.

"Hallelujah," Donal acknowledged. "Ava, Jean-Claude. We could run. I don't advise it. If we meet up with *Sea Lion,* I can turn you over into official Oregon hands. If we turn out to sea now, we're following the ship we just ran away from. Or we could head back to Surrey."

Jean-Claude shrugged. "I'm happy to speak to the Coast Guard. Ava?"

Ava nodded. "Might as well."

OCGS *SEA LION* WAS INDEED NOT MUCH BIGGER THAN *CANADA DAY.* THE white and red motorboat simply drew alongside and threw a couple ropes across to keep them idling together for conversation.

Jean-Claude presented his case, that he was with Médecins Sans Frontières, MSF, and sought to travel and treat disadvantaged groups in Oregon. MSF was concerned and wanted to know more about Oregon's situation. He'd heard there might be need of medical help near the California border, and on the fire lines. He hauled out the medical stash Ava had bankrolled him to bring, and displayed it.

To Ava's eye, the American Coast Guardsmen weren't quite as implacable as Miller and his crew on the bridge from Detroit to Windsor. But they came close. They listened to Jean-Claude's story with nary a twitch.

The skipper, Gonzalez, neither granted nor denied Jean-Claude's request. Rather he turned to Ava, whom Donal indicated was also headed to Oregon. "What's your story?"

"I'm a courier, sir," Ava said. "I have a delivery to make in Oregon." She swallowed. "From Hudson. That's the country that used to be New York–New Jersey, plus New England." Pennsylvania and Delmarva were still in flux, though everyone assumed they would join Hudson. But so far away, she didn't see that the details mattered to these hard men on a boat in Puget Sound.

"Guardsman," Gonzalez corrected on automatic. "Or skipper. I'm not a sir."

"Yes, skipper. Sorry," Ava said.

"You're a long way from home," Gonzalez said. "Who's the package for?"

Ava frowned. This was the hard part. "We're not exactly sure. In Hudson, we have Army officers called Rescos. They manage civilians. Do you have Rescos in Oregon?"

"Haven't heard of that," Gonzalez said. "Rescos."

Ava wasn't surprised. The librarian in Vancouver hadn't heard of them either. "Is Oregon under martial law?"

"It is," Gonzalez agreed.

"Is there a Major Marcus Wetherby in Seattle? Might be a light colonel."

Gonzalez narrowed his eyes, but shrugged. "I'm not Army, miss."

"I'd like to go to Seattle and look, skipper," Ava asked humbly. "I've come a long way to make this delivery."

Gonzalez nodded slowly, keeping his poker face. "Alright. And you, Dr. Friesen. What do you want?"

"To deliver these two to Oregon, then return to the marina in Surrey with my son. Preferably today."

"Alright. You two, grab your gear and transfer across. Doctor, if that junk keeps receding, we can escort you a little way. Get you past Birch Bay, anyway, and headed home."

"Thank you, skipper," Donal replied.

"You *will* head home to Canada," Gonzalez reiterated. "And stay there."

"Yes, skipper," Donal agreed, in his best attempt at meekness. Meek wasn't his forte. Command of a ship, or a surgical team, was more Dr. Donal's speed.

Gordy helped Ava and Jean-Claude haul their stuff from the cabin's bedroom, and pass it across to the Coast Guard Search and Rescue boat. Donal chatted with the guardsmen about boating conditions in the Sound and progress charting the new hazards since the rapid sea level rise in February.

And then it was time to go. Donal and Jean-Claude traded handshake, hug, and kisses on both cheeks in farewell. Ava and Gordy's farewells were physically more shy, but heartfelt. Ava gave the Friesens a burner phone bought just for the purpose, and asked them to contact Kelly back in Vancouver, and let her know Ava got this far.

Donal requested they not contact him again this month. Smuggling people out of Canada could get him in a lot of hot water with the authorities. And MSF might need him to do it again.

Ava and Jean-Claude clambered up a ladder to board the *Sea Lion,* and they cast off.

"Dr. Friesen?" Gonzalez called as a parting shot. "Don't do this again. If this MSF needs to send doctors, and this Hudson needs to send couriers, they need to present themselves at a land border and make their case. These waters are too dangerous."

Donal nodded respect, and got busy adjusting his sails into the wind again.

27

Interesting fact: Oregon's neighbor to the east, the Montane Territory – the ex-states of Idaho, Montana, and Wyoming – did not style itself as a nation.

"Colonel Marcus Wetherby?" Ava asked over the phone. She had an actual land line, with an old-fashioned hefty two-lobed handset attached to its base unit by a pigtail cord. The Coast Guard station dispatcher in Bellingham, Daniels, set up the call for her in a private office.

"Yes?"

"This is Ava Panic. I'm a courier from Hudson. I was hoping you could help me deliver a very special package, from your Resco peers in the Northeast."

"Ms. Panic, I'm sorry, but I don't understand. I'm very busy –"

"Charles Schwabacher sent me," Ava rushed to say, before he could hang up. "The general of Ohio. And his aide, Arturo Porta. He said his nickname was Deck when you knew him, and you were Goonie. I work for Kyle Sullivan, Skull."

Silence came from Marcus Wetherby – Goonie.

"Sir, are you still there?" Ava pleaded.

"Yes," Marcus bit out.

Ava blew out in relief. "Sir, may I speak with you privately in Seattle?"

Dispatcher Daniels had located the man for her. Wetherby had indeed been promoted to lieutenant colonel since Major Porta last knew him. But there was no exact equivalent of the Resco role in Oregon. As in the small state of Connecticut in the East, Oregon's martial rulers had shored up existing local and state government structures to manage the civilians. Lt. Col. Wetherby managed not human, but natural resources. His turf was the northwest quadrant of Oregon, or western ex-Washington state. He was a lead resource coordinator, in a sense.

Wetherby answered slowly. "Ms. Panic... Oregon wants no part of those people."

Oops. "Sir, I'm not sure what you mean by 'those people,'" Ava replied. "Hudson and Ohio are the largest successor nations of the ex-United States. They want to discuss something with their peers in Oregon. Something sensitive. Sir, I've traveled all the way from Cleveland to deliver this. It took me two weeks to get here. Plus a boatload of money, and favors from the Canadian government. Please help me?"

Ava bit her lip in anxiety. If Wetherby said no, her task in Oregon got a lot harder. Her only other lead was the man who murdered California. Contacting him was a last resort.

"Alright," Wetherby said grudgingly. "Meet me in front of Seattle HQ at ten hundred hours tomorrow."

"How do I –" Ava began.

He hung up on her.

How do I get to Seattle? was what she intended to ask.

Ava blew out slowly and laid the phone handset back on its cradle. That wasn't the reception she'd been hoping for.

~

"You don't have to come with me, you know," Ava told Jean-Claude, as they plodded across Bellingham. The Coast Guard dispatcher seemed to think walking was the obvious and only way to cross town to I-5, the interstate highway south to Seattle. There were other pedestrians and bicycles on the city streets. The few motor vehicles were military.

She paused to snap a picture of an 'Oregon Health' clinic, and yawned mightily. She only managed a few hours sleep, sharing the hotel bed with Kelly, before she was up and going before dawn this morning.

Jean-Claude shrugged. "We come so far together. I want to know you are OK. Besides, I do not know Oregon either. Maybe I return to Canada with you."

"Well, thanks," Ava said, and picked up his luggage handle again. For the Oregon leg of the trip, she'd downgraded to the small duffel she could sling on her back. Jean-Claude still bore all his worldly goods, plus the medical supplies she'd paid for. She rolled the wheeled suitcase of those across town for him.

Bellingham offered bus service to Seattle, the dispatcher had informed them. It left every morning at 9 a.m. and cost $160 Oregon. By this time, it was past noon. Ava had no local currency, and needed to be in Seattle by 10 a.m. tomorrow. The dispatcher's next suggestion was to hitchhike down Interstate 5.

They rolled the suitcases another couple blocks, and found themselves at the entrance ramp to the highway.

"Oh, that wasn't bad," Jean-Claude exclaimed. "Less than a mile."

"Yeah," Ava agreed absently, eyeing the establishments clustered about the foot of the ramp. "Let's try the gas station."

She thoughtfully clicked a picture of it when they got closer. 'Oregon Gas' it proclaimed on a painted sign. All the lit plastic signs of the pre-Calm chain store had been removed, as well as the prices at the pumps. Instead an A-frame chalkboard outside the door bore a table of codes she didn't understand. She asked Jean-Claude to stay at the curb with their stuff while she went inside to inquire.

A man looked up warily from his reading tablet behind the counter as the door jingled. She approached him with a smile.

"Excuse me, sir," Ava began. "We're hoping to hitchhike to –"

"Get out," he said. "Deserters aren't welcome here!"

"But I'm not a –"

He drew a pistol on her. "No loitering, or I'll call the cops!"

Ava's hands drifted up in surrender, and she backed out of the store, slowly. She took in what little she could on the way out. The steel shelves were mostly empty. What they did carry seemed more or less in line with being a gas station near a freeway, though. Bread and snacks were offered, and drinking water refills, though not containers. The value of an Oregonian dollar appeared around half of the Canadian, on bread if not on bus fare.

Outside the door she paused to frown at the A-frame sign again. *Ration codes?* she guessed. It didn't list prices. She walked back to Jean-Claude and described her encounter. "Not very friendly here," she groused, and started to pick up the handle of the medicine suitcase to relocate.

"A moment," Jean-Claude said, raising a hand. "I try first." He strode into the gas station, leaving her on the curb with the luggage.

Ava studied the passersby who studied her. A couple glanced at her for more than a moment. She flashed them a model-quality smile and said, "Hi! Beautiful day today, isn't it?" They recoiled and walked past faster.

No, it wasn't her imagination. Bellingham wasn't very friendly.

Jean-Claude returned, looking amused. "Teenagers are trouble!" he greeted her with a chuckle.

"We try," she agreed. "What did I do this time?"

"You should be in uniform at age eighteen," Jean-Claude explained. "Universal draft."

"How do they know I'm not seventeen? Or sixteen?"

Jean-Claude looked her over, and smiled apologetically. "You're an adult. This is clear. But trucks stop here. He will not call the police." He scratched his nose ruefully. "They have universal health care here. Like Canada."

"Good for them," Ava replied.

"Hm." Jean-Claude looked pointedly at the suitcase full of medicines.

"Awesome," Ava said. "I hope you didn't tell him we came from Canada."

"Non," Jean-Claude agreed.

Ava sank to a seat on the pavement. Without stripping on the street, she did what she could to adjust her appearance in a younger direction. Her stylish asymmetric jacket went back into the rucksack, leaving her in a light baseball T-shirt over skinny jeans. She didn't need a jacket anyway. She'd only exchanged her wool sweater for the jacket at the Coast Guard station to look more mature. She replaced her combat boots with her red high-top sneakers again. She uncoiled her wind-blown French braid, and redid it neatly. She rolled one of her silk scarves into a rope and tied it around her head along the hairline.

"There. Do I look any younger?" she asked.

"Not really." By then, Jean-Claude was also on the pavement, lying back against a soft-sider suitcase to nap. "I'm sorry, Ava. You look like you know what you're doing."

She snorted. "Appearances are deceiving."

There was precious little traffic, on the interstate or at the gas station. They fell into a doze.

A GUNSHOT RANG OUT. AVA CAME AWAKE INSTANTLY. SHE FLIPPED ONTO her stomach, propped up on her hands and flexed toes, and peered between suitcases.

A guy around her age was running down the embankment from the interstate, headed for the closest buildings. He wore a once-white T-shirt over army camouflage pants and boots. His head was shaved almost bare, nothing but stubble.

An MP stopped higher on the bank, to aim his shot. This second one felled the runner. The gunner strode closer and shot him again, in the head – an execution. A couple other soldiers slowly followed, their rifles slung across their backs. They picked up the dead body, and carried it back up the embankment, behind the shooter. Ava could only see the canvas top of their transport from this angle.

She drew Jona, and took a careful snap of the tableau. "Jona, caption, maybe shooting a deserter," she murmured.

A woman, maybe in her thirties, had stopped her bike to watch, not 10 yards from Ava and Jean-Claude. "Does that happen a lot in Bellingham?" Ava called out to her. "We're from out of town."

The woman stared back at her, visibly shaken. "No. No, we have no levies here. He must have been trying to run home." She shook her head. "Never run from them," she advised Ava earnestly.

"I won't," Ava agreed. She sized the woman up, and rose. She stepped closer, and asked in an undervoice, "We have some medical supplies. Would you like to buy any?"

The woman stared at the MP's and gulped. "Insulin. Do you have any?"

"We do," Jean-Claude assured her, and dug into his suitcase. "How much do you need?"

"I only have a hundred on me," the woman whispered. "Can I have three bottles?"

Jean-Claude carefully displayed three bottles of insulin. Ava blocked the view from the gas station with her body, and accepted five twenties. Ava was beginning to wonder if Hudson was the only nation using electronic currency. Jean-Claude crowded close and handed over the bottles. The woman pedaled off the moment she had them stowed.

Ava murmured, "I keep trying to tell myself that Hudson might look just as bad."

"Non," Jean-Claude said. "Hudson looks bad in a different way." He waggled his eyebrows.

That surprised a laugh out of Ava. She sat and photographed her Oregon 20-dollar bills, front and back, and captioned them with their price, three vials of insulin. With luck, that might buy them a night at a flophouse instead of a dank alley in Seattle.

Well, there was always one way to make cash. She pulled in her knees and laid her forehead on them. *I could have had a militia job in Soho Ville. Working for Guzman, I'd never have to turn tricks again, or push drugs.*

Three weeks ago Ava Panic set off into Ohio to train a handful of green agents. She had Skull's backing, money, wheels, good people at her back. She could talk to her boyfriend every night. Cade didn't want her to. *Tough.* She called him anyway, and he talked. He was the one who dragged her into this job.

Actually, he tried his damnedest to talk me out of it. But he was glad I chose to join him. Wasn't he?

"Can I help?" Jean-Claude inquired.

"Shut up. I'm feeling sorry for myself," Ava replied.

He chuckled, and lay back down to wait for some magic carpet ride.

Ava snuffled. *Would Cade wait for a magic carpet ride?* No, he wouldn't. She wasn't sure what he could do, though. If Ava couldn't pass, Cade would be obvious as a deserter. *That's not the point, Panic. If Cade were in my shoes…*

He'd change the game.

Ava stood decisively. "C'mon, Jean-Claude. We're going back to the Coast Guard station."

"Why?"

"You'll see."

"DANIELS!" AVA POUNCED ON THE POOR DISPATCHER THE MOMENT SHE was back in the door at the Coast Guard station. She left Jean-Claude outside minding the luggage.

"You won't believe what I just saw!" Ava continued, irate. "Army thugs gunned down a young man before my very eyes on the interstate embankment!" Her arms flew in large gestures back toward I-5. "I dropped into a gas station to ask directions. The attendant pulled a gun on me! Called me a deserter! Threatened to have me arrested!"

Ava was ever so glad to chuck the slow Minnesota round vowels. She squawked a mile a minute in the most raucous, nasal, arrogant New York accent she could drum up.

"Daniels, I am an emissary of the sovereign nations of Hudson and Ohio!" she shrieked. "*Hudson!* And *Ohio!* I shall not be treated like this! Hitchhike down to Seattle indeed! You get that bastard Wetherby back on the phone for me right this minute!" Her finger stabbed the poor man's desk with each of the last half dozen words.

"Ah…" said the horrified Daniels, reaching slowly for the phone.

Ava's conscience twinged. Daniels had been nothing but kind to her. But he wasn't the sharpest tool in the shed. She could use him. She folded her arms belligerently. "Well?" she demanded. "Dial him! I am on a dip-lo-matic mission!" *And proving it by the minute,* she thought wryly.

The call connected. "Yes, sir, excuse me, sir, this is Daniels again. At the Coast Guard Bellingham station? I, um –"

Ava snatched the phone from his hand. "Wetherby?" she demanded.

"This is Lieutenant Colonel Wetherby," he acknowledged, with only a slight stress on his rank.

"Wetherby, this is Ava Panic. The *emissary* from Hudson and Ohio," she said, keeping the Queens accent wince-worthy. "I *demand* you send us transportation to Seattle! And you'd damned well better provide a decent hotel room when I get there, too!"

"Who *are* you?" Wetherby replied.

"I believe we already covered that, *Goonie,*" Ava said. "Would you like me to tell Commander Daniels here all about how you came by that nickname?" Ava didn't have a clue.

"Excuse me, miss," Daniels attempted. "I'm not a commander."

Ava never thought he was. She waved away his objection imperiously, and kept talking fast into the handset. "And about your *association* with *Vulture?* I'm sure the Coast Guard would be *very interested!"*

"Woman, for the love of God!" hissed Wetherby over the phone, "Stop talking! I thought the Coast Guard would arrange transport."

"The *Coast Guard* sent me on foot to I-5, to hitch a ride from a trucker!" Ava shrieked. "Where I saw a deserter shot before my very eyes! And someone pulled a gun and threatened me – *me!* – as a deserter as well! I assure you, *Goonie,* Generals Schwabacher and Cullen shall hear of this!"

"Christ, lady!" Wetherby said. "Please *stop talking.* Look, I asked to meet with you tomorrow because I'm not in Seattle. I'm visiting the fire lines. I can swing through Bellingham and pick you up at the station. It'll be a couple hours."

"We shall see you then," Ava said. "At about four?"

"Sixteen or seventeen hundred," Wetherby allowed. "Alright, I'll see if I can hurry it up."

"Good!" Ava yelled, and slammed the phone down. Mobile phones were so unsatisfying that way. Tapping the end key didn't give nearly the nice percussive *thump* of closure.

Daniels stared at her, frozen in horror. One did not yell at, nor hang up on, a lieutenant colonel. Daniels probably didn't even swear at his wife, the poor man.

Ava smiled at him sweetly, and crooned, "Thank you so much, Daniels. You've been so helpful. Would you like a sedative? We have some."

"Ah..."

"We'll wait outside. It's lovely out. A bit muggy." She left quickly.

"Any joy?" Jean-Claude asked as she rejoined him.

"Yes. A lieutenant colonel will pick us up in a couple hours."

Jean-Claude's eyes lit. "How do you manage this?"

"I asked myself what my boyfriend would do," Ava confided. "Cade would pick the weakest link and go psycho on his ass."

Jean-Claude's grin spread to his whole face. "Go psycho?"

Ava shrugged. "Become the most dangerous person in the room. Somehow. Then make everyone try to placate you. It's very effective. Sometimes."

"And was he? The most dangerous psycho in the room, this boyfriend?"

"Well, yeah," Ava allowed. "I can go either way myself."

Jean-Claude laughed, then pointed at a restaurant up the docks. "We could buy lunch!" They were building a new Coast Guard office up that way. This old one seemed too low-slung for the times.

"Yeah," Ava agreed. "Let's make Daniels watch the luggage."

She dumped half of it inside the station door. Jean-Claude dragged in the rest. "Daniels, we'll return in an hour. Would you like us to bring you back anything from the...crab shack, or whatever it is?"

"Ah, the salmon burger?" Daniels requested. "And maybe that sedative...?"

"Of course! Jean-Claude," she instructed him airily, "a sedative for our friend Daniels."

"Valium?" Jean-Claude offered.

Daniels nodded in relief. "That would be lovely."

28

Interesting fact: Before the Calm, the world's leading microchip manufacturers were Korea, U.S.A., Taiwan, Japan, and Europe. Few wafer fab plants were capable of the leading-edge technologies. A wafer fab cost billions to build, and each specialized in only a certain range of chips it could manufacture. Without the chips, modern computing capacity was impossible to maintain. There were wafer fabs in the Northeast, but they couldn't produce the full chip set needed for, say, a cell phone, or an Internet router. However, the U.S. overall had ensured domestic capacity in the interest of national security.

The ride to Seattle started out rather awkward. And they never did reach Seattle.

"About this delivery –" Lt. Col. Wetherby began, as he steered his compact electric car onto the empty I-5 southbound. He was a tidily built black officer, around forty, and attractive in an excessively erect posture sort of way.

"Jean-Claude isn't part of my mission," Ava interrupted. "We're not going to talk about my delivery in front of him."

Jean-Claude elaborated with his mission for MSF. "Where would you suggest I go, to help the, ah, under-served? Elderly, refugees, poor. Or maybe these 'fire lines'?"

Wetherby considered that. "We have universal health care. Refugees from California are turned back at the border. Oregon Health has strong policies about what kind of health care they offer. So there's a black market in medical extras. But not basics."

"We sold some insulin to a woman," Ava said. "She was willing to pay a hundred for three vials."

"That's illegal, Ava," Wetherby said. "But yeah, diabetic treatment is one of the controversial ones. Adult diabetes. They're ordered to exercise a lot, lose weight, follow an extreme diet, quiet and meditation. Some aren't willing. They want a quick fix."

"Ah," said Jean-Claude. "Oregon Health is correct. It is hard for people to change, maybe."

"Dr. Alarie," Wetherby said, "I don't think you came here to become a black market luxury doctor."

"Non. You are right. Are there maybe rebels? Prisoners who are not served?"

Wetherby considered. "Maybe survivalist enclaves. But the visiting health clinics are supposed to drop by once a month. There's a formula, at least one nurse practitioner for a couple thousand people or something. Gaps happen. But universal health is wildly popular. Props up support for the government. It's not perfect. But compared to the U.S., it's night and day."

"Very nice," Jean-Claude said. "Lovely."

"Sorry, Jean-Claude," Ava said with a grin.

"Sorry I waste your money, Ava," he returned.

"Money?" Wetherby asked.

"We didn't have a way to buy currency quietly," Ava explained. "So I converted a couple thousand Canadian to medical supplies for Jean-Claude. We figured some of it must have black market value."

"Ah." Wetherby looked pained, as though imagining the red tape this would entail.

"So tell us about Washington," Ava encouraged. "Oregon. What happened here in the Calm? People out East want to know." Ava clicked Jona on to record, making a show of it so the colonel knew.

"Well, the earthquakes in California were the turning point,"

Wetherby began. He settled into his story. They had an hour and a half drive before them to Seattle.

Here, far closer to the California cataclysm two years ago, there was little doubt that the disaster was engineered. The earthquakes were carefully planned and executed with American nuclear weapons deployed along well-known fault lines. The tsunamis hit the open Oregon coast hard, though not as bad as Hawaii. The populous Puget Sound coastline was sheltered and accustomed to big tidal swings, as Ava had seen for herself. Fallout was minimized because the nukes were subterranean. But enough radioactive signature escaped to identify exactly where and what was detonated.

The hard-hit Pacific Navy was as irate as Washington–Oregon. The two powers collaborated on the investigation. They sent in special ops teams to scrutinize the California fault lines. Those were high mortality missions, given the crazed chaos on the ground.

Courts martial were convened. Marcus Wetherby, among others, came clean with everything they knew about the secret measures of the Calm Act, the plan to deliberately cull the American population to sustainable levels. The Navy and Washington–Oregon jointly decided to secede from the United States and repudiate the Calm Act, a couple months after the California earthquakes. The Army general responsible for the overall West Coast was among those executed.

"The death angel superior?" Ava asked.

Wetherby glanced pointedly into his rear-view mirror at Jean-Claude.

Jean-Claude murmured, "Ava and I met this general in the East."

Wetherby nodded shortly. "I survived my court martial. Barely. Several of us had worked on vetting the Calm Act. We told everything we knew. One was executed, the death angel for the West Coast. And his minions, when we caught them."

Ava made a show of turning off the recording. "I'm going to erase some of that. Vulture?" she asked. "You ratted on him?"

"Yeah."

"And the Northern League?" she asked.

"I don't know what that is," the colonel replied. "We know that someone absconded with half our troops from Fort Lewis–McChord.

We had to institute a civilian draft even before California, to garrison the borders. Started training everyone age eighteen to thirty for emergency call-up. After California, we called them up. Doctor, the universal health coverage started then. We needed something to offset the public outrage over the draft."

Ava started to record again, and asked him to repeat all that.

Wetherby continued. Getting the name 'Washington' off of their new independent country was also a popular move. Both states were once part of the Oregon Territory, so that name worked.

"And the death toll?" Ava asked. "How much did the population of Oregon fall?"

"Our population rose," Wetherby replied. "It started around eleven million. I think we're up to twelve and a half. The Army is strict about kicking back any refugees we catch. The civilians, not so much. We're not worried about people who are absorbed. The southerners are soft about that. So long as their adopted strays are housed and fed and employed, the martial authorities look the other way. No one's happy to watch California self-destruct. We just can't save them from themselves."

"I survived New York City," Ava said. "One in ten."

"Jesus," Wetherby replied. "California isn't like that, Ava. In New York, there wasn't enough food capacity inside those borders. It wasn't possible for everyone to survive, even without Ebola."

"We noticed."

"That must have been hell on earth."

"It was," Ava agreed.

"California, even with the droughts, is sustainable," Wetherby said. "Well, now anyway. The population fell by a lot. The problem is restoring order."

"The Northeast chose to go in and restore order to the Apple Zone," Ava told him. "Save everyone who was left, like me."

"When the surviving population was small enough," Wetherby countered. "Some would say they went in too soon. Put too much strain on New York–New Jersey."

"They worked with New England and Pennsylvania," Jean-Claude said. "Canada helped, too. A little."

Ava added, "I met one of our kids in Sioux Lookout, coming across Canada. A thirteen year old my gang shielded through the Starve. He lost his foot. A Canadian couple adopted him."

"Wow," Wetherby said. "I suppose it's possible to inflict order on California. If we joined forces with the Rockies and the Montane Territory and the Naval Republic. I just don't think there's a will yet. We have our own problems."

"What's it like in there?" Ava asked.

"Chaos. War lords, gangs, and armies. Too busy fighting to get their act together and distribute water fairly. Not much agriculture. The enclaves that grow food only grow it for themselves, because it takes too much manpower to defend it. We're guessing about eighteen million left. More than us."

Ava nodded thoughtfully. She understood. Even allied with the neighbors, California was too big for them to fix. Oregon would only break itself trying. "So what is Oregon's status these days? Are you in good shape?"

Wetherby waggled a hand so-so. "Fires and drought on the western half. Food production is tight, but enough. It's hot, but our climate can stand that. Storms. Constant infrastructure investment, waterworks and renewable power. Rebuilding to bypass sea level rise. Compared to the U.S., we're doing great."

"The ex-U.S.," Ava reminded him.

"Right. The rest of you."

"You don't talk to the rest of us," Ava prompted.

"Personally," Wetherby said, "I repudiated the Calm Act group. All of us, really. We're loyal to Oregon. We broke all ties. Pardon me, Ava. But no one sent a girl your age as ambassador."

"First toe in the door, maybe," Ava said. "It's a hell of a trip. Is there a national park coming up? Let's exit somewhere and speak privately."

~

AVA REFLECTED THAT HER MENTAL IMAGE OF OLD WASHINGTON STATE owed much to *Twilight* movies. Away from the wild and rugged coast, this main drag between Bellingham and Seattle would look right at home in the I-95 corridor back East, or in the Windsor–Quebec City strip.

No one lacked for potable water on the Pacific side of the Cascade Range. After the day's unnatural midday hours of sunny blue, the sky was drizzling again.

There were no convenient national parks soaring with majestic conifers. But they had to detour east anyway to avoid a drowned stretch of I-5 south of Marysville, about an hour out of Bellingham. They drove through a suburban sea, tiled with partially wooded subdivisions. The hydrangeas were in bloom, blue and pink giant flower balls cheerful on big-leaved mounded shrubbery. Wetherby detoured farther to the bank of Lake Stevens, and a public boat ramp.

Ava agreed that was private enough. They left Jean-Claude in the car, and walked out to the end of a long dock.

Ava took a seat on the wet boards, facing the dark water. The sun hadn't set yet, but the rain made the evening dim. "What I came here to deliver."

In distaste, Wetherby joined her, wetting his pants. "Yes?"

"Microchips," she said. "Your peers in the Northeast want to know how Canada makes a new cell phone like this one." She handed him her ouiPhone, Jona. "We can't make all the chips. Can you?"

Wetherby looked the phone over, front and back, and handed it back to her with a shrug. "Nice phone."

"Oregon makes phones?"

"Not sure," he said. "I don't know of any tech bottlenecks. But I'm not the right person to ask."

Ava sighed. She hadn't expected it to be that easy, though. Wetherby was never her target, merely the person who could point her in the right direction. Her backup guide, Vulture, was dead. She could only approve on that score.

"Who could I talk to in the martial government of Oregon?" she asked.

His eyebrows lifted. "No. Not the Army. I mean, the Army will need to approve anything that crosses our borders. But you want someone to push the project, right?"

"Yeah?"

"That wouldn't be an army officer, Ava," Wetherby explained. "We have a top engineer, but she does civil engineering. The power grid, highways, aqueducts. Army Corps of Engineers stuff."

"Yeah, my boss's boss does that for Hudson. Colonel Tony Nasser."

Wetherby looked impressed for the first time. "You work for Nasser? Skull works for Colonel Nasser?" He seemed surprised.

Ava considered explaining that Skull was a death angel. But given what he'd said, that wouldn't help here. Oregon's context was too different. Wetherby was in on the death angel business at the get-go. He managed to escape, and considered himself well shut of it.

"Skull is a normal Resco," she explained instead. "He manages the southern Finger Lakes district, in western New York, and north-central Pennsylvania. In that role, he reports to Tony. But he also runs agents who cross super-state lines. I'm one of those. We do kinda risky business. Like traveling to the West Coast on a wild goose chase for microchips."

"Yeah? Skull was a quiet one. Gotta watch those, I guess. They're sneaky. You ever met any others?"

Ava went along with the social noises for a bit, to build rapport. She almost lost credibility with him when she said she knew Emmett MacLaren. But she had photos to prove that claim.

Wetherby shook his head in honest amazement. "I never believed they could make a go of it in the Northeast. Ava, you people are a miracle."

"I think I figured that out when I survived the Starve," Ava agreed.

"You got that right."

"Back to microchips," Ava said. "I'm not sure, but I think that was General Schwabacher's idea, out of Ohio. Tony Nasser was interested. But I think high-tech stuff is Lieutenant Colonel Cameron."

"Yeah, I know Cam," Wetherby agreed. "He did a heck of a job on the tech chapters for the Resource Coordinator manual. I wrote the forestry chapter. Dad was a lumberjack here."

"Electronics aren't a bottleneck in Oregon?" Ava asked. "They are, all across the Northeast."

"Yeah, I bet. Ava, what you want is a tech mogul, not an Army officer. Why is the Army even trying, out East?"

"Um," Ava said. "Because the economy collapsed? I'm sorry, colonel. I don't understand this stuff. But we don't have money like you do. In Hudson, our money is basically our cut of the food rations. If anybody wants to build something, open a factory or stuff, they end up asking the Rescos for help."

He nodded. "I get it. Complete economic collapse. They have to bootstrap. We didn't fall that far here. We replaced the currency – well, you're probably not interested."

"I'm interested," Ava said. "But I don't know anything about economics. When I caught Ebola, I was a sophomore in high school. We don't have high schools in Hudson anymore. I'm working on my GED."

"Crap. OK. The quick version is, we converted the old money to the new. Even before California."

"Wait – can I record this?" Ava asked. At his nod, she started recording again.

He backed up, then continued. "But we used the opportunity to flatten wealth inequality to a max ten to one ratio. So the wealthiest became ten times as rich as the poorest. That was cash, all hand-waving and book-keeping through our regional banks. Physical capital stayed in private hands, unless it was already public. The Army only intervened to run operations that failed. If we still needed them. Long distance buses. Phones. Power. Most of that, we handed over to the local governments, or the new Oregon national government. We're not as far from the pre-Calm economy as you guys." He laughed sadly. "That's ironic. We jettisoned the U.S. first. And now we're the closest thing left to what we used to be."

"We're working on it," Ava said defensively. "We fell farther. But we're getting back on our feet."

"I see that. Impressive. So, Ava. If I help you, promise me this isn't some Eastern political scheme."

Almost certainly, Ava thought. But Wetherby clearly wanted to stay out of Calm Act politics. "Microchips," she said. "They sent me to talk microchips."

"OK. Let's find you a tech mogul." He rose and offered a hand to pull Ava up. "We're driving the wrong way."

29

Interesting fact: the Oregon tax code enforced the ten to one ratio of wealthiest to poorest household income. Above the ceiling income, taxation was 100%. Instead of losing it to taxes, high earning individuals funneled income to proteges. They built networks of influence and ready capital.

Half an hour later, Wetherby turned onto a private gated drive. As he requested entry over the intercom – he'd called ahead – Ava breathed deep of the fragrant plantings flanking the gate. The tall walled entrance could have appeared hostile. Luxuriant hydrangeas and snapdragons and evergreens softened it to a welcome, and a whispered promise of a peaceful oasis beyond.

The gates swung open almost silently, admitting them to a hushed curving road flanked with tall conifers. This Arlo Hofer guy liked his privacy. His home wasn't visible from the public road at all. Just as Ava's curiosity began to grow to an uncomfortable pitch, they crested a rise, and the grounds opened up below them in a hollow, nestled between the surrounding forested hills.

A huge modern home spread sideways on multiple levels in an indoor-outdoor style reminiscent of Frank Lloyd Wright. That held pride of place. But a half dozen smaller houses, each uniquely beautiful and harmonizing with the big one, flanked the drive, with other structures beyond. Like the streets of the Apple, this enclave used solar driveway lights to extend into the evening, a golden glow through the misty rain. Dark greenhouses and vegetable gardens mingled with more esthetically inspired landscaping. Glints of red LEDs in the trees spoke of discreet but extensive security.

This place made the Grosse Pointe Lawn & Racquet Club look pedestrian. Ava expected it slept more people, too.

As instructed at the gate, Wetherby drove them to the grand entrance, shielded from the rain by a generously sized portico. A man waited there, lounging against a pillar, enjoying the soft rain. As the guests alighted from the car, he strode out to meet them. Middle-aged but perfectly fit, with close-cropped reddish brown hair, he wore a light sweater and tailored chinos over bare feet in the summer evening. His jaw firm with exercise under a quarter-inch trim beard, Ava guessed he spent a couple hours a day keeping his body tuned. She couldn't figure out if he was security or the butler.

"Colonel Wetherby. Arlo Hofer. Welcome to my home," the man said, extending a hand to shake. "You must be Dr. Jean-Claude Alarie," they shook hands, "and Ava Panic, the courier from Hudson." His eyes drilled into Ava's with intensity as he shook her hand. This guy exuded power and authority, now that he wasn't gazing off into twilit shrubbery. "Come in."

"Actually, Mr. Hofer –" Wetherby attempted.

"Arlo." His intense gaze fell back on the colonel.

"Arlo," Wetherby conceded uncomfortably. "I need to get back to Seattle. Could I drop them off with you? These, um, guests are exhausted. They left Vancouver at oh-dark thirty this morning. I hoped you could take care of escorting them back to the border when you're done with them. Feel free to call if you need me."

"Of course," Arlo agreed. He matter-of-factly helped Ava and Jean-Claude extract their luggage. He carried a third of it. They bid farewell to Wetherby with subdued thanks.

"This way," Arlo invited. They passed a quiet modern living area that wrapped around an internal glassed atrium, doors open to enjoy the soft night. A woman who looked every bit Arlo's match glanced up from her reader and smiled slightly. He waved for her not to get up.

"My wife Moira," he murmured. But he continued to guest rooms on the right wing of the house. The rest of the floor plan seemed labyrinthine, but their route was straightforward from door, past atrium, to guest housing.

"Was this Frank Lloyd Wright?" Ava asked. "The architect. I visited Fallingwater in Pennsylvania. Your home reminds me of it."

Arlo smiled. "An acolyte, I think. Moira will be pleased. We'll speak in the morning about business. Make yourselves comfortable. You're welcome to join us by the atrium for a drink, or a bite to eat. We'll turn in soon ourselves. Early risers."

Ava opted for a shower instead, to sluice off the itchy salt of the Sound. The bath didn't bother with a wall or shower curtain, just a simple rainfall shower head and a drain, in a bathroom tiled in stone. Potted plants stood by a window made private by an evergreen outside. The scent of living flowers and gentle rain pervaded her beautiful bedroom.

Arlo Hofer's compound was a far cry from the flophouse she'd feared to find tonight in Seattle. Ava sank into a deep sleep after a huge day.

"AVA. YOU'RE REFRESHED?" ARLO ASKED.

She walked up the gravel breezeway to join him in his pagoda-roofed open-air office behind the main house, promptly at 9:00 the next morning. A slip of paper under her bedroom door had invited her to this appointment. He was alone, as was she.

"Yes, thank you, Arlo," Ava said, sinking into a teak chair before him. Elegant but hard, the seat matched her host.

And she was refreshed. After her long sleep, she took a run throughout the compound, found and played in the gym, and breakfasted on salmon and fresh eggs. She'd met the source chickens down the road a bit.

"Are we ready for me to deliver my message?"

"No Jean-Claude?" Arlo asked. "Alright." He steepled his fingers. "What brings you all the way from Hudson and Ohio? That's quite a trip."

"Microchips," Ava said. She produced her black box, and her list of parts. She sat forward to write on his desk. He slipped a legal pad under her page before her pen could dent the wood. "I had to memorize a lot of this. Give me a minute to write it down." She wrote twenty-two vegetable names in alphabetical order.

He nodded, and accepted the parts list. He let her finish writing in silence, as she reconstructed the good and compromised times and satellite phone numbers.

Then Ava arranged her two pages and the black box on the desk before him. "Inside the black box is a memory dongle, with engineering schematics. For a cell phone, I think. Ohio and Hudson would like to be able to build that phone. Oh, wait."

Ava extracted Jona, too, and laid in on the desk. "This phone was kind of the inspiration. It's a latest model ouiPhone I picked up in Toronto. In Hudson we're living on recycled electronics. But Canada is still advancing their tech. We want to restore our tech base. But we never had that capacity in the Northeast. I'm sorry, I'm making a hash of this."

Arlo picked up the ouiPhone and studied it, turning it on to flick around its screens. "Just the phone in Canada? I understand you traveled here across Canada. Did you see any other tech advances?"

"Their auto-drive vehicles seem more advanced," Ava said. "Just plug in your phone, like an Uber driver used to, but then it drives the car. Across the Dust Bowl, they've got like one train track. The trains take turns going east and west, or wait for a faster train to pass. But they push through self-driving trucks. They're still mining and stuff in the dust zone. That might be new tech. They've gone down to a thirty hour work-week standard. They claim that's from tech, but I don't know. The phone is incredible. Voice controlled, artificial intelligence, relational databases. That thing is smarter than me. More powerful with a data connection to the cloud."

"Of course," he agreed. He'd found a screen of interest and studied it. "Hm. And why did they let you travel across Canada to talk microchips?"

"I don't think Canada knows that," Ava admitted. "They think I went to Vancouver to hand-carry some sensitive details on PIAGO Power."

"I don't know what that is."

"Oh. My boss's boss, Colonel Tony Nasser, is power czar for Hudson. He heads a big project now to develop next-gen nuclear power for Hudson. Um, rather than make more dangerous waste, it uses old waste as fuel. Unlimited, safe, twenty-four-seven power. No greenhouse emissions. Don't need to mine for fuel, because we have radioactive waste from the old nuclear plants. We had some melt-downs on the East Coast after the tsunami in February. They decided we have to replace them. 'We can, and we must, therefore we will.'"

Arlo stilled through this, listening intently. "A moon shot for clean nuclear power."

"I guess."

He murmured, "What a different world if we'd done that forty years ago."

Ava shrugged. "My boyfriend would say the oil companies had too much money, too much power."

"True. Piago. Does that mean something?"

"It stands for Put It Away in Good Order. It's a Hudson meme. You never know, you might die before you walk this way again. So put your tools away in good order. So some survivor can come by and put them to good use again. It started with the ferries they used to save the survivors of the city. Like me. The ferrymen died. But first they put the ferries away in good order. Kind of heroes in Hudson. Dead heroes."

Arlo's attention was riveted. "You survived New York City?"

"Yes, sir." Ava paused. "I don't know what you heard. But it was probably worse."

"I'd like to hear about that," Arlo said. "But first, what am I looking at here?"

The man's expression reminded Ava of her boss. That bemused look of a powerful man not quite sure what to make of a teenager. She seemed to inspire that a lot. "Sorry. Those are satellite phone numbers. Call them at these times. Oh! Greenwich Mean Time. Sorry."

Arlo circled the times and wrote '-8h GMT' beside them. He paused and translated the first two times to 4:06 p.m. and 7:17 p.m.

Ava was impressed that he didn't need to look that up, or even think hard. This guy must have called London a lot once.

She continued, "Use the 'good' numbers if you're secure on your end, an absolutely private conversation. Use the 'compromised' number if you can't guarantee that. They want to talk about this list of microchips. Which ones you can make in Oregon, I think. The vegetables are code names to refer to the chips. There's more on the memory dongle inside the box. I don't have a key. You just cut open the box."

"And why the secrecy?"

Ava sighed. "We think there are people who will try to stop us. Canada is part of that. We're trying to set up communications that they can't intercept."

"Does this have something to do with the Calm Act?" Arlo asked.

Ava nodded. "The people who enforce the Calm Act."

"I thought the Calm Act was over. I mean, for all the ex-states. Oregon chucked it in under a year."

"Wetherby mentioned that half of Oregon's troops went missing?" Ava waited for Arlo to nod that he was aware of that. "I saw them in Edmonton. They wear the American flag, plus the badge of, um, that alliance. A bunch are on Vancouver Island right now. Doing summer war exercises with their allies."

Ava considered mentioning that those allies included Russia. She was pretty sure Skull would be furious at her if she did. She suspected she was already on thin ice.

Arlo huffed a bitter laugh. "Well, we knew Canada was no friend of ours. I guess this confirms it."

"Excuse me, sir, but Canada is friendly to Hudson and Ohio," Ava said. "They helped save the Apple. New York City. They're all in on PIAGO Power. They were willing to help me cross Canada. I don't know about the rest of the alliance. But Canada isn't our enemy. I thought it might be. But it isn't. I think it's more complicated."

Arlo considered that, then tapped the box with a finger. "We're highly interested in the chips. Like you, we can't make them all. But what does it take to be 'all in' on PIAGO Power?"

Ava shrugged. "I think Hudson wants to save the world. Whatever we come up with will be public. We'll sell equipment and training. But it won't be secret. Other nations that contribute will speed up the project, and benefit sooner." She tapped the vegetable list. "But we wanted to open a dialogue over the chips. We thought if Canada can make a new ouiPhone, maybe Oregon supplied the chips we can't make."

The businessman nodded thoughtfully. "Some of them. Probably. I'll find out." He took out his phone and placed a call. "I need metal cutters. There's a steel box I need to open. Thanks."

With his phone still out, he looked up something on Jona, Ava's phone. He performed some operations on his own phone, then called Jona. After answering his own call to check the connection, he made Jona remember his number.

"Good," he said, handing her phone back to her. "I need to research some things. Please enjoy my home for the day. Keep the phone with you. I'll call if I have questions. I hope to respond this evening, at... 4:06 p.m., hopefully."

Ava blew out, then smiled. "Yay," she said in a small voice. She'd done it! All that was left was... "Um, and can you get us back to the border?"

Arlo frowned. "Without the Canadians knowing you were here?"

Ava's eyebrows flew up. "You can do that? That would be awesome!"

"How did you get here?" he asked.

Ava related their sailing trip with Donal and Gordy Friesen. She got sidetracked on big and little Chinese junks and smuggling and pirates and her forays into Vancouver's Chinese underworld. Arlo had to redirect her several times. Skull was right. She really needed to get better at putting things in order.

"Anyway, I can't go back the way I came," Ava concluded. "If I show up at the border, they'll definitely let Jean-Claude in, and probably me. But Canadian intelligence will be mad at me. Probably my boss, too."

Arlo's eyes lit. "Let me think about it. You won't leave today, in any case. I want to succeed at this phone call first. Even if all I'm ready to tell them is that you arrived safely, and we're interested. But I should be able to tell them more than that. Ah! My box cutter has arrived. Excuse us, Ava."

"Do you want to go back to Canada?" Ava asked Jean-Claude. They were enjoying the Hofer compound heated swimming pool, shared by the whole community. She was right last night. There were over 150 people living in this compound – security, gardeners, livestock tenders, Hofer's proteges and assistants, and their children. This wasn't just a rich man's private estate. It was practically an ark.

"Your business is done so soon?" Jean-Claude returned in surprise.

"Might be. Tomorrow or the next day," Ava hedged. "Not sure yet. I'm just the courier."

"I think… I have not decided yet," Jean-Claude said. "I am curious about California. To walk into California alone, though, no. I need allies."

"Not interested in the Montane Territory? Or Rockies?" Ava asked.

Jean-Claude shrugged. "Still thinking. Ava, you didn't tell them about the American soldiers from Edmonton, did you?"

"Why?" Ava asked. She briefly reviewed, and decided Jean-Claude didn't know that those troops were from Washington. Or rather, he didn't find out from her. What Jean-Claude knew in general, or cross-checked from Laurent, she had no idea.

He tugged a lock of her wet hair. "A courier delivers mail, little one. Don't cause trouble, yes?"

"Mais oui!" she replied. She slipped underwater to escape the conversation and swim some more laps.

He was right, though. In retrospect, telling the Oregonians about the Edmonton troops, and PIAGO Power, was way outside her mission. And Hofer seemed more interested in those than her microchips.

Oops.

Maybe she wasn't cut out to be a courier. The one she met in Grosse Pointe barely said a word. *He had a much more constrained job, though,* she consoled herself. *I'm more of an agent-courier.*

Yeah, that didn't help. She suspected she'd seriously overstepped her bounds. Hopefully the Canadians wouldn't mind too much. Or at least, they'd still let her go home. Oregon was OK, aside from the universal draft. But the familiar suburban banks of Lake Stevens yesterday had left her homesick for Hudson and Cade, so far away. She yearned to head back east.

30

Interesting fact: Until this time the East considered it a draw whether Hudson or the Naval Republic of Hawaii was the first successor nation of the United States. In fact, Oregon pre-dated either of them, but kept quiet for fear of retribution.

"Hello? This is Arlo Hofer, in Oregon. Your courier arrived safely last night. We are eager to talk vegetables."

Ava and several of Hofer's colleagues crowded around his desk in the gazebo. He put the call on speaker.

"Lieutenant Colonel Cam Cameron of Hudson," came the reply. "Martial law administrator for Long Island. Excuse me, but I was expecting a call from a brother officer. Could I speak to the courier?"

"This is me, Cam," Ava piped up.

"Hi, um, Tail," Cam replied. "Tell me something only Tail would know, please."

Ava thought fast. "If the snowman is there," she replied, "tell him I saw Germy. He has a blade foot. We swam in a lake with the pelicans."

"Please hold while I confirm," Cam said, cool and efficient.

The gathering around Arlo's desk remained hushed, mindful of the requirement that this conversation be highly secure. Given their surroundings, that seemed odd to them, but they had to accept Ava's word that this communication had risks. It was likely to be overheard by exactly the shadow powers which Oregon had repudiated.

She didn't mention that she worked for that very same shadow organization. Some nuances were just too complicated. And the death angels were an especially dark shade of grey.

"Confirmed," Cam said, sounding amused. "Tail, the snowman is on the warpath because he didn't hear sooner about the pelicans."

"Send my love," Ava said.

"Will do," Cam replied. "Sorry you had to go all the way south to Oregon. That was unintended. But you made good time."

"Correction, Cam," Ava said. "Washo is now named Oregon. I am currently north of Seattle. I think."

Arlo nodded.

"Got it," Cam said. "Who is Arlo Hofer, and why did you pick him?"

"If I may?" Arlo inserted himself. "Colonel, I hold several patents in the, ah, vegetable space. These days I work as a venture capitalist. To maintain Oregon's agricultural edge in the new economic conditions."

"Tail?" Cam prompted.

"I met with my preferred contact," Ava said. "He took me to Hofer. The system here is really different. This stuff is private sector. I think they can get the government's backing, though. If they need it."

"Easily," Arlo confirmed.

"Cam?" Ava added. "They kept banks and stuff."

"Interesting, Tail," Cam said. "Please save for your report. Let's talk vegetables. Mr. Hofer, would you be able to supply any of our needs?"

"Yes, colonel," Arlo confirmed. "We are strong on artichokes and asparagus. We hope to buy beans, beets, broccoli, and brussel sprouts. We do not currently have a crop, but could supply cabbage and carrots by next year. Please note that I am speaking potentialities here. Trade logistics are a separate concern."

"Understood," Cam acknowledged. "There's more?"

"Yes." Arlo proceeded to divvy out cauliflower through tomatoes.

"We are particularly concerned about kale varieties," he added at the end.

"We believe we can grow kale," Cam said. "Nearby."

"Really!" Arlo said, eyes practically glowing. The others gathered around the table grinned and traded high-fives.

Ava consoled herself that she wouldn't understand what they were so excited about even if they used real names for these things. The decoder list was lying on the desk between them. For the umpteenth time, she wondered dolefully what a PMIC was, and why there were so many in a phone. Porta made her promise back in Cleveland not to look these things up on the Internet, especially not while traveling. It was best that she not know until she was safe home in Hudson, in case anyone asked.

Cam returned, "We are *very* excited to hear that carrots and turnips are attainable. Are you currently exporting any of these to Canada?"

"I'm sorry," Arlo said. "I am told we are not at liberty to discuss our other customers at this time. We do grow more than our domestic needs, but I can't get more specific. We believe Canada does have other import opportunities, however."

"Perhaps another time, then," Cam acknowledged.

Then Arlo ventured off-script. "Tail mentioned several other things, that are also of great interest to Oregon. Arugula, and zucchini."

"I am not familiar with the arugula and zucchini status," Cam said worriedly. "Tail?"

"Wait one," Ava said. She watched as Arlo wrote out his additions. The American GIs in Canada were arugula. Zucchini stood for PIAGO Power. "These are new vegetables, Cam. The smiley boss who sent mine as a delegate is growing zucchini. Arugula bothers my GI tract. Tastes horrible, too. But I learned to eat it where I danced with your husband."

"Where you danced with my husband?" Cam repeated, still puzzled.

Ava was confident that Cam remembered that she danced with his husband at West Point, during Army Basic. The part he would be stumped by was how West Point related to a technical discussion, and what about West Point she meant by 'arugula.'

"Yeah. They produce arugula," Ava confirmed. "I ran across some, way north. I was surprised to find it so far north."

"Hold for one," Cam said, and went silent.

Ava tapped 'arugula' on the decoder page. "Arlo, this is a bad idea. I shouldn't have said anything to you."

Arlo was not Jean-Claude, nor anyone else Ava could push around. This man was a king in his own domain, and they sat in his throne room. "Oregon is *very* eager to discuss arugula," he assured her.

Cam came back on the line. "I believe I understand arugula and zucchini. Tail, your message is 'D-minus.'"

"Yes, sir," she acknowledged with a sinking feeling. Yes, of course Skull was patched in on this conversation.

"Arlo," Cam continued, "we would like to limit our discussion to vegetables."

"Very well," Arlo said. "We hope to send produce brokers to you. A zucchini rep, and a turnip expert. The arugula we will arrange separately with our tropical broker."

"I think I am very confused," Cam admitted. "Hold for one."

Ava didn't blame him. She wasn't sure what Arlo wanted either. Actually, she should do something about that. She got up to whisper in his ear. "What do you want?"

"We want to send a physicist liaison for PIAGO power, and a systems engineer on the chips," he whispered back. "We want the transit permission you got for them to cross Canada. And train tickets."

"I caught that part. But the arugula?"

"Will Hudson take its GIs back if we send them?"

"Hell, yeah!" she said, in knee-jerk reaction. "Or, well… Hm." That had the makings of a thorny international incident, now that she thought of it. And the GIs who served the Northern League, would Hudson truly welcome them back? Or throw them in jail?

Her eyes widened further. Did Oregon intend to demand their troops back?

Cam returned. "We aren't clear on the ask."

"Cam?" Ava said. "Reservations for two, is the ask. Um, that's four, with the girls. Home. Oregon would feel more comfortable with their brokers on site."

"Got it. I cannot grant that one without asking. But we will check. Arugula has us baffled."

"Um, Oregon hopes to return some arugula. No help is required at this time."

Arlo nodded confirmation at her. She gazed back at him in profound reservation.

Arlo asked, "Colonel, could you confirm those reservations later tonight?"

"I can try."

"The return of your courier depends on that," Arlo said.

Ava looked at him in alarm. *I can't leave unless Cam gets Canada to agree to more travelers?*

"Was that a threat?" Cam asked.

"Not at all," Arlo denied. "Logistics. Scheduling. Coordination with our tropical connection."

Hawaii? Ava guessed with deepening misgivings.

"Tail, are you well?" Cam inquired.

"It's all good," Ava replied. "Strawberry day." Ava feared Cam would have to consult again to decode that one. But apparently Cam remembered her photo, of her and Frosty eating strawberries on the Staten Island Ferry, two feral gang rats out on a summer date, who ran across free treats.

On second thought, that image conveyed a little more than she'd intended. *Ships. Tropical. Hawaii. Pacific Fleet.*

Cam may have picked up on the ships. "Are we recalling that D-minus?"

"Yes, sir," Ava said. "I earned that D-minus. Too busy making friends in class."

Please don't channel Frosty now, she begged herself. Cade would tell Cameron to shove it up his ass, because the agent on the spot had to make the call. *But my call is that being rude to Lt. Col. Cameron won't help my case.*

Cam advised, "Try to pick up your grade point average, Tail. But we are very happy to hear you made it. And eager for the vegetables.

So there's two A-pluses. Keep racking up those A's to offset the D's, alright?"

Ava tamped out a grin. If she read that right, Skull was annoyed at her, and possibly worried for her health and safety. But Cam was tickled pink. Skull was an undisputed wizard of the underhanded managerial arts. But from what she'd seen, Cam was the kind of ferocious that made his military superiors nervous.

Cameron signed off cheerfully, with a promise to call with an update on the train reservations at the next available time slot. Or circumlocutions to that effect.

Arlo Hofer and his minions fell into happy discussion of the technical challenges. Such exciting possibilities would open up with the full alphabet of vegetables available. Ava couldn't share in their greedy geeked-out glee. She sat quietly and waited until Arlo caught her eye.

He excused himself, and drew her by the elbow into the breezeway connecting gazebo to house, for a private word. "You're concerned," he invited.

"What does Hawaii have to do with any of this?" she asked plaintively.

"Ah. That. I have good news. I found you a ride back to Canada."

~

Ava stood by the railing, out of the sailors' way, as the guided missile destroyer HNS *Hilo* cruised toward Victoria Harbor early Sunday morning, three days later. She snapped pictures with Jona. Half were shots of the approaching deep water piers by the harbor mouth.

The other half were of a Canadian ship bearing down on them. Ava hoped they were coming to talk, not shoot.

The capital of British Columbia, Victoria lay on the south end of Vancouver Island. Ava hadn't gone north back to Canada. She went west, threading through islands across Puget Sound. Hofer delivered her last night to the naval station in Everett, a Hawaiian enclave on Oregon's shore. The port was just south of Marysville, where they detoured Wednesday night southbound on I-5, heading for Seattle.

She never did reach Seattle.

Her arrival in Bellingham on a Coast Guard search and rescue boat, not much bigger than the yacht *Canada Day* and afraid to face a gun junk, had left Ava with a misimpression of naval power in Puget Sound. It was a shame she hadn't seen Everett before slipping word to Arlo Hofer about the lost American troops from Edmonton. Ava didn't know much about the navy. But Hawaii's two aircraft carriers and three destroyers in port at Everett seemed self-explanatory.

Little smuggler boats might play hide and seek between the islands. But the Sound was owned by Hawaii and Canada.

"Hello, hello!" Jean-Claude greeted her cheerfully, coming to join her at the rail. "The Dust Bowl made me appreciate rain!" It was, of course, raining again, in a blustery spitting sort of way. A darkening sky promised worse to come.

Ava smiled crookedly, and snapped a picture of him.

"Non! A selfie of us together!" the doctor insisted.

He flung his arm around her, and they hammed it up for a series of shots, alternating the background view between the rainy docks, and the Canadian navy ship.

"They're going to kill me," Ava muttered.

"Non!" Jean-Claude said. "Maybe a little. Me, they will be very annoyed with!" He giggled, then bent to whisper in her ear. "They told me to make sure you don't cause trouble."

"But I'm so good at it," Ava quipped, then switched to a whine. "I didn't know it was loaded. I never imagined they'd do *this*."

"Of course," he agreed. "Except I think you like the result! You'll get punished anyway. So enjoy!"

"Fair point," she admitted. She was delighted to stick it to the Northern League. Hudson and Ohio didn't dare cross them. It honestly never occurred to her that Oregon and Hawaii might be insane enough to try. And Jean-Claude was right. She'd answer to the boss in any case. So she might as well have fun in the meantime. "Aren't you worried what they'll do to you?"

"Ah, I will not be here to punish," Jean-Claude said cheerfully. "This is good-bye, ma chère. Thank you! Your company was delightful!"

"What?" Ava said, blinking dumbly. She assumed Jean-Claude would disembark at Victoria with her. She took for granted that they would return together to their funky First Nations art boutique hotel in Vancouver. They'd celebrate their adventure once again over a good meal and a bottle of wine.

It was hard to remember she'd only known him for two weeks. "You changed your mind? You're staying in Oregon?"

"Non!" Jean-Claude said. "Santa Catalina Island. I talk with these sailors. Very interesting! There are islands off the California coast. Santa Barbara to Los Angeles. Safe refuge. Kind of safe."

"Just off the California coast doesn't sound very safe."

"Is maybe twenty kilometers," Jean-Claude clarified. "Not so close. And the Navy adopted them. This ship, the *Hilo,* travels there soon. I go with them."

"Wow, Jean-Claude. Not much communications for a spy."

"There is enough," he said. "When the Navy visits, I can send reports, and learn more. Besides, like I told you. I am a doctor, not a spy. I want to help in California. And not get myself killed. Getting killed does not help!"

They both laughed, and shared a lingering hug. "I'll miss you, Jean-Claude. If you ever make it back East, you contact me!"

"But of course. Don't worry. Enjoy!"

They broke off their embrace when they saw a petty officer bearing down on them with intent. She had Ava's pair of Oregonian envoys in tow.

"Ms. Panic, Dr. Alarie," the young woman greeted them formally. She was about the same height as Ava, dressed in business-like khakis with a navy blue windbreaker thrown over to foil the rain. Compared to the Hudson Army, Ava found the Hawaiian shipboard uniforms somewhat of a hodgepodge. She assumed this was a supply hiccup, but different roles also seemed to wear different clothes. The woman's shirt labeled her CPO Kudo. Ava thought a chief petty officer was roughly equivalent to Sergeant Calderon back at West Point.

"I've been told to brief you," Kudo continued, assuming a parade rest stance, knees flexed to compensate for the slow heave of the deck. "We will begin docking soon. Dr. Alarie, you are to stay hidden below in berthing until after departure. Once our Canadian counterparts are also docked, we will be met by Canada Border Services and the RCMP. They will remove Mr. Tanner and Dr. Wu, then grant them travel visas off-site. I understand the RCMP will escort them to the ferry, and on to your hotel in Vancouver."

"OK," Ava said tentatively. "But not me?"

"You are to remain on HNS *Hilo* as a resource to the captain during negotiations," Kudo said. "When your services are no longer required, we will attempt to disembark you quietly."

Ava dolefully considered the deep water dock, suitable for an Alaska cruise ship, they were now turning to slip into. Arranging security for a pier wasn't much of a challenge. The thing attached to land on one end. Security blocked that end.

Ava asked, "Am I under arrest, Chief Kudo?"

"No, ma'am," Kudo replied blandly. "You are a guest of the Naval Republic of Hawaii. For the next few hours, you will impersonate one of us. For your privacy and convenience. We are about the same height. If you'll come with me, ma'am."

"I guess this is it, then," Ava said. She extended a hand to shake with her Oregonians. "I'll see you in Vancouver. Jean-Claude."

He grinned encouragement. "I'm sure you will be marvelous! Au revoir, ma chère!"

"Au revoir," she agreed, hugging him one last time. He kissed both her cheeks. She hoped Santa Catalina Island was as safe as he claimed. She was so proud of him for finding a way in, to help California. She had to wipe a tear from her eye.

Jean-Claude remained cheerful throughout, his smile lines deeply grooved around cheeks and eyes. The doctor without borders was no stranger to farewells.

Ava turned to follow CPO Kudo back into the grey bowels of HNS *Hilo* to play dress-up.

31

Interesting fact: Hawaii was now headquarters and safe haven for the Pacific Fleet. When the great San Diego naval base fell to the earthquakes, most ships were out on an exercise. But the fleet lost ships to the tsunamis, which also caused tens of thousands of deaths in Hawaii, especially in the city of Hilo. The Navy lost families in port. To say that they held a grudge would be a gross understatement.

"We are here to reclaim a battalion of the Oregon Army," Captain Pulaski of HNS *Hilo* announced to Captain Cote of HMCS *Saskatoon,* the frigate next door.

To Ava's eyes, a frigate appeared daintier than a destroyer. *Hilo*'s apparent edge in tonnage was moot, however, since the home of the Canadian Pacific Fleet was the harbor next door. *Saskatoon* simply cruised around a headland to meet them here. Back within range of excellent Canadian phone data service, Jona happily served Ava a map.

"We have intelligence that this missing battalion is in Victoria," Captain Pulaski continued. "Naturally Hawaii volunteered to help Oregon transport it home."

Captain Cote looked askance at a Canadian Army colonel standing next to him. "It was my understanding that the battalion in question is American, not Oregonian."

"The United States is defunct," the Hawaiian captain replied, his tone implying a swear word. "The battalion was illegally diverted from Oregon. We respectfully request that the battalion present itself here for inspection."

Ava stood hidden in the back row of some kind of honor lineup, stealing peeks between taller sailors in front of her. CPO Kudo turned out to have skinny little chicken arms. Ava's muscles didn't fit in her khaki blouses. So now she wore a baggy camouflage ensemble similar to her old Army uniform, in a different pattern of greens. Her waist pack fit under her shirt with plenty of room left over. The sailors disapproved, but she wore her own combat boots.

She also wore an ear piece and microphone to listen in. She could speak quietly and unseen to Captain Pulaski and Lt. Col. Marcus Wetherby, currently facing off against their Canadian counterparts. A camera feed on Wetherby's lapel gave her a wide-angle view on Jona's screen. The Canadian Captain Cote was beginning to look annoyed.

Ava murmured into her mike, "We need Cote as our ally here. Canada is not the enemy." This was only a reminder. *Stick to the plan, dude.*

Pulaski gave no indication of hearing her, but he did soften his approach. "Captain Cote, I respect you. We are here to investigate a serious allegation from our allies in Oregon. I hope you will join me in getting to the bottom of this."

"There is nothing to get to the bottom of!" the Canadian Army officer insisted, Colonel Tremblay. "Captain Pulaski, you are violating Canadian waters!"

Pulaski and Cote glared at him. Cote said coldly, "This is a formality, Colonel Tremblay. The Hawaiian Navy called ahead to explain their errand. And the Canadian Navy requested in advance that you produce the American battalion here at the pier. They appear to be missing. That is a problem."

"Protocol was followed," Captain Pulaski confirmed. "We docked with permission from our friends in the Canadian Navy."

That was pushing it. The navies of Hawaii and Canada cooperated. The Oregon and Canada Coast Guards worked together closely. But Canada did not offer alliance to any of the ex-U.S. successor states, only membership to a select few. Alaska was its new acquisition in this neck of the woods. Canada's official position was that alliance 'would be premature.' In other words, 'let's see who's left standing a decade from now.'

Jona vibrated with an incoming message from Kelly.

KPrak: Morales incoming. On map.

Ava checked to find a marker migrating on street view. She reported via her mike. "Our contact in the battalion is moving toward us. Three blocks out."

Pulaski made a show of holding his ear phone and asking her to repeat that. He told Captain Cote the happy news.

"How do you know that?" Colonel Tremblay demanded.

"Captain…" his Navy counterpart suggested to him in a growl. One did not bark things rudely at the captain of a vessel on his own deck. Especially not Army someones. "The question is, Colonel Tremblay, why you didn't know that."

Captain Pulaski chose to ignore the rude one. A gust of wind struck them, and the rain strengthened. "Captain Cote, would you prefer to wait in my cabin? While the Army gets its act together."

"Thank you, Captain Pulaski," his counterpart returned, "but I'm quite comfortable."

Pulaski nodded. They all settled in to prove that they could stand firm in a rising gale. The gale meanwhile started hurling rain at them in sheets. A gust caused Ava to stumble into a neighbor in the back, who politely righted her.

"What are we doing?" she asked him quietly. A cloth shopping bag flew by, carried aloft from the city streets.

"Honor," he replied, and resumed his stoic pose, rain dripping from his nose.

After a few minutes of silence, Pulaski and Cote began to chat about the weather. This naturally segued into their respective ships' handling in rough seas. They showed off their familiarity with each other's ship class, by expressing mutual admiration of the model's fine features.

Ava got the impression they could keep this up for hours. *God, I hope not.* She murmured, "Our contact is now at the foot of the pier." Sadly becoming acquainted with the pace at which things nautical evolved, she hoped that meant they were less than an hour from going indoors. Cold rain poured into her collar, then down her back in rivulets. Good thing the ouiPhone was waterproof.

KPrak: Commanders advancing.

KPrak: Morales bitching about the rain.

Ava relayed the news to the Captain, and added, "When the major arrives, ask him to bring forward his non-coms. Then I have names of GIs to talk to, if you need them."

KPrak: Hawaii GI wants to run to boat.

Panic: Hold H GI. Wait until noncoms advance. Safer.

That reminded her. "Colonel Wetherby, Major Haskell bought a mail order bride from the Dakota Dust Bowl refugees. The grunts call them prairie cows. He's their CO."

Wetherby coughed, then restored himself to stoic pose. He so didn't want to be here today. But like Ava, he knew more than most about things Calm Act related. Of Oregon's original 'seed Rescos,' the ones from the dawn of the Calm Act, Wetherby was last man standing. The rest were executed or imprisoned following their courts martial.

Ava's neighbor on the left, Oliphant, the Marine who righted her when she stumbled, pursed his lips at her. "Prairie cows," he echoed.

"I hope we execute the bastard," her neighbor on the right commented, a brother Marine. Both towered over Ava. The howling wind and clatter of rain slashing the deck let them get away with talking in ranks like this, at least at the back. Voices didn't carry.

"Guys, you never heard this," Ava murmured, hand blocking the mike. "You never saw me. This never happened."

"Sure." "Right."

It was a minor thing. But Ava felt her own righteous indignation rising. *Stay cool, be effective,* she warned herself, as she felt her blood start to boil. She murmured into the mike, "Colonel, Canada offered refuge to those mail order brides. America left them to die. Like me."

Her flanking Marines stared at her on that one. Then one after the other gave her a grim nod of respect.

Great. Now they think I'm a prairie cow. But that bit of misdirection could only help her stay anonymous through this. She wanted Canada's leave to go home. Hopefully without the frosted cabbage corps killing her en route.

At last the American officers were escorted to the naval captains and their attendant colonels. Colonel Tremblay introduced them grudgingly. "Major Haskell, battalion commander. Majors Prieto and Chomsky." The latter two were army captains, getting a social promotion so as not to be confused with the lofty naval captains.

Ava recognized one of them. "Chomsky has an attitude toward the states that joined Canada," Ava commented into her mike. "Considers them traitors. Our contacts are in his company. He's grumpy but respected. Prieto is well-liked." She'd spent a half hour on the phone with Kelly, decanting anything they could remember that the GIs told them on the train.

Captain Pulaski didn't appear to give a damn whether the officers were popular. "Major Haskell. Your battalion was assigned to Lewis-McChord, for the purpose of defending the Oregon borders. You abandoned your post."

"We obeyed orders, sir."

Pulaski pressed, "Major Haskell, you do not have the right to obey an unlawful order."

"Captain, I had no reason to believe the order was unlawful," Haskell insisted. "My regiment was diverted to protect – To Canada. My CO and fellow officers believed the assignment to be valid."

Ava murmured, "Colonel Wetherby, how many civilians died doing Haskell's job?"

Wetherby stepped forward. "Major Haskell, civilians had to step in after your regiment deserted. Tens of thousands of Oregonians, with the bare minimum of training, died defending the California border. Captain Pulaski, Colonel Tremblay, Oregon demands that these officers be returned to Portland for court martial, for dereliction of duty."

Ava winced. She hadn't realized there were quite so many civilian casualties. Even though she served in the Hudson Army, she never wondered how many of its soldiers died holding the borders. *Not nearly enough on the Apple borders,* she thought automatically. Nothing could change her feelings on that score.

"I agree," Captain Pulaski said. He turned to the Canadian Army representative. "Colonel Tremblay?"

"Perhaps the court martial could be held here," Tremblay suggested. "With members of the panel from Canada, as well as Oregon and Hawaii."

"With respect, colonel," Wetherby returned, "this battalion was assigned to Oregon."

"Yes, that is the point under contention, colonel," Tremblay returned equably. "Whether Haskell and his officers were legally reassigned, as they believe. Their CO and entire regiment were transferred to Canada."

"That is not a possible legal order, colonel," Wetherby said frigidly.

Tremblay waved his hand. "I misspoke. Deployed physically to Canada, under American command, of course."

"There is no legal American command, colonel," Wetherby said. "Because the United States no longer exists. This is Oregon's position."

Captain Pulaski raised his hand. "Take them below," he ordered the Marines who flanked the officers.

"You can't –" Major Haskell began.

"Go quietly and you will be treated with respect," Captain Pulaski told him. "Respect I question whether you deserve, major." He turned to Tremblay. "Next I wish to interview the battalion's senior non-coms."

The Canadian Captain Cote cut in, "Captain Pulaski, this is extraordinarily high handed."

"Captain Cote, the consequences of their cowardice were severe," Pulaski returned. "As Lieutenant Colonel Wetherby just related. We wonder what this battalion has been doing in Canada, while they were supposed to be defending Oregon. Hawaii also wonders whether Canada is holding soldiers from Hawaii, Oregon, and any other sovereign American nations against their will. I remind you that Canada recognizes these nations."

"You are suggesting this is an extradition, sir?" Captain Cote asked.

"I am suggesting the nations of Hawaii, Oregon, Rockies, the Montane Territory…"

Ava supplied, "Hudson, Ohio, Carolina, Ken–Tenn, Florida, Ark–Lou–Sippi…"

Pulaski rattled those off too. "These nations demand their soldiers back. Hawaii is happy to facilitate. We are open to legal proceedings to retrieve our nationals from the Canadian interior. But this battalion is here and now, and we will start with them."

"Captain, I sympathize with your position," Captain Cote said. "But you've arrested three officers. I'm not sure we can countenance bringing anyone else from the battalion on board. I can't speak for Colonel Tremblay, but I believe I need legal counsel and diplomatic representatives from the Canadian government to proceed further."

Ava commented, "They're on the dock…"

"Very well," Pulaski agreed. "I had hoped to bring them in out of the rain. But let us interview the non-coms and enlisted on the pier. We have no reason to believe any of them will stand court martial. Our intent is merely to return them to Oregon to complete their terms of service. In due course, they will be repatriated to their home nations, if they wish."

Ava tuned out the rest of the posturing as the party broke up on deck. With the Marines, she ducked into a tack room and grabbed her duffel. She feared it stood out like a sore thumb, especially the Project Reunion patch. She worried at it with a fingernail, trying to pull it off.

Her benefactor from before, Oliphant, stayed her hand. He grabbed a marine gear duffel, dumped its contents, and then thrust her bag into it. "I can carry it for you if you want," he offered.

Ava grinned and held out a fist to bop with him.

"You're from the Dakotas?" he asked.

"I'm not here, never was," she reminded him. "But no. I survived the Apple."

"No shit." In the Navy, they'd heard what happened to the Apple, and believed it. The Atlantic Fleet was instrumental in Project Reunion to save the city.

"If anyone sees me," Ava said in entreaty, "I may never make it back. I want to go home, Oliphant. I'm a Hudson patriot. I want Hudson and Hawaii to become allies."

"Cool. Stick with us, short stuff. We'll hide you."

"I need to escape into Victoria," Ava said. "Without the Canadians noticing."

He eyed her uniform. "You got civvies under that?"

Ava nodded. Unfortunately, her T-shirt was white, which would be rather eye-catching when sopping wet. She dug into her bag and pulled her red rain poncho and lavender Chinese jacket to the top for easy access.

Oliphant nodded. "Let's go."

As they moved, Ava kept half an ear on the discussions centered on Captain Pulaski, skipper of the *Hilo.* Occasionally she fed him a piece of information on demand. The name of a sergeant. GIs from different companies to draw attention away from her contacts. The little she knew of what the battalion was doing on Vancouver Island.

Ava followed her contingent of marines down onto the pier, marching to flank Captain Pulaski and the others at the foot of the dock.

The American sergeants, quite rightly, said the officers never consulted them, just told them they'd been reassigned to Edmonton.

"Oh-dark thirty deployment, no advance warning," Ava muttered to her mike. "GIs were re-shuffled into and out of the regiment a couple days before." Pulaski confirmed these 'rumors' with the sergeants, who conceded they were true. They were also rather damning. An international deployment wasn't a spur of the moment thing.

Pulaski requested the sergeants retire to the back, so he could speak directly to their men. Ava was pleased for their sake that the sergeants withdrew but spread out in *front* of their men, at parade rest in the still sheeting rain.

"We stand with our troops, sir," announced the highest ranked of them.

Good for you! Ava thought. The rank and file shouldn't have to face an O-6 level officer, one step down from an admiral, without a sergeant present for moral support.

She showed her map to Oliphant, where her contacts stood on the dock. Morales was near the front, to her left as she faced the base of the dock. Oliphant obligingly veered his group to that side, advancing forward farther than was polite. They were actually beyond the row of American sergeants.

Ava ducked down behind beefy guys and peeled out of her wet Navy camouflage. She quickly pulled on her lavender jacket and red rain poncho, pulling its hood well over her face. She stuffed her drenched Navy uniform into the now-empty duffel Oliphant had provided, and handed it back to him.

On a bright sunny day, she probably couldn't get away with this. But wind and rain made it hard to see. That would change quickly when she stood up from her crouch, a bright red hood bobbing through a sea of wet-dark green uniforms. Oliphant and a few more marines flanked her and percolated forward even further, as far as she dared.

Panic: 30 yds from Morales, red rain poncho.

KPrak: Morales sees you.

"In position," Ava reported over her mike. "Ready to cross lines when the GIs move."

"Godspeed," Wetherby murmured back. "And thank you."

"Thank you," Ava returned. "The East still cares about you. Never forget."

"I won't," Wetherby said. "Give my regards to your boss."

Pulaski suddenly spoke through a loudspeaker mounted on the *Hilo.* "American GIs. You were wrongfully diverted from Oregon under illegal orders. Oregon wants you back. Hawaii is here to offer you a ride, and repatriation. Your officers may face prosecution. But all enlisted personnel and their NCOs are offered amnesty. If you wish to return home, please step forward."

The Americans in front of Oliphant's marines had to step around them. Ava scuttled quickly through, still squatting, threading through until she reached Morales. Other soldiers flowed around them to step forward, or backward in some cases.

Ava popped up and gave Morales a big hug and a kiss. "We'll miss you!" she cried.

He kissed her back with interest, then let her go with a laugh. "Thanks, St. Pauli girl!" The other guys she met in the bar car crowded around to trade high-fives with her.

"Say cheese!" She snapped one last picture of them. "Jona caption. Never forget," she said. Pulaski and Wetherby probably heard that. *Good.*

"Never forget," Morales agreed.

With that, they stepped forward to claim a ride home to Oregon.

Marines from the Canadian side stepped forward to drag her back behind their lines, scolding her severely. Every few steps she turned and took pictures, waved like crazy, and threw kisses to the troops. Some recalled the St. Pauli girl and her rose gold phone from the train concourse in Edmonton. So a smattering throughout the troop waved back at her.

"I'm from Minnesota," she explained to her Canadian Marine escort. They were unimpressed. "Soldiers deserve a sendoff," she elaborated. That earned a grudging nod from one of them.

The battalion mostly finished splitting into two groups, about two thirds forward and one hanging back. If this were a normal parade ground evolution, they'd have finished in under a minute. But these soldiers were saying good-bye to friends they'd served with, far from home, for years.

"Why do we think they hang back?" Pulaski asked the group-think over her ear piece.

"Wives in Edmonton," Ava suggested. "Not many sweethearts. No mingling with Canadians. They're really isolated."

"Fear," Wetherby suggested. "Of consequences."

Pulaski got back on the horn. "Those of you hanging back. Perhaps you left wives in Edmonton. Oregon is happy to extend citizenship to your dependents when they reach the border. This could take time and negotiation. But Oregon honors your service, and welcomes your families. Literally millions of Oregon civilians are fighting on the front lines. They're doing your job. While you sit in garrison in a foreign land, far from harm's way. I urge you to reconsider. You have three minutes to step forward."

Another thirty-odd did so.

One of their sergeants stepped up to Pulaski. "With respect, sir, someone needs to tell those wives that they have the option. I'm willing to carry that message. But I belong in Oregon with my troops."

Pulaski nodded, and got back on the horn. "All of you who remain. We respect your choice. But please carry that promise to the families left behind. Raise your hand if you will tell the wives that they are welcome in Oregon."

Nearly all of them raised a fist, including a couple lieutenants lurking in the rear. The other junior officers had stepped forward. A few more enlisted stepped forward now to elect Oregon.

Still on the loudspeaker, Captain Pulaski asked politely, "Captain Cote. With your permission, I intend to board these troops."

By now, a news crew was filming the circus. Cote didn't have much choice. He stepped out of the way and waved an arm to indicate the Americans were free to board.

Colonel Tremblay was not consulted. With nothing more than a couple honor guards, he wasn't equipped to stop this if the Navy's Cote decided to allow it.

"Board the ship," Pulaski ordered. Marines behind him re-formed to make a corridor and guide the GIs. "Captain Cote, on behalf of the Hawaiian Navy and our Oregon allies, I thank you for your assistance. We will get underway as soon as practical." He snubbed Tremblay.

Cote nodded respect.

We did it! Ava exulted in triumph. *Take that, frosted cabbage!* It was a small thing, but she'd landed her first blow against the Northern League.

Never forget!

"Ava! What are you doing here!" wailed Laurent, scurrying up behind her.

32

Interesting fact: Canadian news only carried the Oregon battalion story west of the Dust Bowl. The viewing public around Edmonton and Victoria were interested, but the rest, not so much. Canadians were growing fatigued by news of the ex-U.S.

"Laurent! What are you doing here?" Ava returned.

"Working," he said. "This...diplomatic incident. What were you doing?"

"Saying good-bye," Ava said ingenuously. "You remember Morales and the guys from the bar car? I was visiting them here in Victoria. Isn't it cool? They're going home to Oregon!"

She'd left her mike on, so Wetherby and Pulaski would catch that she was busted and couldn't contribute any more. Now she surreptitiously turned it off. *Thank you. Never forget.*

Laurent took her elbow and firmly steered her clear of the Canadian Marines. He flashed his RCMP credentials a couple times to excuse himself for wading in here. Once they got free, he didn't stop until they put the news cameras behind them, and ducked into his temporary car.

"Your friend told me you were sick, in Vancouver. Kelly."

"I got better," Ava said. "A couple days ago." Her quest complete, she'd tried to hustle out of Oregon. But Tanner and Wu needed time, as did the Hawaiian Navy. Hofer also made good use of the time, digging up more details about Oregon's microchip manufacturing. Ava was carrying another black box with a memory dongle back to Hudson. Fortunately for her, Tanner and Wu caught the worst of the memorization assignments. Ava only had to memorize contacts for Hudson and Ohio to connect with diplomatic channels in Oregon and Hawaii, not technical code words.

"I thought you didn't trust Kelly," Laurent pressed.

"I really don't," Ava agreed.

"Then why let her stay in your hotel room?"

"You're being awfully nosy, Laurent," Ava replied. "I just wanted to get out and look around a little. Is that so bad?"

"Did you cause this diplomatic incident?"

"How would I do that?" Ava asked, blinking. "Laurent, I'm an eighteen-year-old courier. How would *I* get the Hawaiian Navy here?"

What a fabulously good question. She hoped to have a hilariously good answer ready by the time she spoke with Skull.

Laurent scowled at her. "No, I don't suppose you could. But Ava, you were supposed to contact me before leaving Vancouver."

"I'm sorry, Laurent," she said. "I didn't realize that was, like, an official thing. I thought you were just getting kind of, um…romantic. I really do have a boyfriend back home. We've been together since I was fifteen." She glanced sideways at him through her eyelashes, trying to look young and bashful. "I've never had another boyfriend. Cade is everything to me. I don't know how to deal with, um, romantic."

"You're really in love with him."

"I guess. I mean, I don't know anything else. Cade is my one and only." *Sorry, Cade.* She sincerely doubted he'd get this sappy about her, even to manipulate someone. Cade was a better liar than she was. He was also an accomplished flirt when he chose to be – men, women, he didn't care.

Laurent sighed. "Well, it's an official order. You're not to leave Vancouver again without my permission."

"OK. I'm sorry," she said meekly. "I won't do it again." *Damned straight I won't. Hudson, here I come!*

"Where's Jean-Claude?" Laurent asked, starting the car.

"He went south. Doctor stuff. Médecins Sans Frontières."

Laurent corrected her awful pronunciation on automatic. Then, "South where? You don't mean Oregon!"

"That was the plan, yeah," Ava agreed. *Huh. Maybe Jean-Claude can take the heat for this.* "Oh! You don't think he –? No."

"No what?"

"No, he wouldn't tell Oregon about the American soldiers," said Ava. *Or maybe he mentioned it, not realizing they would go mental. Nah, least said the better. Let Laurent spin his own theories.*

"But how would he cross the border?" Laurent demanded.

"I don't know. I hope he didn't go with Triad smugglers! That sounds dangerous."

"Extremely dangerous!" Laurent agreed. "No. No, he must have waltzed into a border crossing. Then talked too much, to gain entry."

Good theory! "I gave him some money for drugs," Ava admitted. "To help him help others."

Laurent shook his head in disgust. "Americans and drugs."

"We're not all bad," Ava claimed. She sniffed, and wiped her nose on her wet poncho. "Can we go somewhere I can change into something dry?"

He patted her knee condescendingly. No doubt he meant it kindly. "We'll be at the police station in a moment. You can change there. Um, but then we walk to the bus, to the ferry back to Vancouver. To the bus. To the SkyTrain. To your hotel." He sighed.

"I understand," Ava assured him. "It's just very wet here."

"I have a couple more charges waiting for me back at the police station. Agricultural experts from Oregon. Border Services is processing them. They got permission to travel east. They might be on your train, if you leave soon."

"Really? I'm leaving Tuesday."

"I see," Laurent said sadly. He didn't.

And that was a good thing.

The slow ferry trip back to Vancouver was kind of fun. Ava caught more pictures of seals and misty creepy scenery during a break in the storm. And she made the acquaintance of Tanner and Wu again, who turned out to be passable actors.

The teen generously offered to show the men the ropes the next day, to buy train tickets and secure medical clearance to cross the Dust Bowl. Their alarm at this news was most gratifying. Ava couldn't resist adding details about surviving a dust storm and digging out the tracks before a freight train plowed into them.

The Oregon pair had their own generous wads of Canadian cash, courtesy of Laurent. Ava wondered if Skull was selling moonshine futures in PIAGO Power to bankroll all this. Investors sure lined up in a hurry, salivating to jump on board.

But PIAGO Power is real. Right?

Ava decided that if she had any doubts on that score, these were the last people she should share them with. But having met Tony Nasser, and heard his perspective on the founding fathers of Hudson... She wouldn't put it past him to fake it.

~

AVA BLEW OUT TO CENTER HERSELF. SHE NODDED TO HERSELF IN THE ROOM mirror, a large tummy aperture framed with a totem-style bird. *I have nothing to be afraid of,* she told herself. She swallowed.

It was time. She tapped the button to connect her 'videconc' with Skull. She reminded herself that they'd played this trick twice before. Canadian Intelligence were no slouches. By now they were surely getting better at decoding these calls.

"Hi, boss!" she said sunnily, as Skull appeared. "You have a sunburn. I'm jealous. A week ago, Vancouver outdid Noah's Ark. Still raining."

He smiled, mellow. "You missed Solstice yesterday. I opened the border with PA. Held a big party in Ithaca, picnic and boating all afternoon, fireworks at night. Ran buses up from from Towanda, Elmira, and Binghamton. Good times."

Hudson was continuing its new tradition of big public holidays on the Solstices and Equinoxes. Governor Sean Cullen claimed this evenly spaced holidays through the year. Entering the four seasons represented facing the new climate challenges together as a nation.

Ava took her boss's relaxation as a good sign, and blew out more tension. "Was Cade home for it?"

"No. I assume he celebrated on Long Island with Cameron and Perard, his husband," Skull said. "The big Resco training starts...next Monday? Yeah, the twenty-ninth. So he's plowed under with work getting that together. He was supposed to keep it to twenty hours a week." Skull shook his head, resigned.

"Cade doesn't like free time," Ava pointed out. "Or being alone."

"No. You're right. Hey, before we get started. Ava, I asked you to hold off on telling Cade about Jeremy in Sioux Lookout for a reason."

"Oh. Yeah. But it made him happy, didn't it?"

Brow furrowed, Skull searched her face. "Not exactly. There's a video from him, on your file share. For Jeremy. Cameron said he was up half the night with Cade. He was still crying off and on in the office the next day."

Ava stared, mouth open in horror. She wished she could fly this minute to Cade and fold him into her arms. But she was still at least a week away. "I'm so sorry. Can I talk to him? Tell him I'm sorry?"

Skull shook his head. "Cade's alright now. We spoke Saturday. He's busy and enthralled with putting together this circus. Just...please don't bypass me again like that, OK? I wasn't being mean, Ava, keeping you two apart. I won't always tell you everything. You've got to trust me. I care about you two."

Ava wiped a tear from her eye. "I'm sorry!"

"Apology accepted. Enough of that. So! You made it to pin city! Well done!"

Pin city? Seattle? "You said D-minus," Ava reminded him. "On the bitter herbs." *Arugula. The American Northern League troops.*

"Yeah, I was afraid that might blow up in your face," Skull allowed. "But it didn't, right? I mean, you got back to Vancouver quietly. I got the money and train permission lined up for tomorrow. Including Kelly. I trust she's not in the room."

Ava shook her head. "I booked a new room for me, and let her have the old one. Figured that would keep this conversation private." She picked up the tablet she was using for a video camera, and panned it around the room. "Totem birds this time."

"That's an awesome hotel," he said.

"It really is. Laurent suggested it. Tanner and Wu went ga-ga. I guess Tanner is some kind of collector of totem pole modern art. Took us half an hour yesterday to pry him out of the lobby."

"Now Tanner is cucumbers?" *Zucchini, PIAGO Power,* he meant.

"Tanner is generic. Wu's on cukes," Ava replied. "They're alright. We've got a date in an hour to buy the tickets and get medical clearance."

"Got it. What did they mean about handling the greens themselves? We couldn't figure that out. Sounded ominous."

"Yeah, about that. You know how sometimes you say something, and it turns out you accidentally pushed a crazy button? Like, the big red Make My Day button?"

"Yeah?" Skull said, in slow misgiving.

Ava licked her lips. "Turns out, that particular kind of salad was a real sore point. Oh, I didn't tell you. Oregon has a compulsory draft now, every man and woman, age eighteen to thirty."

"That's extreme. And wildly unpopular, I bet. Is it relevant?"

"It's a red button," Ava said. "Turns out someone made off with their border troops, you see. There was this big foofaraw yesterday while I was sightseeing in Victoria –"

"Sightseeing," he acknowledged. "Victoria."

"Yeah. A pineapple boat sailed in, to demand the locals fork over a stolen salad!"

Ava bit a finger and waited while Skull worked this out. He gradually started laughing his ass off.

Wiping tears from his eyes, he confirmed, "And then there were four in Vancouver."

"Yeah, Laurent escorted us back after the food fight."

"So you never actually left," Skull said.

"Nope. No, I'm under Mountie supervision. Laurent was pretty cross that I visited Victoria without telling him. I was afraid you'd be mad, too."

"I am in awe," Skull clarified. "You got away with it? And the pineapple with the salad?"

"Yeah, so far so good. Oregon won its salad, and suspicion fell elsewhere."

"Hopefully on foe, not friend?"

"My friend continued south," Ava said. "He can't be reached."

Skull chuckled some more. "Well. You just erased your D's for the semester."

"I thought you'd average the D's with the A's. More like a low C average."

"No. Overall A-plus. Ava, this is beyond my wildest dreams. Let's not talk any more. I want detail. But it has to wait. Come on home, courier. Stay safe. No prizes left except getting you back. With passengers."

"Want any souvenirs?"

"No, thanks. You can't top what you've already given me." Skull was still grinning when he clicked off the video feed.

I got away with it! Ava exulted. *I hope I got away with it.*

She still had 3,000 miles of frosted cabbage territory to cross before she was home safe. The death angels were perfectly capable of striking into Hudson, too. *But what good would that do them?*

She had no idea. She'd screwed with powers way out of her league. She'd just have to trust that no one thought an 18-year-old courier was an ongoing threat. In any event, there wasn't much she could do about it. One train, one track, led home.

Souvenirs, she decided resolutely. She'd love to get little totem critters for Doc and Cookie and Puño, but they were never to know she left Hudson. She supposed Cerveza and KT might like them.

She'd need to buy another ouiPhone for Kelly in order to pry Jana out of her hot little hands. Ava had removed Jona's battery, and stuffed it into a Faraday cage pouch, where the phone would safely remain until she could gift it to Daneel. Jona's electronic signature was linked to the Hawaiian fiasco now. The burner phone Kelly used on her end had already been tossed.

Kelly showed Ava her final report last night, submitted to the dead drop in Vancouver. *I'm homesick. Going back to Hudson.* She'd formally canceled her application for asylum. She won permission to cross Canada in order to return to Hudson.

No other souvenirs? Ava thought sadly.

This trip had taught her a lesson. She needed to invest in female friends. Maybe she could get something for Butch from her old gang, and Rahema. What would say *Vancouver?*

She stifled a giggle, and reached for the tablet to search for it. Yes, actually, they did sell toy geoducks. There was a kinky boutique nestled among the native art galleries in Gastown. Something to look forward to after herding her new flock through their medical clearance.

~

"CAM? KYLE," SKULL SAID.

"I could actually tell that by the extremely secure line," Lt. Colonel Cam Cameron said dryly. "What now?"

"New development," Skull said. "Ava cracked open an intriguing line of attack."

"Ava did? How intriguing?"

"Magic."

Cam sighed. "I don't believe in magic."

"Remember your trick with claiming a hundred percent?"

"I was voted down," Cam reminded him.

Skull said, "I thought it was clever. We all agreed in principle. We just thought it was more politic to deal in the neighbors. We've got new neighbors this week."

"We do?"

"Hawaii just made off with a battalion of American GIs. They belonged to Oregon, you see. Stolen. By our American command in Edmonton."

"That *is* interesting," Cam agreed. "But I'm still not tracking the hundred percent – oh, my. Edmonton?"

"Let's wait. Next week we'll talk, once the agent is back. She can't speak freely yet."

"I look forward to that very much. Speaking of which. Thanks for the new game cards for the Resco marker game. But I'm still missing your materials on rural torpor. Half hour talk during Tuesday's sessions."

"You'll get it," Skull growled. "Gotta go."

~

AVA BLINKED DUMBLY AND ACCEPTED THE SPRAY OF WHITE CALLA LILY AND red rose, nestled among rain forest ferns. "Thank you, Laurent," she said, at a loss. "They're beautiful."

The line moved, and she kicked her luggage along a few yards, including her replenished survival knapsack and brace of water jugs, empty for now. Business class boarding would begin in a few minutes. Kelly tactfully held back Tanner and Wu, to grant Laurent a modicum of privacy.

Laurent pointed to the handle on the bouquet's plastic water cup, the sort that hooks into a car window. "I thought that would work on the train window," he pointed out awkwardly. "And you know, that spot over your feet in the berth." *In bed,* in other words. He flushed slightly.

"You're not going with us," Ava gathered. "I don't know why I assumed..."

"No," he agreed. "It was a real adventure, Ava. Romantic. I probably ought to grow up and be a more dispassionate sort of Mountie." His self-deprecating smile brought out a cute dimple in one cheek.

Ava suspected he knew that. Laurent was far too cute not to know it. "You were a great time, Laurent. Thank you for looking out for me. And the great hotel, and everything." She tiptoed to kiss him on the cheek. "I think you make an awesome Mountie."

"Yeah, well, you don't have much to compare me to."

Not true, Ava thought. *I have all too much to compare you to. I think he'll always win. That's no reflection on you, Laurent.* But she nodded. "You're my one and only Mountie."

He grinned. "I should go. Good-bye, Kelly. Mr. Tanner, Dr. Wu. I hope you enjoy your stay in Canada. I leave you in experienced hands, with Ava."

He stole another kiss, then strode away, pleats and belt flapping fetchingly on the rear of his executive rain coat.

"He has class, I'll give him that," Kelly said. "Did you sleep with him?"

Tanner and Wu looked offended.

Ava sniffed her rose, hiding her lower face. She arched an eyebrow above the spray. "None of your business. You lack class, Kelly."

Kelly shot a dismissive glance at the flowers. "I get paid better."

Point, Ava conceded.

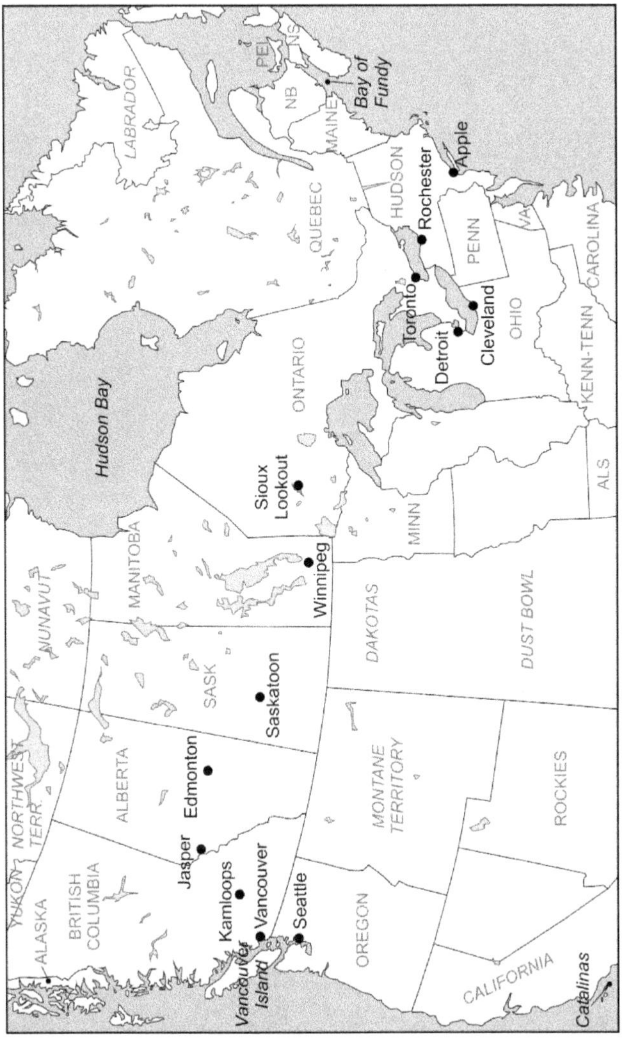
Hudson Bay
LABRADOR
PEI
NS
NB
Bay of Fundy
MAINE
QUEBEC
HUDSON
Rochester
Apple
PENN
VA
CAROLINA
Toronto
Cleveland
Detroit
OHIO
KENN-TENN
ONTARIO
Sioux Lookout
ALS
MINN
Winnipeg
MANITOBA
NUNAVUT
DAKOTAS
DUST BOWL
SASK
Saskatoon
NORTHWEST TERR.
ALBERTA
Edmonton
MONTANE TERRITORY
ROCKIES
YUKON
ALASKA
BRITISH COLUMBIA
Jasper
Kamloops
Vancouver
Seattle
Vancouver Island
OREGON
CALIFORNIA
Catalinas

33

Interesting fact: Ava Panic appeared on the raw video footage of the 'Hawaiian Incident' in Victoria. However the local news editor didn't have her permission for broadcast, and had no way to identify or contact her. So she responsibly edited Ava out.

Ava's memories of the train home were never as vivid as the westbound trip, when the sights and experiences were fresh and novel.

Far less intrigue was on offer. The quartet had facing berths together, Ava and Kelly on one side, Tanner and Wu on the other. Ava stuck Kelly with the top bunk. Kelly loved it, overwhelmingly grateful to have a bunk this time. She had a hard time sleeping through the short twilit nights, and appreciated the claustrophobic dark. And Ava got to keep her treasured window.

The steward was careful to shift her flowers into her berth at night when he rotated and reattached the benches to build their beds.

The quartet ate meals together, and traded stories of Oregon and Hudson, but only in their private row of the sleeper car. In the dining car for supper, or in the viewing cars, they kept their conversation strictly on Canada. Aside from meals, they stuck to their natural pairings, teenage girls versus middle-aged men.

Ava and Kelly caught up in Western Civ. Skull submitted their essays for grading and returned the results. Kelly passed her GED back at West Point. But she didn't like English any better than Ava did. That made her a better tutor than Cade, who could readily rattle off a thousand word essay in an hour. His grammar, spelling, and punctuation were flawless on the first draft, as well as hook, style, and substance. Ava still struggled with the basic mechanics. Kelly coached her to write in distinct passes, the way a high school teacher would advise – outline, expand outline, write draft, then revise for content, then style, then the fidgety correct English. That way she could focus on one aspect of the problem at a time.

Ava objected that was too slow. Kelly told her to adjust her expectations. If she expected an essay to take five hours, would she still be frustrated? With practice, she'd get faster. Kelly was currently managing B's at about three hours per essay.

Ava had to admit, Kelly's approach actually accomplished something in each 45-minute pass, which was about as much sitting and writing as Ava could stand before getting up to move around. So, it worked. She managed an A- on her essay discussing the potential for cities such as Detroit and Cincinnati to become latter-day 'Champagne Fairs' linking trade to the south and north.

Skull and General Schwabacher read that essay after it was graded, and debated its merits in a new section of comments. Their verdict was that her thesis was good but the cities were wrong. Cleveland, Erie, and Buffalo tied the American northeastern tier with Canada, while the Apple and Philadelphia ports linked to the south. Order was a prerequisite for trade, and Detroit had a long way to go to restore anyone's confidence. Schwabacher hoped his new acquisitions in western Virginia might aspire to the Champagne Fair role for a land route, but Cincinnati wasn't seeing much traffic.

As for sightseeing, the coastal mountains, then Kamloops and the desert were hot and pretty again. Jasper and the Rockies were still pretty, and also surprisingly warm.

They caught Edmonton in mid-day instead of pre-dawn this time around, and didn't need dust removal. The group elected to rent an electric auto-cab to tour the city for a couple of their six hours of layover.

Ava and Kelly grudgingly agreed they needed something touristy for camouflage. They let Tanner choose the Works Arts & Design Festival downtown, where he drooled over the First Nations art again. After a strict 30 minute limit for culture, Ava programmed the auto-cab to drive past her best guess for military installations in the neighborhood. They didn't approach too closely. But she took pictures with Porta's camera, the one she never uploaded to the servers. They didn't spot the American compound itself, but Ava did photograph a sign that gave directions to it. That picture she caught on Jana so it would be geocoded, and marked as private, no upload.

"Because we're not spying," Kelly said.

"That would be rude," Ava agreed.

"Oregon would want us to go see," Tanner insisted, and reached for the auto-cab control tablet.

Ava swatted his hand away playfully. "You already had your turn. It was boring."

"I haven't had my turn," Wu pointed out. "But our visa is clear. No spying."

The Canadians devised a new form of visa for the guys. They traveled under their own Oregon IDs, with a detailed itinerary. The train car steward had to sign and date their paperwork each time they left and re-boarded the train. Kelly's deportation progress was similarly monitored. Ava was the only one pretending to be Canadian.

Ava didn't notice any Mounties assigned to watch them this time. But she assumed there were plain-clothes police on the train somewhere, in addition to military MPs in the ever-present troop cars. This train was too critical and fragile a link between eastern and western Canada.

~

THE DUST BOWL WAS WORSE, NOT BETTER, THE SECOND TIME THROUGH. They lost power two hours out of Edmonton, before the dust got bad.

Temperatures inside the train started to climb. Two hours later, they were well into the dust when they pulled onto a side rail in late evening.

No digging was required this time. The breakage was on the far side of Saskatoon. But their train sat there stranded for over twenty-four hours. Dry lightning played through the night. Dust pervaded everything. With dawn, the temperatures mounted again. By 1:00 p.m., it was over 100 degrees in their berthing – 40 Celsius, according to Corporal Singh, their troop steward for the dangerous leg.

Ava stripped down to shorts and sports bra, plus the vital silk scarf and breath mask and goggles. The dust kept clogging her pores to frustrate sweating. Singh advised them to move as little as possible, and use no more than one of their water gallons that day. With only emergency power to Singh's station, the passengers cycled through taking turns on his two breath nebulizers. Ava volunteered to staff that for a while, giving Singh a break to sit and chat with frightened passengers. By 3:00, she was dizzy and needed to sit down again herself. Singh's station reported the temperature as 46 Celsius by then – 115 Fahrenheit outside, and not much cooler inside the car.

When Ava stumbled back to the gang, Kelly rose from Wu's usual seat and asked Ava to take it for a while. Wu sat on Ava's bench. Tanner was not handling the situation well. He was hunched forward, and rigid. Ava sat knee-to-knee with him, and took his hands. He grasped them back hard enough to hurt.

"You'll get through this," she promised softly.

"It's getting darker," he said. "Why is it getting darker?"

"A dust storm is coming. It's impressive. Want to look?" Ava faced the storm, coming up behind him.

"God no. When will we get out of here?"

"There is only now," Ava told him. "This now, I choose another swallow of water. You, too."

He gulped too much, and spilled more down his chest, and splashed some on his head. "I think I have heat stroke."

"Probably," Ava agreed. The storm, a swirling brown wall of menace, miles high, loomed closer. "You know what I have?"

"What do you have." Tanner couldn't care less.

"I have date rape drugs. I bet they'd help you sleep. Maybe a quarter dose. Not enough to knock you out. Just enough that you don't worry so much."

A long grumble vibrated up through their feet. The hiss mounted. Hairs stood up on Ava's arms and neck from the static electricity, and the ozone made her feel wired.

"What was that?" Tanner demanded, squeezing Ava's hand bones together in his panic.

Ava extracted her hands. "Just thunder," she said. She removed a capsule from her waist pack, and poured a couple ounces of water into a cup left from breakfast, after wiping the dust out with a corner of her scarf. She pulled apart the Rufie and tipped about a quarter of its powder into the water. "You see? Only a quarter dose. To calm you."

"I'm afraid," he admitted.

"That happens," she said. "But I'm with you. And I'll stay right here with you. Drink this. I'll keep you safe."

With further coaxing, Tanner drank the drug. Wu, watching intently, asked for the rest of the pill. Ava mixed the dose for him, barely a sprinkle of Rufie on the water.

"Just to take the edge off," she insisted. "You're doing fine. This is a once-in-a-lifetime experience. You want to see it," she urged Alan Wu.

"No, I don't!" Tanner squeaked.

"Shh, no," Ava assured. "But Alan likes physics. He'll enjoy thinking about the –" Yeah, Wu might, but Tanner wouldn't. "Kelly, you've got Alan, right?"

"Absolutely," Kelly agreed. She shifted onto the bench beside Wu, taking his hand. Maybe she whispered, maybe the rising hiss of the dust just blotted out the sound of her voice. But the pair across the aisle fell back out of Ava's universe.

The rising gloom took a sharp step darker as the wall of dust overtook the sun. "Take a look, Tanner," Ava encouraged. "It's always better to face your fear than turn your back." She trusted the drugs were starting to dull his terror. He wasn't clutching her hands so hard anymore.

At last he turned to see the maw of storm curving miles above to swallow them. "Oh my God, oh my God…"

Ava firmly pulled him to her bench, between her and the window. She beat some dust off his breath mask, and pulled out two fresh ones from Wu's survival kit.

"The masks get clogged, Tanner. We have to remember to keep them unclogged. Breathe *out,*" she encouraged, once she had the new mask on him. She was right. His old mask was crusted, and he didn't wear a scarf under it like she did. She hastily fetched another silk scarf from her luggage to augment his face protection. It was the one she'd been trying to save from dust service, Cade's impressionist painting of eating strawberries on the Staten Island Ferry.

Cade would understand.

By the time she got the new scarf back on Tanner, she could no longer see the wall of dust, or the ground, because they were inside the storm. Tanner slithered to the floor and buried his face in her lap. She forcibly turned his face to clear his breathing passage. She stroked his back to keep tabs on whether his chest rose and fell properly. And she listened to the storm.

These things are much easier to take, when I'm protecting someone else, she thought. *That's what Cade told Jeremy, on his video.* She tried to imagine showing it to the boy, when they reached Sioux Lookout. But her reflexes and training didn't allow it. She was in danger, and when in peril, she existed in the Now. *Breathe out…*

Tanner fell asleep, but she sat vigil over his breathing through the roaring white noise, the growling and pealing thunder, the occasional fusillade of pinging gravel, in an emotional whiteout beyond fear. Seconds crept by unremarked, experienced but not judged, neither good nor bad, but eternal and immense.

Eventually she saw the dim disk of the sun again, much lower in the sky. The temperature in the car had fallen to the merely uncomfortable, not life threatening. She roused Tanner for a groggy gulp of water, then let him settle back to sleep on her lap.

Three hours later, the backlog of westbound traffic broke through again, and passed them on the main track, train after train after train. Singh experimentally opened the doors on the car's far side, because the night air was cooler than inside the car. The temperature drop was a blessed relief, worth the clouds of dirt that blew in, borne by dust devils cavorting beneath the murky brown moon.

Ava decided that by now Tanner was merely sleeping, not dangerously drugged. So were Kelly and Wu. She left them to it, to gaze out the open door with fresh air bathing her skin. She climbed out, only a few steps from the carriage. She unwound her scarf and snapped out its dust, to dance with the little brown dervishes. And she laughed.

There was nothing quite like the exhilaration of surviving the threat, making it through to the other side, then laughing her defiance.

Corpsman Enthwaite, Corporal Singh's sidekick at Ava's end of the car, took a seat on the top doorstep. He inquired if she was quite well.

In answer, she threw her head back and howled at the moon. A couple guys clambered out of the troop car door a few yards down-train, and howled, too, one yip-yipping. In a few minutes, Kelly and Wu pushed pass Enthwaite to spill out and challenge the moon. The silliness spread up and down the train, passengers spilling out to howl, giddy with the relief of cool air on the surreal landscape.

Tanner and Wu seemed wary of Ava after that night. She couldn't blame them.

Laurent's flowers filled with dust, and wilted in the hot dry air. Ava threw them out. But she saved the car-window cup.

~

AT SASKATOON, THEY WERE ALLOWED INTO THE TRAIN STATION THIS TIME. In defense of its indoor air quality, the passengers disembarked one car at a time, to be vacuumed before entry.

Ava took a washcloth bath in the washroom, and rinsed her beautiful ferry scarf. She changed into fresh sports bra and underwear and shorts. Kelly babysat the luggage in the hallway. Then they traded places.

Ava luxuriated in feeling downright *chilly,* with bare wet skin, dripping hair, and wet scarf drying across her shoulders. The power was still out on the train. Other passengers waited in line to stand by an evaporative cooler, just a fan blowing hot dry air over water. Refrigeration type air conditioners were outlawed in Canada as in Hudson.

The train picked up another two cars for the leg to Winnipeg. The crew sent out to repair the rails had continued on to Saskatoon for medical attention afterward, because that station was closest. The new cars would take some home today, with their original short crew train from Winnipeg waiting to return tomorrow. Ava volunteered to help nurse. She didn't do any of the yucky stuff or heavy lifting. But the exhausted men enjoyed having a pretty young woman smile at them and hang on their seats to flirt.

Winnipeg came and went. They enjoyed their electronics again, especially their reading tablets and Internet. Summer heat broiled the Canadian Shield. But they turned north. There were lakes again.

Lots and lots of lakes.

34

Interesting fact: Quebec accepted 1200 child survivors from New York City, in need of extensive medical and psychiatric care. The province was very proud of them, and contrary to plan, passed none to Ontario and New Brunswick.

"Ava! Come in!" Mrs. Hodgins enfolded her in an embrace. "Jeremy, Ava's here! He wanted to meet you at the station. But by the time he came in from the woods, you were halfway here!"

Ava called ahead from the train as soon as she had phone service. That wasn't far from the small town of Sioux Lookout. The mid-day heat was waning, but she eagerly accepted the offer to dive into the lake. She and Jeremy ignored the swarming midges. They'd suffered worse than gnats in their time. The chill clean water felt divine.

Pa Hodgins fired up the grill for some walleye and caribou burgers. Mom Hodgins went inside with Ava and Jeremy to watch the video from Cade before supper.

The first part featured Cade alone, a little sun-burnt, but dressed in neat polo shirt and chinos for the office, where he sat. Ava assumed this was Lt. Col. Cameron's office space in Ronkonkoma on Long

Island. There seemed to be a dozen workstations, but no one else there for the moment.

"Hey, Jeremy! Recognize me?" Cade riffled his fingers through his darkening blond hair, fairly short on the sides and longer on top. "Not so Frosty, huh? Yeah, I don't bleach it anymore. I work in an office." He waved around. "For a while. Usually I'm traveling, like Ava. But I'm benched right now.

"The PTSD caught up with me. I don't know if you remember, but I got a bad concussion this one time in Jersey. They call it a 'traumatic brain injury,' TBI. PTSD and TBI go together like fire and gasoline. They make each other worse. So I'm benched to get my head straight. Sometimes it's three steps forward, two steps back, you know? But I'm getting better. Or so the doctor tells me." Cade laughed.

He looked good, relaxed and open.

Jeremy slowly smiled. Frosty the Snowman hadn't laughed often, or even smiled much.

Cade confided, "Ava said you didn't believe I cried a river when you left." A tear leaked now, and he wiped it away. "Well, I did. And you know what? I cried a river all over again when I heard she saw you, and you were doing great, and you had new parents, and lived on a lake, and I saw your picture!" He wiped a few more tears away this time.

"Jer, during the Starve, you and the other kids, you kept me going. If it looked like I wasn't scared, or I didn't hurt – Jer, I was trying to be strong for you. Not to impress you." Cade's hand sliced the air in negation. "Who cares about that. We were friends. Man, I've known you since you were eight. I stayed with you when your mom went into labor with your sister. Your dad was out of town. Remember?

"It's just if I cried, because I was scared, or because the hunger hurt so much, that would make it that much harder for the gang. That's why men don't cry in public, Jer. To protect people from our feelings.

"I owe so much to you. All the kids, but you most of all. You kept me going. And yeah, I cried when you left. And yeah, getting over the Starve, it's hard. Some days I wish I'd died, because I'll never escape it."

Jeremy sobbed out loud. Ava and his mom put their arms around him. Mrs. Hodgins shot Ava a look of concern, as though wondering if she should turn this off. Ava shook her head sharply. Cade knew what he was doing.

"But you know, Jer," Cade said. "Those days happen less and less. And then there are days like today. I'm floating on air. Because you're alive! You made it! You're good! Nah, I don't mean your life is all rainbows. Some days are hard. But look how far you've come." Cade chuckled. "Look at Ava! Man, you remember what a scary bunch of twigs she looked like." He bit his lip. "Now she looks great. And she got past the PTSD. I need more help, because I got sicker. But if she can do it, maybe I can too, you know?"

Cade sat back. "When you're scared, when it hurts. It hurts less if you help someone else. Ava says you got a new little sister. Maybe you can be tough for her, like I was for you. Pay it forward. Not because you owe it. But it meant the world to me. That you're OK.

"I love you, man. Always. Never doubt it."

The video broke to a still picture, taken in a hospital room. Cade must have been a freshman in high school, teeth bright with braces. Jeremy, eight years old, sat on his lap. Their chair was next to his mother's bed, the new baby in her arms. Jeremy's dad was draped across her shoulder, grinning with pride.

The caption read, *My dad saved the picture. Said it made him proud of me – Cade Snowdon (Frosty the Snowman).*

"I have this photo for you, too, Jeremy," Ava said softly. "There's more of the video when you're ready." She paused it in the meantime.

Jeremy nodded in a trance. "Frosty's dad is dead, right?"

"No, his dad's alive," Ava said. "He was in Jersey. But now they're both grown men. Cade sends him money to help out. You can't go backward."

Mrs. Hodgins asked, "Is the rest of the video any easier?"

"Much," Ava assured her. "Ready, Jeremy?"

The boy touched his late parents' faces on the screen, then nodded.

"Hey squirt!" Maz called out, Cade's best friend and now leader of the old gang. The pair sat together, knees and shoulders touching, on the usual sturdy table in the dojo back in Chelsea.

Maz was in a manic mood. His lanky dark blond hair was held

back by a backwards red baseball cap. He wore the dojo's summer black T-shirt with their water tiger emblem silk-screened on the breast. He'd bulked up, more muscular than Cade beside him.

"Damn, man!" Maz continued, "I cried when I saw your picture! Frosty won't tell me where Panic found you." He paused to punch Cade, who casually slapped up a block. "But you look great. Awesome lake! I want a lake like that."

Cade pointed a finger across at Maz. "City type. Allergic to fresh air."

Maz grinned and pointed back. "Wannabe cowboy. Yeah, I like the city."

"The gang is good?" Cade prompted him.

"The gang is great," Maz agreed. "We're all going to school now. Well, not me, because – *ta-da!* – I now have a high school diploma!"

"Me, too!" Cade said, raising his hand. "Couple years late."

"Better late than never," Maz said. "None of the kids are here, younger than you. Nobody's even *seen* them til you. So you're like a complete celebrity now."

"Totally," Cade confirmed. "We're going to plaster your picture on posters. It'll be embarrassing as hell."

"Yeah, you'll be glad you're not here," Maz agreed. "Totally." He grinned.

"They have running water now," Cade said. "Toilets. Power. Laundromats. Food. Like real people."

Maz nodded. "Yeah, and we're still on West 23rd. I ain't going nowhere. I paid blood for this block. I'm keeping it."

Cade chuckled. "I'm good with leaving the blood behind. That was icky, Maz."

"Icky," Maz repeated, and shot Cade a mock-mournful gaze. "I miss the kids!"

"We all miss you kids," Cade agreed, looking straight into the camera. "But don't come back soon. You got out! You live! That's awesome!"

"That is pretty awesome," Maz agreed. "Maybe when you're grown up. Then you can visit."

Cade said, "OK, enough mushy stuff."

"No way! We're going *mushier!*" Maz insisted.

The camera cut to the view down onto West 23rd Street from Maz's balcony, next door to the apartment Ava used to share with Cade, on the third floor above the dojo. Maybe a hundred teens and early twenties stood below. The front rank held sheets of paper, spelling out J-E-R-E-M-Y, not Germy, one letter at a time. On cue, the crowd yelled *"JEREMY!"* and cheered and waved like crazy.

Maz stuck his head into the camera angle from one side. "Love ya, bro!"

Cade stuck his head in from the other side. "We remember you. Always."

The video cut to another still picture of the gang and the sign.

Jeremy grinned from ear to ear. Mrs. Hodgins mouthed *Thank you!* to Ava over his head.

AFTER SUNSET, IN THE LONG SUMMER TWILIGHT, JEREMY WALKED AVA BACK to the train station. Three men sat on the curb drinking from flask-size liquor bottles. They rose ungracefully as the younger pair approached.

"Friends of yours?" Ava asked softly.

"Bad eggs," Jeremy confirmed.

One of the men swaggered ahead of the others. "Give us your money. You. Boy. Run along home. We're gonna party with the little lady. We seen you, off the train from Winnipeg, fat with cash."

"Maybe you should, Jer," Ava murmured. "Get help."

Jeremy pulled his knife. "Fuck that."

"Oh, ho! The little shit thinks he can fight!" The leader broke the end off his bottle, with a shattering to outrage the quiet night. Somewhere a dog barked in protest. "Bet mine will hurt more."

Jeremy's eyes lit. He started taunting, loudly. *"Ar-ar-ah, ooh-ooh-ooh!"* He shifted left. Their eyes followed him.

Ava took a sudden running jump and kicked the leader in the chest, as high as she could reach. Her wet towel was still in her hands. The bathing suit dropped to the pavement, and the rest snapped out to slap a second wannabe mugger.

Now the drunks' attention was fixed on her. Jeremy took a running leap and kicked the third man's right hand with his blade foot, sending his half-full bottle flying. The man made a grab for the kid, but Jeremy danced away. He did a back-flip and started up the annoying taunting again.

Ava held her towel as a shield waist-high, matador style. *"Toro, toro!* Beef for brains! *Andele, andele,* morons! *Too-wheet! Too-wheet! Ha, ha, ha!"* She swiped the towel right and left with a little dance.

"Caw caw caw!" Jeremy yelled.

Bullies are cowards. That's what they taught in the dojo, what Ava taught the girls and children as queen bee. *Ridicule makes them stupid. More stupid. Always stand up to a bully.*

Quite a lot of dogs were objecting by now. Doors opened, though not where Ava could see them. This was the commercial main drag. The houses were out of view, behind the single front row of business establishments.

"What the fuck?" yelled the leader. "Just gimme your money, bitch!"

Ava snapped the towel into his face, then backed away. *"Toro, toro!"*

"Toro, toro!" Jeremy echoed in a shrill mocking falsetto. "Big men! Attack a cripple and a girl!"

Ava heard footfalls pounding down a side street now. "Better run, cowards! They're coming to get you! *Woo, woo, woo!"*

"Andele, andele, toro!" Jeremy mocked, weaving behind her. "Run, rabbit, run!"

"Bunny hop, bunny hop, hop-hop-hop!" Ava screamed, sashaying side to side with her shield towel.

"Fuck this!" the addled leader decided. He started running, just as the approaching footfalls turned the corner. His cowardly sidekicks hesitated for a fraction of a second in confusion, then took off after him.

One set of footfalls skidded to a stop, apparently for aim, because a shot rang out. There sure were a lot of dogs in Sioux Lookout. They were all baying now, half out of their minds.

"That was fun!" Jeremy said, bouncing with adrenaline. "Chicken-shit *cowards!*" He yelled down the street after the fleeing attackers. Ava folded over laughing.

"Are you alright?" the first rescuer called, jogging to reach them. He held a pistol. The one who paused to fire his rifle took a little longer to catch up.

"Drunken Indians," Jeremy accused, spitting on the pavement. "Wanted to mug and rape my friend from the train."

Ava elbowed him. The rifle shooter was First Nations. "Not nice, Jer. One of the muggers was native," she clarified for the white man with the pistol. "Maybe one of the others was mixed, the third white. Three of them. They were drinking on the curb. You see their bottles." Ava swooped down to reclaim her bathing suit. She shook out the broken glass.

"Ava needs to catch the train to Toronto," Jeremy said.

The two armed Samaritans escorted them back to the station. The steward Macdonald – he rejoined the train in Winnipeg – let Jeremy board the sleeper car to look around. Macdonald made up Ava and Kelly's beds for the night for the boy's clambering enjoyment. Everyone was amazed at how nimble the kid was with his prosthetic.

Everyone but Ava – Jeremy always was a gifted little monkey. He was the most talented of her students at the dojo, before Ebola.

She stepped out of the train with him for a final private word before the waiting gun men walked him home.

"I don't know when I'll see you again, Jer," Ava said. "One thing. I know Canada looks safe. But it might just be slower than America to fall apart, you know?"

"Where'd you go?" Jeremy asked suspiciously. "What'd you see?"

"Never mind that. It's just, make friends where you are, OK? You need allies here. And don't get stuck on old solutions from the Apple. That racist thing – that was New York. Could be totally different in Quebec, or wherever you are when things go down."

"I guess," he allowed.

"I *know,*" Ava insisted. "And you got too big a heart for that. Stay flexible. Roll with the punches." She punched him once, then gave him a big hug, and kissed him on the cheek, which embarrassed him no end. "Good bye, Jeremy."

Back in her cocoon-like berth, waiting for the train to move, Ava watched Cade's videos to Jeremy again, tears flowing silently.

He didn't send one for her.

35

Interesting fact: Not all Apple 'gang royalty' were blacklisted on the Hudson citizen database as criminals. In fact, the most successful adult gang leaders were appointed as Community Coordinators – Cocos – and even Resource Coordinators – Rescos. The difference was whether the gang existed primarily for crime, or to protect a community. This distinction was murky at best.

Art Walsh, Daneel's boss, stood waiting on the Rochester train platform with a placard seeking 'Tanner Wu Prak.' Ava reflected that she would probably forever think of the older man as Ike, the false name he traveled under on their mission to tap communications from Mount Weather.

Today marked one month to the day since Ava departed from Brooklyn to hand-carry a funding proposal to Ohio and Ken–Tenn. *What a long strange trip it's been.*

As the train squealed and jerked to a stop, Kelly visibly gulped. Ava grabbed the other girl's bags to compensate for her flagging resolve. Kelly was terrified what Skull would do to her.

Ava privately suspected that the worst of her punishment would be the anticipation until Skull had time to meet with her. Which wouldn't be this week. In the meantime, Kelly would stay at Art's place in Binghamton and perform whatever grunt work he could think of for her penance. Yard work, most likely. Summer had arrived in Hudson late, but hot and humid under a leaden sky.

Ava hustled out Tanner and Wu with their gear, and waved Art over. She introduced everyone on the platform, not daring to get more than 10 feet from the train door. She needed to jump back in to continue east to Albany, then south to the Apple. She exchanged quick hugs with her discharged charges, and a much bigger hug with Art.

"I got this for Daneel," she said, showing him a ouiPhone. "Is he with you?"

She considered this her crowning achievement of the last couple days. She negotiated with Mr. Clark to let them cross the border with their ouiPhone collection. Well, that and she convinced Tanner and Wu not to stay in Toronto for Canada Day. That would have added another two days to the trip, driving Ava up a wall with impatience.

Art's hand reached for the phone, fingers flexing claw-like in greed. But he reluctantly admitted, "You'll see Daneel on Long Island."

Ava promptly withdrew the phone. "Kelly has one, too. And Alan Wu."

"Oh, good!" Art said. He shifted his clutching fingers toward Kelly. "Gimme."

"When will we see you again?" Tanner asked Ava.

Ava shrugged. "No idea. But you'll be happy here!"

With that, she hopped back on the train, with a final wave. She sank back to her seat alone. Sprung springs and torn sticky vinyl greeted her legs. The damp heat loosed months of foul aromas from the patina of grunge coating the interior of the train.

Home. We should clean up the place. Once upon a time, only months ago, everything outside the Apple looked positively wonderful to her. She saw Upstate Hudson more clearly now, much of it overgrown and ramshackle, with signs everywhere of making do, or doing without.

"Jana, message boss," Ava murmured to her phone. "Delivery complete."

"Message queued," Jana replied. "No signal."

Oh, yeah. That. She got to keep her fancy phone, but not the communications infrastructure that made Jana so awesome. Reluctantly, she tucked Jana away as a souvenir and memory device. She pulled out her old phone to tap in the text. She wondered if she could teach Jana to operate her company phone. It would be nice to keep the dictation and AI-assisted database, and let Jana run the older phone as a slave.

Boss: A+! See you in Ronk.

She tried to text and call Cade again, but got the same auto-responders. He was unavailable this week and would not see her message.

After changing trains for the evening leg down to the Apple, her phone rang. *Skull.*

"Hi, boss," she said, subdued. "I'll reach the city after curfew."

"That's alright. Daneel will pick you up at Harlem and drive you out here. You'll stay at his place tonight."

"Not Cade?"

"No," Skull said. "You alright?"

"I want to talk to Cade."

"He's busy, Ava," Skull said. "Cade's doing miracles with this Resco training week. Having a blast. Half the Rescos are trying to hire him away from me."

"His contract is up next month, isn't it," Ava said. She swallowed. Their contracts were twelve months. Hers ran until next April.

"It is," Skull agreed. "But let's talk about you. You're back! *Impressed as hell,* Ava! Well done!"

"Thanks," she whispered.

"Tomorrow you need to pull together your report. A presentation again. The seminar attendees will leave Friday mid-day. Then you'll debrief to the lead Rescos before they split."

"OK."

"More than OK! You've got great material. Dying to see it."

"Thanks."

"I need to get back to a party," Skull said. "You done good, Ava. Don't be offended that Cade is too busy for you tomorrow. He'll be free after your debrief. Then you'll catch up. And I'll work with you on your slides tomorrow. Got it?"

Ava started to get angry now, not just scared. "Cade's too busy to see me?"

"Right. Give him space."

Ava growled, "He's had over a month of space."

"Yes. And he used it well."

"What's going on with Cade?" Ava demanded.

"Ava," Skull said in a warning tone. "You and Cade need to talk. But not now. And not through me. Got it?"

"Got it," she bit out.

"Don't worry," Skull said. "He's fine. He cares. He's busy. The rest will work out. Just be patient."

After Skull signed off, Ava noted that she had three train seats to herself. By train standards, she had enough privacy to work. She decanted everything from Porta's camera and Jana, the images and notes she'd never shared for fear of Canadian intelligence intercepting them. She got that organized. She came up with a first-pass outline for her report, and fidgeted with it for half an hour. Then she killed time selecting her best photos. At last she pulled into Harlem Station at 125th Street, the latter-day Apple terminal for points north.

No placard here. Daneel stood on a bench looking for her, wearing his marbled scarf from Sayre market. When he spotted her, he waved the scarf like crazy, then darted through the crowd. He nearly tackled her with an enthusiastic hug.

Daneel had her laughing in no time. He wanted to hear everything about her adventures in Canada and Oregon. He loved his new ouiPhone. He dismissed Cade's inner demons with an airy wave.

"He's hopelessly in love with you, Ava. Don't sweat the messy details. He's just working full out on this Resco course production, you know?"

They swung by the curfew-free, 24-hour Chinatown for dinner and ogling the nightlife, then headed out on Long Island. Before bed, Daneel even forwarded her files to the analyst section. Unlike her, Daneel knew these people.

His apartment had a spare bedroom waiting for her, fresh and clean, windows open to the summer night rain and singing toads and insects. The island was mercifully cooler than inland.

It wasn't home. But after a few hours with Daneel, it felt close enough.

~

"– ANOTHER COMPANY AGENT PICKED UP TANNER AND WU AT THE Rochester train platform Wednesday afternoon. I arrived Long Island oh-two-hundred yesterday," Ava said, completing her chronological walk-through.

The same Rescos were in the room today as for her proposal last month that sent her to Schwabacher, and inadvertently launched the mission to Oregon. Skull clapped, instigating an ovation all around. Cade and Daneel sat in the back, and stood to clap. Daneel whistled enthusiasm.

Skull turned and shot a neck-slicing gesture at Daneel. But coming off a week of seminars and camaraderie, the officers were laid back this Friday afternoon.

"That wasn't the end," Pete commented to the room. Everyone settled down. Skull – newly promoted Lt. Col. Kyle Sullivan in this context – rose to take the slide controller from Ava. She moved to sit, but her boss gestured for her to remain standing on the opposite side of the projection monitor.

"Analysis," Skull announced. "Early results. My people are still working on it. Good news first. Although Canada remains understandably guarded, Ava saw much to indicate that its people are not antagonistic to Americans. They seem sympathetic to Hudson. We built a powerful store of good will with Project Reunion."

His slide included an image of Ava and Jeremy straddling the sides of a canoe, trying to rock each other off into the lake. Mrs. Hodgins caught that shot with Ava's phone.

"That was the strategic argument for Project Reunion," Pete agreed. General Ivan Link, sitting next to Pete, shot him a pained look. Pete ignored him. "Ava, do you agree with these statements?" he asked. Apparently he'd noticed a reservation on her face.

"Mostly," she said. "I think the Canadians see themselves as superior. Because they haven't fallen so far yet. Maybe they think they never will. The stereotype is that Americans are destroyed, kinda pathetic, dope addicts, violent. But one on one, they let it go easily enough. With me, anyway."

Skull nodded a fair-enough, and switched to another slide. "We estimate Canada is running about six years behind us on the collapse. Ava's photos and notes are consistent with that model. Canada has our experience to learn from, and a less fractious political landscape. They shouldn't crash as hard. But they are falling."

"Better real estate under climate change," Pete suggested.

"I disagree," Cameron said. "The southern tier of Canada isn't that different from us. There's a limit to how much warming can benefit them. Thawing permafrost won't make agricultural land out of taiga and tundra. Much of their landmass is too far north. We both remain in the Goldilocks zone. This century, anyway."

Pete asked, "Do we think they'll remain a single country, Kyle?"

"Less clear," Skull replied. "The Dust Bowl is getting worse. Their current transport across it is inadequate. As travel and trade decrease, the Quebec separatist tendency strengthens. And with Maine added to the mix, the Maritimes are more viable. We could see Canada breaking into four nations, plus resource-rich territories." He threw up a quick map and sketched his suggested split, circling the population centers of the Canadian West, southern Ontario and Manitoba plus Minnesota, then Quebec, and last the Atlantic provinces with Maine.

"But we can add vector," Skull continued, switching to another slide. "Canada is entranced by the PIAGO Power initiative. And microchips without dealing with China. They are still getting chips from Asia. Oregon, too."

"Damn," said Cam.

"They prefer us as a source," Skull countered. "Schwabacher is taking the lead on this."

"We will be able to manufacture phones," Ava inserted, lest that point be missed.

Skull nodded. "Yes. Also, between PIAGO and the chips, Schwabacher is negotiating to buy dedicated communications bandwidth between the Northeast and Oregon. From there we can reach whoever Oregon is talking to. Hawaii, Rockies, and Montane, certainly. We're pretty sure he'll get us the Internet bandwidth. He's also agitating for another rail line, or at least to add another track to what they've got. Steel sourced by PA and Ohio, of course."

Ava liked that. Even doubling the track would halve the time to cross the continent. It could more than double the food and resource throughput.

"We want freight rights on that," Ash Margolis suggested.

"You talk to Schwabacher," Pete told him.

"Always happy to chat with Charles," Ash agreed.

It seemed odd to Ava that the most aggressive Rescos, Ash and Cam, were also the ones who handled diplomacy and public relations. But Hudson had a martial government, and so did the neighbors.

Skull flipped to the next slide. "Canada's birth control is interesting. Oregon's currency is truly interesting. And we've got a capitalist expert to mine for details. Emmett, remind me why we didn't do that? Save the banks."

Emmett MacLaren rubbed his furrowed brow. "I suck at banking. Um, the proposal just seemed arbitrary to me. Who got how much, and why. Also, Portland and Seattle survived. Our financial cities didn't. Ava, do you know who spearheaded the currency in Oregon?"

"Deke Fowler," she supplied. "They executed him. For killing California. I really liked that about Oregon," she couldn't help adding.

"Yeah," Emmett said. "Fowler advocated that proposal. Never trusted Fowler."

Skull tamped down a grin. Apparently he agreed.

Ivan Link commented, "Emmett, in general. When the argument goes, 'If not here, where? If not now, when?' Your conclusion is supposed to go, 'here, and now.' Would you rather I take over banking?"

"Yes!" Pete and Emmett agreed emphatically. "Kyle, let's move on," Pete added.

"Right, sorry," Skull agreed. "Was distracted by whether to make a bid for Albany as the banking center." Skull was Resco of Albany before he accepted the death angel role.

Ash Margolis grinned at him. Albany was his now. "Point taken. I'll follow up."

"Boston," Ivan told them with finality.

Ava was floored by the contrast between these Army officers and Arlo Hofer, pushing the economy around. "Sir? I think the main thing Oregon did different was empower people like Arlo Hofer. Instead of the Army."

Ivan Link nodded agreement, and made a note. His Boston was once the high-tech entrepreneurial hub of New England.

Skull belatedly put up his next slide. "Ava captured some detailed reports on Northern League natural resource extraction agreements and Canada's mining. Ash, I'll get you the raw data." He showed a summary from the pages Ava photographed from Camille's luggage.

"Do we even have this for Hudson?" Pete asked. "Our mining and stuff?"

Ivan Link said, "We tracked it for New England. Get me a copy, too, Kyle. I can add this to my new 'banking' duties."

"Please," Pete agreed.

Skull nodded, and flipped the slide again. "And here is the American command bunker, now that we know where to look. Best guess, three regiments like Oregon's, sundry Air Force, etc. Still low confidence on identifying the people pulling the strings."

"Can we bomb them?" Ava asked.

Skull glanced at her, eyebrows raised. "No."

"We prefer 100% control," Cam Cameron said, with a crooked smile.

Ava pointed to that bunker on the projection screen, the other fist on her hip. "We're not going to take them down?" she demanded.

"Take them over," Cameron clarified.

"Not this week," Pete sighed.

"Living well is the best revenge," Skull told Ava softly. "And with that, I think it's time my agents left the room. Any last questions for Ava before they go?"

There were a few. Pete limited the discussion to 10 minutes. After that, she received a standing ovation.

Skull wrapped up, saying, "I'll send this presentation along to Ohio by courier."

"I should go," Ava offered instantly. She hadn't thought that through, but after a moment's reflection, gave a firm nod. "Charles Schwabacher will want to talk to me."

Skull's smile slowly bloomed. "Agreed. I'll talk to you later."

I could get used to this, Ava thought wryly, not realizing that she already had.

36

Interesting fact: The eventual aPhone, as it came to be called, was not a clone of the ouiPhone, though it did share much of the same chip set. The Ohio-Hudson design was more rugged than pretty, and supported many connection alternatives to cell towers. The aPhone sold in Canada as a superior option for remote small towns. This took years, however.

"Hey, you did awesome," Cade said quietly, as the three death angel agents exited the debrief with the lead Rescos. The officers were still in there, a lecture hall in the defunct community college they'd used for the Resco training week. "Impressed as hell. Got a minute?"

Daneel hastily split, with a quick wave and a vague excuse.

"Got an hour at least," she said, glancing at the closed door behind them. "I wish I thought they planned to attack the frosted cabbage league." That was her theory on why they'd been dismissed before the meeting broke up.

Cade shook his head. "No. Plot a slow takeover, more likely. And not in this meeting."

Ava stilled, and shot him a quizzical look.

"Ava, they won't fight the Northern League," Cade clarified. There was no one in earshot. He double-checked that point. They strode along a walkway through the wet hay field that used to be a campus lawn. "They loved what you started. Evict the current Americans and replace them with our own troops and commanders. Hudson, Ohio, and Oregon, most likely. America's northern successors, to replace the pawns of a defunct nation."

Ava scowled. "No punishment for killing the Apple?"

Cade shrugged. "Separate issue. Ava, it isn't up to us."

"Yet," Ava quibbled, through gritted teeth.

Cade chuckled softly. "Not what I wanted to talk about. Haven't seen you in a month."

"You're finally ready to talk, are you?" she growled.

She couldn't help it. Daneel and Skull practically sat on her to keep her away from Cade since she arrived in Ronkonkoma. Cade was busy directing logistics for the Resco training workshop. He even presented at a couple sessions, plus running the office. She could see that. She still resented his not finding just five minutes to drop everything and fly into her arms.

Well, she wanted a minimum half hour, really, in private.

And he still hadn't touched her. That scared her, which made her tongue extra sharp.

"Yeah. Here is good." Cade pointed to a dilapidated picnic table in the tall grass of the college lawn.

Ava contemplated her good wool coat-dress. She contemplated the bird droppings, broken clam shells, and years of dirt littering the dented aluminum picnic table. She elected to remain standing, while Cade dropped to a seat on top, unconcerned for the state of his chinos. It was hot and sticky, the hazy bright July swelter arrived at last. They'd both change into shorts soon.

She waited, emotional barriers drawn.

"You did not get a video from me, right?" Cade verified first.

"No. Skull said he had one," she replied. "But you reneged." Actually, Skull said he talked Cade out of it. That some things were best handled in person.

"Good." Cade visibly gathered himself to speak.

Ava interrupted him. "You are not breaking up with me."

Cade shook his head, looking down at his minimalist broken-down sneakers. "I hope not. Ava, this is hard for me. Let me talk?"

Only if you're not going to break up with me. "Yeah." She blew out to control rising anxiety.

"My blowup, in May," Cade started slowly. "Before I started the new treatment for PTSD and the traumatic brain injury. I think people misunderstood. Maybe they thought it was about remembering that time we were raped. But that wasn't it. I never forgot that."

"No," she agreed softly. They both remembered. It stalked their dreams.

"What I couldn't handle, Ava," Cade said, "was how angry I was at you. And I lashed out, couldn't get myself back under control. If Cam and Carlos weren't there, I could have killed you. You know how it is when you get too angry. It snowballs. All the different angers come flying out of storage like harpies."

"Yeah?" she said. "Cade, you're not getting mad now, are you?"

He blew out slowly, then cracked his neck to both sides. "Damn. Almost brought it on again. No. I'm OK. Anyway, while you were away, I was dealing with *that.* While you weren't here to hurt. Except by my not talking to you."

Questions popped like firecrackers through Ava's mind. But this wasn't the time to say anything at all. It was time to listen very quietly indeed. She swallowed.

"Thanks," he whispered. "Maybe I could just speak my piece. Then we talk."

She nodded, eyes on her navy ballet flat shoes. Staring at him would encroach on his emotional space. She dug into her computer bag and offered him a protein bar from her stash. He was more dangerous when hungry.

Cade grudgingly took a small bite and chewed. "Ava, I never got over how angry I was at you for leaving me last August. Your note. You said you gave me my soul back. Did you mean to tell me to commit suicide? Because I did business with White Rule?"

"What?!" Her resolve flew out the window. She stared directly into his eyes aghast. That was their deal, during the Starve. It was a group of them, not just between her and Cade. Some were dead now. But she

and Cade, and his best friend Maz, they weren't allowed to give up unless one of the others agreed it was time. Unless they got permission, suicide wasn't an option.

Her knee-jerk reaction was to deny it. Unfortunately, his earnestness gave her pause. This mattered too much to him. She licked her lip. "I think…not exactly. I was angry at you. I think all I meant… Damn. It doesn't matter, Cade."

"What did you mean?" he whispered, hurt eyes holding hers.

She blew out slowly, tears in her eyes. "That soul thing. We held each other's conscience, Cade. Not just, that we couldn't give up living. We couldn't give up our morals. Not without hashing it out. But if we talked, and agreed some vile crap was the best we could do, under the circumstances, then OK. It was forgivable.

"Cade, what I meant was, White Rule stepped over the line, for me. You decided, for all of us, to team up with scum like that, instead of trying out Soho Ville and the Cocos. Cade, I meant to hurt you. You know how angry I was. But I didn't mean you should kill yourself. I meant, you didn't consult me. You didn't let me say, *No! This is not OK!* So here, mind your own conscience. Because you wouldn't listen to me."

His face was in his hands, elbows on his knees.

"We never talked that out, did we," Ava said more softly. "Why we broke up. I just…wanted so badly to be back together."

"Me too," he said, muffled and hoarse. "And I was angry, too. That you would dare to cut a deal with Soho Ville behind my back."

"I wanted it bad," she admitted. "I wanted to wrangle a better offer before I came to you with it. You knew the villes weren't hot and cold running water and three square meals a day. But I didn't want to hear it. I wanted to believe in some kind of paradise. That it would all be magically *over* and comfortable again."

"I know. We did talk it out," he said, wiping tears from his eyes. "But I was still angry. Hey, before we go any farther." He pulled a list out of his pocket. "I want to suggest a keyword system. 'Honey, not now, I have a head-ache.' Either of us says that, it means, just stop. I can't handle this. And we break away and cool off."

Ava's eyes narrowed. "How many things are on that list?"

"We're still on number two," he grumbled. "Welcome to my world. I've been crying this crap out all month."

"That sucks. So…you have a head-ache?" she asked hopefully.

"No. Next," Cade said doggedly. "Pet peeve. Don't hit me, and then hide behind your 'little girl' status. Dammit, you hit hard. You kick even harder. And ninety-nine times out of a hundred, you hit me first. But God forbid I hit you back. Ava, that's not fair. Don't make it look like it's all on me. It's not. Is it."

"No," she agreed. "Maybe ninety-seven out of a hundred. But I never tell them –"

"Don't even try," he cut her off.

Fair, she admitted. People did automatically assume Cade was in the wrong. And she used it, rather than correct them. "Yeah. Sorry. Formal matches only?"

"For now, yes, please. Thank you. Next." He consulted his list and considered for a few moments. "Thank you for giving me space to finish my job here on Long Island. I didn't really expect you would. But this mattered to me. Our careers in the company won't always include each other. I didn't get to see Jeremy, or sail Puget Sound. You didn't get to play Resco aide. We can share it afterwards. But we won't always be partnered for work."

"I'm proud of you," she said. "I peeked in on your Resco marker game yesterday. Daneel showed me the card designs. That was really cool, Cade. All of this."

"Thanks. I'm proud of you, too." He crumpled his note sheet and shoved it into his pocket.

"Only four?" Ava asked. That list looked longer.

"Screw it," he said. He stood and folded her in his arms at last, cheek to cheek. As usual, their bodies initially tensed, then relaxed into each other. Only then did he turn her face for a deep kiss. *Home.*

He broke off the kiss to suggest, "The rest would work better as pillow talk."

She traced a finger along the scar on his face, then along his jaw to his earlobe. "Got a pillow?"

CADE LAY NAKED FACE-DOWN ACROSS THE BED, WAITING FOR HER TO FINISH up in the bathroom. Done playing with his new nunchucks for the moment, he drew a toy geoduck out of Ava's souvenir collection, and powered it on. "Trying to make me feel inadequate?"

"No!" Her face was already flushed. It burned brighter still. "Wait. Cade? That doesn't hurt your feelings, does it?"

He flopped onto his back, shrieking with laughter. When he calmed down, he reached for her, with one of the happiest, most relaxed smiles she'd ever seen on him. "Ava, physically, we match great. Intellectually. Morally. Emotions are hard. We've got too many that suck. But physically? We're awesome."

"I always thought so," she agreed. "I'm kinda fat at the moment."

"Yeah, mushy from all that sitting around," Cade agreed, poking her. "That's a fun change."

"I'll burn it off," she insisted.

"For now," Cade agreed. "But you won't be a tiny little hard-body forever, Ava. Women flesh out. I'm a major fan of your body. Whatever it does."

In net, Ava decided that was a pretty good compliment. "Yours, too."

She grabbed back the geoduck, and poked him with it before putting it away. "Those are souvenirs for my girlfriends."

"You have girlfriends?" he inquired, liquid in relaxation.

"I plan to," she said defensively. "Female agents unite."

Ava didn't recall ever seeing Cade this mellow. He earned the nickname Frosty the Snowman long before Ebola broke out. "This month has been good for you," she said. "I'm sorry I couldn't be good for you."

"Hey," he said. "Come here." He touched her with a fingertip.

She sat beside him, draped in her towel.

"You've always been good for me," Cade told her. "The way this got started? Doctor Keillor asked what I wanted. Like, a goal. I told him I wanted to marry you someday. But I was too screwed up. I thought you'd be better off choosing someone else." He paused, and swallowed. "But our third anniversary is coming up in September. That's a long time."

"I'd say yes in a minute, Cade," Ava said. "You know I would. But you push me away."

"Yeah, I finally realized that," he said. "How I push you away. Sorry." He rolled up onto an arm and reached a hand on her leg. "But you leave again in the morning."

"Do you mind?"

"Just wondering," he said.

"I want to be as good an agent as you," Ava said. "The Governor of Ohio gave me this mission. Maybe Skull thinks I'm a little girl who needs to be protected. Maybe if Schwabacher thinks otherwise, so will Skull."

Cade nodded thoughtfully. "And how do you think you did?"

"Well, I didn't have a team –"

"Didn't you?" Cade asked. "Ava, Skull is our boss. Team leader isn't a supervisor job. She's the mission holder, the one who improvises, pushes through, adapts the plan, gets it done. You pulled in people as needed. Lots of them. Most were grown men. Right?"

She thought about that a moment, her face warming again. "Yeah. I did."

He nodded. "I'm impressed. Ava, most men aren't low-lifes. You're suited for a different class of mission. Just don't get stuck in Ohio, OK? Come back, and we can take some comp time together."

"Vacation? You?" she asked skeptically.

"Well, an *active* vacation," he qualified. They both fell together chuckling. "We could canoe the length of Seneca Lake. Or bike around it. We'll think of something. Just come back. Tell Schwabacher you've got plans, partner."

"And if he offers me a mission I can't refuse?" Ava asked archly.

"Then have a blast, succeed, and come home safe. I'm benched another month. The lake won't go anywhere. We'll talk on the phone."

"OK, I will," she agreed, taking the challenge. "Cade, what was your assignment here?"

"You saw," he said. "Help Cameron stage the Resco training so Skull didn't have to." He didn't meet her eye while he said it, though.

Maybe if she couched it as a joke, she thought. "I got jealous, you know. Thought you were assigned to seduce him." She kissed his shoulder.

But he replied, "As a friend, yeah. Not lover. Cam and Skull were friends back at West Point. Sang in a traveling choir together. After, they grew apart. They were both at Leavenworth before the Calm. Skull pushed Cam away to protect him. But we need other patrons if we're going to shrug off the Northern League. For protection. So Skull sent me here to mend fences, build contingency plans. We're double agents now. Long Island is about as safe as it gets in Hudson."

"Did it work?" she asked.

Cade nodded. "I'm welcome back anytime. You too, and Daneel. Skull's safer with MacLaren. His house has remote-controlled gun emplacements and a militia barracks next door. Skull's screwing over some seriously powerful people."

"So Long Island is our way out of the cross-fire."

Cade chuckled. "Says she who won the first battle."

EARLY THE NEXT MORNING, CADE DROPPED HER OFF AT SANDSEND, THE terminal point of the Apple rail system, and beginning of the miles-long gap before the Long Island trains began. He returned to Ronkonkoma, to finish his followup on the successful Resco training marathon. After a few days, he'd wander back to company HQ in Elmira.

Ava hoped to meet him there. But first, she'd finish what she started, and hand-carry her report to Schwabacher in Cleveland. Their client deserved the opportunity to question her directly.

She didn't want to take the train, though. She had a better idea.

"Hi, I'm Brenda," Kelly introduced herself, grabbing one of Ava's bags to throw in the back of the miniature SUV. Skull had been only too happy to offload Kelly on Ava.

Kelly added, "That's Carla. She's new to the road, June class from West Point."

"They didn't take me," Carla admitted apologetically.

Big-framed, Carla looked like she stood a better chance than Kelly or Ava ever did. Apparently the Army still hadn't caught on to how the Rescos benefited by their turning away the bottom 20% of each class. The company faced steeper competition this round, as other Rescos bid harder to snatch up the trained 'rejects.' Tough young female recruits were particularly prized. Learning to deal with men in Basic polished some useful social skills for a harsh world.

"Ashley," Ava said, offering her hand to shake. "From Manhattan. Who's driving?"

"I've got the city. Which way?" Kelly inquired.

"We cross the border near Port Jervis," Ava replied. She wondered what Carla's real name was, but wouldn't ask. "We're not carrying contraband, are we? This trip is people only."

"Just a few bribes," Kelly said. "Small weapons. Cash."

"Sounds good." Ava settled into the passenger seat, propping her red high-top sneakers on the console, as Kelly started driving. "So Carla, tell us your life story. Don't leave anything out. It's a long drive to Cleveland."

No one doubted that Ava was team leader.

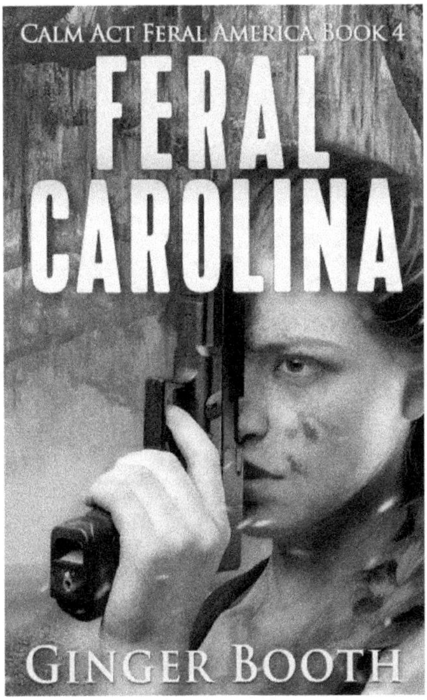

Dear Reader,

I hope you enjoyed Ava's trek to the left coast!

She's rather cunning, isn't she? Skull thought he was hiring Cade's girlfriend. He hadn't bargained on how potent a queen bee was in her own right.

Alas, our little gang rat has developed a taste for revenge. But what can one small girl hope to accomplish against the Northern League?

When the League fires her boss in revenge for her antics in Canada, Ava is demoted and reassigned to Carolina. Right in the middle of her honeymoon, too. How rude.

Can Ava break in her new boss, strike another blow against the Northern League, and win back her honeymoon?

Ava kicks butt in Dixie!

Get it now!

Thank you for reading!

Ginger Booth

ALSO BY GINGER BOOTH

Calm Act Feral America: Ava Panic

Feral Recruit

Feral Agent

Feral Courier

Feral Carolina

Short Prequels

Ebola Day (Ava & Cade)

Civilly Disobedient (Dee) **

Dust of Kansas (Emmett) **

Road to Humble Texas (Kayden)

** *free for reader group*

Calm Act, Books 1-4 : Dee Baker

End Game

Project Reunion

Martial Lawless

Tsunami Wake

The Calm Act Books 1-3 (box set)

Thrive Space Colony Adventures

Skyship Thrive

Spaceship Thrive (~April 2019)

Nonfiction:

Indoor Salad: How to Grow Vegetables Indoors

FREE E-BOOKS

CALM ACT GENESIS
SHORT PREQUELS

Join my reader group at
gingerbooth.com/freeferalbooks

to receive free prequels, bonus content, news, etc.

ACKNOWLEDGMENTS

I'm deeply grateful to my test readers. My beta readers put up with reading the manuscript while I'm still writing it. The team for *Feral Courier* included Terry Bader, Kimberley Bridgwater, Gerry Ford, Jim Hunt, Brett Jarman, Ron Kaminski, Bonne Kelley, Jenniffer LaPointe, Karen Reinertsen, Robert Slater, Suella Tucker, and WMH Cheryl. Thank you so much for your time and insights, and most importantly for your friendship, and urging me on.

Thanks as well to the advance review copy readers, who read the almost-final manuscript, ready to write reviews for book launch.

And thank you, for reading my book. Without you, I couldn't do what I do, so I really appreciate that you give my work a chance. Drop me a line! I respond personally to all messages. Books take a long time to write. Feedback is the fuel that powers the next story.

Ginger Booth
ginger@gingerbooth.com

CPSIA information can be obtained
at www.ICGtesting.com
Printed in the USA
LVHW021131010419
612522LV00003B/254/P

9 780960 068579